The Hired Man

The Hired Man

A Dick Hardesty
Mystery by

Dorien Grey

GLB PUBLISHERS® San Francisco

Published in the United States by
GLB Publishers
P.O. Box 78212, San Francisco, CA 94107 USA

Cover by GLB Publishers

ISBN 1-879194-76-7

Library of Congress Cataloguing in Publication Data

Grey, Dorien.
  The hired man : a Dick Hardesty mystery / by Dorien Grey.-- 1st ed.
    p. cm.
  ISBN 1-879194-76-7
  1. Hardesty, Dick (Fictitious character)--Fiction. 2. Private
investigators--Fiction. 3. Gay men--Fiction. I. Title.
  PS3557.R48165 H57 2002
  813'.6--dc21
                    2002005422

First Published 2002

Reprinted 2004, 2006

To those for whom a closet is
just a place
for hanging clothes.

CHAPTER 1

Have you ever noticed that when people talk about "the oldest profession" they never seem to include, or even realize that there is, a sizeable male contingent of the group? Sexism, pure and simple, that's what it is. Any gay male who lives in or has even visited a place with a halfway decently-sized gay community knows that hustlers are part of the landscape, like the Boston ferns in upscale bar/restaurants. Hustlers, like their female counterparts, are most often individual entrepreneurs who stand on street corners and wait for a car to pull up with an offer, or lounge around specific bars that always remind me of the shark tank in an aquarium. But just as there are considerable differences between "hookers" and "call girls" so there are differences between "hustlers" and "male escorts." Not more than one straight guy in 10 can afford a "call girl" and few gays have the money (or, let's face it, the inclination) to indulge their whims on the pretty high-quality talent discreetly available through a growing number of businesses providing the services of a "male escort."

But for those who can afford it, there's a whole fun new meaning to the term "hired man."

* * *

I was sitting at the bar at Napoleon—early as usual— waiting to have dinner with a brand-new client. Napoleon is a very nice, quiet gay restaurant in a former private home on the edge of The Central—the city's rapidly growing gay business district in the heart of what some still called "the gay ghetto." The client, Stuart Anderson, was from out of town—the C.E.O. of an expanding chain of trendy kitchen supply boutiques which was opening two new stores here. He'd called me from Buffalo the week before to set up an appointment. While I was dutifully impressed to think that my fame had spread beyond my local area code, he'd been really vague when I asked him how he had heard of me, or who had referred him. He'd just said "a business acquaintance" had made the referral, and I didn't press it any further, though I was curious. Also, though the subject of sexual orientation never entered the conversation, I automatically assumed he was gay (hey, I automatically assume *everyone* is gay) since I have had very few straight clients.

Part of the mystery of his secretiveness was solved within two minutes of his walking into the office for his 4:30 appointment. Stuart Anderson, it turned out, was an average height, average looking, pleasant-enough man in his mid 40s, dressed casually but expensively, and carrying a slim briefcase. He had no sooner taken the seat in front of my desk when I noticed that though he had a healthy tan, the third finger of his left hand had a wide, untanned circle where he had obviously taken off a wedding ring. *Oh, great, I thought, one of those.*

Rather than just sit back and wait for the expected pass, I thought I'd nip in the bud any little game he might be intending to play.

"I appreciate your calling me, Mr. Anderson," I said. "But I think we should clarify something before we proceed: I assume you know that I'm gay and generally specialize in gay clients?" His only response was a small smile and almost imperceptible nod, but since he said nothing, I continued. "I mention this only because it *is* an issue for some people, and I don't want there to be any misunderstandings or awkwardness between my clients and me."

He never lost the small smile, but I noticed that his right hand unconsciously found his left and his right thumb and index finger went to cover the telltale untanned circle. "Not a problem," he said. "My business here has nothing whatever...directly...to do with...anyone's ...sexual orientation. I was simply told you were very good at getting information." His right thumb and forefinger slowly twisted the missing wedding ring. I wondered why in hell he'd bothered to take it off in the first place if he was going to make it so obvious he wore one.

It turned out that he merely wanted me to do a careful background check on the prospective managers and assistant managers for the new stores, which was apparently something he did routinely and was probably a good idea given that he himself wouldn't be around every day to check on things. I estimated it would take only a couple of days to do the checking. Hardly the most exciting of assignments, and certainly not one that any other private investigator in the city couldn't handle in his sleep, but I wasn't in a position to turn away any source of income. I had a couple other minor assignments I was working on, but they could be put on hold for the few days it would take to complete this one.

I told him my rates and when he didn't bat an eye, I reached into my desk and handed him a standard contract, which he signed without reading. I signed below his signature and, as I went to my new Xerox machine to make him a copy, he opened his briefcase. When I handed him his signed copy, he gave me the resumes of the four men and two women he was considering for the managerial positions. I glanced at them briefly to be sure they had all the necessary information, and put them in the top drawer of my desk.

Business over.

Well, that was easy, I told myself.

Anderson made no move to get up from his chair. "I was wondering if you'd like to join me for dinner?" he asked.

Ta-Dah! I thought.

"That's very nice of you, Mr. Anderson," I began, "but..."

"It's Stuart, please," he said with a smile. "And please don't misunderstand—I'm not trying to come on to you. It's just that we have a mutual...friend...whom I'm meeting for dinner this evening and I thought you might like to join us. I know he's looking forward to seeing you."

He had me. I still suspected there might be a hook in there somewhere, but decided I didn't really have too much to lose...except a client, of course.

"Well, sure," I said. "That would be nice." I didn't ask who the mystery "friend" might be, but got the distinct impression that Anderson was giving me a little test to see how curious this detective he'd just hired might be.

Anderson got up from his chair, still smiling, and reached across the desk as I got up to shake hands.

"Seven thirty, then? At Napoleon—you know it, don't you?"

"Of course," I said. "I'll see you there. And thank you."

"My pleasure," he said, and I somehow had a mental picture of a cat and a mouse.

And with that, he picked up his briefcase and left.

* * *

At exactly 7:25, Stuart Anderson walked in...alone. *Uh huh. Here we go,* I thought. He came over and took the stool next to me. Noticing my drink was still about 3/4 full, he nonetheless asked "Ready for another?"

I shook my head. "I'm fine, thanks," I said as the bartender came over.

"Tangueray with a twist," he said, reaching into his pocket to extract a roll of bills large enough to choke a pony, if not a horse. He peeled a $20 off the top, laid it on the bar in front of him, and stuck the wad back in his pocket.

"And our friend?" I couldn't resist asking.

Anderson smiled. "He'll be along in a moment," he said. "Actually, I made the reservations for eight o'clock, to give us a few minutes to get to know one another."

Sigh.

"I don't normally mix business with pleasure," he continued, "but I so seldom have the chance to just relax it's nice to be among kindred spirits when I can."

Kindred spirits, I thought, listening for the sound of imaginary hairpins hitting the floor.

"Yes," I said. "I noticed you're married."

He glanced quickly at his left hand, splayed his fingers, and grinned. "Yeah," he said. "Fifteen years, three kids; a different world. And a totally separate world," he added.

Indeed, I thought.

"Any problem juggling them?" I asked. Bisexuals have always been a puzzle to me. Like the Easter Bunny and the Tooth Fairy, I wasn't really sure I believed in them, but what other people did or thought was none of my business.

The bartender came with his drink, took his money and went to the register to ring up the sale and make change.

"Not at all," Anderson said, jump-starting me back to where

the conversation had left off. "When I'm in the straight world, I'm straight. When I'm in the gay world I'm...not straight. Obviously, most of my life is strictly heterosexual, but I've always enjoyed the things gay men can do that women can't."

Well, that was certainly cryptic, I thought, but didn't choose to follow up on it. If he expected me to ask "Such as...?" he'd just have to wait. I still wasn't convinced that this wasn't all part of some game he enjoyed playing; and if he thought for one minute I wasn't aware that he was playing....

"Fortunately," he said, "I get to travel quite a bit, and when I do, I like to indulge myself a little." He took a sip of his drink, then turned to look at me, full face. "How about you?" he asked. "Totally gay?"

I took another drink from my Manhattan before answering. "About as gay as they come," I said.

"Hmm," he said. "How old were you when you knew?" he asked. I sat back on my stool. "I was really a late bloomer," I said. "I think I was five before I was absolutely sure."

Anderson looked a bit surprised. "And you've never...?"

I grinned and shook my head. "Never the slightest interest," I said, rather hoping we could drop this whole line of conversation pretty soon.

Luckily, at that moment I noticed someone else coming into the small bar: tall—about six foot three—with black wavy hair, incredibly handsome. When he saw me he smiled, revealing about 72 of the whitest, most perfect teeth I've ever seen.

"*Phil?*" I asked, turning around on my stool and getting up to greet him. I noticed Anderson smiling broadly as Phil came over and grabbed me in a huge bear hug, which I returned. When we released one another, Phil turned to Anderson and shook hands: "Stuart," he said warmly. "Good to see you."

I managed to sit back down and, while Phil and Anderson exchanged a few words and Phil gave the bartender his order, my mind went back to my first meeting with Phil...or, as I first knew him, "Tex/Phil"...at Hughie's, a hustler bar not far from my office. He'd been in full Marlboro Man drag at the time— though I thought even then that he had the Marlboro Man beat by a mile. Seeing him now, looking like he'd just stepped off the cover of a fashion magazine, only underscored the fact that Phil was an amazingly handsome—and sexy—piece of work. But clearly, there had been some dramatic changes in his life.

Obviously it had been Phil who had recommended me to Anderson, and I was secretly very pleased to know he'd remembered not only me but what I did for a living, though I was pretty much in the dark as to the details. Anderson did not strike me as the kind of guy who would spend much time in Hughie's (though I knew you could never tell), and Phil was certainly not the same readily-identifiable hustler I'd known. I was curious as all hell about what was going on, but decided to let discretion be the better part of valor and just see what I could pick up as the evening progressed.

Phil had ordered a Black Russian—again, quite a change from his beer-bottle-butch days, and he stood beside Anderson with his free hand casually on Anderson's shoulder.

"So how long has it been, Dick?" Phil asked.

"Don't ask," I said. "Too damned long," and realized I meant it. I realized too that until I knew exactly what was going on between Phil and Anderson—though it wouldn't exactly require a caliper and slide rule to figure out—I had better watch what I said. "You're looking spectacular, as always," I said, "and it looks like you're doing well for yourself." I immediately hoped Anderson wouldn't take that last sentence the wrong way, but if he did, he didn't let on.

"As a matter of fact, I am," Phil said, giving Anderson's shoulder a squeeze and exchanging grins with him. "I've been working through ModelMen for about six months now. A great outfit."

ModelMen! I should have guessed! The ModelMen Agency, though less than a year old, was a hugely successful business venture which cleverly doubled as both a legitimate talent agency specializing in strictly male fashion models and an extremely discreet "male escort" service which provided …um…companion-ship… to very, very wealthy men like Stuart Anderson. Well, that pretty much explained how Phil and Anderson had gotten together, but I was still intensely curious as to how Phil had made the transition from diamond-in-the-rough street/bar hustler to this highly-polished gem standing three feet away from me. I'd make it a point to find out when I could manage to talk to Phil alone, though I realized it probably wouldn't be tonight.

"They were damned lucky to get you," I said and again meant it wholeheartedly. "I guess I have you to thank for referring Stuart to me."

"Guilty," Phil said, grinning. "You're kind of a hard guy to forget, and when Stuart mentioned he was going to hire an investigator to look into the backgrounds of his prospective management teams, I naturally suggested you."

While trying (with only moderate success) to keep my crotch from reacting too strongly to that "hard to forget" line and stripping him naked on the spot, I was glad when Anderson entered the conversation.

"If any of the applicants for the managers' job might be gay," he said, "I didn't want to risk his—or her—chances by putting the responsibility for checking them out in the hands of some potentially-prejudiced straight investigator. Of course," he said with a grin, "I'm taking the chance that you won't go off in the opposite direction."

"Guaranteed," I said.

The maitre d' came over to announce that our table was ready, and we followed him into the dining room.

I must admit that Phil really impressed the hell out of me at dinner. We hadn't spent all that much time talking in the couple times I'd seen him, actually, but I did know that Phil had come from a lower-middle-class background and had never gone to college. That wasn't to say that he wasn't a pretty intelligent and self-confident guy, but I never had the feeling that he was ever too concerned about knowing which fork was for the oysters. But I had no doubt but that he knew now. How, when, and where he'd learned was added to my "things to find out" list. He talked easily with Anderson about stock trends and market shares and things about which I could barely venture an opinion. And it was all blended together so smoothly and effortlessly that it was as though he'd been that way all his life.

Dinner was very nice, actually. The food was, as always, excellent, although Anderson did bring up his other life in greater detail than I'd have needed to know. His youngest son, aged 8, apparently was giving the family a lot of trouble, and they had decided to send him away to private school where they would hopefully be able to address his problems before they got completely out of hand. I gathered Phil was familiar with the situation from his previous encounters with Anderson. But other than those fascinating insights into the life of the average heterosexual, the rest of the conversation was pleasant enough, on a wide range of subjects.

Anderson, I decided, was one of those nice guys easy to talk with, but about whom I felt nothing in particular one way or the other. He was returning to Buffalo the next day, but was due back in town Sunday evening for dinner with a prospective cutlery supplier, and then set up personal interviews Monday with any of the prospective managers my research had not eliminated. I made sure I had his office address and phone number and told him I would have my report waiting at his hotel—the Montero—when he arrived.

But Anderson had other ideas, apparently.

"No," he said, "why don't you bring them around to the hotel first thing Monday morning —say around 7:15? I go for a 20 minute run every morning at 6:30, so that will give me time to get back and shower. We can have breakfast and go over your report—it will save me some time, especially if I have any questions."

I really don't like being jaded, but I immediately had the mental image of Anderson opening the door in his robe, which would conveniently manage to come open when I stepped inside the room....

Still, he hadn't really even come close to making a pass, and it was unfair of me to think that just because his gay side was repressed most of the time, he wouldn't be able to keep it under control. I was mildly embarrassed to realize I was using exactly the same kind of specious logic many straight men use against gays.

"Fine," I said.

As we said goodbye outside the restaurant, I told Phil how good it was to see him again, and asked him to please give me a call. He said he would and, when we shook hands, I got the definite impression that he meant it.

Can crotches smile? I wondered.

* * *

I'd been lucky enough (if "lucky" is the word), about six months before, to handle a case for Mollie Marino, a lesbian who worked in the Clerk of Courts office in the City Building. Mollie's ex-husband had threatened to expose her sexual orientation to her notoriously homophobic boss—which would, at the time, have put her job at risk or at least effectively ended any chances she may have had for advancement. When I was able to discover that the ex-husband was dumb enough to be having a secret affair with his boss's seventeen-year-old daughter, that pretty much resolved the case then and there. But Mollie was very grateful, and I'd been able to get priority treatment whenever I needed information on someone's arrest record, which I made a standard part of most of my investigations.

After stopping briefly at the office to check for mail and phone messages, I wrote down the names and basic information from Anderson's resumes on a single sheet of paper, folded it, put it in my shirt pocket, and headed for the City Building. Mollie was, I was glad to see, on duty, and she accepted the list without giving it more than a cursory glance.

"When do you need it?" she asked.

"As soon as you possibly can without going out of your way," I said.

She smiled. "Give me a call around 3:00—I'll see what I can do."

As they say, it's not *what* you know....

* * *

I was pleasantly—to put it mildly—surprised to find, on returning to the office, that I'd had a call from a Phil Stark. Though I don't think I'd ever known Phil's last name, I was sure it was him, and I hastened to return the call.

When the phone was answered, I didn't recognize the voice.

"Phil?" I asked, wondering if I'd been wrong and this was another Phil.

"No, this is Billy. Phil should be back in about half an hour. Can I have him call you?"

Billy, huh? He sounded pretty young—and pretty sexy, if voices count.

"Yeah, if you would," I said. "This is Dick Hardesty returning his call. I'll be in the office for a couple hours."

"I'll give him the message," Billy said. "Thanks for calling. 'Bye."

Billy, huh? my mind asked again.

Yes, 'Billy, huh', I answered. *Why in hell couldn't you have been born a Gemini instead of a Scorpio? There's more to life than your fucking crotch.*

Like, for instance...?

I reached for the phone and called downstairs to the coffee shop to order lunch—a chef's salad, blue cheese dressing, and a large black coffee to go, then immediately got up from my chair, left the office, and took the elevator to the lobby. My order was waiting for me when I got to the cash register. Either Eudora or Evolla—the identical twin waitresses who, I was sure, had voted for Coolidge—handed me the bill and the white paper bag. After all these years, I still couldn't tell them apart without their name tags, which they often did not bother to put on or, as I strongly suspected, frequently switched—which would be the only oblique concession to humor (or any other emotion) I ever saw them display. *They knew who they were; if nobody else did, tough.*

I didn't want to tie up the phone while I waited for Phil's call, so I spent the time looking through the phone book with one hand and eating with the other. I went through each applicant's past work history and then checked for and wrote down the phone numbers of the companies/ organizations for which they had worked. A couple of the applicants had moved into the city from elsewhere, so that meant a little more work and some calls to Information. One of the women applicants had included phone numbers and extension numbers in her list, and she immediately moved to the top of the heap in my estimation—which admittedly probably wasn't going to be much of a factor in Anderson's final determination.

The phone rang just as I was wiping a dab of blue cheese dressing off one of the resumes.

I let it ring twice—which gave me time to move the salad safely out of the way—before answering.

"Hardesty Investigations," I said.

"Dick, hi. This is Phil." Of course it was. "Sorry about the phone tag. I had an appointment for a haircut and just got back."

"No problem," I said. "And before I forget, I want to thank you again for referring Stuart Anderson to me. I really appreciate it."

"Well, like I said, I never really forgot our little get-togethers, and when Stuart said he needed some help, I thought of you immediately."

"I owe you," I said. "And speaking of get-togethers, I'd really like to see you whenever you have the chance—I want to hear all about what's been happening with you since you sort of disappeared."

"I'd like that," he said, and sounded as though he meant it. He paused, and then said: "Tell you what; my evenings are pretty much tied up, but how about meeting me at Hughie's Saturday afternoon around 4:30?"

"You still go to Hughie's?" I asked, a little surprised at myself for being surprised to hear that he might.

"I haven't in a long time," he said, "but I always say, you should never forget where you came from—you never know when you might have to go back there."

"Well, Phil," I said. "I somehow suspect you've moved a bit beyond Hughie's. But it'll be fun to see you—there or anywhere. Until 4:30 Saturday, then."

"Looking forward to it," he said. "So long...."

* * *

When my crotch finally allowed me to tear my thoughts away from some very interesting fantasies involving Phil, I started calling the phone numbers I'd written down on the resumes.

As so often happens, one minute it was 1:45 and the next it was 3:00 and time to call Mollie at the Clerk of Courts office. The three resumes I'd managed to go through produced nothing but good-to-glowingly positive ratings, and I was rather hoping Mollie might have at least come up with an ax murder conviction to make it interesting. No such luck.

"A total of three speeding convictions," Mollie said; "one destruction of property conviction—breaking a window at an abortion clinic during a protest rally—one assault and battery charge stemming from a mini-riot after a football game, and one violation of a restraining order issued by an ex-wife filing for divorce. Kind of vanilla."

I agreed, but noted the appropriate information on the appropriate resume and promised Mollie I'd take her and her new lover Barb out to dinner one night soon by way of thanks.

* * *

By the time Friday afternoon rolled around, I had finished the background checks on all the resumes Anderson had given me and typed up my report. Not a single ax murderer among them. While assignments like this paid the bills, they were hardly the kind of stuff of which impressive resumes—mine, in this case—are made.

And while I had resolved some time ago not to work on weekends, I stopped by the office Saturday morning just long enough to type up my bill, put it in the envelope with the resumes and my report, and bring it home so I wouldn't have to take the time to go by to pick it up Monday morning.

While I was really looking forward to seeing Phil, I knew my tendency to always be early, so I deliberately took my time puttering around the apartment until I was sure that I had it timed perfectly to make it to Hughie's by 4:30. And, of course, I arrived fifteen minutes early.

Hughie's was a time warp. No matter when you went in—no matter the hour or the day or the month or the year—it never changed. Bud, the bartender, was behind the bar as he had been all but a handful of times I'd been there; the individual hustlers changed, of course, and so did the individual johns, but they were still cookie-cutter hustlers and still cookie-cutter johns

I ordered my usual dark beer on draft—actually, I never had to actually *ask* for it—Bud only needed to spot me out of the corner of his eye as I walked in the door for his hand to immediately reach for the cooler where the iced mugs were kept. Something both a little comforting and a little disturbing about that, I thought.

I sat at a stool near the end of the bar as Bud brought the beer over, flourished a napkin onto the bar in front of me, and set the mug on it. As always, by the time I'd fished a bill out of my pocket to pay for it, the napkin had turned sopping wet from the condensation running down the sides of the mug. But it was part of the routine, as was Bud's "How's it going, Dick?" and my "Fine, Bud, how about you?", his shrug, and his taking my money to the cash register.

"Got a match, buddy?" a voice behind me said, and I turned to see...Tex/Phil. Not the "new" Phil from dinner, but the original Tex/Phil I'd met in Hughie's that afternoon what seemed now like an eternity ago. Full Marlboro Man drag—cowboy hat set sexily back on his wavy-black hair; Levi's jacket open to the navel, no shirt, incredibly tight Levi's jeans, a silver belt buckle the size of a small hubcap, scuffed cowboy boots.

I couldn't help but grin from ear to ear. "My God, man!" I said, "You're incredible. You did this just for me?"

He put one big hand easily on my shoulder while he pulled up the empty stool next to mine with the other.

"Mostly," he said with a grin. "Actually, Billy's meeting me here around 7:00; we've got a Double Shit-kicker Special on for tonight."

Still grinning, I shook my head. "Lost me," I admitted.

"I'm not surprised," he said, motioning to get Bud's attention. "I guess we've got a lot of catching up to do."

"I'm all ears," I said, and he grinned again.

"Like shit you are," he said, giving a rather obvious eye-slide down my body to my crotch.

"Glad you remember," I said.

Bud came over and Phil ordered a Miller's. Bud nodded without a word and moved off to get it. Phil started to reach into the very small front pocket of his Levi's, but I waved him off, taking another bill out of my pocket. "You hustler," I said, putting it on the bar. "Me john. John pay."

Phil gave me a quick, raised-eyebrow grin.

"So fill me in," I said when Bud had put Phil's beer in front of him and left.

Phil clicked the top of his bottle against my mug and took a long drink before beginning.

"Long story," he said.

"I like 'em long," I replied, straight faced, which produced another of his raised-eyebrow grins.

"Well, about six months ago now…maybe seven..," he began, "I was working Beech Street one night around eleven when this Jag pulls up. Older guy, average looking, nice grey hair, obviously not worried where his next meal was coming from. We go through the usual, and I get in. But instead of taking me someplace, or even making a pass in the car, we just drove around for about half an hour, talking. That's a little unusual, but not unheard of. He's asking me all sorts of questions on all sorts of things. Mostly about me, but a whole bunch of other things too. Seemed like a pretty nice guy. Finally he says 'How would you like to work for me?' I told him I thought that's what I was doing, but he smiled and said 'No, a real job; same line of work, but it will pay a great deal more.'

"I was a little leery, but he asked me to hear him out, and I agreed. 'Good,' he said. 'But first, I'd like you to meet my wife.'"

Now I was the one with the raised eyebrows, and Phil grinned and raised his hand. "Yeah, I know, that was my reaction too, but it wasn't like that at all. I told him I didn't do that kind of kinky stuff, and I sure as hell didn't do anything with anybody who doesn't have a cock. He just looked at me and smiled again. 'My dear boy, you misunderstand,' he said and then explained the whole thing."

Phil looked at me, and then took another long drink from his beer, draining it. He set it on the bar and pushed it toward Bud's side. I did the same.

"Am I telling you more about penguins than you care to know?" he asked.

"Hell no," I said, and meant it. "Tell all." I waved at Bud and took another bill from my pocket and put it on the bar. Phil shook his head, reached out and handed the bill back to me, and fished in his own pocket, coming up with a folded $100. Then he picked up his story where he'd left off.

"Well, his name's Arnold Glick," Phil said. "He's bisexual and a retired stock market analyst from New York. If he'd been giving me this line in a bar, I'd probably have thought 'uh-huh' and dozed off; but when I'm driving around town in a brand new Jaguar with less than 1,000 miles on the odometer—I looked—I tended to give the whole thing a little more weight. Though why he chose me is still a mystery."

Gee, I wonder? I thought. *Six-three, a body and face to die for, a great personality...go figure.*

Bud brought our drinks, took a look at the $100 bill and walked over to a small light by the cash register, where he carefully examined it before opening the till and counting out the change, which he brought back and laid in front of Phil.

"Business must be good," he said.

"Oh, yeah," Phil said, and left the change sitting on the bar. When Bud walked off, Phil picked up his story. "Glick's wife, Iris, is a lot younger than he is by about a third—she's only about 40 now—and she started out as a showgirl in Vegas. Iris isn't exactly what you'd call a shrinking violet: she's got bigger balls than a lot of the guys who used to pick me up. Anyway, when she got too old to be in the shows, she decided to start a sort of finishing school for showgirl wannabes and some of the more enterprising hookers. She met Arnold in Vegas about three years ago, and they decided to get married. He'd retired from his stock market job in order to concentrate on his real estate investments. He's got a lot of property here, and when they moved here to keep an eye on it, she was pretty unhappy about having to give up her school. So they took stock of the situation and somehow hatched the idea of opening a modeling agency and male escort service. Arnold had a lot of rich friends who dig guys, and Iris figured she could extend her finishing school talents to include guys. Their goal was to offer class without bullshit, and strictly legit in that everybody involved, on both sides of the fence, knows all the rules going in, and no-body...*nobody*...breaks them."

I hadn't taken my eyes off him for one second since he started talking, and I was totally absorbed in every word. Talk about a different world!

Suddenly Phil indicated my left arm with a head-lift nod. "What time is it?" he asked.

I looked at my watch. "Five fifteen," I said. "You've got plenty of time, if you don't have to meet Billy until seven."

Phil gave me a big grin. "You don't think I planned to sit around here for two and a half hours, did you?"

I hoped I was the only one who could hear my crotch shouting: *Wheeeeeeeeee!*

"Well," I said, "we could always continue our talk at my office. As I recall, you do some of your best talking in offices."

We looked at each other, still grinning, then in unison drained our drinks, set the empties on the bar, and walked out.

* * *

I had no idea what Phil's professional rates were, but there was no question whatever that they were a steal no matter how much it cost! And though Phil had undoubtedly undergone some polishing of his social skills, in a horizontal position he was as natural and spontaneous as the first day I'd met him.

When the fireworks display was over and we'd regained our respective breaths, I lay back against the arm of the office couch with Phil semi-on top of me, his head on my chest.

"And you have to go through this again tonight?" I asked, my chin on my chest so I could look down at Phil. "How in the hell do you do it?"

He smiled. "All part of the business," he said. "And Billy and I know how to pace ourselves."

I had been curious about Billy ever since he'd answered the phone. "If you don't mind my asking," I said, "just what is the 'family relationship' here? And what is a 'Double Shit-Kicker Special'?"

Phil's smile widened into a full grin. "We've got this one client, a businessman from Tokyo, who grew up watching American westerns. So whenever he comes to town, he arranges for Billy and me to come over in full cowboy drag and put on a little show for him. He never gets involved himself—he just pulls a chair up beside the bed and watches while we go through this little 'bunkhouse buddies' playlet we improvised the first time. We do it exactly the same every time; no variations—he wants it that way. Then when we're done, we get dressed and leave, and he hands us each a $100 bill as a tip."

"Jeezus, am *I* in the wrong business," I said.

Phil grinned again. "Hey, if you're interested…" he said.

I put my hand behind his head and pressed it quickly into my chest, then released it. "I appreciate that," I said, "but I'm kind of used to what I'm doing now."

"Well," Phil said, "if you should ever change your mind…." Then his eyes fell on my watch, which was lying on top of my pants on the floor beside the couch. "Oh, oh," he said, "I'd better get going; it's six thirty."

We untangled our arms and legs and got up, rummaging through our clothes to get dressed.

"Wish I had a shower here," I said. "We both could use one."

Phil, slipping his shorts up over his hips, shook his head. "Nah," he said, "that's fine—my being all sweaty just adds to the hard-riding cowboy image. The guy'll love it."

"So," I said, "it's none of my business, but are you and Billy…."

Phil reached for his Levi's jacket. "Oh, no," he said without looking at me. "Billy's like my kid brother. I got to know him when he first came to town, and I sort of adopted him. We room together, and we trick…well, we, uh, *work*…together from time to time, but that's about it."

"Billy works for ModelMen too, then?" I asked, tucking in my shirttail and looking for my shoes.

"Yeah," Phil replied. "I convinced the Glicks to hire him, too. They needed a type like Billy."

I was going to ask what he meant by that, but Phil, having sat back down on the couch to pull on his boots, stood up, adjusted himself, hooked his belt buckle, and said: "Why don't you come back to Hughie's with me? You can meet Billy before we head off. I think you'd like him—and I know damned well he'll like you."

This whole new world Phil was living in had me fascinated, and I very much wanted to get a look at Billy. "Sure."

Taking a last look around the office to be sure we hadn't forgotten anything, we went out into the hall. I double-checked to be sure the door was locked, and we made our way to the elevator.

* * *

It was a warm evening, but fortunately not so warm that we would have needed the air conditioner in the office—which still didn't work anyway. As we walked the two blocks to Hughie's, I couldn't help but ask Phil more about his new life.

"Are you seeing Anderson when he comes back into town tomorrow?" I asked.

Phil shook his head. "No, not tomorrow. Maybe Monday or Tuesday before he goes back to Buffalo on Wednesday, but I'm not sure. All those arrangements are handled by the Glicks."

"So no freelancing?" I asked.

"Not with ModelMen clients," he said. "Everything goes through the Glicks. We can still do whatever we want on our own time, but not with anyone we meet through ModelMen. And they generally keep us pretty busy."

"Makes sense," I said. "So how many guys work through ModelMen's escort service, if that's not privileged information?"

"There are only six of us in the escort end of it, actually. Each one a different physical type, each with his own…uh, specialties. But we're all pretty…uh…versatile. And we all do modeling, too, to keep the whole thing legit. That gives ModelMen the widest range of flexibility when it comes to meeting a client's specific needs."

He sounded like some young business executive outlining the benefits of his company's profit-sharing plan. Which in a way is exactly what he was doing.

When we arrived at Hughie's, the door was just opening to disgorge a mean-looking leather-clad hustler and a timid-looking suit-and-tie'd businessman. *Shark and chum,* I thought.

The place was about as busy as when we'd left it, and a couple of the same guys were still there. Bud, to my considerable surprise, was not. Another bartender I had seen once or twice before was holding sway with the usual total-lack-of-interest expression Bud usually wore.

As we entered, I had immediately spotted a little blond dressed in faded Levi's pants with a hole in one knee and a matching Levi's short jacket—and a cowboy hat. About 5'10", slim, an angelic teenager's face….

Phil, of course, walked us right over to him. The kid looked up from his beer and, spotting Phil, his face broke into a wide grin that was totally disarming. Then he realized I was with Phil and, his eyes darting quickly from Phil to me and back again, his grin made just the slightest change from cherubic to innocently naughty.

"Dick," Phil said, wrapping one arm around the younger guy's waist, "this is Billy."

Billy quickly set his beer down so we could shake hands. "Nice to meet you, Dick," he said, and his voice, as it had been on the phone, was warm and sincere.

"You too, Billy," I said, and really meant it. I could readily see how engaging in a little voyeurism involving the tall, dark Phil and the slight, boyish blond could well be worth whatever the Japanese businessman paid.

"We got a call from Mr. Glick just as I was leaving the apartment," Billy said, looking up at Phil. "He wants us to be at the hotel a little early."

"Like how early?" Phil asked.

Billy shrugged. "Like now," he said.

"Got your inhaler?" Phil asked.

Billy patted his pocket. "Right here," he said.

Noticing my look, Phil grinned. "Billy's got asthma and strenuous…activity…sometimes brings on an attack. I have to watch over him like a mother hen." He and Billy exchanged grins.

Phil gave a long sigh, then turned to me. "I'm really sorry, Dick; I was hoping we could all have a drink and you and Billy could get a chance to know one another."

You're not the only one! I thought. "No problem," I said. "Next time."

"I'll look forward to it," Billy said, smiling.

"So, partner," Phil said, looking at Billy, "we'd better be moseyin' down the trail."

Billy looked at him, his face taking on an expression of wide-eyed total innocence. "Whatever you say, Tex." He then turned to me and gave me a wicked grin and a wink. "See'ya, Dick," he said. I shook hands with both of them, and they turned to walk out of the bar, side by side.

Oh, to be a fly on that hotel bedroom wall! I thought.

CHAPTER 2

I had a quick beer at Hughie's after Phil and Billy left, then headed home. Normally, I'd have grabbed dinner and then taken a shower and headed back out to the bars. But my little afternoon romp with Phil had pretty much taken the edge off my usual drive to get out there and look for Mr. Right. So instead, I fixed dinner, took a shower, put on my robe, made a big bowl of popcorn and settled down in front of the TV. It was all sort of oddly decadent, since I so seldom did it, but what the hell?

Sunday morning was my "B" schedule—I had an "A" and a "B": the "A" was a "wake up with a trick" schedule, which had several variations depending on how I felt about the trick, and the "B" schedule, which had very few variations at all. Under the "B", I woke up whenever I damned well felt like it (a game I play with myself since even when I had absolutely no reason to, I was almost always awake by 6:45), stumbled into the kitchen, fixed coffee, went out into the hall to see if I could figure out where the paper boy had left it *this* time, read the paper, did the crossword puzzle, made more coffee, took a shower, then thought about breakfast. Here's where the only "B" schedule variation came in: eat in or go out to brunch.

I tried calling my friend Jared—a beer delivery man working on his Ph.D. in Russian Literature, who was built like a battleship complete with 18" cannon. No luck—knowing Jared as I did he was undoubtedly operating under a schedule "A" of his own. I hung up before his answering machine kicked in.

I next tried Bob Allen, a longtime friend and owner of my favorite bar, Ramón's—but again, an answering machine. He'd probably spent the night with Mario, the guy he'd been dating pretty heavily for a while now.

Now, about this time most rational people would just give up and go into the kitchen and make their own damned breakfast. But not me. I took not finding people home as a personal challenge. And then I thought of Tim Jackson. I'd not seen Tim in far too long, but that was sort of our pattern. We always had a great time whenever we got together, but we each tended to get easily distracted. Tim was a medical examiner in the coroner's office, and he'd been a real help on a couple of the messier cases I'd handled, so on a whim I dialed his number—rather pleased that I still remembered it.

When I got Tim's answering machine, I left a generic sort of message about having been thinking of him and wondering how he was doing, and that he should give me a call when he had the chance. Then when I hung up I figured 'the hell with it' and went into the kitchen to fix breakfast.

So much for Plan B.

* * *

Five thirty is much too early for any civilized human being to get out of bed on a Monday morning, but I forced myself, taking absolutely no consolation in the thought that I didn't have to do it very often. Fixed a pot of coffee—I'd set it all up the night before and then forgotten to turn on the timer switch—and bumbled into the shower.

About the only good thing about that time of morning was that downtown parking places were still possible to find. I parked about half a block from the Montero and seeing I was about ten minutes early, I took my time walking to the hotel, forcing myself to look in store windows that I normally never would have bothered looking in—and, having looked at them, realized why—and walked into the Montero's lobby at exactly 7:12. I went to the registration desk and asked for Mr. Anderson's room. The clerk smiled, looked at something I could not see just below the counter, then picked up the phone and punched in a number. She held the phone to her ear for about half a minute before hanging it up, saying "I'm sorry, sir, Mr. Anderson is not answering."

Figuring he was probably still in the shower after his run and didn't hear the phone, I asked if she'd mind trying again in a minute or two, then stood there by the desk, idly looking around the cavernous lobby while I waited. The Montero was one of the city's older and more prestigious hotels and had recently undergone a multi-million dollar renovation to restore it to its original elegance. They did a nice job, I decided.

After a few minutes, I turned back to the clerk, who was busy doing whatever registration clerks do when they're not taking registrations.

"Would you try Mr. Anderson's room again, please?" I asked. She smiled her registration clerk's smile and again picked up the phone. Another half minute wait and again "Mr. Anderson is not answering, sir. Perhaps he stepped out."

I doubted that, but thought I'd check out the dining room, just in case I'd misunderstood him. I thanked the clerk and headed toward the huge mahogany French doors which separated the main dining room from the lobby. There were perhaps a total of six early-risers sprinkled around the large room with only a click of coffee cup on saucer or fork tapping plate to break the thickly carpeted silence. Anderson was not there.

I returned to the registration desk.

"Did Mr. Anderson by any chance leave a message for me? Dick Hardesty?" She again checked the area under the counter, then said "No, sir. Nothing."

"He was supposed to go running this morning," I said. "I wonder if you might have seen someone in a running suit go through the lobby?"

She shook her head. "We have quite a few runners," she said, "but they generally leave through the parking garage."

Hmmm, so much for that, I thought. "Perhaps I should go up and see if he might still be sleeping," I said. I didn't know how set in stone his running ritual might be. "May I have his room number?"

She looked at me as if checking to see if I were wearing bib overalls, a straw hat, and had hayseeds behind my ears. "We do not give out our guests' room numbers, sir," she said with a condescension that made me want to reach across the counter and throttle her. I realized immediately that of course they did-n't/wouldn't.

"Then would you mind seeing that Mr. Anderson gets these," I said, handing her the envelope with the resumes, "and tell him I will…" I noted her slight raised eyebrow. I changed course in mid sentence. "Would there be a way I could leave him a note?"

She nodded and reached under the counter. I swore that if she tried to hand me a pencil to write with, I would throttle her. Instead, she came up with a piece of Montero stationary, a pen, and an envelope. I jotted a quick note for Anderson, telling him I would be in my office, and for him to please call me if he needed anything more from me.

Mildly pissed, I left.

I wasn't particularly hungry, but when I got to the office I deliberately took the time to go to the diner and order a Denver omelet and coffee, and took my own sweet time in eating. Then I stopped to pick up the paper from the lobby newsstand. But when I got into the office and checked my messages, there was nothing from Anderson.

I didn't know the guy well enough to know if this was standard operating procedure for him, but I somehow doubted it. Something must have come up, though if he'd just gotten into town the night before, there wasn't really all that much time for anything to have distracted him. Oh, well.

I read the paper and started to do the crossword puzzle, but my heart wasn't in it. I called the Montero and asked them to ring Mr. Anderson's room. When they said there was no answer, I asked if he had picked up the resumes. He hadn't.

Since I knew he was intending to set up interviews for his prospective managers, I couldn't imagine that he would just ignore their resumes. I even toyed with the idea of trying to call Phil. I knew he said he wasn't intending to see Anderson Sunday night, but things might have changed. But even so, I couldn't imagine their spending the night anywhere but in Anderson's room. Very odd, indeed.

At eleven thirty, the phone rang. Finally! I thought. I let it ring twice, then picked up the phone.

"Hardesty Investigations," I said.

The voice was not Anderson's. "Dick, this is Mark Richman. Could you come down to headquarters right away?"

Mark Richman? What the hell did I do now? I wondered. Mark Richman was Lieutenant Mark Richman of the City Police Department. A nice guy I'd worked with before, but I'd been on his—and the department's—shit list for a while.

"Sure," I said. "I'm expecting a client to call any minute, though. Could you tell me what this is about?"

"Stuart Anderson," he said.

Shit! "I'll be right there," I said.

* * *

I thought about the possible scenarios all the way to the City Building: Anderson had been busted trying to pick up an undercover cop posing as a hustler. Or, worse, somehow he and Phil had gotten busted together. I wished I'd taken the time to call Phil before I left the office. Or, third possibility, they'd busted the whole ModelMen Agency and Anderson had been caught up in it.

But if any of those things had happened, why wouldn't Anderson, or Phil, just have called me directly? What was Richman doing in all this?

I parked in the underground garage beneath Warman Park and walked the two blocks to the Police Annex of the City Building. Wending my way through the sea of blue uniforms that always washed back and forth in the lobby, I went directly to the elevators and up to Richman's floor. I'd not so much as talked with Richman since my little falling out with the department, and had no idea of the kind of reception I might expect. *Well, too late to worry about that now,* I thought as I knocked on the door with the "M. Richman" written in black letters on the opaque glass.

"Come," Richman's voice commanded from within the office. Taking a deep breath, I turned the knob and entered.

"Dick," Richman said, his face expressionless as he got out of his chair to shake hands.

"Lieutenant," I replied, hopefully with a matching lack of expression and reaching across his desk to take his extended hand. A very quick shake-release, and he motioned me to the nearest chair.

"You were at the Montero this morning, looking for Stuart Anderson?" he asked.

The question took me aback for some reason. "Yes, I was..." I said. "Why?"

"What was your business with Mr. Anderson?"

Come on, Richman…what are you getting at? I thought.

"He had hired me to check out some prospective managers for his new stores here in town," I said. "I was bringing him my report, as he'd asked me to. Is…."

"Your clients are all gay, aren't they?" he asked. As usual when we talked, he never took his eyes off me.

Whoa, there, Charlie! I thought. "That's hardly a fair question, Lieutenant," I said. "Most of my clients are gay, of course, but I don't make sexual orientation a qualification for accepting a client. Mr. Anderson is married and has three children."

A smile as quick and as subtle as far-off summer lightning flashed across his face. "Well, then…" he said, and I realized that not only was Richman not stupid, but that I certainly sounded as if I were.

"So," I continued, hoping we'd both forget that unspoken 'oh, then he can't be gay' reference, "exactly why am I here?"

Richman sat back in his chair. "Because your client, Mr. Anderson, is dead."

Jeezus H. Kryst! I thought, feeling as though someone had just tossed me a 40-pound medicine ball and I'd caught it with my stomach. My total confusion must have been written all over my face. "What happened?" I asked.

Richman gave me a moment to calm myself down. "He was found in his hotel room at around 9:15 by the contractor working on his new stores. They had a 9 a.m. appointment at Anderson's room. When Anderson didn't show up, and in light of your earlier visit, hotel security went in to check. "

"What happened?" I repeated. "Heart attack? Fall?"

Richman shook his head. "Murder. He was…choked to death."

"Good God!" I said. "Do you have any idea who…." And suddenly my already queasy stomach dropped down to my toes. *Phil! Do they know about Phil? Could Phil possibly…don't be stupid, you idiot…that's totally ridiculous.*

Richman was quiet again for a moment, never taking his eyes off me. "So Anderson was not gay?"

I shook my head, more to clear it than anything else. "Lieutenant," I said, choosing my words as carefully as I could under the circumstances, "As I've told you, I never ask my clients their sexual orientation. When someone mentions having a wife and children, the assumption is that they're straight."

"And how did you come to Mr. Anderson's attention?"

"He told me he'd been referred to me by a business acquaintance," I said, hastening to add "but he never said who it was. But part of the reason he wanted me to do the checking was because he wanted to give all the applicants an equal chance. He thought that if any of them happened to be gay, a straight investigator might let his prejudices influence his report."

"And were they?" he asked.

"Were they what?" I asked. "Gay? What does that have to do with..."

Richman made a small, dismissive wave with one hand. "Sorry," he said. "A stupid question and it has no bearing on anything. I guess I've found out everything I need to know for now."

The 'for now' wasn't lost on me.

He rose from his chair and I followed suit. We shook hands.

"Thanks for coming over," he said.

"Nice to see you, Lieutenant," I replied. I was greatly relieved that apparently I might be pretty much off their official shit list. He was sitting back down as I turned and left.

* * *

Jeezus, Hardesty! I chastised myself as I walked back to my car. *Why in hell didn't you tell Richman that Anderson was gay...well, okay, bi....*

Because it wasn't my place, I answered defensively. *Anderson had a family; they don't need to have their noses rubbed in the fact that he wasn't the man they thought they knew.*

Like that's going to make a difference now? I thought. *My God, the man was murdered —and probably by some wacked-out hustler who you might have helped to stop by letting the cops know where they might start looking. Shit! Shit!*

The first thing I wanted to do was to check with Phil. I knew he couldn't possibly be involved in any way with what happened to Anderson, but I had to be absolutely sure. And maybe he might possibly know something about Anderson's sexual interests outside of ModelMen.

When I walked into the office, I didn't even sit down before picking up the phone and dialing Phil's number.

"Hello?" a young voice I recognized as Billy's said.

"Billy, hi…This is Dick Hardesty," I said. "Is Phil by any chance around?"

"No, he's not. He hasn't come home yet. He had an all-nighter with a client."

Oh, Jeezus! "Do you know who he was with?" I asked, hoping my anxiety wasn't too obvious. "It's really, really important!"

There was a long pause, then: "Well, yeah, I know, but I'm afraid I really can't tell you, Dick. We're never allowed to talk about our clients. Not to anybody."

"Billy," I said, "I can appreciate that, but you have no idea how important this is." Then I had an idea. "If I give you a name, can you at least tell me if I'm wrong? That way you won't be violating any rules."

"Tell you if you're wrong?" I could picture him thinking that one out. "Yeah, I guess I could do that. But don't tell anybody, okay?"

"I won't, I promise," I said. Then I took a deep breath. "Stuart Anderson."

Another pause, then: "No."

Damn! "No?" I said. "'No,' I'm right, or 'no,' I'm wrong and it wasn't Anderson."

Billy laughed, obviously having no idea of what I was trying to find out. "'No,' you're wrong. It wasn't Stuart Anderson."

I let my breath out in a great, long sigh. "Thank you, Billy," I said. *And thank you, God!* I thought.

"Sure," Billy said. Then: "Are you okay? You sound kind of funny."

"Well, I feel better now," I said, "but please have Phil call me the minute he gets home, will you? I've really got to talk with him right away."

"Sure," Billy said. "Is there anything else?"

"Not now, I don't think," I replied. "Oh, my home phone number—I don't know if he has it. I'll be here until 4:30 and home right after 5."

"Let me get a pencil," Billy said, and I heard the phone being put down. A moment later, he came back on and I gave him the number.

"Got it," he said.

"Thanks again, Billy," I said. "I owe you."

"I'll remember that," he said cheerily. "See you, then."

"Bye," I said as we both hung up.

* * *

I was still torn about calling Richman back and letting him in on the fact that Anderson was bi, and frequented hustlers—well, okay, semantics: make that 'and paid men for sex.' But if I did that, a background check might well bring Phil into it. I decided I'd wait until after I talked with Phil to see just how likely it might be that ModelMen might also be dragged in to the picture.

If a street hustler had killed Anderson—and I suspected that was a pretty good bet—that was one thing, but to bring Phil and ModelMen into it unless it was absolutely necessary wouldn't do anyone any good.

I was just getting ready to leave the office when the phone rang.

"Hardesty Investigations."

"Dick…Phil. Billy said you wanted to talk to me. What's up?"

"We've got to talk—someplace private. I know you just got home, but can you come over here? Or to my place?"

"Gee, Dick…I don't know. I'm really, really beat, and the Glicks said that Stuart called last night after his dinner with his supplier and wanted me to come over. When they told him I was on an assignment, he asked for tonight. So I've got to grab a few hours of sleep and then get over to his hotel."

Definite change of plans, Phil! I thought. But I still didn't want to say anything on the phone.

"Phil, can I come over there? Right away? It's important, believe me."

There was only a slight pause, then: "Sure, I guess. If we can make it kind of short. I don't mean to put you off, Dick, but…"

"I understand, Phil," I said. "Give me your address and I'll leave the office the minute we hang up."

"Billy's here, of course," Phil said. "It's okay if he stays?"

"Of course," I said.

"Okay, it's 1933 Partridge, Apartment 4—you know where it is? About six blocks east of Barnes Park?"

"I'll find it," I said. "And I'll be there in about fifteen minutes. Bye."

* * *

1933 Partridge was in an area of solid older apartment buildings, mostly three-story, mostly well kept up. I rang the buzzer for Apartment 4 ("P. Stark/W. Steiner") and the door immediately clicked open. Apartment 4 was on the ground floor, in the rear. I was just raising my hand to knock when Billy opened the door.

"Hi, Dick, come on in." he said, stepping aside as I entered then closing the door behind me. I was favorably impressed—a lot cleaner than my place; comfortable-looking furniture, including an obviously new couch, nice prints on the walls; a few plants on the window ledges. Absolutely no evidence of Phil's "Tex" persona.

"You want some coffee, Dick?" Phil's voice called from what I assumed, being the astute detective that I am, was the kitchen.

"Yeah, please," I said, loudly enough to carry the distance. "Black."

"Have a seat," Billy said, and I did. Billy seemed hesitant to sit himself, looking toward the kitchen where Phil was emerging with a coffee cup in each hand. He started to give one to Billy, but Billy shook his head. "I'll go get it," he said, and headed toward the kitchen, discreetly leaving Phil and me alone.

Phil handed me my coffee, then sat on the edge of the couch, leaning forward, elbows on knees, both hands on his coffee cup.

"So tell," he said, and I did.

The color drained from his face, and he quickly moved forward to put his coffee cup on the table lamp beside the couch. He started to say something, then merely shook his head and put one hand over his mouth.

"Billy!" he finally managed to call, and Billy came into the room, looking mildly puzzled.

"Yeah?"

"Tell him, Dick," Phil said softly, and I repeated what I'd told Phil.

Billy's eyes grew wide and he plopped down on the couch next to Phil, nearly sloshing the coffee out of his cup. "Holy shit!" he said.

We were all quiet for a moment until I said: "When you couldn't go over night, did ModelMen send someone else?"

Phil shook his head: "I don't think so," he said. "I'd have to check with the Glicks to be sure, but..."

"Did Anderson go for street hustlers, do you know?" I asked.

Again a head-shake. "I don't think so—he said a couple times that he liked the discretion of ModelMen—a lot safer all around. But who knows?"

"Did he have any...uh...special interests in guys?" I asked.

Phil thought a minute. "Not really. He was really pretty vanilla; way too uptight for anything at all kinky...at least not with me. He did seem to like darker-haired guys over blonds, but other than that...."

"What do you mean by 'way too uptight'?" I asked.

Phil gave a barely perceptible shrug. "Well...just between us, he was pretty limited. He just wanted to get fucked. Period. Didn't suck, didn't want to get sucked; casual cuddling, but no kissing. That was fine with me, and other than his, uh, limitations, he was really a nice guy."

There were a million questions I wanted to ask, but decided that now was not the time and this was not my case. The main thing was that Phil had an alibi if he really needed one.

"Well," I said, taking a drink of coffee, "if the police find any links between you and Anderson or ModelMen, you and the Glicks had better be prepared for a pretty rough time."

"Jesus!" Phil said.

We finished our coffee in silence, and I decided it was time I left so Phil could get some sleep. I got out of the chair and looked around for something to do with my empty coffee cup. Billy got up and took it from me, then picked up Phil's cup from the lamp table and headed into the kitchen.

"I'd better get going," I said. "I just wanted to give you a heads-up about all this. And I'm really sorry about Anderson—he sure as hell didn't deserve this. There are just too damned many sick people in this world."

"Both hustlers *and* johns," Phil said. "It's pretty damned dangerous out there for hustlers, too—but not many people think about that, or care. Which is one of the reasons both of us went with ModelMen—our clients are pre-screened and we don't have to worry about any deadly surprises."

He was quiet for a minute, his eyes on mine. Then he sighed and said: "Stuart was a nice guy. You're right...he didn't deserve this." He moved forward to give me a hug. "Thanks, Dick. I appreciate your concern."

"Call it a vested interest," I said, smiling as we released from the hug.

Billy came back into the room and the three of us moved to the door. I shook hands with both of them.

"Watch yourselves," I said as Billy opened the door and I went out into the hall.

* * *

I'd been home all of ten minutes and was just thinking about what to have for dinner when the phone rang. I figured it was probably Jared, or maybe Tim Jackson returning my message.

I answered with my usual "Dick Hardesty," even though I didn't get many business calls at home and friends hardly needed to be told my last name. Habits are odd.

"Mr. Hardesty," an unfamiliar voice said, "my name is Arnold Glick. I'm sorry to bother you at home, but it's extremely important that I speak with you privately, and as soon as possible."

Arnold Glick of ModelMen. Well, Phil hadn't wasted any time in getting in touch with him, obviously.

"Of course, Mr. Glick," I said. "When and where?"

"Could it possibly be this evening?" he asked, and though his voice was casual, I could sense a definite urgency. "At my home, perhaps?"

I looked at my watch...it was 7:25. "Well," I said, "I was just about to have dinner, but I could come by around 9 or 9:30, if you'd like."

Glick sounded relieved. "Excellent," he said. "I do appreciate it. Let me give you my address—and phone number, in case you are delayed."

I reached for the pencil and pad I always try to keep by the phone and was pleasantly surprised that they both were there—I invariably walk off with the pencil and leave it God-knows where. I took down his number and address, told him again that I'd see him between 9 and 9:30, exchanged goodbyes, and hung up.

* * *

Glick's address, I recognized, was in the Briarwood area, which wasn't exactly subsidized housing. Part of it sided the golf course of the Birchwood Country Club, the most exclusive country club in the city. It was rumored that the lobby of the main building had a large model of the Mayflower, since so many of the club's members claimed—rightly or wrongly— direct lineage from its passenger list.

It would take me at least half an hour to get there and since I hadn't even started dinner, I decided to grab something on the way. I changed my shirt, made a quick inspection to see if I needed a shave or not—I could pass—and headed out the door.

* * *

I pulled into the circular drive of 6811 Edgemont Court at exactly 9:00, after having driven up and down several nearby streets killing time. I didn't see a single house that didn't look like it cost more than the gross national product of Guatemala. *Where in hell does all this money come from,* I wondered, *—and why in hell don't I have any of it?*

The Glick residence made its neighbors look like squatters' shacks by comparison. "Quiet ostentation" would pretty much describe it, if you took away the "quiet." I decided immediately that however much money ModelMen pulled in, it wasn't nearly enough to finance a place like this.

I parked in a mini-mall-sized parking area on one side of the house, found my way to the front door, and rang the bell.

CHAPTER 3

There was about a 30-second wait, and the left side of the massive double door swung open to reveal a tall, rather striking woman in her early-to-mid 40s, jet black hair almost to her waist, and eyeliner that reminded me of Cleopatra. She wore a gold lame tank top and black leather toreador pants. *Probably not the maid,* I decided. "Mrs. Glick," I said, risking it, "I'm Dick Hardesty. Your husband is expecting me."

She smiled warmly and naturally, and extended her heavily jeweled hand "Please come in, Mr. Hardesty," she said. "My husband is on the phone, but should be off shortly. Why don't we go into the study?" She closed the door behind me, then led the way through the marble-floored circular foyer whose focal point was a staircase like the one at Tara, only nicer, then through a large, doric-column-flanked doorway into a surprisingly comfortable study complete with floor-to-ceiling bookcases and a fireplace. I would not have been the least bit surprised to see Sherlock Holmes in a smoking jacket, seated in one of the wing-back chairs by the fire.

"Please," she said, with a sweeping-hand, full-arm game-show-hostess gesture toward one of the wing-backs, "have a seat. I'll go check on my husband." And as I sat, she turned and left the room, the soft click of her stiletto heels echoing her path across the foyer.

I took the time to look more carefully around the room. A large, French-pane window flanked by wooden shutters rather than curtains; rich, dark paneling—walnut, I think—a muted rose carpet; an elegant writing desk that managed to look both fragile and sturdy at the same time, some very nice paintings on the wall areas between the bookcases. One of the paintings was a marvelous French city-scape by Raoul Dufy—I had a print of it in my bedroom hallway. I got out of my chair to verify what I already knew...this wasn't a print.

I heard the clicking of Mrs. Glick's shoes approaching, and turned to see her enter the room, accompanied by a small, grey-haired, distinguished looking gentleman in...I swear!...a smoking jacket with a casually open-at-the-collar white shirt. I was mildly disappointed not to see a pipe.

He walked quickly across the room, hand extended, which I stepped forward to take when he reached me.

"Mr. Hardesty," he said in a smooth, rich voice, "I can't tell you how much we appreciate your coming over." He motioned me toward the chair I'd just left. "Please, let's sit. May I get you a drink?"

"Not right now, thanks," I said, and he gave me a quick smile.

He and I sat, and Mrs. Glick stood beside her husband, as though protecting him.

When we'd settled in, Glick pushed himself slightly further into the chair back and said: "We have a serious problem."

I nodded. "Stuart Anderson," I said.

He nodded and glanced up at his wife, reaching over to pat her hand gently. "You have no idea how distressed we are over what has happened," he said. "Stuart was a long-time business acquaintance, and a friend. Phil tells me you and Stuart were doing some work together. While your business arrangement with him is none of my business, I would assume that he died before it was completed, and therefore you were not paid for your services."

I realized with something of a mild shock that he was right.

"That's true," I acknowledged, "but I'm certainly not concerned about money under these circumstances."

"That's very noble of you," Glick said, and I knew he wasn't being sarcastic. "However, we would like to reimburse you on Stuart's behalf: it is the least we can do."

I was both grateful and impressed by their kindness, but felt awkward about taking their money. "That's very kind of you," I said, "but it's really not necessary."

"We insist," he said, and I nodded my thanks. "Stuart's death creates a very complex set of problems and potential problems for the ModelMen Agency," he continued, "and we would like to utilize your expertise in helping us resolve or avoid them. Would you be interested?"

"As a matter of fact, I would," I said.

Glick looked up at his wife and exchanged smiles. "Wonderful," he said. "I assume you have a standard contract you would need us to sign?"

I did, of course, but since I had no idea that I'd be taking the Glicks on as clients, I hadn't brought one with me. "I will get you one, of course," I said. "Shall I drop it by your office?"

"Would you mind bringing it here?" Glick asked. "While all our escorts are also registered models, we prefer to keep the two aspects of the Agency as separate as possible. And my wife should be here all day—we're having a fountain put in beside the pool house, and Iris likes to oversee these things." He turned slightly to smile up at his wife, who returned his smile.

I realized I had not even mentioned my fee—but it was in the contract and I sincerely doubted that the Glicks would have a hard time meeting it. I'm sure the cost of a fountain beside the pool house would be considerably more than the cost of my services for several months—full time.

"But perhaps we should go over a few things first," I said.

"Of course," Glick said, and Mrs. Glick moved to sit on the arm of his chair.

"I recognize the importance of…discretion…to the escort service branch of ModelMen, and I will consider myself bound by it. I will not ask questions in what you consider sensitive areas unless I feel it is absolutely necessary." They both nodded. "However, should there be something I feel I really need to know, I will expect your full cooperation. If any limits are set on where I can go and where I can't, I can't do the job you're paying me to do and you might as well just save your money and hire someone else from the start."

"Understood," Glick said.

"Good," I said. "I have several questions already, but if you'd prefer, since it's getting late, we can take them up at our next meeting."

Mrs. Glick slipped a hand behind her husband's head to rest it on his far shoulder. "We can start now, if you'd like," she said, and her husband nodded agreement.

"Good," I said again. "I'll try to make this brief. First, I understand from Phil that Mr. Anderson had called you when he got into town Sunday night, asking if Phil might be available for the night. May I ask how he was able to reach you?"

Mrs. Glick smiled. "All ModelMen escort calls come here. As

we've said, we prefer to keep the modeling aspect of the business separate from the escort service. I'm not sure exactly what time he called. My husband was out of town on a business trip, and I'd asked Gary over for dinner. We were just finishing when Stuart called. We told him that Phil was on another assignment, and he set up an appointment for what would have been tonight."

Gary? I decided to let it pass for the moment. "He didn't ask for anyone else from ModelMen?"

Glick and his wife exchanged quick glances, and then Mrs. Glick replied: "No, Phil was his...favorite companion."

"And your other escorts are...?" I asked.

Again the exchanged glances, and a hesitation before Glick said: "Other than Phil, we have Mark, Billy, Aaron, Steve, and Gary."

Ah, that Gary—whoever he was.

"So Phil was the only ModelMen escort Mr. Anderson utilized?"

There was a momentary pause before Glick said: "When Stuart first registered with us, he did spend an evening with Gary, but on his next trip into town he asked for someone else."

"He and Gary didn't get along?" I asked.

"Oh, no, no," Mrs. Glick said quickly. "It was nothing like that. It's just that many of our clients enjoy variety. It just so happened that we sent Phil, and they got along so well Stuart never found the need to ask for anyone else."

"I see," I said, immediately remembering how much I hate it when people say 'I see.' "Approximately how many times did Mr. Anderson and Phil see one another?"

"Is that important?" Mrs. Glick asked.

Test time, I thought. I smiled. "Yes, I think so. The more times Phil was with him, the more likely someone will remember their having been seen together, and the more curious the police will become."

"Well, while I'm afraid it's inevitable someone will remember Phil in Stuart's company," Glick said, "I hope no quick conclusions will be drawn. Stuart always stayed at the Montero, which is nothing if not discreet in guarding the privacy of its guests. But in order to allay any suspicion of Phil's real purpose in visiting, Stuart felt unnecessarily obligated to imply that Phil was a company employee working on the new stores. I think there were four visits in all."

"Five," his wife amended.

"Any overnighters?" I asked.

"Oh, no," Glick said. "Stuart was too cautious for that. Phil would go over usually around eight, they would go out for dinner, then return to the hotel for a couple hours, then Phil would leave, always through the lobby so that he could be seen leaving. I really doubt anyone was paying attention, and even if they had been, it would all appear quite innocent."

"Undoubtedly," I said. "But Mr. Anderson's murder changes all that, dramatically. I understand Phil has an airtight alibi in that he was with a client. But here we may have a potential major problem: any alibi has to be verified, and if his client is reluctant to come forward..."

Glick smiled broadly and heaved a large sigh. "I'm sure if it becomes necessary, this particular client will not be hesitant," he said. "He is a very prominent local figure, but thank God he is also gay and his sexual orientation is an open secret. He normally does not utilize our services, but he met Phil at a social function and took a liking to him. Phil is very likable."

Oh, my, yes! I thought. The clock over the mantle was striking ten, and I decided it was about time to leave.

"Well, I think I've covered the most immediate bases," I said. "I appreciate your cooperation, and there are several things I can start on as far as damage control is concerned. I'll do my best to keep the police at bay, but I'm obligated to advise you, quite unnecessarily, I'm sure, that if you are contacted by the police, do not lie. Evade and avoid if you think it's necessary, but outright lies are dangerous, as I'm sure you know."

I got up from my chair, and both Glicks also rose. We shook hands and Mrs. Glick walked me to the door.

"Thank you for coming," Mrs. Glick said, smiling warmly as she opened the door. "We look forward to seeing you again."

"It was a pleasure meeting you," I said, not insincerely, but well aware we were doing a little etiquette pas de deux.

We exchanged our good nights, she closed the door, and I went home.

---

* * *

On the way home, I kept thinking about Stuart Anderson and what might have led to his death. Tim Jackson might well have some ideas, and I was very glad I'd called him on before Anderson was killed—I didn't want Tim to think I only called him when somebody turned up dead.

And as for the Montero. That it was extremely protective of its guests and discreet in its dealings with them was fine, but it occurred to me that the Montero was several cuts above your run-of-the-mill No Tell Motel, and the average street hustler would stand out like a sore thumb if he was seen walking in with a guest...or walking out, alone. I felt Stuart Anderson was too concerned about maintaining his surface heterosexual image to risk it by bringing just any street hustler home; the Glicks had said as much themselves. But there were places like Faces, a gay bar/restaurant which catered to rich guys looking for far-above-average hustlers. Faces was sort of a halfway house; I mean, halfway between the street and ModelMen. Anderson could very well have picked up someone there who wouldn't have raised an eyebrow at the Montero. I'd have to check it out...or let the police do it.

I was still bugged about having been so evasive with Lieutenant Richman that it teetered perilously close to outright lying to him. And especially after having given the Glicks my "don't lie" spiel. Richman had always played fair with me and I might very well need his help in the future. I couldn't afford to jeopardize that. I decided to call him in the morning and try to extricate myself from the hole I'd dug.

* * *

As soon as I got to the office in the morning, even before I opened the paper or took the lid off the coffee I'd picked up in the ground floor coffee shop, I called Tim. I knew he would already be at work, but I wanted to talk to him as soon as I could.

His machine picked up on the fourth ring. "Hi, this is Tim. Obviously I'm not home, so leave a message. 'Bye."

"Tim, it's Dick again. Tried to reach you , but you're a busy boy.

Please call me at home tonight if you can. Thanks."

I hung the phone up, took the lid off the coffee and forced myself to read the paper as I drank it. The article on Anderson's death was on page 2, and gave only the barest essentials, not even mentioning his name ("ending notification of next of kin"); just that a guest at the Montero had been found dead in his room and the police were conducting a full-scale investigation. *So much for the Pulitzer prize for investigative journalism on that one*, I thought. I just shook my head and kept on reading. I got as far as the crossword puzzle before my impatience with myself forced me to pick up the phone again and dial police headquarters and Lieutenant Richman's office.

"Lieutenant Richman," the now familiar voice said.

"Lieutenant, hi…it's Dick Hardesty. I've been thinking over this Stuart Anderson thing, and I'm afraid I wasn't quite honest with you. I apologize for that. I'm afraid knowing that Anderson was married and had a family clouded my judgement a little. I realize now he's well past trying to protect his reputation."

There was a frustratingly long pause before Richman said: "And what did you want to tell me?"

"I'm pretty sure Anderson was bisexual," I said. "I realized that the minute he came in to my office and had obviously taken off his wedding ring—I could see the untanned circle on his finger. Straight guys don't normally take off their wedding rings when they know they're going to be around gay guys unless they don't want you to know they're straight. And that means he may well have picked up a hustler, and was unlucky enough to get the wrong one. I could be wrong…hell, he could have picked up a hooker whose pimp got in on the action…I don't know. I just felt bad about not being totally honest with you."

Another pause, then: "Well, I appreciate your calling, Dick. We'd pretty much figured out the same thing"

"Oh?" I asked. "Can you tell me how?"

"Not in detail," Richman said. "But there was…well, a definite indication other than the brutality of the murder, that whoever did this is a pretty sick puppy who just might have a grudge against married men. Keep your eyes and ears open, would you? We want to get this guy, and soon."

"I promise I'll let you know if I find out anything," I said.
"I'll hold you to that," he said, and I got the message.
We exchanged good byes and hung up.
"*A definite indication*", *huh?* I knew I had to find out what he was getting at, even while I realized I probably wouldn't like it. It was sort of like approaching a car wreck ahead of you on the freeway—you don't want to look, but you know you will.

* * *

I took a contract out of the drawer, filled in the few blanks, ran off a copy on my new copier, then folded it and the original and put them in an envelope. I wouldn't have been the least bit surprised if the Glicks had a copy machine of their own somewhere in the house, but didn't want to chance it.

I waited until around 10:30, then left the office and drove to the Glicks. There were two or three small work trucks in the parking area, and a couple late-model sports cars parked at the far end. I parked and walked to the front of the house to ring the bell. After the second ring, the door was opened by a very large, pleasant looking black woman wearing an apron.

"Is Mrs. Glick in?" I asked.

"Yes, sir," she said. "She's in the back by the pool house. You can just go around, if you'd like."

I thanked her and retraced my steps, going through the parking area to the back of the house. The already huge house was made even larger by the attached four-car garage at the far end—and beyond that stretched an 8-foot high wall surrounding the pool, pool house, and about an acre and a half of park-like grounds.

A heavy wooden stockade-type gate stood open wide, apparently to allow the tanned, shirtless, sweaty and well-muscled workers I could see milling around what appeared to be a small man-made hill to move back and forth to the trucks in the parking area. As I entered, mentally playing my favorite kid-in-the-candy-store games (*I'll take one of those, and one of those, and...*), I noticed that the little hill totally surrounded three sides of the pool house. And the parts of the hill facing the pool were being terraced to provide what would be cascading rapids of water. Bucolic as all hell.

When I was able to tear my eyes away from the workers, I looked around for Mrs. Glick and spotted her—the tiger-striped tank top and gold toreador pants made her a little hard to miss—standing between two tall, very handsome guys in white shirts, ties, and sports jackets. One was very butch-looking, in his mid 20s; the other roughly the same age, sandy hair, nice tan and had, when he looked in my direction, the most spectacular sea-green eyes I think I've ever seen. Aside from the fact that they were fully and very well dressed, it was fairly clear they weren't here to work on the fountain.

I was about fifteen feet away from them, after nearly tripping over a bag of concrete while exchanging a warm smile with one of the shirtless wonders, when the green-eyed one moved his head closer to Mrs. Glick and said something which caused her to turn toward me, her face breaking into a warm perfect-hostess smile.

"Mr. Hardesty!" she said, all warmth and never losing the smile. "How very nice to see you!" She extended her hand as I was still about ten feet away, and I took it when I got there. "Won't this be nice?" she said, indicating the work in progress.

"Yes, it certainly will," I said. I glanced from one of her companions to the next and saw they were both looking at me, each with just the hint of a smile, and I somehow felt like it was feeding time at the lion's cage. Mrs. Glick reached out to touch each of them lightly on the arm. Without looking at them, she said: "Aaron, Gary, I'd like you to meet Mr. Hardesty."

"Mr. Hardesty," she said, turning to the guy with the sea eyes, "this is my brother Gary. And this," she said turning her entire body very slightly toward the butch-looking one, "is Aaron. Gentlemen, this is Mr. Hardesty."

"Dick," I amended, as each of them took a small step forward in turn to shake my hand. Firm grasps. Sincere. Disarming. Practiced.

"Nice to meet you, Gary...Aaron."

"My pleasure," they echoed, almost in unison. But Aaron's was accompanied by a grin that managed to be both friendly and wicked at the same time.

Aaron and Gary...Glick had mentioned both names when he was listing the escorts in ModelMen's employ. Very interesting. The fact that Gary/Sea Eyes was related to Mrs. Glick came as something of a surprise, since there wasn't all that much of a family resemblance. And not to be unkind, but he was obviously her *younger* brother.

"Gary designed this," Mrs. Glick said with obvious pride, again indicating the work in progress. "He is a true Renaissance man." Gary looked at me with a serene smile.

I've got a bedroom ceiling that could use some work, I thought. *Maybe he'd like to come over and spend a couple hours looking at it.*

"I'm impressed," I said honestly, and I wasn't just talking about Gary's being a Renaissance man.

"Would you like to come inside for coffee?" Mrs. Glick asked "My husband had some things he had to see to at the office, but he should be back in about an hour, and I know he'd be sorry to have missed you. I assume you brought the contract for us to sign?"

"Yes, I did," I said, "but don't worry about it...I'll just leave it and pick it up another time. There's no rush. But I really should be getting back to the office, and I can see you're busy. May I have a rain check on the coffee?"

She smiled warmly. "Of course."

I handed her the envelope with the contracts, which she in turn handed to Gary. "Be a dear, Aaron, and walk Mr. Hardesty to his car, while Gary does me a big favor and takes this in to the study. Would you mind, dears?"

Both smiled on cue and echoed "Of course not."

I glanced at Aaron just in time to catch his eyes on mine. "I'd be happy to," he said, giving me a decoder-badge-secret-message smile.

Mrs. Glick extended her hand, which I again took. "Thank you again for coming over," she said.

"My pleasure," I said. "Please tell Mr. Glick I'm sorry I missed him." I then turned to follow Aaron toward the gate.

I increased my pace slightly, deliberately avoiding looking at the shirtless workers as we passed them, to walk alongside Aaron. Well, actually Aaron didn't *walk*—he sort of *panthered* along like some jungle cat, practically exuding an aura of raw sexual energy.

"You're pretty good," he said.

"Thanks," I said, having absolutely no idea what he was talking about. "At what?" I asked.

"Playing the Alice at the Tea Party game. 'How nice of you to come.' 'How nice of you to have me.' 'One lump or two?' 'How very kind of you.' God, I get so fucking sick of that crap!"

He really had me, and I was just a little embarrassed because I knew exactly what he was saying.

"Well," I said, "next time I'll just belch a lot and scratch my crotch."

He grinned, then sighed. "That would be a breath of fresh air," he said. "I know she means well, but sometimes she reminds me of a drill instructor. I guess it pays off, though... we're all doing pretty well. But the thing that gets me with all this 'gentlemen of the world' training is that a lot of our...clients...are vanilla pudding on the surface—martinis and polite conversation at dinner, but the minute that bedroom door's closed, they wanna rut like pigs."

We'd reached my car, but Aaron kept right on talking. "Of course, I'm probably being a little unfair—rutting's my specialty. I'm like the rest of the guys in that I can do anything, and do, but we each have our little 'specialties' for the more discriminating clients, and mine is down and dirty." He smiled again, and it was pure satanic glee. "You like it down and dirty, Dick?"

He had me on that one. "I'd have to see the menu first," I said.

"Yeah," Aaron said. "You think about it." He extended his hand, and I took it. He slowly but steadily increased the pressure of his grip, and I automatically matched it. Neither of us said a word, but our eyes were locked on one another's, our faces impassive as hand tightened on hand. Just before I was sure I was going to start hearing bones cracking, he quickly released his grip and smiled again.

"You'll do," he said. And again I hadn't the slightest idea what he was talking about.

He held his right forearm unconsciously with his wrist lightly touching the side of his chest just about level with his pecs, his elbow and arm drawn back like a piston stopped in mid-stroke. His hand, again apparently unconsciously, was in the position of a lightly formed fist, and his thumb worked itself slowly and lightly back and forth across the top of his index finger, as if bringing the circulation back. For some ungodly reason, I found it erotic as all hell.

Jeezus, Hardesty, I thought. *Get a life!*

I reached for the door handle. "See 'ya, Aaron," I said, opening the door.

"Bet on it," he said, grinning, then turned and walked back toward the open gate.

* * *

I really couldn't do much more, I felt, until I could talk to Tim. I had to find out whatever he could possibly tell me about Stuart Anderson's death and what Richman meant by "certain indications".

I puttered around the office for a couple hours, then headed for home. Around 5:30 I started playing my little "don't watch the clock" game. You've done it. You find yourself looking at the clock so often you determine *not* to look at it. You look. It says 5:43. You force yourself not to look for a good 20 or 25 minutes. Then you look at the clock again. It says 5:44.

Oh, the hell with it, I thought, and was just reaching for the phone when it rang, scaring the shit out of me.

"Dick Hardesty," I said after the second ring.

"Hi, stranger," Tim's voice said, cheerful as always. "It was great to hear from you. It's only been...what...six years?"

"Oh, come on!" I said. "It can't have been more than three years next Michaelmas."

"Well, however long it's been, it's been too long," he said "But of course, the phone line does have two ends, so I'll forgive you one more time."

"You're a saint," I said. "When can I make it up to you? I won't ask how."

"Well," he said, "that part goes without saying. But Gay Pride's coming up this weekend. You want to go to the parade with me...maybe the carnival afterwards?"

"Sure," I said."That'd be fun. But, uh, there was something else I wanted to mention..."

"Here it comes," he said with a long, dramatic sigh.

"Hey, no..." I said, "this just came up, I swear! I called you before it happened."

"Stuart Anderson," he said.

"You got your diploma from Mind-Reading school, I see. But, yeah, I'm afraid you're right. How the hell did you know?"

Tim gave a little laugh. "You…a murdered gay guy…well, a murdered bi guy—you must be expanding your territory…it figures."

He had me shaking my head. "And how in hell did you know he was bi?"

"Because there was evidence of semen—his—on the sheets from his bed. He was taking an active part in the sex."

I was now stepping over a threshold I didn't really want to cross. But…

"I understand he was strangled—do you have any idea how? A chain? Belt? Could you tell from the ligature marks?" I asked.

Tim paused. "Well, there weren't any ligature marks, actually. He wasn't strangled so much as choked."

"I'm sorry?" I said, confused. Then I remembered Richman had used the word 'choked,' too.

"He had semen in his throat, if that gives you any idea. And the insides of both his forearms had large bruises."

It took a minute for it to sink in. "So you're saying someone knelt on his arms to hold him down and face-fucked him to death?"

Tim sighed. "Apparently so. The guy must have been both pretty strong and pretty rough. Anderson couldn't breathe and couldn't struggle with his arms pinned down."

"Jeezus!" I said, then paused to think. "So it might have been an accident in the course of rough sex?"

"Well, I could almost go along with that, but…" Tim said.

"But…?" I coaxed.

Tim sighed. "Something was inserted into a body cavity."

I paused. "Meaning…?" I asked.

"Meaning whoever did it shoved Anderson's wedding ring up his ass."

CHAPTER 4

Like you had to know that, right, Hardesty?

I didn't say a word. In fact, I didn't say a word for so long that Tim finally had to say: "Hello?"

"I'm here," I managed to say. Then I paused again, but forced myself to ask: "How in hell do you do it, Tim?" I knew I didn't have to explain what I meant.

"It's my job," he said calmly. "A lot of times I don't like it, but like the cliche says: somebody's got to do it. And if something I find rummaging around in a chunk of meat that used to have a person inside helps find out exactly how and why the person left it, it's worth it. I just always remember that a body isn't a person any more; nothing I have to do to it matters to the human being it used to belong to."

"I guess you're right," I said, and I knew that he was.

"So," Tim said, his voice once more the chipper little hunk I always think of him as being, "are we set for , then? Around noon at my place?"

"Sure, but why don't we make it a little earlier and grab an early brunch. The parade starts at 1:30, I think."

"Great idea," he said. "But we'd better call for reservations like tonight—every place will be jammed."

"I'll do it," I volunteered "I might have to call around though to see what's available, though, but I'll call you later." Then I had a thought. "Have you ever met my friend Jared?" I asked.

There was only a slight pause before Tim said: "No, I don't think so. Should I?"

"Oh, yeah!" I said. "I was thinking of asking him to join us at the parade, if you don't mind."

"Fine with me. You can ask him if he wants to join us for brunch, too, if you'd like. Are we doing our 'Dick Hardesty, Boy Yenta' number here?"

I laughed. "No way! Shit, if I get you married off we couldn't have our far-too-infrequent-as-it-is little bedroom chats. But Jared's a special piece of work, and I know you'll like each other. I'll give him a call."

"Ok," Tim said.

After we hung up, I dialed Jared's number, not really expecting to find him home, and was surprised when he answered on the first ring.

"Just waiting for my call?" I asked without identifying myself. Obviously I didn't have to. "Dick, hi," Jared said. "I was just picking up the phone to call you. Chalk another one up to E.S.P. What's up?"

"I was wondering if you'd like to join my friend Tim Jackson and me next Sunday for the Gay Pride parade." I said. "We're going to try for brunch beforehand, too, if you can make it."

Jared didn't hesitate a second. "Sure," he said, "sounds great. Tim's your buddy at the coroner's office, right?"

"That's him," I said, "and I'm pretty sure you'll like each other."

"Meaning?" he asked.

I laughed. "Meaning I'm pretty sure you'll like each other. Don't worry, I'm not trying to set anybody up." I paused for only a second before saying: "So let me check around for reservations, then, and I'll call you back with the time and place, ok?"

"I'll be here," Jared said. "I'm starting the forty-fifth draft of my dissertation, so I'm not going anywhere."

"Talk to you soon, then," I said, and we exchanged good-byes and hung up.

I immediately called Calypso's and Rasputin's—both were booked solid. Then, on a whim, I tried Napoleon—they normally didn't do brunches, but it being Gay Pride, I figured they might. I lucked out. They were, indeed, having a special brunch for the occasion and I was able to get a reservation for 11:45. Actually, I felt just a little bit uncomfortable even thinking of Napoleon since that was where I'd last seen Stuart Anderson.

Well, life goes on, I told myself.

Yeah, but not for Stuart Anderson, my mind answered.

* * *

I couldn't get Anderson—and what had happened to him—out of my mind. How could someone not have seen something? The two of them coming in through the lobby— assuming Anderson had gone out and picked up a hustler.

And, technically, the Glicks hadn't hired me to find Anderson's killer, but to run interference for ModelMen. But to my mind, one thing equaled the other: if there was a tie-in, I wanted to know it. If there wasn't, that would still be to their advantage in defending themselves.

I thought of the reception desk clerk's comment about the parking garage—that runners often used it rather than going through the lobby. I had no idea whether or not Anderson might have rented a car, but if he had, and driven in with a hustler, or if the killer might have somehow left through the garage, I wanted to know about it.

And, of course, there was the problem of the police and me stumbling all over one another's feet. I had the feeling that I might be allowed a little more leeway than a straight p.i., not because of my irresistible charm and razor-sharp insights, but simply because when it came to serious cases involving the gay community, I was a hell of a lot better able to move around in it than they were, and Lieutenant Richman and possibly Captain Offermann, head of the Homicide Division, realized it. And until the department got around to hiring openly gay police officers, it was a lot easier for them to do a little quid pro quo with me. But I wasn't stupid enough to take this little arrangement too much for granted, or to try to press my luck too hard.

Was Anderson robbed? Were any of his things missing? Shit! How would I know? Richman might well know, but I'm pretty sure he wouldn't or couldn't tell me. Maybe if I could find out something I could offer in trade....

* * *

At the office the next morning, I tried to rough out exactly what I might do to earn my keep from the Glicks. I wished I had a photo of Anderson, since I planned to go to Faces that evening to see if anyone might remember his being there, and if he'd left with anyone that last night. On the far outside chance that Phil might conceivably have a photo, I waited until I was pretty sure he'd be up, then called.

Billy answered, and when I asked if Phil were around, he said: "No, he's doing some catalog stuff for ManSport Outfitters. He won't be back until late this afternoon. Anything I can do to help?"

Uh, now that you mentioned it, I thought.

"Probably not," I said, forcing myself to shift my thoughts from crotch to brain, "unless you might know: did Phil ever have his picture taken with Stuart Anderson?"

Billy thought a minute, then said: "Yeah! He did! He went with Stuart to some function that big lawyer Glen O'Banyon gave, and they had their pictures taken with O'Banyon and Senator Marshfield. It's right here. Do you need it?"

"I'd like to borrow it for a day or so, if you don't think Phil would mind," I said.

"Nah, I'm sure he wouldn't," Billy said. "You want to come by and pick it up?"

"Great," I said. "I'll be right over. Thanks, Billy…I'll owe you."

"Mastercard and Visa gratefully accepted," he said. "See you when you get here."

* * *

It was interesting to hear that Anderson had known Glen O'Banyon. O'Banyon was one of the wealthiest and most prominent attorneys in the city and though his being gay was no secret, his wealth and power gave him access to the city's straight upper crust; he was constantly hosting or attending both straight and gay fund-raisers and social events of one sort or another. Anderson would have felt comfortable in those surroundings and evidently even sufficiently so to take Phil with him—no doubt as a "business associate."

I'd done some work for O'Banyon and liked him, though we hadn't been in frequent touch recently. It occurred to me that I might try to contact him to see how well he might have known Anderson. I called his office and was put through to his secretary, Donna.

"Donna, hi…this is Dick Hardesty. I was wondering if you could leave a note to ask Mr. O'Banyon if he could call me when he gets a chance. Nothing urgent, but I would like to speak with him for a moment. He has my home number, I believe, if that's more convenient for him."

"I'll give him the message, Mr. Hardesty," she said in her usual cheerfully efficient manner.

When I hung up, I finished up a few things around the office, then headed out for Phil and Billy's apartment.

* * *

Billy answered the door in nothing but a pair of gym shorts, his face and torso glistening with sweat. I noticed he had a small tattoo on his left pec, just above his nipple—a little field mouse sitting back on its haunches. I'm not big on tattoos, but this one somehow suited him perfectly.

"Come on in, Dick," he said. "I was just working out a little. Have to keep the merchandise in mint condition," he added with a big grin.

After I'd entered and closed the door behind me, Billy motioned me to a seat. "Would you like some coffee?" he asked.

"No thanks, I'm fine," I said.

"So I've heard," Billy said with another wicked little grin. It really fascinated me how such a cherubic, innocent face could suddenly turn so...well, *sexy*.

I wasn't sure whether I should let that one pass or not, but being a Scorpio... "Phil been telling tales out of school again?" I asked.

Billy picked a framed photograph off the top of a bookcase and brought it over, standing directly in front of me.

"He didn't go into detail, if that's what you mean," Billy said, holding the picture out just slightly in front of his gym shorts, and I couldn't help notice that little Billy may have been small, but oh, my! I reached out for the photograph, but somehow my hand kind of got...um...sidetracked, and Billy just pushed his hips slightly forward to meet it.

There was a moment of silence in which I could almost hear the crackle of electricity, until Billy said: "I was just thinking of taking a shower. Care to join me?"

I looked up into his absolutely beautiful face and his wide nodoubting-what-it-meant grin. I took the picture from him and laid it carefully on the chair next to me, then grabbed him by the hips with both hands and started to slide his gym shorts toward the floor.

"How about a tongue bath instead?" I asked, pulling him forward toward me.

* * *

Remember when you were a senior in high school, and there was that little blond your gut ached for every time you saw him, but you for one reason or another never got to do anything about and always kicked yourself because you hadn't? Well, that guy, whoever he may have been, grew up to be Billy, and he fulfilled the fantasy in spades! He didn't have to say a word, but his every action made it clear that you were the one in control, and that was exactly what he wanted you to be, and that he'd be more than glad to follow your lead wherever you wanted to go. Think about it. That was Billy.

I did end up joining him in the shower: by that time we both needed one. God, he was an incredible mixture of sweetness and sex, and I'm sure he brought out the "Me Tarzan" side of every guy lucky enough to go to bed with him. And as I'd thought with Phil, the Glicks found a gold mine when they found Billy. If Phil's "specialty" was 'whatever you want' and Aaron's was 'down and dirty', Billy's was definitely 'ego-fluffing.'

* * *

I took Phil's photo to a local quick-service photo place a block from my office and had them crop Anderson's face out of the photo and blow it up to a 4X6, and then headed back for the Montero. I drove around the block, looking for the entrance to their parking garage and, upon finding it on the side street flanking the hotel, was interested to note the sign above the ramp said "Guest Parking Only." I found a place to park about a block away, and walked back around to the side of the hotel and down the ramp to the Montero's garage. Both the entrance and exit lanes were blocked by those retractable railroad-crossing type barriers, but about six feet inside the barrier was a small attendant's booth between the two lanes. No one was in the booth or in evidence in the garage itself. I noted that entrance was apparently gained by punching numbers into a small keypad on box on a pole about 10 feet from the barricade—the barricade on the exit side was probably triggered automatically when a car approached from inside the garage.

I walked around the barricade and went up to the attendant's booth. There were no signs of recent occupancy, and it occurred to me that they very well may not have a regular attendant. I just walked on through the main part of the relatively small garage, which apparently had been added during the recent renovation as a convenience to the hotel's guests. Visitors and those attending social functions at the hotel probably used the large public garage across the street and a few doors down from the hotel. I reached the wall at the far end of the garage where two doors were set in the wall: one an elevator, the other a stairway. Instead of just a single button beside the elevator door there was another small key pad—apparently the elevator could not be summoned without punching in some numbers—probably the same ones which gained entrance to the garage. I took the stairway, and found myself, not surprisingly, in the lobby.

So it would be difficult for anyone to gain access to the hotel's guest floors without having the key-pad combination or being with someone who did—but not at all difficult to leave the hotel via the garage without being seen. Out of curiosity I stopped at the registration desk to ask about the garage attendant; I was told they had one on duty between 10 p.m. and 7 a.m., largely to keep an eye on the visitors' cars against late-night vandalism. I made a note to return after 10 to check to see if he'd noticed anything unusual that night.

On my way back to the office, I stopped at the photo place to pick up Anderson's photo.

* * *

I stayed at the office a little longer than usual, planning to catch the tail end of the Happy Hour—if they had one—at Faces. I wanted to be there before the dinner rush really started, but when I could be pretty sure all the waiters and bartenders would be on duty.

Faces, as I've mentioned, was several steps above the usual hustler bars—considerably more discreet. The hustlers tended to be generally better looking, better groomed, and subtler than the guys, say, at Hughie's. There was some crossover traffic, of course, but not much. The guys at Faces might deign to check Hughie's out on a really slow night, but most of Hughie's hustler clientele didn't want to bother with the little games—like getting dressed up—hustling at Faces pretty much required. The hustlers at Faces seldom drank beer. And, finally, at Faces, generally you wouldn't be moved in on without your giving some indication of interest first.

While I was hardly a regular at Faces, I had been in often enough either for dinner—they had a fantastic French onion soup—or on other cases to know some of the staff casually. I'd tricked with one of the maitre d's a couple years before when he worked at another restaurant, and the turnover among the waiters and bartenders tended to be lower at Faces because of the money that could be made on tips from the wealthy businessmen who made up the other half of the clientele.

I got there at around 7, just at the end of the cocktail hour and just when the early diners started to arrive. I was happy to see that the bartender I'd spoken most often with…Kent… was on duty, and so was one of the waiters…Tod?… I'd gotten info from before. That would make it a lot easier. And of course I always made sure to fulfill my part of the quid pro quo with a sizeable contribution to their personal charities.

As usual, there were a number of U.S.D.A. Prime specimens seated at the bar, though it was a little early for most of the…um, what to call them?…johns was what they were, just as hustlers was what the guys waiting for them were, but somehow they were a cut or two above the Hughie's brand of either. And once again I wondered where in hell all these good looking guys had come from, and how they'd gotten into hustling and where they'd be in ten years.

'Yeah, yeah…and do they like puppies and do they spend Christmas with their folks, and…yawn,' my mind said, neatly bringing me back to reality. I took a seat at the bar, noticing a few casual glances from the other customers, probably wondering which category I fit into—buyer or seller.

Kent came over immediately. "What'll it be tonight, Dick? Old Fashioned?" Two marks of a good bartender...remembering names and remembering drinks.

"You talked me into it," I said.

He grinned and moved a few feet down the bar to put it all together. I watched as he emptied the last from a bottle of bourbon, then expertly snapped the neck off the bottle on a little device kept just below the bar. I'd always wondered why they did that, until I realized that was to guarantee the customers that the bottles wouldn't be refilled with cheaper stuff. While he was doing that, I reached inside my shirt for Stuart Anderson's photograph.

When Kent returned with my drink I set the photo on the bar in front of him. "Would you happen to know this guy?" I asked. He picked up the photo, looked at it carefully, then handed it back to me, shaking his head.

"Sorry, Dick. Never seen the guy before."

"No problem," I said, as Kent went back down the bar to attend to a customer.

I sat nursing my drink, looking idly around the bar. At a table not too far from me, I couldn't help but notice a double-take hot guy about 30 seated with a rather attractive man in his early 50s. They looked like two successful executives, and I wondered idly if they were just business associates here for dinner, or if the younger guy were part of the menu. But if there was such a thing as looking too butch to be gay, this guy was it. Though I tried not to stare, my eyes kept wandering back to him. Now, if he wasn't ModelMen material, I didn't know who was. At one point he looked over and caught me looking at him. He gave me a quick, warm smile and a wink, then returned his attention to his companion.

I engaged in some healthy erotic fantasy until Tod, the waiter, came over to the service area of the bar to place a drink order. He saw me, smiled, and nodded. I returned both the smile and the nod, then waited while he gave Kent his order. When Kent turned away to make the drinks, I took advantage of the momentary lull in Tod's schedule to call him over. Keeping an eye on Kent so as not to keep his customers waiting one second longer than necessary, he walked the four or five steps from the service area.

"Can I help you, Dick?" he asked. I'll bet he could remember what I drink, too.

I slid Anderson's picture along the bar so it was in front of him. "Would you happen to remember seeing this guy around here? Especially last Sunday night?" I asked.

Glancing quickly in the direction of Kent to check his progress with the order, Tod picked the picture up and looked at it closely, as Kent had done.

"Well, I was working Sunday, but he wasn't here." Tod said. "I recognize him, though. He's been in a couple times. But not for a long while, now—maybe two, three months."

Well, that was a mixed bag of news. "Do you remember anything special about him?" I asked.

"He was a damned good tipper," Tod said with a quick grin. "But other than that, no."

"He usually pick someone up?" I asked.

Tod pursed his lips. "Usually, yeah. Guys like him don't just come in for the food, you know." He grinned again, then noticed Kent setting drinks on the tray at the waiter's station. "Gotta go," Tod said, and turned quickly to pick up the tray and head off toward a group of four guys at one of the farther tables.

Okay, I thought. *So we've established Anderson wasn't a total stranger to town.* But that he hadn't been in lately may be linked to when he started seeing Phil. I'd have to remember to ask the Glicks when Anderson had become a client.

And just out of curiosity, I'd have to take his photo down to Hughie's. ModelMen was the top of the hired man ladder, Faces just a couple rungs below. I wondered just how far down the ladder Anderson climbed.

I had a couple more questions for Tod, so I sat nursing my drink until he returned to the waiter's station with an order from another table. I picked up my drink and moved a couple stools closer to where Tod stood waiting.

"A couple more things, Tod, if you don't mind," I said.

Tod smiled. "Sure."

"Do you happen to remember any of the guys the guy in the photo I showed you went home with? I know it's been a long time, but...."

Tod chewed the corner of his lower lip for a moment, then looked toward the far end of the bar, where most of the... younger gentlemen...were sprinkled.

"Paul," he said, "the one in the tan jacket and white shirt."He gave an almost imperceptible head nod to indicate a very nice looking guy about two-thirds the way down the bar. "I know he left with Paul one night. The others...I'm not sure about."

At that point, Kent brought Tod's order and set the drinks on his tray.

"Thanks again, Tod," I said. Tod just smiled, picked up his tray, and left.

I fixed my eyes on the guy Tod had pointed out, and continued to stare at him until I caught his eye. He glanced at me, looked away, then brought his eyes back, and his face broke into a small but definite grin, and he nodded an acknowledgment. The universal language of cruising.

I had to take a moment to explain carefully to my crotch that *I* was going to be in control of the situation this time, not it. I smiled at Paul, who got up off his stool and came down to take the stool beside me.

"Hi," he said, as though we'd known each other for years. "What's up?"

"You're Paul, right?" I asked.

He looked at me with just the slightest trace of suspicion on his face. "Yeah," he said. "Do we know each other?"

"I'm sorry to say we don't," I said sincerely. Up close, Paul was pretty typical of Faces' younger clientele, which is to say, pretty damned attractive. Dark brown hair, eyes so dark brown they were nearly black, just the hint of freckles—Irish heritage, I'd guess.

I reached into my shirt pocket and took out my business card and Anderson's photo, giving him my card first. He looked at it, then up at me with a raised eyebrow. "And...?" he said. I laid Anderson's photo in front of him. "I understand you went home with this guy a couple months ago," I said, "and I'd just like to see if I could find out a little more about him."

Paul shook his head. "Sorry," he said, "I don't talk about people I meet."

"That's commendable," I said, "but I'm not out to get anybody into any trouble. Just the opposite—I'm trying to maybe save somebody's life."

He looked mildly reassured, but still skeptical. "His?" he asked.

I shrugged. "I'm afraid it's too late for that," I said. "He was killed Sunday night."

Paul looked truly shocked. "Killed? You mean somebody...?" Then a look of realization spread across his face. "The guy at the Montero?"

I nodded, wondering how he'd made the connection..

"I..." he started to say, then just shook his head. "What can I tell you?"

"Anything you can tell me about him...any preferences? Any special requests? Anybody else you may have seen him with?"

Paul set his drink down and ran his hand across his face, his eyes cast to one side in thought. Then he slowly shook his head again. "No. Nothing. Really. I met him here one Friday or Saturday night about three or four months ago. The usual routine. He was staying at the Montero, and he took me there."

"Did you drive or take a cab?" I asked.

"Drove. A Caddy. He said he always rented a Continental but they didn't have one this time, and he was pretty unhappy about it."

Hey, I sure would have been pissed, I thought.

He was quiet for a moment, then said: "I only saw him that one time, though I gathered from what he said that he'd been here—Faces—a couple times before. We didn't talk all that much, really, other than general stuff. He did tell me all about how one of his kids was driving him nuts and he didn't know what he was going to do about him. As for the sex, nothing at all kinky. He was a bottom—a lot of married straight guys are bottoms, since that's something they can't get from their wives. Not wham-bam-thank-you-ma'am, but not all hugs-and-kisses either." He was quiet again, then sighed. "That's it. God, I'm sorry to hear he's dead. He seemed like a nice guy."

"Yeah," I said. Noticing his drink was nearly empty, I said: "Can I at least buy you one for your time?"

He smiled. "Sure. Thanks."

"No, thank *you*," I said, motioning to get Kent's attention.

* * *

Okay. I was pretty sure from what the Glicks had said and what I'd seen myself in both Phil and Paul, that the chances Anderson would have picked up a street hustler were pretty remote. He apparently liked well-groomed brunettes/dark hair, neat, who didn't look like hustlers. Not out of the question that he might have just picked someone up, of course, but given the Montero...

I went home, had some dinner, then headed out again around 9:30 for the Montero, hoping the garage attendant would be the same one on duty Sunday night. I wasn't able to find a parking space within two blocks of the hotel, and was really pissed. Patience was never one of my greater virtues.

As I walked down the ramp to the parking garage, I saw that there was, indeed, someone in the attendant's booth—a guy so large I wondered how he ever managed to fit in there—the effect was not unlike a full-rigged sailing ship in a bottle. He made no attempt to either get out of his chair or leave the booth as I came up.

"Help you?" he asked as I approached the half-open window on the "entrance" side.

I handed him my card. "Yeah," I said. "I was wondering if you were on duty Sunday night."

"You're wasting your time," he said, setting his magazine on the small shelf which pressed up against his more-than-ample belly. "I already talked to the police."

"I'm sure you did," I said. "But would you mind telling me what you told them?"

He sighed and shifted his enormous weight on the fragile looking stool. "I told 'em I didn't see nothing. People come in, people go out—not many, but enough. As long as they've got the key combination and don't try to steal things from the other cars, that's all I care about."

I noticed that the booth was equipped with large...well... rear view mirrors on either side, which enabled the attendant, seated facing toward the street, to keep an eye on what was going on in the garage without turning around: a blessing for this guy, I'd imagine, who I doubted could turn around if he wanted to.

On a hunch, I said: "Did anybody leave the garage on foot?"

He thought a minute, then said: "Just the regular."

"The regular what?" I asked.

"One of the guests who comes in pretty regular, he's a runner. He went out around 6:30 as always."

"You recognized him?" I asked.

"Sure. Knit cap, grey sweatshirt and sweat pants. Runs every morning at the same time when he's here."

"You recognized his face?"

He shrugged. "I guess so. I didn't pay any attention. Same guy, though."

Why did I not think so?

"Did you mention him to the police?"

"I mentioned it, yeah. They were more interested in who came in."

"Did you see two guys drive in together?" I asked.

He shook his head. "No. My wife made lasagna for supper Sunday night, and it gave me the runs. The cops checked all the entry times, and I was able to match all of 'em up to specific cars, except one. I guess I must have been in the john when that one came in."

"Does each guest get a special number, or is it a universal number?"

"Universal...changes every day at noon."

So Anderson very well might have driven in with his killer. Of course, from what I gathered about this guy, even if he had seen Anderson come in he wouldn't be able to describe who was with him.

But the runner....

"Anything at all different about the runner this time?" I prodded.

He shook his head. "Nope; except he was carrying a gym bag...and he had on funny shoes."

"Funny shoes?"

"Well, I just caught a glimpse as he went up the ramp, but—they didn't look like running shoes to me; just regular shoes. Figured he left his running shoes at home."

"You told the cops all this?"

He shrugged. "Maybe; maybe not—I don't remember. I don't think they asked."

Jeezus!

"Well, thanks for your help," I said, and turned to go.

"We're allowed to take tips," he said, and I turned back, reaching into my wallet for a bill, which I passed through the window to him. "Thanks again," I said, and left.

*   *   *

That's how the killer left! Anderson must have mentioned that he ran every morning at the same time! He'd put his own clothes in Anderson's gym bag, put on Anderson's running outfit—including the knit cap, which would hide his hair, then just taken the elevator down to the garage, and left. But what about the shoes? That was easy enough to figure out: a sweatshirt and sweat pants are baggy enough to fit a variety of sizes, but if the killer were larger...or smaller...than Anderson, the shoes wouldn't have fit. And if I were to guess, I'd say the killer had bigger feet than Anderson's—if they were smaller, he might have made do with Anderson's running shoes and not called any attention to himself at all.

But now the question was: where did Anderson pick up his killer? If not at Faces or through ModelMen, where? Any of the nicer gay bars or restaurants, I'd imagine. And there were any number of possibilities there. And in that case, perhaps the guy he picked up may not even have been a hustler. But I rather suspected that Anderson, like a lot of guys in his position, would prefer the...well, *control* or the emotional distancing...that paying for sex with a guy would provide. Just picking up another guy might be putting himself too much on the guy's level—too much of a concession to his own gay side. But then what did I know about bisexuals?

And if the garage attendant had not gone into what, for him, passed for detail with the police, I might have that bargaining chip to use with Richman.

CHAPTER 5

First thing Thursday morning, I called Lieutenant Richman's office. I wanted to talk with him, but was still leery of being seen too often around police headquarters. He agreed to meet me by the fountain in Warman Park at about 12:30, and I took his willingness to go out of his way to accommodate me as another indication that the police didn't have too many leads of their own to follow up on. I also took it as further tacit recognition of their need for links to individuals in the gay community when dealing with crimes directly involving that community. Progress, slow but sure.

I was surprised, shortly after hanging up from Richman, to hear a knock at my office door and to see, though the opaque glass, the outline of an imposing male figure.

"Come on in," I called, and the door opened to reveal Gary...I never did get his last name; Iris Glick's brother, he of the sea-green eyes.

I got up from my desk and went over to take his hand. "Gary," I said: "this is a surprise. Have a seat."

He took the chair to the left of my desk, and I went around it to sit down. "What can I do for you?" I asked.

He smiled—he *did* have a nice smile, I noticed.

Oh, fer chrissakes, Hardesty, can it! my mind chastised.

"Iris was going to call you to tell you they'd signed the contract," he said, "but I told her I'd bring it over. I've always been curious about what a private investigator's office looks like." His face spread into a slow, somehow very sexy grin.

Okay; sexy. Yeah. We get it! my little voice said with no little exasperation.

"Not much to see, as you've noticed by now," I said, my eyes wandering over his very nice looking face and equally nice looking torso. He was wearing a white pullover Polo shirt which showed off both his tan and his muscles to full advantage. He hoisted his rear slightly off the seat to reach into his back pocket, from which he pulled out my original envelope with the contract.

"I'm glad you're working for Iris and Arnold," he said. "A terrible thing to have happened to that Anderson guy, but...."

"I understand you spent some time with him," I said, my mind formulating a couple hundred questions I'd like to ask him.

"Yeah, when he first became a client," Gary said. "Whenever possible, Iris likes to have new clients over for dinner with as many of the escorts as are available that night. A little extra touch of personalized service, and it gives the client a chance to see what's available for him."

Nice touch, I had to admit.

"Then," he continued, "the next time he came into town we got together."

"Was there anything...well, unusual...about him? I understand he was pretty vanilla in bed."

Gary grinned. "Vanilla is right!" he said. "I mean, I get paid to do whatever the client wants, but it's nice if there's a little...well, *involvement*. He could have saved a hell of a lot of money if he'd just gone out and bought a dildo."

"So you just saw him...one on one as it were...that one time, then?"

"Believe me, once was more than enough, thanks. I'm glad he moved on to Phil."

"I'm curious," I said. "I hope you don't mind my asking, but how did you happen to get into the business?"

He grinned again. "I like sex," he said. "*Like* it? Hell, I *love* it! And I'm afraid Iris was getting a little worried about me just giving it away left and right; thought I might get into trouble. And since I'd always been sort of the black sheep of the family, I guess one of the reasons Iris wanted to start ModelMen was to save me from my wastrel ways. Now I've got the best of both worlds: lots of sex *and* I get paid for it, too."

"Any drawbacks?" I asked.

Gary shrugged. "Oh, sure—there are drawbacks to everything, I guess. The biggest one is that I don't always have a choice in who I fuck...or who fucks me. But when that happens, I just close my eyes and go with it. And I still have quite a bit of free time...as it were," he added with a grin.

He held the grin, but I noticed that his eyes were now locked on my own. I suddenly had the urge to go swimming.

Are we getting a message here, boys and girls? I wondered.

"How about you, Dick?" he asked. "You like sex?"

"You might say that," I said.

"Good," he said. "You're pretty fucking hot."

Gary got up from his chair and moved around to sit on the edge of my desk. He was wearing a very subtle but very nice men's cologne and he was close enough that I could almost feel the heat radiating from him. And I couldn't help but notice a very respectable bulge running down the inside of his left pant leg. He saw me looking.

"You want a little?" he asked.

I got up from my chair, went to the door and locked it, then returned to push him back onto the desk, which was fortunately pretty clear of obstacles.

"If a little's good, a lot's better," I said as I reached forward to unbuckle his belt.

* * *

Well, we may have started out on the desk, but by the time we'd finished, we'd managed to cover just about every foot of the office, and I'm surprised we didn't break anything. I believe in enthusiasm when it comes to sex, but Gary took enthusiasm to a new level, and by the time our mutual blastoff arrived, I was momentarily reminded of Aaron's quaint phrase: "rutting like pigs." Not a very polite description, or a very pretty picture, but in intensity....

And why did I have the very odd impression that I'd somehow just been conned?

* * *

I just made it to Warman Park at 12:18, after a quick trip home for a badly-needed shower and a change of clothes. After my little session with Gary, I was more firmly convinced than ever that the Glicks had a great thing going for them. I also realized, with a mixture of mild embarrassment and considerable pleasure, that I had been privy to half of the escort wing's offerings. And from my brief chat with Aaron while he had walked me to the car, I suspected that I'd be chalking up another before too long. I'm sure the Glicks probably wouldn't be too happy to know that I'd been getting for free what should have cost, at their going rate—whatever that might be—a tidy fortune.

I walked to the central fountain, enjoying the flora and fauna—and particularly the two legged fauna (male variety)—and idly looking around for a police lieutenant's uniform, which it occurred to me would stand out like a sore thumb in these peaceful surroundings. So I was a bit surprised, as I sat on one of the marble benches surrounding and facing the fountain, to see a nice looking guy in casual dress walking toward me carrying a gym bag, and realize it was Lieutenant Mark Richman in civies. And if he cut a handsome figure in his police uniform, he was even more impressive in street clothes.

'You really are a slut, aren't you, Hardesty?' my mind-voice asked.

I got up from the bench to shake hands, and then we both sat down, his gym bag at his feet between his legs.

"I try to make it to the gym a couple days a week when I can manage to take a lunch hour," he said, thereby explaining the civies. "What did you want to talk about?" As if he didn't know.

I started by asking if they had determined yet how the killer had managed to leave the hotel without being noticed.

"We're still working on that one," he said. "We're pretty sure he had to have left through the parking garage. But from what we can gather, the attendant saw only one person leave on foot, and that was somebody he knew."

Aha! "Well, two things, there," I said. "First, as you probably know, the attendant had…stomach problems…that night and was back and forth to the bathroom, leaving the entire garage unobserved several times—the Spanish Army could have marched through the place and he wouldn't have known it if he was busy on the toilet. I know Anderson had a rental car—a Continental, probably—and that one unaccounted-for car entry was during one of those times, as you also know. But as for the guy the attendant saw leaving…" I proceeded to tell him what I knew of Anderson's running habits, and the scenario I'd patched together as to how the killer had left, including the fact of his not wearing running shoes and what that might imply.

Richman looked at me impassively, but with one eyebrow just slightly raised.

"Hmm," he said, followed by a long pause. "Interesting theory. But why wouldn't he just have driven out of the garage in Anderson's rental car?"

"He might have, if the attendant hadn't been in the booth—but in the driver's seat of a car he'd have to pass close enough for the guy to have seen his face—and for all he knew, the attendant might have been able to recognize it wasn't Anderson. On foot he could stay close to the far wall. I think he covered his bets by wearing the jogging suit just in case anybody else might have seen him in the hallway or in the elevator. The attendant wasn't in the booth when they drove in, but he couldn't count on his not being there when he tried to leave." I made a wild guess: "Anderson's keys were missing, right?" I shot Richman a quick glance, but his face remained totally impassive.

I'd learned that the police, as a group, tend to hold their cards extremely close to the vest, but with Richman there were ways to take a peek at their hand. "So," I said, "anything in there you didn't already know?"

He gave a non-committal shrug: "A little," he said. "Thanks."

Realizing I might be walking on thin ice, I decided to risk it: "Is there anything you can tell me about the murder without compromising the investigation?" I asked.

"Such as?"

"I assume he was robbed?"

"We didn't find his wallet," he said, then added "…or keys. We're checking to see if the credit cards have been used since the murder."

Something told me nothing would show up. Even if the motive weren't robbery the killer probably would have tried to make it appear it was.

I noticed he was watching me again—a habit he had that would have driven me nuts if anyone else did it. He had his lips semi-pursed as though trying to decide whether or not to say something.

Apparently he decided to go with it.

"There's one thing you might keep your eyes and ears open for," he said.

He had me. "Sure," I said. "What's that?"

"Well," he said after another quick semi-pursing of his lips, "When we contacted the supplier Anderson had met for dinner the night he was killed, we found out the guy had given Anderson a set of really expensive cutlery—six chef's kitchen knives in a red leather case. Antonio Vivace's the manufacturer, and the name is engraved on the handle of every knife. Anderson wasn't stabbed, and they weren't in his room, and they weren't in his car. We figure the killer took them. We're checking all the pawn shops and fences of course—the supplier says they're worth at least $1,800."

Interesting, I thought. Either the killer knew what he was getting when he took them, or the fact that they were in a red leather case clued him that they were probably valuable.

"What time was he killed?" I asked.

Richman kept watching me, as always, and he was quiet a moment, as if thinking of just how much he should tell me and how much he shouldn't. He'd obviously already overstepped some invisible line by telling me about the knives.

"The car entered the garage at 11:15; from what we can tell, he was probably killed somewhere around 1:30 or 2 a.m."

So that means we've got a pretty cool killer here—he sat around the room with the body for over four hours until he knew it was time for Anderson to go on his run. He had plenty of time to go over the room carefully to remove any evidence, and to decide to take the knives.

"I don't suppose any prints were found in Anderson's room, or in the rental car? Especially on the passenger's side?"

"There were some partial prints in the car, yes," Richman said. "But nothing conclusive."

"Any in the room?"

"Again, nothing conclusive. We think the killer did a pretty good job cleaning up, under the circumstances. But if, as you say, he knew Anderson had a set running schedule, he could have used that fact to get away unnoticed—and he'd have had plenty of time."

Two great minds with but a single thought.

I decided to take one more tentative step. "I know you can't be specific," I said, "but can you at least tell me if you do have any solid leads?"

"Not until we find the knives," he said, which to me meant "No." "If the killer tries to pawn them, though, that red leather case will be pretty easy to spot." It was fairly obvious that if they did have any solid evidence, Richman wouldn't have to be sitting here talking with me now.

He stared at me for a moment, then said: "Now let me ask you a question."

Oh, oh, here it comes, I thought "Sure," I said.

"Just what is your interest in this case? Did someone hire you to investigate it? If so, I'd like very much to know who...and why."

I'd been anticipating that, and fortunately I was able to give a straightforward, if not totally all-inclusive, answer. "I'm curious because Anderson was my client and because it's pretty likely that his death involves the gay community. No one has hired me to investigate it."

And that part was true. The Glicks hired me to run interference for ModelMen, not specifically to find who killed Anderson.

"And have you found out anything you're not telling me?" he asked.

"No," I said honestly. "I just want to keep the lines of communication open between us. I appreciate what you've done for me and the community in the past, and I think I might be able to be of help to you on this case, too. But in order to do it, I need as much information as you can give me without jeopardizing the official investigation."

Richman gave a small smile. "I'm afraid that's not going to be very much," he said.

I shrugged."I'll take what I can get," I said.

* * *

The weekend finally arrived, with relatively little accomplished. I was able to tentatively assure the Glicks shortly after my meeting with Richman that the police were apparently still unaware of Anderson's association with ModelMen: given the discretion on both sides of the client/escort arrangement, it was unlikely that there would be any obvious links. I was glad Richman was not officially a member of the homicide division, though, because if anyone in the department might make a connection between Anderson's apparent taste in hustlers and the existence of ModelMen, it would be him.

I did make the rounds of several of the bars and restaurants where more upscale hustlers could occasionally be found, showing Anderson's picture to waiters and bartenders, but with no luck at all. Which brought me reluctantly back to ModelMen and the obvious possibilities there. But from all I'd been able to gather, everything passed through Iris or Arnold Glick, and direct contacts between the individual escorts and the clients were strictly prohibited. And it would be unlikely for one of the escorts, unless he were truly stupid—which none of the ones I'd met thus far appeared to be—to risk losing a very lucrative job for a few extra bucks on the side. I'd have to remember to ask the Glicks, though, if they might ever have had to fire an escort for trying to moonlight ModelMen's clients. Though I was tempted to call on Saturday, I forced myself to observe my "weekends off" rule and instead paid my extremely reluctant obeisance to the Gods of Domesticity—laundry, shopping, dishes, etc.

But a little of the "Happy Homemaker" routine goes a very long way with me, and by the time 6:00 rolled around, I was feeling pretty…what's the word?…antsy? That feeling you get that isn't quite boredom, but an odd mix of wanting to do something and not wanting to do something and not knowing what you'd want to do if you did want to do something. I don't like feeling antsy. I missed my old Saturday-night-out-to-dinner tradition Chris and I had upheld for the five years we were together. Hell, I missed Chris.

Poooooor Baby! I knew practically every bar and disco in the city would be jammed to the rafters with Pride Weekend parties, but being wedged in with too many people in an enclosed space was not my idea of a good time. I guess the memory of the Dog Collar fire was still too strong.

I made my evening Manhattan, broiled a steak, and fixed a salad, then sat down in front of the boob tube. By accident I stumbled into the opening credits of "San Francisco"—one of my favorite movies of all time. Clark Gable, Jeanette MacDonald, Spencer Tracy, and the greatest earthquake sequence ever put on film. I'd seen it about three dozen times, but every time Jeanette gets up there at the Chicken's Ball and belts out "San Francisco" followed by that deep rumble....

By the time Jeanette and Clark and Spencer and 8,000 or so extras march over the crest of that hill to look down on what's left of the city, my antsys were gone and I didn't even think of going out. Unusual for me, I know, but the next day was Jared and Tim and thousands and thousands of my closest friends at the Gay Pride Parade. I could spare one night.

* * *

The three of us had arranged to meet at 11:15 for a couple pre-brunch Bloody Marys, but just as I was leaving the apartment, the phone rang. It was Chris, my ex, calling from New York. He knew it was the day for the parade, and he was waxing nostalgic about the fun we'd always had going together every year. We talked a lot longer than we probably should have, given my compulsion to never be late, but it was good talking with him...and his new lover Max, whom I'd never met but who seemed like a pretty nice guy from our having talked on the phone. Hard to imagine they'd been together as long as they had.

So I didn't get to Napoleon until about 11:20. I should have known parking would be impossible, and it was. The parade didn't start until 1:00, but gays and lesbians were already pouring into the Central from all over the city and all over the state. The first thing I saw when I walked in the door—other than that it was crowded—was the back of Jared's massive 6'3", football-player's frame, standing a little way back from the bar, obviously engrossed in somebody sitting in front of him. I didn't see who it was until I got closer to Jared and noticed it was Tim who Jared was engrossed in. Why was I not surprised? The two of them were talking and laughing like old friends. Considering they had never met before, that might have struck some as a 'small world' coincidence, but I knew Jared and I knew Tim, and I was obviously right in thinking they'd hit it off. Apparently they had found each other with no help from me.

Tim saw me first and gave me a heads-up nod. Jared turned around and grinned. "Hi, Dick," Tim said. "I don't think you've met my new husband."

"Jeezus," I said. "I can't turn my back on you for ten minutes and you're off picking up sailors."

"I thought you'd gotten lost," Jared said, his left leg trapped firmly between Tim's knees. "It's not like you to be late."

I signaled the bartender and ordered, then said: "Sorry...got a phone call from Chris in New York just as I was leaving. Glad to see you two managed to find one another—I guess you didn't need the name tags after all."

They exchanged grins. "We managed," Jared said.

"Yeah," Tim said. "Jared was just telling me all about your adventures in Leatherland. I didn't realize you were so... versatile."

"Well," I said, "maybe if you are a very good little boy, Jared might ask you over to play on his sling set."

Jared grinned again. "That offer's already been extended," he said.

The bartender brought my Bloody Mary and took the bill I'd reached past Tim to lay on the bar. "My God," I said, "I was only five minutes late. You two have been busy, haven't you?"

Tim laughed and said: "Yeah, but you're usually fifteen minutes early, so both of us figured we'd come early too. Pure kismet."

Uh huh, I thought.

* * *

Brunch was great. We got seated exactly on time, all ordered what proved to be world-class Eggs Benedict, and had a really nice, easygoing conversation. I was delighted to see that Jared and Tim were instant old friends, and while the sexual undercurrent was clearly there, I was rather surprised and pleased to see that it wasn't all just between the two of them.

We found a spot on the corner of Beech and Evans, about halfway down the parade route and on a slight rise. We could look down Beech in either direction and see an almost solid wall of people on both sides of the street. Tens upon tens of thousands of us, and it never failed to give me an indescribable sense of wonder and empowerment to know that at least right here, right now, *we* were the majority, *we* were the norm.

The parade itself, when it finally got moving, was a lot of fun. Some pretty impressive floats, lots of as-naked-as-they-could-get-away-with flesh, some local politicians who were beginning to realize that the gay vote could be crucial at election time; the banners, the flags, the marching groups, the local gay and lesbian chorus on a huge flatbed hauled by a rainbow flag-bedecked semi-trailer belching thick black smoke signals from its dual diesel exhaust pipes. People who have never been in a minority simply have no idea what a gay pride parade means to the gay community.

And, as was traditional, when the last float passed by, the crowd spilled into the street and became part of the parade itself, heading to the end of the parade route and the annual Gay Pride Carnival in Barnes Park.

Tim, Jared, and I joined the throng, our arms around each others' waists. Then I heard a voice behind us call out "Dick!" and I turned to see Phil and Billy in full shirtless splendor, wending their way through the shoulder-to-shoulder crowd. When they caught up with us, I introduced Jared and Tim to Phil and Billy, all of whom seemed mutually impressed, as well they should have been.

The crowd was so large that we realized, while still about two blocks from Barnes Park, that we'd never be able to move in the crush of people trying to get in to the carnival.

"You guys all want to come over to my place for awhile?" Jared asked the group. "I'm not all that far away. We can relax for a while then maybe come back early tonight when the crowd dies down."

Phil and Billy looked at each other, then shook their heads. "Wish we could," Phil said, "but I've got an assignment around 6, and Billy's got an actual, non-work related date."

"Ah," I said. "Who's the lucky guy?"

Billy gave me a wicked grin. "A gentleman never fucks and tells," he said.

"Maybe next time," Jared said.

Phil reached over and grabbed Billy's wrist so he could look at his watch. "Wow! I didn't realize it was this late! We'd better head for home—it's going to take forever to fight our way back as it is."

We all shook hands, and Phil and Billy and I exchanged hugs, and they turned and disappeared into the mob.

"How about you two?" Jared asked.

"I'm game," Tim said.

"Sure," I said.

Feeling not unlike salmon swimming upstream against the rapids, we made our way back to Napoleon. Tim's car was closest, but he drove a little two-seater sports car with a minuscule back bench that would have been a tight fit for an average-sized Munchkin, but I'm no Munchkin, and Jared sure as hell wasn't. So we walked the extra block to Jared's car and rode together to his place.

* * *

We sat around drinking beer and shooting the shit, when the conversation inevitably got around to the universal favorite male topic, sex. Tim and I were seated on the couch, with Jared in a large overstuffed armchair directly across from us. He was sitting back, relaxed, with his legs unselfconsciously spread apart, which pulled the fabric of his pants tight against his crotch. Tim's eyes zeroed in on the unmistakable bulge. Jared caught Tim looking and grinned. Tim blushed, but looked away only for a moment, then returned to his staring. Finally, he leaned toward me, the back of one hand covering one corner of his mouth and said in a stage whisper:"Is that for real?"

Jared and I exchanged grins. "Meat for the multitudes," I said and Jared, his crotch reacting to Tim's interest, had to shift his legs to try to relieve the growing pressure.

"Wow!" Tim said.

Finally, Jared had to stand up to try to rearrange the package.

"Want a look?" he asked, having to unbuckle his belt in any event, in order to reposition himself.

Tim, eyes still glued to the impressive display, merely nodded, and I glanced down to see that Tim himself was having a little difficulty in the tight pants department. And it goes without saying that I wasn't exactly Mr. Impartial Observer myself.

Jared, seeing both Tim and I in an equal stage of readiness, though still confined, said: "Why don't we all make ourselves a little more comfortable?" and kicked off his pants.

* * *

Even though I was totally but happily exhausted Monday morning, I made it to the office on time, and went through my little coffee-and-crossword puzzle ritual and, around 9:30, decided to call the Glicks to check on the possibility of any of their escorts having left their employ—and especially if they had ever had occasion to fire one. The phone was answered on the third ring by a woman's voice I knew wasn't Mrs. Glick's, so I assumed it had to be the maid.

"Glick residence," the voice said.

"Good morning," I said, hoping I sound cheery. "Are either Mr. or Mrs. Glick in, by any chance?"

"No, sir," she replied; "they are both at the office."

"Thank you," I said. "I'll try to reach them there," and I hung up after exchanging goodbye's.

I would have preferred not to bother them at ModelMen—I knew they liked to keep the two aspects of the business completely separate, but I didn't really have anything else to go on at the moment without following up on my hunch.

I had to look up ModelMen's number, and was somewhat surprised to hear the phone answered by Iris Glick.

"ModelMen Agency," she said, sounding very professional.

"Mrs. Glick, good morning," I said. "It's Dick Hardesty, and I'm sorry to bother you at the office, but I have a question I really would appreciate your helping me with. Would it be possible for me to come by for a moment?"

There was a pause, and then: "Why yes, of course. Would now be convenient?"

"I'll be right over," I said, then added: "Is Mr. Glick there, too? I'm sure either of you could answer the question, but I probably should discuss it with both of you."

"Yes...we're taking on a new ad agency this afternoon, and my husband is going over the details of the contract."

"Well, congratulations," I said. "I won't take up much of your time, I promise."

"We'll look forward to seeing you," she said.

* * *

The ModelMen offices were located on the second floor of a very nice new low-rise office building close…but not too close…to the Central. The glass double door had a neatly but subtly scripted "ModelMen Agency," and opened into a small reception area tastefully but not ostentatiously furnished and decorated. Mrs. Glick was seated behind the reception desk, which was flanked by two highly polished wooden doors. She'd been doing something with an open file folder in front of her when I approached, and she looked up and smiled as I entered. I went over to the desk to take her hand.

"Thank you for seeing me on such short notice," I said, as she got up from her chair and led me to the door to the right of the desk.

"Our receptionist is out ill today," she explained, "so I'm filling in for her. I rather enjoy it, actually." She knocked lightly, then opened it. Inside was an office about the same size as the reception area, but considerably more elegantly furnished. On one wall were an array of probably twenty professional portrait photos of extremely handsome men ranging in age from late teens to probably early fifties—the main agency's stable of legitimate models, I gathered. It did not escape me that Phil, Billy, Gary, and Aaron were among them. Mr. Glick was seated behind a polished mahogany desk. He rose as we entered, and moved around to greet me. We shook hands and he motioned me to a seat, returning to his own chair. Iris Glick stood by the open door, where she could keep an eye on the reception area.

"What can we do for you?" Mr. Glick asked, leaning back in his chair.

I turned my own chair slightly so I could see both of them. "I know ModelMen has only been in business a relatively short time, but have you had any turnover at all in your escorts?"

The Glicks' eyes immediately found each other, until Mr. Glick broke his look and returned his eyes to me.

"Yes," he said. "One. Only one. May I ask why you want to know?"

"The more I know about ModelMen and how it operates, the better I'll be able to protect your interests," I said without going further into detail. "May I ask the reasons for his leaving?"

Again, an exchange of glances and a pause, then Mr. Glick's: "We had to let him go."

"May I ask why?" I could tell they weren't going to release the information without considerable prodding.

Mrs. Glick said: "It was a matter of an infraction of the rules all our escorts are contractually obligated to follow. Why is this important?"

I'm pretty sure she knew damned well why it was important but was somehow reluctant to admit it—maybe to me, or maybe to herself.

"Well," I said, "If there is a possibility of there being a disgruntled former employee...."

Mr. Glick shook his head strongly. "Oh no, no! That's inconceivable. Are you suggesting...?"

It was my turn to shake my head. "I'm not suggesting anything," I said. "But I don't want to overlook anything that could possibly link ModelMen with Stuart Anderson's death."

Mr. Glick continued shaking his head. "Out of the question," he said. "Out of the question!"

"You're undoubtedly right," I said. "But could you tell me his name and the circumstances?"

"Matt," Mrs. Glick said. "Matthew Rushmore. He stepped outside our strict rule against initiating contacts with clients. We felt terrible about it, but infractions are infractions."

Mr. Glick sighed and added: "Our escorts are extremely well paid," he said, "and because of that fact we insist that they have no contact with our clients except through us. Matt, we discovered, approached a client we'd originally referred to him, offering his services on a freelance basis. That was completely unacceptable."

I had a suspicion there was something a little more to it. "You don't give a warning or a probationary period for transgressions of the rules?" I asked.

"No," Mrs. Glick said. "Each of our escorts fully understands our rules and why we have them before they are hired. A violation is a violation."

"May I ask how you found out about it?" I asked.

Again the Glicks looked at one another, but said nothing.

I knew something was being left out. "Please excuse me," I said, "but this is one of those instances I told you about when we first met, wherein I would not ask unless I really thought I had to know."

Mrs. Glick nodded almost imperceptibly to her husband who gave another deep sigh before speaking:

"Among the criteria we use in selecting our escorts is that they have certain areas of...well, specialization. Matt's was ...shall we say, catering to clients who enjoy a moderate degree of...discipline."

"S&M, you mean?" I asked.

"Oh no, no, nothing quite like that. Nothing...serious," Mr. Glick hastened to add. "Never beyond what the client requests. However..."

I resisted the temptation to say anything and instead just kept my eyes locked on Mr. Glick's until he looked mildly uncomfortable and glanced at his wife, as if for guidance.

"However," Mrs. Glick picked up her husband's faltering explanation, "Matt crossed that line too. We would never have known about it had not the client contacted us and explained the situation." She paused, looked into the reception area and moved to stand beside her husband. "I should add that we of course also removed the man from our client list—our clients, too, are expected to observe the rules as stringently as our escorts."

She laid a hand lightly on her husband's shoulder. "This particular client claims that Matt had arranged a freelance meeting with him, and then had gone considerably beyond the bounds of what he had expected or wanted. He had, as a matter of fact, had to go to the emergency room for treatment of his injuries. He had the good sense to tell the hospital and the police that he had been mugged by an unknown assailant."

And, I was sure, the fact that he was probably married and wouldn't care to have his family know he was into rough trade, however discreet, might have played a part.

"And how long ago was this?" I asked.

"About three months," Mr. Glick said.

"So you once had seven escorts, then?"

Mr. Glick shook his head. "No, we've never had more than six. After Matt left, we were lucky enough to find Aaron, who was coincidentally also a friend of Gary's."

Aaron had told me, I remember, that his specialty was "down and dirty"—which I suspected might include a bit of innocent B&D if not downright S&M.

"And how did Matt react to his…termination?" I asked.

Mrs. Glick gave a small smile. "Quite well, I think," she said. "You must remember that our escorts are also selected for and trained in being civil and adult. Matt had most of these qualities, but unfortunately neither he nor we foresaw this happening. We lost one or two of Matt's regular clients when he left, so we can only assume Matt is still seeing them."

"And where is Matt now?" I asked.

Mrs. Glick removed her hand from her husband's shoulder and walked again to the door where she could see into the reception area. "Part of our regret over this entire incident," she said, in effect talking over her shoulder as she looked out through the glass doors into the hallway, "was that each of our escorts becomes almost like family. Even given the severity of Matt's transgressions, we could not just throw him out into the street—plus the fact that we did not want to put him in the position of feeling animosity toward us. We arranged with another model agency to take him on. He is a very accomplished model—one of our most popular. But under the circumstances we thought it best to sever all ties with him. I understand he is doing quite well."

"And may I ask which agency he is with now?" I asked.

"Charter," Mr. Glick said.

I glanced at my watch and saw that I'd been there far longer than I'd intended. But I still had a few more questions.

"I'll be leaving in a moment," I said. "But would you mind answering just a few more questions?"

Apparently relieved that the interrogation was about over, Mrs. Glick said, "Of course."

From everything I knew of Stuart Anderson, his being involved in anything even hinting of other-than-pretty-vanilla sex was remote in the extreme. Still, I had to ask. "First, did Matt ever meet Stuart Anderson?"

"No," Mrs. Glick said, but Mr. Glick raised his hand to correct his wife.

"Yes, he did, as a matter of fact," Mr. Glick said. "We had Stuart to one of our dinners the night he became a client, so that he could meet our escorts. Everyone was there except for Phil and Billy, who were on an assignment, and that was the very night before we...had to let Matt go. But it was only in a setting with the other models. When Stuart next returned to town, Matt was no longer working for us, and as I think we told you, the first escort he spent time with was Gary."

"As a matter of fact," Mrs. Glick added, "I believe he asked for Matt, but when we told him Matt had left us, he selected Gary."

"And did he have any reaction to the news that Matt had left ModelMen?" I asked.

Mrs. Glick thought a moment. "He seemed mildly disappointed," she said, "and asked if Matt had gone to another service. I told him that Matt had left to pursue his modeling career full-time, and that was that."

"Could you tell me how the...uh...financial aspect of the business operates? I don't want to know exact fees, of course, but do the clients pay the escorts, or ModelMen?"

"ModelMen," Mrs. Glick said. "We felt the direct exchange of cash between escort and client was somehow...cold. As the escort is leaving, he presents the client with a ModelMen business card, and the client's signature on the back is our acknowledgment. The client is then billed a set fee. If the client wishes to give the escort a little something extra in appreciation, that is between the two of them."

"Thank you," I said. "I very much appreciate your candor."

It was about time for me to leave, but I had one final thought: "Do you promote your escorts'...specialties...to each new client?"

Mr. Glick shook his head, rather emphatically. "No, definitely not. Our escorts are all equally versatile in the more...traditional... forms of service. If a client asks for something specific, we will direct him to the appropriate escort. But we do not want to risk prejudicing any client by calling attention to...certain activities they might find objectionable."

"Ah," I said, pushing myself forward to the edge of my chair preparatory to standing up. "Well, again, I think I've taken up enough of your time for now. Thank you again for your cooperation. I'll be in touch."

Mr. Glick and I rose in unison, we exchanged handshakes all around, and Mrs. Glick once more walked me to the door.

* * *

Just as I was finishing dinner, the phone rang. I was pleased to hear Phil's voice, but immediately disturbed by it's tone.

"Phil," I said. "Is anything wrong? You sound strange."

"I'm worried, Dick," he said. "Billy's not home."

My confusion must have sounded in my voice. "I don't understand," I said.

His voice was tense. "I mean he didn't come home last night."

"Well," I said, hoping I sounded reassuring, "he did have a date, didn't he?"

"Yes," Phil said. "But he hasn't been home all day, either. And he hasn't called. He always calls. Always—if for no other reason than to see if he has an assignment."

"Well," I said again, "why don't you give the guy he had the date with a call? He might know."

There was a slight pause, then: "That's just it," Phil said. "I don't know who he was going out with. We usually tell one another, but not always. I've checked with everybody I could think of. I even just called the Glicks to see if he'd checked in with them. Nobody's heard from him."

I was at something of a loss for words. "I'm sure it's all right, Phil," I said. "There could be a hundred reasons."

"No," Phil said. "This isn't like Billy. I've got a really bad feeling and I don't know what to do about it."

"Look," I said, "it's still early. I'm sure he'll show up or call before long. But if by some chance he doesn't, give me a call in the morning and I'll see what I can do, okay? I wish there were something I could do now, but..."

"I understand," Phil said. "I'm sorry to bother you."

"Hey, don't ever say that! You could never be a bother, and I'll do anything I can to help. Just try to relax, and see what happens, okay?"

Not sounding as though he meant it, Phil said: "Okay. Talk with you later. Thanks, Dick."

"Take care, Phil," I said.

Maybe it was just a matter of emotions being contagious, but Phil's concern was beginning to give me an all too familiar feeling in my stomach, and I didn't like it.

* * *

I was in the bathroom the next morning, getting ready to step into the shower to get ready for work, when the phone rang. It was Phil.

"He's not home," he said. "He's not home and he hasn't called. Something's wrong, Dick. What can I do? I've called the hospitals; he's not there." I could literally *feel* Phil's anxiety.

"I'll be heading to the office soon," I said, "and when I get there, I'll make a few calls, okay? Did you get any sleep?"

"Not much," he said. "I kept waking up every time I heard a noise, thinking it was Billy coming home."

"Well, let me see what I can find out," I said, "and I'll give you a call the minute I know anything. And you call me if you hear from him."

"I will. Thanks, Dick. I really mean it."

"I know, Phil," I said. "Now go lie down for a while, hear?"

"I'll try. 'Bye."

"'Bye," I said. I put the phone back on its cradle and stepped into the shower.

* * *

The phone was ringing when I walked into the office, and I ran across the room to catch it.

"Hardesty Investigations," I said.

"Dick?" I recognized the voice, but it sounded strange. It wasn't Phil.

"Yes?"

"It's Tim. Are you sitting down?"

Oh, God! I thought, and hastily moved around my desk to sit in the chair.

"Yeah," I said, my voice sounding hollow.

"You remember the guys we met at the parade? Phil and Billy?"

"Yes."

"Have you talked to them since the parade?"

"To Phil," I said. "Billy…Billy hasn't been home." *Oh, Jeezus!*

"Billy's the one with a little mouse tattoo over his left nipple?"

Aw, God, no! I thought. *No, no, no!* "Yes," I said.

"Well…we have a body, with a little mouse tattoo over the left nipple…."

"Billy?" I asked. "Is it Billy?"

"I'm afraid so," he said.

That didn't register at first. "What happened to him?" I asked, not even knowing where the question came from.

There was a pause, then: "He was found last night in a Dumpster behind one of the bars on Arnwood.. He'd been suffocated."

I was totally numb by this time, but heard my voice saying something. "Well maybe it's not Billy. You only met him once. Maybe it could be somebody who…"

"I'm afraid not," Tim said, gently. "I recognized him. I'm really, really sorry."

CHAPTER 6

I must have finished the conversation with Tim somehow because suddenly I was aware that I was sitting there, with the phone still in my hand, listening to a dial tone, afraid to move for fear I would throw up. Slowly, I eased the phone back onto the cradle and leaned forward with my elbows on my desk and cupped my hands over my nose and mouth, forcing myself to take slow, deep breaths.

I had to tell Phil, but I couldn't do it by phone. When the nausea had subsided, I let my motor responses take over. They got me out of the chair, walked me to the door, made sure it was locked behind me, then walked me to the elevator. By the time I reached my car, I was sufficiently pulled together to let my mind, which had been spinning wildly out of control, shift into gear.

How was I going to tell Phil? What could I say? I didn't even know Billy's last name, which meant that Phil was going to have to go with me to the coroner's office to try to identify the body.

Having sex with a guy doesn't make you best friends, and I'd only met Billy a handful of times, if that. But what I knew of him I liked. A lot. He was funny and sexy as all hell, and sweet and young, and beautiful and full of life and some son of a bitch had taken all that away from him and I still thought I might throw up.

A blaring horn from the car behind me made me realize the light had turned green, and I moved along.

I parked about half a block from Phil's apartment and idly thought I should have brought the photo Billy had lent me of Phil and Anderson and Glen O'Banyon and whoever else in hell it was in there with them. I walked down the hallway to Billy's.... no, to *Phil's*...apartment and knocked on the door. A full minute went by and I was about to knock again when the door opened. Phil took one look at my face and all the color drained from his own. His eyes riveted onto my own, as though he thought they might help keep him from falling down. "What is it, Dick?" he asked, though I think he knew.

"It's Billy," I managed to say. "He...."

"Is he hurt?" he asked. "Is he in the hospital?"

I shook my head.

Phil looked at me and duplicated my head shake, in slow motion. His eyes filled with tears and his lower lip began to quiver. He started to say "No," but couldn't make it. I moved forward and put my arms around him as he put his head on my shoulder and started crying like the very little boy who lives somewhere deep inside us all.

* * *

Some time later, when the immediate tidal wave of grief had ebbed away to be replaced by a numb state of semi shock, Phil was able to tell me Billy's last name: Steiner, which I should have remembered from seeing it above the buzzer in the entry to their building. I asked Phil if I could use his phone, and he motioned toward the kitchen. I got up and called Tim at work—something I would ordinarily never do, gave him the information, and told him Phil's address and phone number. Then I returned to the living room to sit with Phil. I had a thousand questions, but they could wait. We just sat there without saying anything. Twenty minutes later, there was a knock on the door. While Phil continued sitting on the sofa, staring off into space, I answered the door to find two plainclothes policemen.

"Mr. Stark?" The shorter of the two asked.

"No," I said, "I'm a friend."

"And your name is...?"

"Hardesty. Dick Hardesty."

I stood back to let the two officers enter, then closed the door behind them. Phil looked up, but said nothing.

The taller of the two turned to me and said: "Well, Mr. Hardesty, we'd like to speak to Mr. Stark in private, so if you wouldn't mind..."

Like shit I wouldn't mind, I thought.

But before I could say anything, Phil said: "No. I want him to stay."

The two men exchanged glances which made it clear they would have preferred to be alone with Phil but apparently didn't want to make waves. Instead, they simply ignored me and walked over to stand in front of Phil.

"Mr. Stark," the shorter one said, "I'm Detective Carpenter and this is Detective Couch." They did not extend their hands, and Phil just looked from one to the other without lifting his head or speaking.

"May we ask your relationship to Mr. Steiner?" the taller one...Couch...asked.

"My roommate," Phil said, his voice flat, then added: "My friend."

The two detectives exchanged glances. "I see," Couch said.

What the fuck is that supposed to mean? I thought, but I said nothing and the two men appeared to have forgotten I was in the room. I folded my arms and leaned back against the door.

"Do you mind if we sit?" they asked, and Phil merely nodded. Carpenter sat in the chair facing the sofa and Couch pulled another chair up to sit beside him. Couch took out a notepad and pencil while Carpenter leaned forward on the edge of his chair, elbows on knees, hands folded between his legs. They proceeded to ask Phil the usual questions—when he'd last seen Billy, if he knew where Billy had gone—or with whom—the night he disappeared, where Phil had been, if Phil had noticed anything unusual in Billy's behavior lately, if he had any known enemies. Then they began to zero in on Billy's relationship to Phil: how long they'd known one another, how they'd met, what they each did for a living. When Phil said they were both models, the two officers again exchanged glances, and then immediately asked if Billy was 'a homosexual.'

Yeah, you assholes, I thought. *Everybody knows if you're a male model you've got to be a fucking faggot!*

When Phil nodded 'yes', they went off on a long string of questions they probably had to ask, but their tone made it pretty clear what they thought about 'homosexuals': did he bring a lot of guys home? How promiscuous was he? (Not *whether* he was promiscuous, of course—all faggots are promiscuous—but *how* promiscuous was he?) Did he use drugs? Was he into S&M? What bars did he frequent? What kind of 'crowd' did he hang around with? Did he hustle tricks? All phrased with the firm assumption that Billy was obviously a slut.

To the question of whether Billy hustled tricks, Phil answered "No," which was technically—and semantically—true.

I was glad I was there—not only because the cops' questions skirted some I had, but because my presence might reign in any open display of homophobia only implied in their phrasing and tone. Phil wasn't in much of a condition to protect himself against being pressured, but I wasn't about to let them even try.

Carpenter reached into his jacket pocket and pulled out a photograph and handed it to Phil. Phil looked at it and what little color he had regained in his face drained away again.

"Is this Mr. Steiner?" Couch asked.

Phil's head moved almost imperceptibly up and down, very slowly. He handed the photo back to Couch, who returned it to his jacket pocket. Phil got up quickly and went down the hall to the bathroom, closing the door behind him.

With Phil out of the room, the two detectives turned their attention to me.

"And were you a friend of Mr. Steiner's?" Carpenter asked.

"I'm afraid I didn't know him all that well," I said. "Mr. Stark and I have been friends for some time now."

"What do you know about Mr. Steiner's sexual habits?" Couch asked, completely out of left field.

"No more than you know of Detective Carpenter's, I'm sure," I said, as calmly as possible.

Couch's face flushed in anger, but before he could say anything, Phil came out of the bathroom and returned to living room. He didn't sit down.

Looking at his notebook, Carpenter then asked for the name and phone number of Billy's employer, and the names and addresses of Billy's family, which Phil provided.

"Should I call Billy's folks?" Phil asked.

"We'll call them," he said. "They'll have to come down to positively identify the body."

"They live in Leeds," Phil said. "And Billy's dad is in a wheelchair—getting around is hard for them. Do you have to put them through this? Can't I do it?"

The detectives looked at one another. "Well, it's preferable to have a relative make the identification," Carpenter said, "but..."

"Could I do it?" I asked, not wanting to put Phil through the trauma.

"No," Phil said. "I want to. I want to see him." He was struggling to keep his composure, and I wished the detectives would just get the hell out of there.

"Well, I guess that would be all right, if you're sure you want to put yourself through it," Carpenter said.

Phil merely nodded.

"Would you like to come down with us now?" Couch asked.

"I'll bring him," I said.

The detectives got up, thanked Phil for his cooperation and said they would be in touch shortly. I stood aside as they approached the door. Carpenter nodded to me as he opened it, and Couch merely glared. Neither said a word to me, which was fine with me.

When they'd gone, I went over to Phil, who was still standing in the same spot and in the same position as when he had reentered the room.

I walked over to him and put my arms around him. He just stood there. After a moment, I backed away, my hands still on his arms. "You want to rest for a few minutes?" I asked.

He took in a deep breath and shook his head. "No," he said. "Let's do it now."

So we did.

* * *

It was one hell of a rough two hours. I'd been to the morgue before, unfortunately, and gone through the entire process of identifying someone. I knew the ritual. It never changed, and it never got easier.

Phil was in that protective state of mental numbness that semi-shock often produces. I insisted on staying with him every minute. When the curtain opened, and they uncovered Billy's face, Phil just looked at it. He lifted his hand and put his open palm on the glass closest to Billy's face. Then he looked at me as though asking who that person was and what he was doing there and what should he do next? I nodded at the attendant, who replaced the sheet, and Phil turned and walked out the door without a word.

* * *

"Why don't you try to get some sleep now?" I asked when we got back to the apartment, but Phil shook his head.

"I can't sleep," he said, though he looked completely exhausted.

I'd tried to convince him to come to my place, but he refused and I didn't want to make an issue of it. I guided him to the sofa.

"Well, then," I said, "why don't you at least lie down here on the sofa for a few minutes. I'd like to use your phone if I could—I should let the Glicks know what's happened and tell them to be ready for a visit from the police."

Phil nodded, then reluctantly sat on the edge of the sofa. I moved over to push him back, gently.

"No, lie down," I said, turning his shoulders to one side and pushing him back against the arm of the sofa, then lifting his legs to put his feet on the cushions. He was much too tall to be able to totally stretch out, so I grabbed a cushion from one of the chairs and put it behind his head. "Now just rest a minute," I said, and looked around for the telephone.

* * *

I called the Glicks' home from the kitchen phone. The maid answered, but put me through to Mrs. Glick. Since I have yet to figure out a casual way to tell someone of a death, or to find an acceptable way to segue into the information, I simply told her directly what had happened, and that ModelMen should be prepared to be contacted by the police. When I told her Billy was dead, I heard the sound of the receiver being dropped and there was a long pause before I could tell it had been picked up again. I had to ask if she were still there, and there was another long delay before she replied. It was rather like talking to someone on the other side of the moon. She seemed to be in shock, and little wonder. When she had composed herself to the point of asking for the details of Billy's death, I told her I would tell them everything I knew a bit later, but that she should probably break the news to Mr. Glick immediately and get ready for a visit. I cautioned her once again not to directly lie, but knew they were sharp enough to be able to evade the issue of Billy's involvement in—or if possible, even the existence of—the escort service branch of the business.

I knew, too, that what I was doing could well—and undoubtedly would—be taken as hampering the police investigation. While I tried to kid myself into thinking there might be no connection between Billy's death and the escort service, my gut told me otherwise. But until I had a better idea of whether there was or not, I needed time. I had been hired to protect the Glicks and ModelMen, and if that put me in trouble with the police, well…I told myself that the cops would have enough to keep them busy with the information they already had.

When I returned to the living room, I was relieved to see that Phil was sound asleep. I went back into the kitchen for a pencil and sheet of paper I'd seen beside the phone and wrote a note to Phil, telling him to call me at the office when he woke up. Taking the phone off the hook and putting it on the counter, I left the apartment as quietly as I could, making sure the door was locked behind me.

* * *

There were two calls waiting for me when I got to the office, neither of them a surprise: Lieutenant Mark Richman and Arnold Glick. I gave Glick's call priority, since I knew that Richman would want to see me at police headquarters. I was relieved to see, however, that it was Richman who called rather than Captain Offermann, head of the Homicide Division. Richman I felt fairly comfortable with—Offermann was pretty much an unknown quantity. And though Lieutenant Richman was technically in the Administrative Department, I knew he worked closely with homicide.

The voice announcing "Thank you for calling ModelMen" was one I did not recognize, but I assumed it was the regular receptionist who had been out ill during my last visit. When I identified myself and asked to speak to Mr. Glick, she put me through immediately.

"Mr. Hardesty," Glick's voice said, not quite able to conceal the tension, "I appreciate your call. You have no idea how shocked and devastated Mrs. Glick and I were to hear of Billy's death! I've been trying to call Phil—I know how close he and Billy were—but his line has been busy."

I explained that I had left the phone off the hook so that Phil could sleep, then said: "We have to talk privately and soon. I explained the situation to Mrs. Glick and am sure you understand I'm doing whatever I can under the circumstances. I suspect I'll be called down to police headquarters, since I was present when the police questioned Phil, but could we meet later this afternoon?"

"Just call when you're ready," Mr. Glick said.

"I assume you've not been contacted yet?" I asked.

"No," he said, "but we expect to be at any time. Of course we have nothing whatever to hide. Billy was one of our most popular and in-demand photographers' models, as you know...."

I got the message.

"Well, until later, then," I said, and we hung up.

I immediately dialed Police Headquarters and asked for Lieutenant Richman's extension.

"Lieutenant Richman," the now-familiar voice said.

"Lieutenant, it's Dick Hardesty. I got your message. I gather you want to see me?"

"As soon as possible," he said.

I looked at my watch. "I can be there in half an hour," I said.

"Okay. I'll see you then." And he hung up.

Hoping Phil would be able to sleep and not try to call me while I was gone, I left the office and headed for the City Building Annex.

* * *

I'll spare you the details of the meeting, mainly because while I was driving over to the City Building, I couldn't help thinking of Billy, and the numbness set in again. So I can't recall word for word what was said or in what order, other than that Billy had been found in a Dumpster behind the Bull Pen by one of the area's homeless, though there was no indication of where he had been killed. His tee shirt was on inside out, his belt loosened and his pants unbuttoned. His shoes were found in another part of the dumpster, as if the killer had tossed them in after the body was dumped. The police suspected he had probably been murdered while he was nude, then hastily dressed. That information in itself would have been enough to make me totally tune out to what followed.

The gist of it was clear, though: Richman was not happy, to say the least. He let it be known that had Captain Offermann not been out of town at a conference, this meeting would have been between me and Offermann, and if I could sense Richman's displeasure, I could fairly well imagine how Offermann must be feeling. The fact that there were now two murder victims, both victims gay—well, one gay and one bi—and that I had known both of them was somehow very disturbing. *Like I was happy about it?* And even though there was absolutely no hint that they thought I was even remotely involved in the deaths, the Scapegoat Principle is a pretty strong one and I was somehow being made the oblique outlet for it, however illogically.

Richman, of course, wanted to know what Billy and Anderson might have had in common. I was able to pull myself together to do a little fancy footwork around that one, but based on the Glicks saying that Billy had not been present when Anderson met the other escorts, I could honestly say that I had no indication that he and Anderson had ever met. He asked if Billy was a hustler, and again I was able to step out on the weak limb of semantics between "hustler" and "escort" and say no, he was not. He asked about Billy and Phil's relationship and I told him honestly that it was strictly a close big brother/ little brother friendship.

Obviously Richman had talked with Carpenter and Couch and was just doing a little cross checking.

He asked what I knew of Billy, and I told him…again honestly…that he seemed like a really nice kid with no apparent problems, and not the kind to get mixed up in anything kinky. But then neither was Anderson.

One little exchange I do remember, though, since it says a lot about the mind-set of the average heterosexual male—well, the average heterosexual male homicide detective, at any rate.

"I hear you managed to piss Detective Couch off pretty effectively," Richman said.

"How was that?" I asked.

"When you implied that he and Detective Carpenter were sexually involved with one another."

"When I *what?*" I asked, incredulous. Then I told him exactly what I had really said, about my knowing as much about Billy's sexual habits as Carpenter knew about Couch's. Obviously, since Billy was a fag and Phil is a fag, and I was most probably a fag, I was inferring the two detectives were as well.

Richman heard me out, then merely shrugged and gave a dismissive wave of his hand. "Ah," he said. "Well, they're good cops, but they learn slow. Interesting how their minds work, though. Give 'em time." He sat quietly for a moment, then said: "So just off the top of your head, what do you think we're dealing with here? Is there such a thing as a gay homophobe?"

"Well," I remember saying, "thanks to having been raised in a wholesome, Puritanical society where far too many gay kids grow up with the idea that homosexuals are disgusting perverts, it's hardly surprising that there are quite a few gays who hate themselves and, by extension, other gays. This guy may well be one of them."

The meeting ended with my usual promise to keep him posted on anything I might learn, though I realized that under the circumstances of this case, that was going to be a mighty hard promise to keep.

* * *

I hurried back to the office to see if Phil had called. He hadn't, so I tried calling him on the basis that if he were still sleeping, I'd get a busy signal. It rang, and was picked up on the second ring.

"Yes?"

"Phil," I said. "It's Dick. Did you get my note? I hated to leave you there, but I know you needed the sleep."

"Yeah, I did," he said, his voice still flat, "and I appreciate your being here. I was going to call you, but...."

"That's okay," I said. "Listen, why don't you come over and spend a couple days at my place? I...."

"That's really nice of you, Dick, but the Glicks just called and they insisted I come over and stay with them until all this settles down. I didn't really want to, but they insisted, so I said I would. Just for a day or two."

"I think that's a good idea," I said, thinking that it was really nice of the Glicks to offer. "Are they home now?" I asked.

"No, they're both at the office. I think they're waiting for the police."

That figured. "I'm going to be seeing them later today, I hope," I said, "so if you'd like me to pick you up and take you over...."

"No, that's not necessary, Dick," he said. "I can drive okay. And getting a little sleep helped a lot."

"Well, okay, if you're sure."

"Yeah," he said, "I'm sure." There was a pause and then: "I've got to call Billy's folks first."

"I understand," I said. "If there's anything I can do to help...."

"Thanks, Dick," he said. "I really appreciate everything you've done. I'll probably see you later, then."

We exchanged goodbyes and I immediately called ModelMen, identified myself, and asked for either Mr. or Mrs. Glick. The secretary/receptionist said that both Mr. and Mrs. Glick were occupied at the moment, but would be happy to call me back as soon as they were available. I pretty much could guess with whom they were occupied, and was anxious to hear how it went.

I tried to pass the time with busy work—reorganizing the file cabinet, straightening out my desk drawers—anything at all to not think of Billy and what had happened to him. I hadn't yet gotten past the sadness stage to the anger, but I could feel the transition starting, and I knew I'd have to work hard on controlling it.

Half an hour later, the phone rang. I didn't wait for the second ring. "Hardesty Investigations."

"Mr. Hardesty, this is Arnold Glick. Could you meet us at our home in about an hour?"

"I'll be there," I said

And I was.

* * *

Mrs. Glick greeted me at the door—though it was not the Mrs. Glick I was used to seeing. Her makeup was subdued, and instead of the bright colors she apparently so favored, she had on an attractive and expensive-looking plain white blouse and dark grey skirt. We exchanged quiet greetings and she led me into the study/library, where Mr. Glick was standing by one of the large windows, talking on the phone.

"No," he was saying, calmly; "no, we won't hear of it. You will not be an imposition at all, and Johnnie-Mae has already started dinner. She knows how you love her back ribs, and she's making them especially for you. You don't want to disappoint Johnnie-Mae, now do you?" There was a pause, and then: "I thought not. And the pool is just sitting empty, waiting for you to use it whenever you feel like it. All right? We'll see you shortly, then. Our home is your home. Goodbye."

He had noticed my entry a moment or two before he finished his conversation, and he shook his head as he hung up.

"That was Phil," he said, sighing—which I had already assumed from what I'd heard. "He had changed his mind about spending some time with us; said he didn't want to impose. But he shouldn't be alone now, and I managed to convince him."

I was again impressed by the Glicks' kindness and generosity, and actually a bit relieved to find that Phil had not yet arrived. I didn't think Phil needed to hear what the Glicks and I had to talk about.

The chairs had been rearranged around the fireplace, with three in a small semi-circle. Mrs. Glick motioned me to one, and she and her husband sat next to one another in the other two.

"This has been an incredibly difficult and sad day for us," Mr. Glick said, reaching out to take his wife's hand. "And we are grateful to you for your kindness to Phil, and for being so considerate as to be the one to break the news to us and prepare us for our meeting with the police."

"How did the meeting go?" I asked.

He gave a slight shrug. "About as well as could be expected, I think," he said. "There were two detectives…a detective Carpenter and a detective…" he paused, looking to his wife, who shook her head.

"Couch," I supplied.

"Yes, Couch. Thank you. They had the usual questions and some not so usual." He looked again to his wife, who picked up the conversation.

"They asked if we knew Billy and Phil were gay, and if we made it a point to hire gay models. We told them that the sex lives of our models was none of our business, and mentioned several of our models who are indeed married. We keep portfolios on all our models and the work they've done, and they asked if we could provide them with head-shots of all our models—I'm not sure why."

I was, and I wasn't happy about it. "Did you give them to them?"

"I told them it would take us a while to get them all together, but that we would call them as soon as we had them," she said.

"At least they were apparently satisfied that Billy was, indeed, a legitimate photographer's model," Mr. Glick said. "They asked what our relationship was with Billy, and we told them honestly that we consider all of our models to be an extended family, and that Billy was a member of that family. When they asked what we knew of Billy's personal life we were once again able to answer truthfully that we had control over Billy only insofar as his employment with us was concerned, but that the personal lives of our models are their own affair. They seemed convinced, however reluctantly."

"They did ask," Mr. Glick said, apparently on reflection, "whether we had ever had any problems with any of our clients—whether any of the photographers or advertising people who employ our models had ever approached them sexually. We told them we had never had any such complaint. I think the police have a very warped view of models, photographers, and the art world in general."

"Indeed," I said, and found myself relaxing considerably. Of course, I probably should not have worried in any case...the Glicks didn't just fall off the turnip truck; they were shrewd business people or they wouldn't be where they were.

We were all silent for a moment, while I thought of how to gracefully approach my main reason for wanting the meeting. Finding there was none, I just gave a mental shrug and plowed ahead. "Which brings us," I said, "to a very sensitive area, and I must once again ask your indulgence if I step over a line or two."

The Glicks looked at one another, then at me, and nodded in

unison. "Proceed," Mr. Glick said.

"I'm afraid we have to face the possibility—however unaccept-able it may be—that Stuart Anderson's death and Billy's death were more than merely coincidental tragedies. And if they were not coincidences, the finger points directly to a link with ModelMen."

The Glicks sat in complete silence. No protestations, no look of shock. Impassive.

"May I ask how closely you check out your escorts?" I said.

Mr. Glick sighed and gave a small wave of his hand. "As closely as we possibly can," he said, "though I'm sure you realize that isn't always easy, given the nature of the business. We of course check for criminal records and interview each applicant thoroughly—as a matter of fact, both Mrs. Glick and myself interview them separately, to look for discrepancies in their responses. Both Mrs. Glick and myself consider ourselves quite astute at judging character and knowing when we're being misled."

I waited for another moment and then continued: "You mentioned, when you were telling me about having fired Matt Rushmore, that he was apparently pretty heavily into…discipline. Are you confident there wasn't any S&M involved? You aren't present during the…meetings, after all."

Mr Glick sat forward in his chair, no longer impassive. "Oh, no! We're quite sure. S&M has such negative connotations. Some of our clients do, as we mentioned previously, request a certain degree of discipline, but we would never tolerate outright sadomasochism. Surely you can't be suggesting…?" he said.

"I'm not suggesting anything," I said. "But there appear to have been evidence of possible sadomasochism in Stuart Anderson's death; I don't have all the details on Billy yet, but hope to have them soon. Given the circumstances, Matt Rushmore is the obvious first person to look at. Can you tell me anything at all about him? Anything you found out from your background check…anything at all you might know from his past…?"

The Glicks exchanged a gunshot-quick glance which did not escape me, then were silent a moment, until Mr. Glick said: "Gary and Matt were our first two escorts, as a matter of fact, and our screening process has evolved considerably over time. We did note that there seemed to be certain areas of Matt's past that he was reluctant to go into in detail, and we did not press him on it. We did know, from both Matt and Gary, that Matt was having serious financial problems, we gather, relating to child support issues—and had taken to hustling to make ends meet. And since Gary and he were so...close...."

Now what in hell did that mean? I wondered.

"Close?" I asked.

Mr. Glick merely nodded, and his wife said. "Matt and Gary had served in the Marines together, and had become very good friends—which of course made it all the more difficult for us to terminate Matt. He is very ingratiating—that's one of the things we look for in our escorts, of course. And while part of Matt's appeal is his overtly masculine, no-nonsense exterior, I suspect it is more of a defense mechanism than a reflection of his true character."

Interesting, I thought. "And while we're on the subject of the escorts," I said, "I've met four of them: Gary, Aaron, Phil, and...Billy," I noticed Mr. Glick reach out to take his wife's hand, "...but I think it might be helpful if I met the other two: Mark and...Steve?" Mr. Glick nodded. "Did they both know Matt?"

"Yes," Mr. Glick said, "and of course you are welcome to meet them. My wife and I were just discussing, before you arrived, that it might be a good idea to get everyone together here for one of our group dinners as soon as Phil is up to it. I'm sure they will all want to express their concerns and sympathy over Billy's terrible loss. Perhaps you could join us? It would give you a chance to talk to everyone."

"That's kind of you," I said. "I appreciate your including me."

"And on the subject of dinner," Mrs. Glick said, "would you be able to stay for dinner this evening? I know it is short notice, but Phil might feel a bit more comfortable if a friend were here."

"If it wouldn't be an imposition," I said.

"Not at all," Mrs. Glick said, smiling as she got up from her chair. "I'll just go tell Johnny Mae."

* * *

Dinner was, as I'd expected, difficult. Phil arrived just before seven, and we went almost immediately into the formal dining room which, like the study, was elegant without being overpowering. The table, though, was gigantic, and looked as though it could seat 20 without even putting in an extra leaf. One end of the table was set for four and managed not to look like everything had just been shoved to one end. Though the food was delicious, no one was really very hungry. Phil was still in something of a state of…well, withdrawal, though he tried valiantly to pretend this was just a casual dinner. The Glicks were marvelously kind—solicitous without being overly attentive. Mr. Glick in particular, I noticed, was subtly keeping a close eye on Phil's every response and reaction. What talk there was was as light as could be managed under the circumstances. Mrs. Glick asked how Phil and I had met, not knowing that it was related to an earlier case involving murder, and I rather hoped Phil might not remember that aspect, either, but of course I knew he did.

After dinner—Johnnie-Mae had somehow found time to make an angel food cake with whipped cream, which she knew Phil loved—we sat around over coffee and Cointreau until I sensed it was time for me to leave. As we all rose from the table, Mr. Glick turned to me and said: "Would you mind helping Phil get settled in?" Which was, I knew, his subtle way of giving Phil and me a moment or two alone together.

"Sure," I said.

"Turn left at the top of the stairs," Mrs. Glick said, "and it's the third door on the right—the room with the small balcony overlooking the pool." Then she turned to Phil and hugged him. "Good night, dear," she said and kissed him on the cheek.

Mr. Glick moved forward to shake his hand. "We'll see you in the morning, then," he said.

Phil merely nodded, and tried to smile. "Thank you both," he said, and I followed him up the stairs and down the hall to his room. Johnnie-Mae had turned the bed down and opened the sliding glass doors to the balcony, which overlooked not only the pool, but the golf course beyond. Phil's small overnight bag was at the foot of the bed. We just stood there a moment then, not knowing what else to do, I gave in to the urge to reach out and hug him.

"Hang in there, kid," I said, rather embarrassed at having to resort to a cliche to express my feelings.

"I will," he replied.

I stayed with him until he got undressed and got into bed, nude. It was the first time I'd ever seen Phil nude that my crotch didn't automatically spring into "ready" stage, but I guess even it knew there is a time and a place for everything…and this was not it.

"I'll talk with you tomorrow," I said as he pulled the sheets up around him. "Okay?"

"Okay."

I closed the door behind me and went back downstairs.

The Glicks were in the study, and I stopped at the door to say my thanks and goodnights, and to ask for Matt Rushmore's home phone number.

* * *

When I got home, just before ten o'clock, I found messages from Tim and Jared. Tim's said he had nothing new to report, but just wanted to see how I was doing, and how Phil was holding up. Jared's simply said he'd heard about Billy— obviously from Tim—and for me to give him a call when I could. Both of them sounded sincerely concerned, and I reflected again on how much easier life is when you're lucky enough to have good friends—and how important they are.

I'd been wanting to call Tim to see if there was anything else he might be able to tell me about how Billy had died, and as soon as I reached him and we'd exchanged greetings, I got right to it. I told him of my meeting with Lieutenant Richman, and what little I'd been able to find out from him.

"Two things I want to know," I said. "Was there any evidence that Billy put up a fight? And was there any evidence of sexual activity?"

"There was semen in the rectum," Tim said. "And he was definitely suffocated—there were traces of Eider down in his mouth and lungs, probably from a pillow. Do you happen to know if he might have been asthmatic?"

I remembered the night I'd met Billy, at Hughies. "Yeah, he was," I said. "Why?"

"All the autopsy results aren't in yet," Tim said, "but we were pretty sure he had asthma. He probably had an attack while he had his face pushed down into the pillow. There was slight bruising on the backs of his shoulders at the base of his neck. Whoever did it was pretty damned strong, I'd say. But as to a fight…bruised knuckles, cuts, scratches, other marks; no. It looks like it started out as consensual sex and went really wrong somehow. It's pretty obvious that Billy's bruises came from the force of the guy on top of him pushing him face-down into the pillow."

"So it could have been an accident?" I asked.

A slight pause, then: "It could have been, I suppose."

But then I remembered that Phil had said that Billy refused to have sex without a condom; the fact that there was semen in his rectum pretty much indicated to me that the sex hadn't been totally consensual.

Anderson had bruises on the inside of his forearms which suggested that somebody may have been straddling him with his knees resting his full weight on Anderson's arms, which would have kept him from moving. And Billy's…

Tim's mind must have been working along the same lines as mine. "But *two* accidents resulting in death?" Tim asked. "Not impossible—just a tad not likely."

Well, that gave me something more to think about, as if I needed it.

The conversation switched, by unspoken mutual agreement, to the general details of the day: the police's visit to Phil, the fact that he was staying with the Glicks for a few days, our dinner…that sort of thing. With Tim's promise to call if he had any more information, we hung up.

It was getting pretty late, but knowing that Jared stayed up until the wee hours working on his dissertation, I tried giving him a call. He was up, and I just sketched in the details of the day, not mentioning ModelMen at all. While I was sure Jared knew about ModelMen—it was hardly a secret in the gay community, but then it wasn't a topic of general conversation, either—those who knew about it just considered it another gay business like the stores, bars, and restaurants along Beech or Arnwood. But I didn't think it was necessary to spell everything out at this point, and realizing that it probably wouldn't take much for him to connect the dots if he had a mind to.

* * *

The morning paper carried a small article on page 3 to the effect that a body had been found in a Dumpster behind a bar "frequented by homosexuals" near Skid Row. Identity was being withheld pending notification of next of kin. End of story.

Though the Glicks had given me Matt Rushmore's home phone number, I made a quick check of the phone book to see if he might be listed. He was, which would pretty much eliminate the necessity of my explaining how I'd gotten it. I didn't want to put the Glicks in an awkward position if I could help it.

I forced myself to finish reading the paper, and tried to do the crossword puzzle, but my mind just wouldn't cooperate, so even though I'd wanted to wait until I was sure Rushmore would be either at work or out of bed, I gave up and dialed his number.

A very masculine voice said: "Hi, this is Matt," and I was just about to say something when it continued "I'll be glad to return your call if you'll leave your number."

I identified myself and left both my work and home numbers—I don't usually like to give out my home phone, but very much wanted to talk to him as soon as possible.

I next called the Glicks to see how Phil was doing. Johnnie-Mae answered the phone. I had found out, I can't recall how, that her last name was Dabbs, and I made a point of addressing her as "Mrs. Dabbs" rather than "Johnnie-Mae". Before asking to speak to Phil, I complimented her on her cooking and on her consideration for Phil. She seemed truly pleased, and when I asked to speak with him, she said he was in the pool but would go tell him I was on the line. I had momentary visions of Phil paddling wetly across the marble foyer, leaving a long trail of water from the pool to the phone when I realized the Glicks just might possibly have more than one telephone in the house, and there was probably one out by the pool.

A moment later, I heard Phil's voice: "Hi, Dick." He sounded almost like the old Phil I knew.

"Just thought I'd check to see how you're doing," I said.

"That's really nice of you," he said. "I'm just taking a dip—Gary came by and insisted I get in the pool with him. I'm glad he did; I feel a lot better...physically, anyway."

"Well, I'm glad," I said, "I just wanted to say 'hi', and now I'll let you get back to Gary."

"No," Phil said, "I'm glad you called. I was going to call you. I've been thinking about Billy and trying to remember anything at all that might help find out who...who did this to him."

My "alert level" went up a couple of notches. "And did you?" I asked.

Phil's lowered his voice noticeably, and I wondered how close Gary might have been to the phone. "I told you Billy didn't tell me who he had the date with," Phil said, "and that was unusual but I didn't think that much about it. Then I thought about it and remembered that he'd only not told me who he was going out with twice before, and both those times it was because he was going out with somebody he knew I didn't like for one reason or another. One was a guy I tricked with once who I suspect stole some money from my wallet, the other guy was a really sleazy druggie who I was afraid might try to pull something on Billy—you know, slip him something without his knowing it."

I was listening intently to every word, and when Phil paused for just a second, I had to hold myself back from jumping in immediately with an "And...?"

"I think," he continued at last, "that maybe Billy had a date with somebody he thought I wouldn't want him to be with."

Aha! I thought. "Any ideas?" I asked.

Another pause, much longer this time, then: "No. I really can't think of who it might be."

Maybe I could. "Billy knew Matt Rushmore, didn't he?"

Yet another pause. "Yeah; Matt left ModelMen just a week or so after Billy joined. Why?"

"Do you know why Matt left ModelMen?" I asked.

"No," he said. "The Glicks just said he decided he could make enough money just modeling. What are you saying?"

"Nothing," I hastened to assure him while lying through my teeth. "Nothing. What did you know about Matt?"

"Uh...not all that much, I guess. I knew his 'specialty' was light S&M, bu..." There was complete silence until finally I had to ask: "Are you there?"

Then finally: "Yeah, I'm here. Jeezus, Dick! I remember that Matt really seemed to be hot for Billy, and Billy was really tempted, but he never would have gone with him."

"Oh?" I asked, genuinely curious; "Why's that?"

"Two reasons. When I got Billy on at ModelMen, I'd told him I didn't think it was a good idea to fuck around with any of the other escorts except in the line of business. I never did, and as far as I know, he didn't either."

"And the second reason?" I asked.

"Matt used to brag that he never wore a condom—even though all the escorts are supposed to—and Billy would never go to bed with a guy who didn't wear a condom. Never."

I remembered.

"Well," I said, again trying not to get him too worked up, "Matt stopped being an escort, so the no-fraternization thing wouldn't have applied. And there are other forms of sex that don't demand a condom. Did you have any reason to dislike Matt, or to make Billy think you did?"

Phil's voice had returned to its regular volume. "No, not at all. Matt *is* pretty hot and he seemed like a nice guy. I figured the S&M thing was just part of his act for the clients. I don't think he was serious about it. Billy was always attracted to guys who came across as really butch, but he was way too smart to ever get into an S&M scene with anyone he didn't know he could trust."

Well, I thought, *maybe Billy thought Matt's S&M image was just an act, too.*

What was obvious was that the Glicks had tried to protect Matt, and I could understand their not wanting to let the other escorts know the real reason he left ModelMen.

"So if Billy did have a date with Matt, you think he would have told you?" I asked.

"I can't imagine why not," he said. "But we—at least I—haven't seen Matt since he left, and I'm sure if Billy had, he'd have mentioned it."

"Okay," I said. "I was mainly just curious. Thanks for the info.

And if you come up with anything else you think might help—anything at all—please give me a call."

"I will," Phil said.

"Okay, well you'd better hop back in the pool. Tell Gary hello for me."

We exchanged goodbyes and hung up.

* * *

I found Phil's comment about why Billy may not have told him who he was going out with very interesting. It occurred to me that maybe Billy didn't follow Phil's rule about not dating the other escorts, but just didn't want Phil to think he wasn't following his advice.

And if Billy *had* been playing around with one of the other escorts…the one who popped immediately into mind only because of his "specialty" was Aaron—Matt's "replacement." If Billy liked 'em butch, Aaron certainly would qualify. But of course I hadn't met the last two of ModelMen's stable—Mark and Steve?—yet.

I was just getting ready to run downstairs for lunch when the phone rang.

"Hardesty Investigations," I answered after the second ring.

"Hi," a very warm, very masculine voice said. "This is Matt Rushmore. I got your message. What can I do for you?"

Well, from the sound of your voice, buddy, I can think of several things, my mind said, and I realized with mild surprise that I was starting to think about sex again, which I hadn't done since Billy's death.

"Thanks for calling," I said aloud. "I have some questions you might be able to help me with. It wouldn't take long."

"Questions about…?" he asked.

"About your time with the ModelMen Agency," I said.

"I'm not sure I…" he began, but I decided there was little to gain by beating around the bush and interrupted him.

"You know Billy Steiner, don't you?" I asked.

"Sure," he said.

"Something's happened to him," I said, "and I need to talk to everyone who knew him…especially everyone associated with

ModelMen."

"...*knew* him?" Rushmore asked, his tone not quite hiding the tension. "What are you talking about?"

"It's a long story," I said, "and I really think it would be better if we could talk face to face."

There was a long silence and then, suddenly, Rushmore blurted: "The Dumpster? Billy was the guy in the Dumpster? Holy Shit!"

"Can we get together?" I pushed.

"Yeah. Sure. Whenever."

"Are you working today?" I asked.

"Just got back," he said. "You want me to come down to your office?"

"If you could," I said, and gave him the address.

* * *

The minute Matt Rushmore walked in the door I recognized him—the really butch guy I'd been eying at Faces, sitting at the table near me. Chalk another one up in the "small world" column. The last thing you'd ever think by looking at him would be that he'd get a kick out of S&M—or even that he was gay. He reminded me in a way of Lieutenant Richman; very outwardly hetero, very discreetly but definitely butch. He was wearing a short-sleeved pullover shirt, and extending below his tight-fitting left sleeve (which molded a very impressive bicep), I could see the tattooed letters "U.S.M.C."

We exchanged introductions and I motioned him to a seat.

"So what's going on?" he asked. "What happened to Billy?"

I told him.

He sat there, silent, for a minute, staring at me, then gave a small shrug and a sigh. "That sucks," he said. "I really liked Billy. He was one hot little fucker." And that was that.

I waited for another moment, giving him time to add something, and when he didn't, I moved ahead. "Did you know Stuart Anderson?" I asked: "One of ModelMen's clients?"

He thought a minute, then said "Yeah, I think I met him when the Glicks had one of their 'new client' dinners. He didn't impress me. Why?"

"Anderson's dead, too."

Suddenly, his head gave a slight backward jerk and his eyes opened wide for a brief instant...a typical "Whoa!" gesture.

"*Whoa!*" he said, then his eyes narrowed slightly and his eyebrows moved imperceptibly toward one another. "That guy at the hotel! I get it!" he said. "The Glicks told you about that fuckin' perv who begged me to give him what he deserved, and then when I did he got me fired. You think just because I like it a little rough that I wouldn't know when to stop? You think I'd do something to Billy or that Anderson guy?" He shook his head. "Shit! What kind of a psycho do you think I am?"

"I'm not making any accusations," I said, "but I've got to find out everything I can about these deaths and about anything anyone might know about either Anderson or Billy." He still looked more than a little skeptical, so I took a slight turn in my questioning. "Tell me the circumstances around your getting...terminated...from ModelMen."

He reached into his shirt pocket for a cigarette and offered me one, but I shook my head and reached into my desk drawer for an ashtray—a souvenir from my three-packs-a-day past. He fished in his front pants pocket for a lighter, raising his ass off the chair and displaying a sizeable basket of goodies in the process, and lit up before answering. I slid the ashtray across the desk and he leaned forward to take it.

"Perkins," he said. "Daniel Perkins, the guy's name was. Owns a construction company here in town. He'd been with Gary a couple times, but apparently didn't get what he wanted; Gary told him about me, so the next time he called ModelMen he asked for me. A real case, that one—he kept begging me for more, but I knew damned well the Glicks wouldn't stand for going as far as he wanted me to go, and I told him so. So one night he called me at home—I'm not sure how he got my number—and wanted me to meet him without going through ModelMen. I told him I couldn't, but he offered me twice the going rate, so... Stupid of me, but I did it. I gave him exactly what he wanted, but when we were done and he saw himself in the mirror, he panicked. He had a black eye and started yelling at me like it was my fault. 'How am I going to explain this to my wife?' he kept asking. I told him that was his problem and I took my money and left. The next day he called the Glicks and said I'd been the one to approach *him*."

He blew out a long stream of smoke and tamped his cigarette out in the ashtray. "Not that it mattered who called who," he said. "The point was that I'd broken the rules."

I started to say something, but he cut me off.

"Yeah, I like it rough." he continued. "I can take it, and I can give it out, and there are a hell of a lot of fuckin' pansies out there who haven't got the fuckin' guts to just go after a man when they want one. No, they hide in their fuckin' closets behind their wives' skirts and their wedding rings until they get so fucking sick of themselves they can't stand it any more and then they come crawling out looking for somebody like me, who'll treat them the way they know they deserve to be treated for being the ball-less cowards they are!"

'Yeah, but what do you really think of them?' my mind asked while I remained silent.

He stopped abruptly and gave me a small, weak smile. "Sorry," he said, "I guess I get a little carried away at times." He paused, aware of what he'd said. "*But not with sex,*" he added.

"Why did you go to work for ModelMen?" I asked.

He shrugged again, then reached into his shirt pocket for another cigarette and lit up before answering.

"Gary's idea, mostly. That and the fact that I needed the money," he said simply.

"You and Gary are pretty close?" I asked.

"Were, once," he replied, and I couldn't tell from his tone if it was regret or anger. "Gary and I had been in the Corps together. I'd never met anybody like him before, and I guess I really looked up to him. Me, if anybody crossed me, I'd just punch them out and that was that. But Gary, he's got other ways of getting what he wants. He can talk his way into or out of just about anything. He sort of took me under his wing and showed me a lot of different ways to get what I wanted. We got...well..." He paused as though not knowing exactly how to say what probably didn't need to be said about their relationship. "We kept in touch after...we got out...and a year or so afterwards, he called and said I should come out and join up with him in Vegas."

"Was that before or after the Glicks got married?" I asked.

"Before. Gary and I were witnesses. When the Glicks moved here and got the idea to start ModelMen—actually, I think it was Gary who suggested it to Iris—Gary and I came out to be part of it. It wasn't bad. To be honest, most of the clients I was assigned to were pretty decent guys. Discipline was my specialty, but like all their escorts, the Glicks expected a maximum versatility. And the money was damned good."

"How did you get along with the Glicks?" I asked.

"A lot better than I'd thought I was going to," he said, tapping his cigarette on the edge of the ashtray to dislodge a nub of ash.

I wondered what he meant by that, and waited for a follow-up comment. When there was none, I decided it was worth a prompt. "Meaning...?" I said.

He took a long drag on his cigarette and let the smoke out slowly.

"Well, from the way Gary had always talked, I expected Iris to be some cold, heartless bitch. Turned out she's not like that at all."

...*the way Gary had always talked?* "I gather Gary had some sort of resentment against his sister?" I asked, and noted the flicker of a smile.

"Yeah," he said. "You could say that. Of course, he'd never let it show—not to her. That's not the way Gary operates."

"They seem to get along pretty well," I said, opening up a mental file drawer to store everything Matt was saying—while wondering just why he was saying it.

Again the small, quick smile. "Yeah, that's the way it *seems*" Did I detect a slight emphasis on "seems"? "The Glicks treat all their employees pretty well, though Gary's pretty much got Iris where he wants her. Like I told you, he can talk his way into or out of anything. Iris'll give him anything he wants. Only natural, I suppose."

"Well, he is her brother," I said, and noticed a slightly raised eyebrow and that damned hint of a smile. *What the hell is that supposed to mean?* I wondered.

Once again I found myself in a position of not wanting to push too far, but having little other option. "So," I said, "if you don't mind my asking, what happened between you and Gary to split you up?"

He carefully crushed out his cigarette before moving his eyes slowly from the ashtray to my own eyes. "Personal," he said.

"Did it have anything to do with your getting fired?" I asked.

"Not directly. We were pretty much over by that time. But it didn't help when he didn't lift a finger to help me. All he had to do was ask Iris to keep me on."

I had the impression that there was a lot more in there than he was willing to volunteer but decided I'd gone about as far as I could for the moment, and switched tracks. "Did you ever make it with Billy?" I asked.

"We never had the chance. I think Billy wanted it," he said "and I sure as hell wouldn't have minded. But I left a week or so after Billy came on, so we never had the chance. Why'd you ask?"

"No reason," I said, "I just understood Billy liked really butch types."

He idly moved his cigarette butt around in a circle on the bottom of the ashtray, but kept his eyes on mine. "How about you?" he asked. "You like 'em butch?"

"I like 'em male," I said.

"Well I guess I qualify for both," he said. "You ever get the urge to find out first hand, give me a call."

What the fuck are you doing Hardesty? my mind demanded, truly shocked. *Here you are talking to some guy who digs S&M and who for all you know may have killed both Billy and Stuart Anderson, and you're cruising the guy? Get a grip, for Chrissakes!*

My mind was right, of course, so with a great deal of effort, I whip-and-chaired my testosterone tigers back into their cages. "I'll keep that in mind," I said. Hey, if Matt Rushmore turned out *not* to be the killer…

You're hopeless, my mind said, disgustedly.

I asked him several more questions, mainly about anything he might have known about Billy, how Billy got along with the other escorts, if Billy had ever mentioned anything at all that might have a bearing on his murder.

He really couldn't tell me anything, so after a while I thanked him for coming over and for his information, and he got up to go.

"I meant what I said about that call," he said as we shook hands at the door.

"As soon as I get this case finished, you can count on it," my crotch said, using my voice.

CHAPTER 7

On the one hand, I'd found Matt Rushmore to be a rather likeable guy—an opinion I realized just might be slightly influenced by my crotch, and by the fact that whether deliberately or not he'd done some pretty shrewd ego fluffing by coming on to me, though unlike with Gary I didn't feel like I was being conned. He certainly didn't seem like the kind of guy who would murder anyone. But on the other hand was my ever-present paranoia. *Well of course he doesn't, you stupid shit! That's the whole point! Every time some TV reporter interviews the neighbors of some guy who put his entire family through a meat grinder, have you ever heard one who didn't comment on what a really nice guy he was: "Always so quiet; went to church every Sunday," etc. You and your fucking crotch!*

And his visit had given me quite a bit to think about. He obviously wasn't wild about a lot of bisexual men. Anderson had his wedding ring shoved up his ass. But while I should have but hadn't outright asked him, it was pretty obvious to me that Matt was bisexual himself—he sure as hell looked   straight, and the Glicks had said something about financial problems because of child support. And how would Matt and Anderson ever have gotten together? They'd only met the one time, at a group dinner, and it's unlikely that Matt would have passed Stuart Anderson his phone number. All ModelMen's client/escort contacts were made through the Glicks. Matt's "specialty" was discipline: Anderson was by all accounts as vanilla as they come.

Well, I definitely wasn't going to rule Matt out, but there were a lot of other loose ends I had to pull together before zeroing in on him completely.

And just what the hell was it he was trying to tell me about Gary? For damn sure I'd be paying a lot closer attention to him—both of them, actually—from now on.

Just as I was getting ready to call it a day, the phone rang. It was Jared, wanting to know if I wanted to join him for Happy Hour at Ramón's. I figured I deserved a break, and agreed. Though I knew Jared didn't get off work until around 5, I got to Ramón's a little after 4:30, figuring I could do a little catching up with Bob Allen, whom I felt kind of guilty about not having seen in quite a while. Jimmy, the bartender, smiled and waved when I came in and took a seat at the end of the bar. He was engaged in conversation with a guy at the opposite end, and took a moment before coming over.

"How's it goin', Dick?" Jimmy asked when he finally broke away and came to take my order. "We haven't seen you around the last couple days. Old Fashioned or Manhattan?"

"Old Fashioned, I guess," I said. "And yeah, I've been busy." I didn't feel like mentioning—much less thinking much about—the whole Billy thing. The not mentioning I could handle, the not thinking much about I knew was impossible. I just wished to hell I could find a way to leave work at the office, but of course I hadn't been able to do that since I took out my p.i. license.

"Bob around?" I asked.

"Not 'til later." he said, and then turned to grab a bottle of bourbon for my drink. I took a bill out of my wallet and put it on the counter.

"No charge," Jimmy said.

"Hey, thanks, Jimmy," I said, surprised. "That's really…"

"Not me," Jimmy said, nodding his head toward the guy he'd been talking to; "Him."

The guy was in the shadows and I couldn't see who it was, but I raised my glass in a silent toast directed at him and smiled a 'thanks.' The guy got up from his stool and came toward me. The minute I saw him walk, I knew who it was: Aaron, ModelMen's "down and dirty" specialist. I wondered what the hell he was doing in Ramón's at 4:30 in the afternoon. I set my drink down and swivelled around on my stool to shake his hand.

"Small world," I said.

He smiled, but the cockiness I remember from our first meeting was missing. I assumed he'd heard about Billy. "I didn't know you came in here," he said.

"A regular," I said. "How about you? Ramón's isn't exactly on the beaten track."

Aaron pulled out the stool next to me and sat down. "I just took a new apartment in the neighborhood," he said. "Right down the street, as a matter of fact—that new building on Hersh."

I knew the building. "Nice place," I said.

"Yeah, well, I can afford it now," he said. "You should have seen the dump I was living in before." He was quiet for a minute, then said: "You heard about Billy."

"Yeah."

"I still can't believe it," he said. "He was a nice kid."

"That he was," I said, and began formulating a long list of questions I wanted to ask Aaron.

He raised his glass. "To Billy," he said, and I raised mine and clicked it lightly against his.

"To Billy," I repeated, and we each took a long drink.

Just as I was ready to start asking Aaron exactly what he might possibly know about Billy that would be of any help in figuring out what had happened to him, the back door opened and Jared came in. The questions would have to wait.

"Dick," Jared said by way of greeting, then surprised me by nodding to Aaron and adding: "Aaron."

"Jared," Aaron acknowledged.

"You two know each other?" I asked, though I really shouldn't have been surprised. Jared seemed to know just about everybody—especially the hot ones.

"Yeah," Aaron said. "We see each other at the Male Call from time to time." The Male Call was one of the more popular of the leather bars and Jared's favorite when he was in one of what he called his 'leather moods.' "Jared was the one who told me about this place," Aaron said. "Nice to have a bar close to home."

"So you're all moved in?" Jared asked after getting Jimmy's attention.

"Just about," he said. "Still got some stuff to unpack…and some equipment to install." They exchanged grins, and I didn't have to wonder too hard what 'equipment' he might be referring to. "You'll have to stop by to check it out," he said, then turned to me. "You, too."

Uh, sure, I thought.

Jared grinned. "Dick's not much into leather," he said, winking at Jimmy as he exchanged cash for his drink. Jimmy looked from Jared to Aaron to me, and returned the wink.

Aaron looked at me and shrugged. "Too bad."

"Have you heard anything more about your friend?" Jared asked. "I left a message at Tim's place after I called you— thought he might like to join us for a drink."

"Well," I said, "Tim keeps pretty odd work hours—depends a lot on what they have going on. But no, I haven't heard anything more."

I wondered if Jared knew Aaron worked for ModelMen, and that he had known Billy, but I didn't say anything.

We sat around talking for about an hour, until Jared drained his glass and got up from his stool. "Well, I've got to get home," he said. "Still doing the final polishing on my dissertation. God, I don't think I'm *ever* going to finish that damned thing."

Aaron looked at his watch. "Yeah, I'd better take off, too. I've got a client at eight."

Jared said: "Wow, you keep late hours."

Aaron just grinned and said: "Yeah. No rest for the wicked," and gave me a knowing look.

I gathered from that exchange that Jared did not know what Aaron did for a living, or for whom.

I hadn't quite finished my drink yet, so we all shook hands and Jared and Aaron left—Jared out the back door, Aaron out the front. When Jimmy came over to pick up the empty glasses, I asked him what if anything he knew about Aaron.

"That is one fucking hot dude," Jimmy replied. "But he's got a tendency to want to play a little rough."

"Oh?" I said.

Jimmy put the glasses in the sink under the bar. "Yeah; he came in around closing a couple nights ago…first time I'd ever seen him…and we sort of got to talking. I took him over to my place after I got off work, and we got going kind of hot and heavy, but the more we got into it, the rougher he got. I finally had to tell him to back off a little."

"And did he?" I asked.

Jimmy shrugged. "Well, I had to tell him twice so he'd know I really meant it, but then, sure," he said, then he grinned. "I have to admit some of it was kind of interesting, though."

* * *

I knew that Tim would call me if there was any news on Billy, but tried calling him as soon as I got home. I felt like talking with him anyway—and I was none-of-my-business-curious to follow up on my hunch that perhaps he and Jared were getting together for a little action. No Scorpio jealousy involved, I might add—to me, they both fell into that rarified category known as "fuck buddies"—what somebody once defined as "a friend, with benefits." It's really hard to find someone who can be both a good friend and a casual sex partner, but with no romantic attachment. I doubted anything serious was going on between Tim and Jared, since I knew both of them liked to play around too much to think about settling down. But still....

Tim wasn't home, so I left a message, then thought about calling the Glicks to arrange for me to meet Steve and Mark, but reminded myself again that I needed to separate work from my personal life. I'd call them in the morning. So I fried up some pork chops (crisp to the point of being burnt), made some instant mashed potatoes and my world famous homemade gravy (flour, water, salt and pepper stirred like crazy to dissolve the flour, then poured into the fry pan and stirred with the grease from the pork chops). Cholesterol City. Then I sat settled in for a night of TV.

Some personal life.

* * *

I'd planned to call the Glicks as soon as I got to the office on Thursday, but on checking my messages, I saw I'd just had a call from Mrs. Glick from her home number. There was also a call from Lieutenant Richman, to which I gave preference.

My call went directly through, and I identified myself—though I suspected that by now Richman could recognize my voice without it.

"Dick," he said, "thanks for returning my call so quickly."

"No problem, Lieutenant. What can I do for you?" I asked with more than a little trepidation. Richman's calls were seldom good news.

"I was wondering what you could tell me about local male call boy services?" he asked.

'Here we go,' I thought, immediately envisioning myself between a very large rock and a very hard place. "I think they call themselves 'escort services'," I said, stepping out onto my tightrope without a balance bar, "and I know there are a couple around. Why do you ask?"

"We're looking into the possibility that Anderson may have used their services; the Montero staff has said that he was frequently seen in the company of a very well groomed young man who didn't fit the image of your average street hustler. They thought he was one of Anderson's employees, but we checked and couldn't find anyone of his description on Anderson's regular payroll, so we figured he might have been a…an 'escort.'"

Shit!

"Well, that's possible," I said, "but I'm afraid I've never had the opportunity—or the money—to utilize them." I sincerely hoped Richman couldn't hear me tap-dancing around his question.

"So you think it's possible one of these call boys…escorts… whatever you want to call them might be involved, then?"

I took a deep breath. "Well, Lieutenant, to be honest with you…" *Shit! Why the hell did I have to say that!* "…from what I do know of these services, I'd say that while Anderson may well have used them, it would be pretty unlikely that they would be involved in his death. From everything I know about them, these services screen their…employees…pretty thoroughly. And as you say, they're several steps above street hustlers in more ways than one. And while Anderson could easily afford some high-priced company, Billy certainly would never have had the money or the need for it. He could have anybody he wanted just for the asking."

"Hmm," Richman said. "Yeah, I suppose you're right. I've checked out the local gay papers and found three 'services' listed: Hunks, Company, and Call Guys. Do you know them?"

Jeezus, I thought, *he's getting close and when he finds out, if he thinks I've been screwing him over, I'm in deep, deep shit.*

"Well," I said, "I'm pretty sure that the guys who work through Hunks and Call Guys aren't quite in the same league as you're talking about—they're pretty much available to just about anybody looking for a quick roll in the hay and willing to pay for it—basically home delivery street hustlers." I said.

"And Company?" he asked.

"I honestly don't know anything about them, but I can check if you'd like."

"Yeah, if you would. I figured you'd know more about these places than we would, and the more time the department can save on not having to go on wild goose chases, the better." There was another pause, and I started to give a mental sigh of relief when he said: "Any others that you know of?"

Oh, oh! Careful how you word this one, kid!

"Let me think on that one and get back to you as soon as I can," I said. "Today, if possible, but..."

"Yeah," he said, "That'll be fine. Thanks for your help, Dick."

"You're welcome, Lieutenant," I said.

'Shit!' I thought. 'Shit, shit, shit!' What sort of game was Richman playing? Couch and Carpenter asked for head shots of all of ModelMen's models. If they didn't know damned well already about the escort branch, it would only be a matter of time—and a very *short* time, I'd wager.

* * *

I dialed the Glicks' home number immediately and, after a brief exchange of pleasantries with Johnnie-Mae, asked to speak to Mrs. Glick. There was only a momentary pause until I heard a receiver being picked up and Mrs. Glick's voice.

"I'm glad you called," she said, her voice a bit more relaxed than the last time we'd spoken. "Mr. Glick and I we were wondering if you could join us for dinner tomorrow evening, say around 6:30? All our escorts..." there was a slight pause as she apparently suddenly realized that not all of them would, in fact, be present "...will be here. It might be a little soon after...Billy's loss, but Phil insists he is up to it, and I know you still have not met Mark and Steve. Perhaps meeting with the entire group at once might be helpful to you in some way."

"That sounds fine, Mrs. Glick," I said, "but something has just come up and I think it is imperative that I meet with you and Mr.

Glick immediately."

"I was just on my way to the office now," she said, the tension back in her voice. "Mr. Glick is already there. Let me give him a call to make sure he's free, and if you've not heard back from me in five minutes, why don't you come directly over to the office?"

"I'd appreciate that," I said. "I hope to see you soon."

* * *

I fidgeted around the office for about ten minutes and, not hearing otherwise from the Glicks, headed out for the ModelMen offices. The receptionist, obviously expecting me, merely smiled and motioned me directly to Mr. Glick's office. I knocked, and hearing him say "Come in" I did so, closing the door behind me.

Mrs. Glick had apparently not yet arrived, and Mr. Glick got up from behind his desk to come over and shake my hand.

"Mrs. Glick will be here any moment," he said. "Have a seat, please."

I sat and then, not wanting to get into the details until Mrs. Glick arrived, asked:"How is Phil doing?"

Mr. Glick returned to his own chair and sighed. "He left this morning right after breakfast," he said. "He's insisted on returning to his apartment. Both my wife and I urged him to stay with us a few more days, but he said he had to start getting on with his life. Would it be an imposition to ask if you might look in on him to see that he's all right?"

"Of course," I said. "I'll stop by later today. And if I may, I'd like to express my admiration and thanks for how kind you and Mrs. Glick have been to Phil. Not many employers would be nearly as caring."

"Thank you, Mr. Hardesty," he said. "But Mrs. Glick and I were serious when we said we consider all our models much more than employees."

At that point the door opened and Mrs. Glick entered, wearing a black skirt and white blouse, her hair pulled tightly back into a pony tail. She looked very businesslike.

After we exchanged greetings and she sat down, I got right to the point, telling them of my conversation with Lieutenant Richman and the fact that the police were very close to zeroing in on ModelMen.

"I've evaded and eluded about as much as I can at this point," I said. "Our only hope is in diverting as much attention elsewhere as possible. But with both Stuart Anderson and Billy directly linked to ModelMen, this won't be easy. What can you tell me of Company, and of any other model agencies you might know of, which, like ModelMen, provide escort services but don't advertise them? Does Charter?" It had occurred to me that Matt Rushmore might have switched more than his modeling talents over to his new employers.

The Glicks exchanged glances, then Mr. Glick cleared his throat and said: "Well, it isn't really quite ethical for us to reveal what we know of other services…" he began, but I cut him off.

"I can appreciate that," I said, "but we're a bit beyond ethics here if there is any hope of keeping the police from coming down on ModelMen with both feet. All I need is some basic information as to their operation."

Mr. Glick sighed. "Yes, you're right, of course," he said. "Company is quite successful, from what I understand, and considerably more broad based than ModelMen. I believe they have ten or twelve escorts. Like it or not under the circumstances, we *do* stand out in the quality of our service, and in our discretion and protection of both our clients and our escorts. As for Charter, I don't believe they provide an official service…although any model always has ample opportunity to freelance his…other talents…if he so chooses."

"We will do anything we can to help find out who did this terrible thing to Stuart Anderson and Billy," Mrs. Glick said, "but I'm sure you understand that under no circumstance can we or would we reveal our client list. I'm sure the police would love to have it, but it could have absolutely no bearing on Stuart or Billy's deaths."

"Well," I said, "If you've not already done so, I would strongly suggest you consider engaging a good lawyer, just in case. I assume you have an attorney?"

The Glicks exchanged glances and a small smile, and Mrs. Glick said: "Did you have anyone in mind?"

"You could not find a better attorney than Glen O'Banyon," I said. "I would recommend him highly."

"I'm delighted to hear you say that," Mr. Glick said. "Mr. O'Banyon has, in fact, been our attorney for some time now. We had a meeting with him early this morning, as a matter of fact, regarding the current situation. We were delighted to find out that you and he have worked together in the past, and he seemed pleased to hear we had engaged your services."

I thought immediately of the photo of Phil and Stuart Anderson taken with O'Banyon and wondered if there were more to the picture than met the eye.

We were all silent for a moment, lost in our own thoughts, until I said: "It would be nice if he could be at dinner tomorrow night, but I know that's probably out of the question given his work load. But I feel better just knowing that he's available if things get tough. So here's what I would suggest for the present: Tomorrow at dinner, I—or you—can lay everything out to the escorts and gear them up for the fact that they're probably in for a lot of tough questions by the police and urge them to tell us beforehand if they know anything they think the police might latch onto. If there is anything, we can pass it on to O'Banyon. That way, everyone can be prepared, and the chance for unexpected surprises can be reduced. Then I'll approach Lieutenant Richman and try to arrange a swap: your and the escorts' total cooperation in exchange for not demanding your clients' names. I think Richman will go along with it…he's not one of those cops who seem to think his badge gives him the right to pass judgment on matters that don't concern him or the case in question."

Mr. Glick sighed. "Very well," he said, "though I'm very sorry it has come to this. Of course catching the killer takes precedence over everything, but I still cannot believe that Stuart or Billy's deaths could possibly be related to ModelMen. However unlikely it may seem, it has to be some incredibly tragic coincidence. That anyone we know could be capable of such acts…."

Mrs. Glick merely nodded in agreement.

"We can always hope that is the case," I said, "but whenever logic comes up against coincidence, the odds are pretty heavily on logic's side."

* * *

I left the Glicks' shortly thereafter and returned to the office to check for messages, and was mildly relieved to find one from Glen O'Banyon's office. I returned the call immediately, and was put through to Donna, O'Banyon's secretary.

"Mr. Hardesty," she said, in her usual bright, efficient executive secretary voice. "Mr. O'Banyon is expecting your call, but he's on the other line right now. Would you want to hold, or shall I have him call you?"

"I can hold for a few minutes, thanks." I said.

"Fine; he'll be right with you."

I pulled the morning paper out of my top drawer with one hand, laid it out on the desk, and idly paged through it—again with one hand—seeing if I could find if any of the stores might be having a sale on air conditioners. I didn't get very far before I heard a click, and then O'Banyon's voice:

"Dick!" he said. "It's been a long time."

"That it has," I said.

"I understand you're working for the Glicks on these God-awful murders. What a terrible business! I met Stuart Anderson, you know, and I understand you knew both of the victims."

"Yeah," I said, "I didn't know Anderson very well, or Billy either, really, but Billy was a real sweetheart. Neither of them deserved this. But I can't tell you how relieved I was to hear that you're the Glicks' attorney. This whole thing is getting messier—and stranger—by the minute."

I then told him of the forthcoming dinner and the plan I'd laid out with the Glicks. "Since I'm not a lawyer, I just want to be sure I don't give these guys the wrong information on how they should react if they're questioned."

"Just tell them if they feel they're being unduly pressured at any point, to very respectfully ask to see their lawyer, say nothing more, and give me a call. The Glicks have my emergency number. And tell them to answer every question as best they can, but not to volunteer any other information. And under no circumstances should they divulge the names of any of their clients."

"Yeah," I said; "well, on that point, the cops will probably claim it could have been one of the clients who did the killings. That might work for Billy, but not for Anderson, I wouldn't think. One client killing another…?"

"You're right, it's shaky ground. If it comes to that, and I'm sure it will, I'll handle that part directly with the police. Tell the escorts to respectfully refuse to answer. Period."

"I'll do that," I said. "Thanks."

"Well, I've got a client coming in in about two minutes, so I'd better go. Keep me posted and let me know if there's anything I can do."

"I really appreciate that," I said, and meant it.

* * *

Feeling a lot more confident, I waited a moment, then put a call in to Phil. He answered on the third ring.

"How's it going?" I asked.

"Ok, thanks," he replied. "Strange, but okay. I just keep the door to Billy's room closed for now. In a couple days I'll start packing his things up. But I'm not quite ready for that just yet."

"I understand," I said. "And if you'd like some help when you do…"

"That's nice of you, Dick, but I…we'll see."

"I was wondering if you'd like to go out for an early dinner tonight," I said. "I don't feel much like cooking, and I could use an excuse to go out."

"Well, thanks, Dick, but I…"

"So you're going to force me to stay home and slave over a hot stove? Come on…it'll do us both good."

He was quiet a moment, then said: "Ok…sure. Where would you like to go?"

The one place I did *not* mention was Napoleon, and we settled on Calypso because of its patio.

"I'll stop by around 7, then, okay?" I said.

"Sure. See you then."

* * *

I was right, dinner out did do both of us good. We managed to avoid any mention whatsoever of ModelMen in general or Billy in particular, but still found plenty to talk about. We exchanged family histories, and growing up stories, and favorite memories, and most embarrassing moments. There was even a laugh or two, and I could both see and sense Phil relaxing. He still had a long way to go, but it was a start.

* * *

I spent much of Friday morning going over just what I'd say to the gathering at the Glick's dinner and how to say it. I tried to figure out ways to couch questions that would elicit the most information, realizing that I was at something of a disadvantage when it came to Mark and Steve in that I'd not yet even met them. And I knew that no matter what I said or how well I said it, it would be extremely painful for Phil. I wanted very much the chance to talk with each of the escorts individually, and in private, and perhaps I could have a chance to do that, maybe after dinner.

I realized, too, that I'd promised Lieutenant Richman I'd get back to him, and that wasn't going to be an easy task. I'd have to tell him my involvement with ModelMen and I knew damned well that I was risking the destruction of the relationship—however undefined that might be—we'd built between us. I couldn't blame him for feeling I'd not been truthful with him, but I could counter, at least as a form of justification within myself, that however evasive I may have been, I had never outright lied to him. And my first loyalties were, after all, to my clients.

Reluctantly, I phoned Police Headquarters and asked for Lieutenant Richman's extension. When he answered the phone, I told him I had the information he wanted, and that I thought I should talk with him in person.

"That's fine, Dick," he said, "but there's been a new development, and I'm going to be tied up for some time with it. Let me give you a call, okay?"

"Sure," I said, totally puzzled. "Uh, can you give me some idea what sort of new development?" I asked.

"I can't talk about it right now, I'm afraid," he said. "But I'll tell you what I can as soon as I can."

"Okay," I said. "I'll look forward to hearing from you."

We exchanged goodbyes, and hung up.

What in the hell's going on? I wondered.

It was about 11:30, so I debated on whether I should just call downstairs to the diner for lunch and bring it back to the office, or to go down and eat it there. Realizing that other than the questionable ambiance of being in the company of Eudora and Evolla, I'd be much more comfortable eating at my desk, I called down to order a ham and turkey club and a large coke to go.

Of course all the way down to the lobby and all the way back up to my office, I was thinking—and worrying—about just what Richman's "new development" might be. Since he had not asked me to come down to headquarters, I hoped I could rule out the discovery of yet another body, and I was mildly reassured by the fact that he had not done so. Still, I wondered.

As I unlocked the door to the office, holding the coke in one hand, my keys in the other, and the paper bag containing the sandwich in my teeth, the phone was ringing. Hurrying across the room, I tossed my keys on the desk and, taking the bag out of my mouth, I reached across the desk for the phone.

"Hardesty Investigations," I said.

"Dick, it's Tim. I'm on my lunch break and thought I'd better call."

"Tim, hi!" I said, hoping he might have some information on Richman's 'new development.' "What's up?"

Tim sighed. "We have another body."

'Oh, Shit! Why didn't Richman tell me, or yank me down to headquarters as usual?' I was glad I hadn't already eaten lunch. "Same pattern?" I asked, hoping against hope that it wouldn't be another ModelMen client...or escort.

"This one's a stabbing. And it's a woman."

CHAPTER 8

"A woman?" I heard myself saying. "And you think there's a connection to Billy or Anderson?"

Tim sighed. "Other than the fact that she was found in a Dumpster like Billy, not much, really. But they found the murder weapon, and when we matched it to the wound, the police seemed to think they'd struck oil. I heard one of them mention Anderson."

"It wouldn't have happened to be an Antonio Vivace knife, would it?" I asked.

Tim's voice registered his surprise. "Yeah, it was. Monogrammed handle—I'd never seen one before, but I dated a guy who was a chef, and he swore by them. How the hell did you know?"

"I'm a detective...remember?" I said.

"Oh, yeah," Tim replied. "I keep forgetting." There was a slight pause and then: "Hey, I've got to get back to work. We'll talk later, okay? I just wanted to let you know what's going on."

"Thanks, Tim," I said. "I really appreciate it. Later."

I had the phone halfway back to the receiver when it struck me: the latest victim was a woman.

Iris Glick is a woman, my mind observed, while kicking me squarely in the stomach. I dialed the Glicks' home.

"Glick residence," Johnnie-Mae's voice said.

"Mrs. Dabbs," I said, hoping my voice didn't sound as tense as I felt, "is Mrs. Glick in?"

"Yes she is, Mr. Hardesty. I'll get her for you."

I released a huge rush of air from my lungs: *Thank God!*

When Mrs. Glick came to the phone, I told her about the third victim—and that it was a woman. I didn't go into any of the specifics.

"But how does this relate to Stuart and Billy?" she asked.

"Trust me...it does," I said, not wanting to go into detail at the moment, and she didn't pursue it.

"However, I don't think that we should alter our plans for talking with the…group…" I don't like being paranoid, but wiretapping was not an unknown practice "at dinner this evening. We're not off the hook yet. And if possible, after dinner I would like to talk with each of them separately, including Phil."

I specifically included Phil in part so as not to make him—or the other escorts—feel I was treating him any differently, and in part because we had not really talked much about Billy since his death, other than what he'd said when we talked on the phone, and there was the outside chance he might have remembered something he'd not mentioned before.

"Of course," she said.

"Well," I said, "I'm sure you want to contact Mr. Glick, so I'll let you go, and will see you around 7."

"Yes…and thank you, Mr. Hardesty!"

* * *

As usual, Tim hadn't had the time to tell me much about the latest victim, and I wanted to find out more from him as soon as I could. I also wanted to talk to Lieutenant Richman, but knew I'd have to wait until news of the discovery of the latest victim was made public—I couldn't risk putting Tim's job in jeopardy by letting Richman know I had another source of information; as smart as Richman was, it wouldn't take much for him to follow the breadcrumbs to the coroner's office and Tim.

In the meantime, I had to sort carefully through the bits and pieces of facts and conjecture now scattered all over my mental landscape, trying to see which ones I could discard. Strangely enough, I found they all tended to go back in pretty much the same order as I'd had them before the discovery of the third victim, and I had that all-too-familiar gut level sensation that that fact alone was telling me something. I really hate those stupid games I play with myself—if I knew something, why the hell didn't I tell me? But that wasn't the way it worked, I knew, and I had to live with it.

* * *

Around four o'clock, the phone rang.

"Hardesty Investigations."

"Hi, Dick...Jared. I was thinking maybe you might want to go out for dinner tonight—maybe we could call Tim and see if he wants to come along?"

Well, well, Jared, my lad, I thought. *Tim must really be making an impression.*

"I'd like to, Jared," I said, "but I've got plans...business, unfortunately. But why don't you call Tim? I'm sure he'd like to go." I somehow suspected that Tim would very *much* like to go. Then I remembered Tim's call. "Ah," I added, "I forgot—Tim called at lunch today, and it's possible he may be having one of his late nights. Wouldn't hurt to call and leave a message, though."

"Yeah, I think I'll do that," Jared said. "Oh, and I meant to tell you: I stopped over at Aaron's last night to see his new place. You really ought to go—if you think you're up to playing with the big boys."

"Which means...?" I asked, suspecting that I already knew.

"You'll find out," he said. "But don't worry; he won't go too far."

"Uh-huh," I said.

"So," Jared said, "I'd better get going. Got a few more stops before the shift ends."

"Do you have Tim's number?" I asked.

"Yeah, I do. I'll give him a quick call now. See ya."

"Later," I said, and we hung up.

* * *

I had just enough time to get home, take a quick—for me—shower, put on some clean clothes, and head out for the Glicks'.

There were several other cars in the parking area when I arrived at 6:20, and Johnnie-Mae greeted me at the door.

"They're all out by the pool, Mr. Hardesty," she said. "If you'd like to follow me..."

"Don't bother, Mrs. Dabbs," I said. "I can find my way if you don't mind. I know you're busy."

She smiled broadly. "Well, yes, I am...but then I'm always busy."

"Don't you ever get a day off?" I asked, only partly joking.

She smiled broadly. "Oh, I do have my Sundays," she said, leading me across the foyer and pointing down a hallway not visible from the front door, behind the massive staircase. "Right that way, sir," she said, and then disappeared in the general direction of the dining room.

I emerged from the house to find myself at one end of the vast swimming pool. At the far end, in the space between the pool and the pool house, I spotted Mr. Glick standing in the center of a rough circle of pool chairs, on which sat four of ModelMen's escorts; Aaron, Phil, and two guys I did not recognize; obviously Mark and Steve. The doors to the pool house were open wide, and I could hear music coming from inside. As I walked around the pool, Mr. Glick noticed me and waved, as did Aaron and Phil. I noticed that the new fountain was in full operation, with water cascading down from about the roof level of the pool house, to splash into matching smaller pools. Inside the pool house, I could see a small bar set up, behind which stood Gary, who was just handing a drink to Mrs. Glick.

All the guys got up from their chairs as I approached. I shook hands with Mr. Glick, Aaron, and Phil, and then Mr. Glick introduced Mark and Steve, and the handshake round was completed. Though there was a lot going on, I was able to take quick stock of Mark and Steve in turn, and decided immediately that they were definitely ModelMen material. Mark was the taller of the two, with strawberry blond hair and a subtle sprinkle of somehow very sexy freckles. He looked to be about 30, extremely handsome—surprise!—and filled out his form-fitting shirt and tight trousers admirably. His handshake, like all the other escorts, was very firm, confident, reassuring, and…practiced.

Steve, now…Well, if Phil reminded me of something by Michelangelo, Steve was definitely Botticelli: almost breathtakingly beautiful, without being effeminate—almost androgynous but definitely sexy. But his handshake, too, was solid and confident, and masculine.

I thought again of how brilliantly the Glicks had chosen their escorts: Gary and Aaron, definitely butch types; Phil and Mark, every gay man's all-inclusive fantasy; Steve and…and Billy, charm and innocence. I was, indeed, impressed.

"Why don't you go get a drink," Mr. Glick asked me, as his wife came out of the pool house to greet me. "Gary has bartending honors this evening."

I exchanged greetings with Mrs. Glick as I moved past her into the pool house. Gary grinned as I approached.

"Well," he said, "aren't you going to ask?"

"I'm sorry?" I said. "Ask what?"

"'Who does a fella have to fuck to get a drink around here?' I've got a great answer."

"I'll just bet you do," I said, and we both laughed.

When everyone had their drinks, Gary came out from behind the bar and joined the group. We all small-talked for about half an hour, and I was very much aware that while the conversation covered a wide range of topics from politics to arts and literature, two subjects were never mentioned: sex, or Billy. I had the definite impression, by observing how Mrs. Glick's attention was focused on whomever was speaking at the moment that these little dinners served as training exercises to hone the social skills of the escorts, and that each of the escorts was somehow subtly being graded. Interesting, to say the least.

At almost exactly 7:00, Mr. Glick rose from his chair and, nodding across the pool to Johnnie-Mae, who stood in the doorway of the main house, hands folded in front of her crisp white apron, announced: "I believe dinner is ready." All the escorts rose in unison, rather like a drill team, and I had to scramble not to be left sitting. Mrs. Glick looked around the group, and gave a warm smile and nod to Mark, who gallantly offered her his arm and led the group toward and into the house. Fascinating.

Seated again around one end of the enormous dining room table, but taking up considerably more of it with eight present rather than four, wine glasses already poured, Mr. Glick rose from his chair at the head of the table and lifted his glass. It was then that I noticed that a ninth place had been set at the table, the chair pulled back as though someone were sitting there.

Everyone rose, and lifted their glass as Mr. Glick motioned toward the empty chair.

"To absent friends," he said.

I got an instant lump in my throat and could see Phil's eyes fill with tears, one of which ran down slowly down his cheek, but aside from an almost imperceptible biting of the corner of his lower lip he ignored it and his face remained impassive. Mrs. Glick, I noted, took a quick wipe of her eyes with her free hand. It was an awkward moment, and painful, and very nice.

Dinner was of course delicious, though none of us appeared to be overly hungry. The conversation was subdued, though everyone, again, made a conscious effort to contribute something.

After Johnnie-Mae had removed the dishes and served coffee and a marvelous peach cobbler—how in the world she managed to do it all and with such quiet efficiency amazed me— Mr. Glick said: "The purpose of tonight's dinner was, as you know, to quietly honor Billy's memory. I say 'quietly' because I don't think any of us has the words to express the sorrow I know we are all feeling. But we must now address the inevitable consequences of the terrible circumstances surrounding Billy's death…and, as you know, the earlier death of one of ModelMen's clients." He motioned to me with one hand. "Mr. Hardesty will explain the situation."

I decided it would probably be better if I stood, so I did.

I outlined the similarities of the two murders without going into too many specifics. The fact of Anderson's body having been violated with his own wedding ring, and the exact methods of death had never officially been made public record and I saw little point in mentioning them

The police, I explained, were putting two and two together and with ModelMen the only obvious link between the two deaths, it was almost inevitable that everyone at the table would be contacted and questioned thoroughly. I cautioned them that while the police would have legitimate grounds to ask questions about Stuart Anderson and Billy, the names of ModelMen's other clients were irrelevant. I told them the police would try to get around the issue on the grounds that perhaps one of Billy's clients had been involved, but that unless they knew for a fact that Billy had been violating ModelMen rules and had been secretly seeing a specific client the night he died, they should respectfully decline to answer without the presence of the Glicks' lawyer—and by extension, their lawyer—Glen O'Banyon. In fact, I stressed, if the questions touched on any areas they felt uncomfortable discussing, they should ask to have Glen O'Banyon present before answering.

I ended by urging them strongly to go back over everything they knew or could think of about Billy, or even Stuart Anderson, to see if there were anything at all they might come up with—however insignificant it may seem—that might help find the killer.

I did not mention the latest murder, or the obvious implication, however remote, that the killer may be one of the people seated at the table.

I sat down amidst a silence so deep I could hear the tick of the grandfather clock in the foyer.

After a moment, Mr. Glick broke the silence by saying: "Mr. Hardesty would like to have a short talk with each of you individually in the study, if you don't mind. Aaron might like to go first, since he has an appointment with a client at 9. This whole thing is very hard on all of us, I know, and Mrs. Glick and I want to thank you all for your cooperation."

Aaron and I got up from our chairs and left the dining room.

* * *

As I'd really more or less expected, my individual talks with the escorts didn't produce much of substance, other than the not totally surprising revelation that despite Phil's having the impression that Billy didn't fool around with the other escorts, there had apparently been a little "fraternization" with most of them at one time or another—as I suspected might well be the case among all or most of them with one another. He had no enemies, never had a run in with any of the other escorts—or any of his clients, had no apparent personal or family problems, no addictions, hadn't been depressed or worried or distracted prior to his death.

As for Anderson, no one other than Phil and Gary, who had gone with him shortly after he first became a client, had ever spent any time with him other than at the "introduction" dinner. Gary's accounting of their one get together had pretty much backed up Phil's assessment: that Anderson was pretty vanilla in his sexual preferences and not at all into anything that might smack of "kink."

I of course tried, as subtly as possible, to determine where each of them had been at the time of his murders, and they all had plausible alibis for the night Anderson died. Gary had been at the Glicks having dinner, Steve, Phil, of course, and Aaron had been with clients, and Mark was out of town for his brother's wedding. Their whereabouts the night of Billy's murder was a little less certain, partly because it was the night of the Gay Pride parade. Phil, Steve and Mark were with clients, Gary and Aaron were supposed to meet at one of the bars and go to the carnival together, but had missed each other in the crowds and had no definite proof of exactly where they were. I encouraged each of them to keep thinking, and to contact me or the Glicks if they came up with anything at all that might have a bearing on the case.

* * *

Saturday morning's paper—which I got up early to go out and buy—headlined what promised to be a prolonged strike by city sanitation workers over a wage dispute. A subhead in the report noted that, in the last Dumpster pickup before the strike, a woman's body had been found in a Dumpster in an area known to be frequented by prostitutes. No references were made to the fact that this was the second body found in Dumpsters in recent weeks. It was handled more or less as an aside, and if it weren't for the subhead, I probably never would have seen it.

I'd realized about halfway to the newsstand that it being Saturday, Richman probably wouldn't be at work. I held out the hope that he might contact me, but also realized that since the victim had not been male, the focus of the police investigation had undoubtedly shifted gears, and my value to it had been moved aside.

Nonetheless, I wanted to find out anything I could that might help me figure out where to go next.

I stopped at the local deli for a bagel and coffee, finished reading the paper—saving the crossword puzzle for later, and returned home. I figured by that time that Tim might be up, and that there might be something else he could tell me.

I dialed Tim's number and heard the phone being picked up, followed by Jared's voice: "Hello?"

"Jared?" I asked, momentarily flustered. "I'm sorry, I thought

I dialed Tim's num..." *You're an idiot, Hardesty,* my mental voice said as I realized that yes, I *had* dialed Tim's number.

Jared laughed and said "Tim's in the shower. See what happens when you put business before pleasure? You missed out on a great night." Then he hastened to add: "We sure missed you...but we managed somehow."

"Gee," I said, "I'm glad to hear that." My crotch was very unhappy to think about what it had undoubtedly missed. "Can you ask him to give me a call when he gets a chance?"

"Sure," Jared said. "I've got to be heading home pretty soon—got a ton of work to do, and there's still that damned dissertation—I don't know why it can't just finish itself."

"You have my deepest sympathy," I said.

"Thanks. Oh, you got any plans for tomorrow? Thought maybe we could go to brunch."

"Sure," I said. "And you can give me a blow by blow of last night."

He laughed. "How about I just give you a blow?"

"You got it!" I said. "Give me a call in the morning and we'll set up the brunch details."

"Will do," he said. "Later."

* * *

Just as Jared's dissertation refused to write itself, my apartment wasn't self-cleaning, so I reluctantly went into my Saturday-chores mode. Actually, it was probably just as well, since the sound of the vacuum and the clatter of dishes in the sink tended, however briefly, to drown out thoughts of the case and my trying to figure out what my gut hinted it knew but wouldn't tell me.

I was piling up clothes to take to the laundry when Tim returned my call. He sounded tired but happy.

"Sorry you couldn't join us last night, Dick," he said.

"Not nearly as sorry as I am," I said. "I had to work on this damned case—which is just about *all* I've done since I took it. And your little bombshell yesterday really threw me."

"Yeah," he said. "Well, imagine what it must have done for the cops."

"So they have no doubt it's the same guy responsible?" I asked.

"They seemed pretty sure. I'm still not sure what that particular knife had to do with anything, but the cops seem to think it was a definite tie-in."

I explained to him what the tie in was—the knife's having been apparently stolen from Anderson's hotel room. I was sure the police had verified that fact with the cutlery supplier Anderson had met for dinner the night he died. But for the killer to make it so easy for the police to make a connection they might otherwise have overlooked struck me as weird in the extreme. Well, killers do weird things.

"Anything similar to the wedding ring thing with Anderson?" Part of me was sitting back listening to the other part of me, amazed at how matter-of-factly I could talk about such incomprehensible things.

"Not that we can tell," he said.

"Were there any signs of a struggle…any mystery bruising? Any indication that, like Billy, she'd been killed while she was naked and redressed before being put in the Dumpster?"

"Well," Tim said, "she was wearing a pretty standard Hooker uniform—halter top, bare midriff, low-cut toreador pants. She was stabbed just above the navel, which would have been exposed in either event. No evidence that she'd been naked and redressed, though. No sign of a struggle, no bruising," Tim said.

"Any sign of sex?" I asked.

"Well," Tim said, "she was a prostitute, and there was indication of recent sexual activity, both vaginal and oral, but there's no way to tell if it was whoever killed her."

"Hmm," I said. "And nothing new on Billy?" I asked.

"Yeah!" Tim said, "I'm sorry—I've been so damned busy…the M.E. released Billy's body to his folks. It's being sent up to Leeds."

I realized that my mind had reached that point of saturation beyond which not much registers, so it was time to back off for the moment.

"Well, I really appreciate everything you've done, Tim," I said truthfully. "Can I buy you dinner tonight, by way of appreciation?"

Tim laughed, and once again I was struck by how easily he could switch between his work life and his personal life—and again realized that in a job like his, it would almost have to be a necessary survival skill . "Oh, sure, Hardesty! I read you like a book. What you really want is to take me out, get me drunk, then have your vile, masculine, lustful way with me time and time again. What kid of guy do you think I am?"

"Well, we've already pretty much established that," I said. "And of course you're right about my intentions. But that would be *after* dinner."

He laughed again. "Actually, I'd love to," he said, "but I'm afraid last night pretty well did me in for awhile. I'm still walking bowlegged. Can I take a rain check?"

"Sure," I said. "Jared wants to go to brunch tomorrow; you think you'd be up to it?"

"Up to brunch, probably. Up to the two of you again so soon, I doubt it."

"Hey," I said, "we don't *have* to have another three-way."

"Oh, yes we do!" Tim said emphatically. "And damned soon. But I really do have something else I've got to do tomorrow—a birthday party for one of my god-kids. I have to be out in the suburbs at around one o'clock. That wouldn't give us nearly enough time...for brunch," he quickly added.

"Okay," I said. "You get some rest today and have fun tomorrow, and we'll get together whenever you can. And thanks again. As I may have mentioned a couple dozen times, I don't know what I'd do without you."

"It's always nice to be appreciated," he said. "Later, then."

* * *

Again, that damned knife. Without it, it just might be possible, after all, that the three deaths...or at least the prostitute's...were unrelated. With it....

And easy enough to say that there was more than one set of Antonio Vivace cutlery floating around out there. But who was it who said "Circumstantial evidence is finding a trout in the milk"? If there was ever a trout in the milk, this was it. But again, could the killer have been so incredibly stupid to use such an easily-identifiable knife stolen from one victim to kill another? What kind of game is he trying to play? What the knife did was to all but shout that the killer had to be bisexual, since it had ties to a gay murder—OK, a bisexual's murder—and a straight's murder. Why would he do that? Or, maybe, since one of the victims was bisexual, one was gay, and one was straight, maybe the killer was telling us he's omnisexual, or just that he doesn't discriminate on the basis of sexual orientation, in which case maybe Anderson's and Billy's deaths were coincidence after all and we can all go back to square one and...

Shit!

I'd almost been willing to go along with the idea that Anderson's and Billy's deaths were semi-accidental; that the killer was somebody who liked rough sex a little too much and it got out of hand. That would conveniently put Matt and Aaron right at the top of the suspects list; they both liked to play rough. Unfortunately, I'd noticed that killers do not always take my convenience into consideration. And it didn't take into account the fact of the woman, or that Tim said she didn't have a mark on her other than the stab wound. Somehow...damn! another one of those infuriatingly elusive thoughts just streaked across my conscience and darted around a mental corner and out of sight again. I really, truly, hate it when I do that.

* * *

Not seeing any practical way to put off the inevitable, I slung the laundry bag over my shoulder—immediately having a physical deja vu of being back in the navy, toting my seabag up the gangplank onto the "Ticonderoga" for the first time—and headed out for the laundromat. Though it wasn't the closest one to me, I liked the people who owned it, and they had a 17 year old son, Jeff, who not only was hot as hell, but always came on to me pretty damned strong. He was way too young for me to even consider following up on it, of course, but my ego sure liked the stroking.

Sure enough, Jeff was on duty, and there was only one other customer in the place, just taking a load of wet laundry out of a machine. She carted it over to a dryer, tossed it in, fumbled in her pocket for change, then when she was convinced the dryer would do its job, she picked up her clothes basket and left.

Jeff, who'd given me a big grin when I walked in (which I of course returned strictly as a matter of common courtesy), watched carefully as I filled up two machines and shook in probably too much powdered soap. Reaching into my pocket I realized I'd forgotten to bring change from my apartment.

Yeah, you 'forgot,' my mind said sarcastically. *Who do you think you're kidding?*

I walked over to Jeff, whose eyes had never left me. "Can I get some change, Jeff?" I asked, giving him a big smile.

His eyes dropped deliberately and obviously to my crotch. "You can get anything you want," he said, moving his eyes back up to my own.

Was I that subtle at that age? I wondered.

"Thanks," I said noncommitally. "The change'll do for now." I handed him a bill, and he opened the register, scooping up quarters with two fingers from one of the trays.

"My folks are gone for a couple hours," Jeff said, carefully and slowly placing each coin into my outstretched hand, making sure his fingers touched my palm with each coin. "You want to come into the back room with me for a while?"

Yes! Yes! Yes! yelled my crotch.

No! No! No! countered my conscience.

"How old are you now, Jeff?" I asked.

"Nearly 18," he said.

"Well, if you're still interested in 3 years, I'll be glad to take you up on it," I said.

As I returned to put the money in the machine, leaving Jeff looking disappointed at the counter, my little voice said: *Prickteaser!*

Hey, I thought, *he's just a kid. He doesn't know he's prickteasing.*

Not him, stupid, my mind said contemptuously: *you!*

* * *

It being Saturday, and me being me, I knew I couldn't just sit home contemplating my navel—not when there was the possibility of contemplating someone else's. As so often was the case, I knew

I didn't *have* to go out, but going out was more than just a perhaps-too-deeply entrenched habit, it was my way of taking a much needed break from thinking continuously about the case.

I did, however, give Phil a call to see how he was doing and if he knew that Billy was going home to his parents. He said he had talked with Billy's folks, and that he was leaving in a few minutes to drive out to see them and take them some of Billy's things. He said he'd probably stay the night, but would call me when he got back.

That pretty much put a damper on my real urge to go out, but I decided I really had to have some time away from the case. After debating the pros and cons, I thought I might just swing by Ramón's for the start of their Happy Hour, then go on to the store for the week's groceries. I figured that maybe just a quick one at Happy Hour might satisfy my need for a Saturday bar fix, and I could just go home and relax for a change. Fat chance, but...

I got to Ramón's at around 5:30, and was rather surprised to see so many people already there. Bob was behind the bar and I took a stool fairly close to the front door, just at the end of the bar, which provided me a good vantage point to play my little "observation" game. (I like to pick out someone I don't know, at random, and see what I can find out about them, just by watching. Body language, laugh, whether they smoke or not, whether they're right handed or left handed—stuff like that. Like I said before, I get a kick out of the little things in life.)

I ordered my usual Old Fashioned, and Bob and I had a chance to exchange little snatches of conversation whenever he had a spare minute. He told me that he had asked Mario to move in with him, which delighted me—I really liked Mario, and knew he was good for Bob. It was a major step in Bob's healing process, and a sign that while Ramón would always be part of him, he could at last let him go and move on with his life.

I took my time nursing my drink, rather relieved to find that my mind had shifted into neutral and I had actually gone more than ten minutes without once thinking about Billy or Stuart Anderson or the Glicks, or...

I felt a hand on my shoulder, and turned to see Aaron, all in black and looking sexy as hell, smiling at me.

"Hi, Aaron!" I said. On the one hand I was unhappy to be plunged right back into the pool I'd been trying so hard to climb out of; on the other hand, he *was* looking sexy as all hell.

Crotch: 1, Mind: 0.

Aaron sat down on the empty stool beside me and waved at Bob, who came right over.

"What'll it be, Aaron?" he asked. That Bob knew his name implied that Aaron might have been becoming something of a regular.

"Pabst...no glass."

Bob nodded and went to the beer cooler just down the bar.

When he'd been served, and given Bob his money, I asked: "Not working tonight?"

"Yeah," he said, picking up his beer and taking a long drink. "I've got a client later on tonight, around 8:30. Still plenty of time for you and me to get it on," he added with a grin.

So much for foreplay, I thought.

"Aren't you afraid I'd tucker you out? You wouldn't want to shortchange the paying customers," I said.

He looked at me and grinned. "Takes a hell of a lot to tucker *me* out," he said. "And besides, no problem in this case—the guy's a regular and all he wants is for me to tie him to the bed, slap him around a little bit, tell him what a rotten sonofabitch he is, and what I'm going to do to him—I'm king of the dirty-talkers, by the way. I never have to actually *do* anything with him—just thinking about it gets him so worked up he goes off like a rocket. I don't touch him, he doesn't touch me. I untie him, he gets dressed, and I go home."

"Interesting job," I observed.

"You have no idea," he said, smiling. "Anything happening with Billy?" he asked, after taking another long swallow from his beer.

I told him about Billy's body being released. I didn't know if he was aware of the latest murder, and didn't want to muddy the waters by asking him.

Aaron shrugged. "Really tough for his folks. And Phil, I know."

"What did you think of their relationship—Billy's and Phil's, I mean."

He shrugged again. "I dunno, really. I was glad for them—guys in our business don't usually have a chance to make real friends.

Phil seemed to be pretty protective of Billy—not jealous, but just like he thought he was Billy's big brother. Billy went along with it, and in his own way he tried to look out for Phil, too. I think Billy was a lot more street smart than Phil or any of the rest of us gave him credit for. He could take care of himself."

I shook my head and paused a second before saying:. "Apparently not," and Aaron took another swig of beer and looked away.

"Yeah," he said.

I finished my Old Fashioned and Aaron, noticing it, chug-a-lugged the rest of his beer.

"So," he said, "you wanna come over and see my…" a significant pause, while one hand dropped to his crotch "…place?"

As Oscar Wilde said: *"I can resist anything but temptation."*

* * *

I will admit, it was different. And not at all bad. True to his advertising, Aaron liked to play rough, but nothing I couldn't handle—and return in kind, which seemed to turn him on. I think he was pretty good at sensing my limits, and he never tried to push them. I even asked him for a sample of his "dirty talk" while I was…um…otherwise occupied, and I must say he did have a way with words.

As we were standing in the shower afterwards—we both sure needed it, and there's no point in wasting water—I forced myself to shift back into work gear for a moment, and asked Aaron if he'd thought of anything more, since our talk after dinner Friday night, about Billy or anything that might be helpful.

He turned me around so he could soap my back, then said: "Not really. Except I always got the feeling that there was a lot more to Billy than he let on."

I turned around to face him and let the water rinse off my back, our chests touching. "Such as?" I asked.

"Hard to say," he said. "Just a feeling. One thing was I think he really got a kick out of being a prickteaser," he said, "and he was damned good at it. He was just playing, most of the time, but I could see where some guys might take it the wrong way and think he was more interested than he was."

Well, that opened up yet another door of possibilities. Maybe Billy played his game with the wrong guy, and it cost him his life. But if that were true, his date for the evening could be pretty much ruled out—you don't usually prick tease a date. But somebody he saw on his way there, or on his way home...probably on his way home, or the guy he had the date with probably would have called to find out why he didn't show. Or maybe.... *Damn!*

* * *

Sunday went by relatively fast, smoothly, and enjoyably, with only an occasional parking-brake slowdown whenever my mind decided to think about the case. Brunch was nice, as always, and Jared and I knew each other well enough by this time to really have become good friends. And after brunch, we came by my place for a different but equally enjoyable form of conversation. He had to leave early to get home to work on his doctoral dissertation, and I didn't even bother to get fully dressed—just threw on a pair of cutoffs and enjoyed the all-too-rare sensation of being sinfully decadent.

Phil called in the early evening after he got home from Billy's parents. It had been a pretty rough time, I gathered. Fortunately, Billy's folks had been totally supportive of his being gay, so Phil didn't have to do too much evading or outright lying about his and Billy's relationship. The important thing was that as far as his folks knew, Billy was a successful model and nothing more.

The body was to be cremated Monday, and a simple memorial service held the following Saturday at the little church Billy's family had belonged to since he was a kid. Phil asked if I'd like to go with him to the service, and I was touched that he'd ask me. I said of course.

CHAPTER 9

The minute I walked in the office door on Monday, I went directly to the phone to call Lieutenant Richman, not even bothering to take the lid off the jumbo styrofoam cup of coffee I'd picked up from the diner in the lobby. I knew he may very well not even be in yet, but I couldn't have just sat around waiting for when I thought he might be available.

Luckily, when the receiver was picked up on the other end, I heard the familiar, "Lieutenant Richman."

"Lieutenant—Dick." I hoped he knew which Dick, since I was just a tad paranoid about having my full name become too well known around police headquarters. I had no reason to think anyone would be listening but, hey, this *was* police headquarters and as I said, I was paranoid. "I saw the paper," I said, again not being specific, "and noticed that 'development' you were referring to Friday. Is there any chance of our getting together to talk?"

There was a pause, then: "We're really pretty busy around here," he said. Then another pause and: "Do you still go to Sandlers' for lunch?"

Aha! I thought. *Maybe I'm not the only one a little bit paranoid.*

I'd never been to Sandler's for lunch, of course, but since that's where we'd met a couple times for breakfast on another case, I got the message. "Yeah," I said. "Regular as clockwork...noon every day."

"Well, maybe I'll see you there one of these days. Sorry, but I've got a meeting in about two minutes, so have to run."

"No problem," I said. "Take care."

* * *

Finding a place to park near Sandler's at 7 a.m. was one thing; finding a place to park at noon was something entirely different. Finally I gave up in disgust and pulled into a public parking garage—one of those that charge so much the guy in the booth taking your money should be wearing a mask and carrying a gun.

By the time I found a place to park inside the garage—I went up and down every aisle for three levels before I found one—I practically had to sprint to the restaurant in order to make it on time. Not to worry, though, Richman was nowhere in sight. I found a booth within easy sight of the door and sat facing it. The waiter came and I told him I was expecting someone momentarily, but that I'd have some coffee while I waited.

I was on the end of my second cup and debating whether I should order or just leave when I saw Lieutenant Richman walk in the door. He was in civies again, like the day I'd met him at Warman Park, and once again as I watched him approach I speculated on the gay world's loss when Richman took out his Breeder's permit.

We shook hands as he sat down. "Sorry," he said; "the meeting ran a lot longer than I thought, and I had planned to go to the gym at lunch today."

"Well, I'm sorry if I screwed up your plans," I said, "but I really do appreciate your seeing me."

The waiter arrived with water for the lieutenant and a full coffee carafe for both of us.

"Do you have any idea of what the hell is going on?" Richman asked as the waiter left and we looked through our menus.

"Uh…no," I said, a little surprised by the question. "I was hoping maybe you did." I resisted adding: "You *are* the police, you know."

Richman shook his head. "We had a pretty good idea when it was just the two men," he said, "but with the prostitute…"

I caught that one. "She was a prostitute, then?" I asked.

"Mmmm," Richman replied, stirring about a quarter cup of sugar into his coffee. "She was found in a Dumpster in an alley well known to be a place hookers take their johns. A couple of the local working girls recognized her. Her name was Laurie Travers and she was relatively new to town, apparently. We're checking with all the girls who work that area to see if they'd seen her with anyone on the night she was killed."

"Any evidence she'd had sex with her killer?"

Richman shook his head. "Pretty hard to say, but there was no exterior evidence of semen, if that's what you mean. He could have worn a condom, of course, and she'd apparently had sex at some point during the evening, but whether with her killer or not, we can't say."

I'd already gathered that from what Tim had said, but didn't want to let on to Richman by not asking the obvious questions.

The waiter brought our lunch, and we began to eat, though talk of murder victims always tends to make me less hungry than I might have been. It didn't seem to slow Richman down, though. He dug in with gusto.

"And no leads?" I nudged.

"None that I can talk about," he said, scooping a forkful of meatloaf through the little lake of gravy sunk into the mound of mashed potatoes. From his tone of voice, I understood that "None that I can talk about" meant "None."

We ate in silence for a moment—well, again, Richman ate and I just concentrated on getting three peas and a kernel of corn out of my mashed potatoes and moving them back to their corner of the plate where they belonged.

"So," I asked, "what does this do to your 'gay homophobe' theory?"

His head was bent down slightly in anticipation of another forkful of meatloaf, but he paused the fork in mid air and without moving his head glanced up at me through his eyelashes. "As I recall, that was your theory, too," he said.

Touché!

"So where *are* the police on this, if I may ask," I…uh… asked.

"We're really not sure," Richman said. "I think we all thought, when Steiner was killed, that we have an apprentice serial killer out there, even though the cause of Anderson's death was slightly different than Steiner's, and we were prepared for the idea that he wouldn't stop at two. But serial killers almost always stick to one gender. This is a new one for us."

"She was suffocated or choked, then?" I asked, knowing full well that she wasn't, but didn't want Richman to know that, and thought it would be a logical question if I hadn't already known.

"No. Stabbed." He looked at me a little strangely, I thought, and I wondered if he knew I already knew. Well, I was in too deep now not to ask the next logical question.

"So what makes you think her death is related to the other two, other than the Dumpster, which only ties her in with Billy."

He looked at me again and I was almost sure he was going to call me out on this little charade.

"We have specific evidence," he said simply, and I decided it best not to take it any further.

He scooped the last dab of mashed potatoes into his mouth, laid his fork on the plate, and pushed it to one side. "But tell me," he said, after wiping his mouth with his napkin and laying it beside the plate, "you're the man with the hunches and the gut feelings. What are they telling you? One killer? Two killers? Or three? Gay, straight, or bi?"

Actually, I realized that my little barely heard voices had indeed been whispering some things among themselves, but not loudly enough so I could make it out yet. I shook my head. "Sorry," I said, "nothing's coming through at the moment. I was as thrown by this latest victim as I'm sure the police were."

"But do you think there might be anything in the fact that one victim was bi, one gay, and one straight?" He asked, pouring another cup of coffee for both of us.

"I thought about that, yeah," I said. "Like you, when it was just Anderson and Billy, I would have taken bets that the killer had to be gay. Now with the woman thrown into the mix, it makes it points pretty strongly to his being a bisexual. But then it could just be some whacko going through a Whitman's Sampler of sexual preferences. If that's the case, he's running out of possibilities—unless a lesbian is the next victim, and I sure as hell hope not. Three is three too many. But regardless, I still think we're just looking for one guy."

The waiter came by to pick up the dishes, and leave the check, which I grabbed before Richman could reach it. "My turn," I said. "I'll take it out of *my* informant's fund."

He grinned. "Okay, but let me get the tip," and he reached into his wallet for some singles.

As we got up from the booth and headed for the register at the front, he said: "You'll let me know when your hunches kick in, won't you?"

"You got it," I said, reaching for my billfold.

We went out into the street, shook hands, exchanged goodbyes, and went our separate ways. I realized about halfway to my car that I hadn't even mentioned ModelMen.

* * *

Richman's reference to my hunches had forced me to zero in on whatever it was that I sensed was in fact going on in there. Richman was right: from everything I'd read about serial killings, almost without exception where sex is an element in the killings, the killer, whatever his warped motives, tends to concentrate exclusively on one gender or the other.

But a bisexual as a serial killer…? Well, there was John Wayne Gacey, so it's not impossible, of course, but even though he was bisexual and unbalanced, all his victims were male.

Regardless, the one thing that kept rising to the top no matter how hard or how often I stirred the pot, was the strong feeling that there was somehow, somewhere, a definite link to ModelMen. And while the fact that one or more of ModelMen's current escorts might be bi crossed my mind, now was obviously the time to try to find out.

I was already pretty sure about Matt Rushmore, of course, and had to include him in the ModelMen group. As I thought the first time I saw him, if there is such a thing as being too butch to be gay, Matt came close—at least on the surface. And Aaron hardly walked around with a sign around his neck. Well, neither did Gary. Or Phil. Or….*oh shit*! For somebody who hates people who stereotype others, what the hell was I doing if not just that?

* * *

Rather than approach Aaron or any of the others directly, I thought it might be a good idea to check with Phil first, on the grounds that he would know. As soon as I got back to the office, I called him.

The phone was answered on the second ring: "Hello?"

"Phil, hi. How are you doing?" I asked.

"Fine, Dick," he said. "But I'm just on my way out the door to meet a client."

I was a little surprised. "Back to work already?" I asked.

"Yeah," he said. "I can't just sit around here for the rest of my life. The bills have to be paid. I told the Glicks yesterday that I was ready to get back to work. They were a little hesitant, but this morning they called and said they'd gotten a request from one of my regulars for this afternoon, so I took it."

"Any idea what time you might be done?" I asked. "There's something I want to talk to you about."

There was only a slight pause, then: "It's quarter to two now; I've got to meet him at the El Cordoba at 2:30; I should be through around 4. You want to meet me at Hughie's around then, or do you want me to come over to your office?"

"Hughie's is fine," I said. I figured I'd be ready for a beer about that time. "I'll see you there."

"Okay," Phil said. "So long."

As I hung up, I thought of his mention of the El Cordoba. That had really surprised me—the El Cordoba defined the word "sleazy": a hotel which would definitely have been "on the wrong side of the tracks" if there were any tracks around. It was not at all the kind of place I'd expect a guy who could afford a ModelMen escort to even know about, let alone frequent. But I was learning that the only thing you can tell for sure is that you never can tell.

* * *

I did some paperwork, made a few phone calls, and did some filing until 3:30, then headed for Hughies.

Bud, the bartender, noticed me coming through the door and had my dark draft waiting when I reached the bar. It was kind of quiet, but it was early yet. There were maybe four or five hustlers standing around, and no discernable johns. One of the hustlers I didn't recognize came directly over and pulled out the stool beside me to sit down.

"How's it goin'?" he asked, not smiling. Not a bad looking guy, a little skinny, needed a haircut.

"Fine, thanks," I said. "How about you?"

I noticed his beer was nearly empty, and assumed he'd probably been nursing it for quite a while.

"Just lookin' for a little action," he said, eyeing me closely but without expression. "You lookin' too?"

"Just waiting for a friend," I said.

He gave a slight shrug. "I'm a friendly guy," he said, his free hand dropping down to grab his crotch. Interesting, yes: subtle, no.

"I have no doubt," I said, "but I'm..." A momentary increase in the light level announced the opening of the door, and I looked around to see Phil coming in. "Speak of the devil," I said.

Phil walked directly over to stand beside me. The hustler on the stool got up without a word and moved off, and while Phil signaled Bud for a beer, I had a chance to really look at him. He was wearing a black, form-fitting sleeveless tee shirt, a wide belt, and faded jeans just beginning to fray at the knees. He looked like a character from the musical "Grease", but a lot better.

"You're lookin' good," I said. Phil was the kind of guy who could wear a burlap bag and still look good.

"Thanks," he said with a smile. Bud brought his beer and I pushed one of the bills I'd left on the bar from my change toward him. Bud nodded and took it. "Thanks again," Phil said.

"What's with the El Cordoba?" I asked, after we'd both taken a drink of our beers.

Phil pulled out a stool and sat down, his back to the bar. "The client gets turned on by games," he said. "Sort of like that Japanese businessman Billy and I used to see."

I noticed with some relief that he was able to say Billy's name conversationally, without any pause or evidence that it hurt to do so.

"He really digs hustlers," Phil continued, "but I think he's leery of them, too, so he uses ModelMen because he can afford to. So sometimes he'll meet me in here, and I'll pretend we've never seen each other before and we'll go through the whole courting ritual; or like today, I'll stand on the corner near the El Cordoba and he'll come strolling by, we'll go through the usual pick-up routine, and then we'll walk down to the El Cordoba and get a room."

"Sounds like fun," I said, truthfully.

Phil took another drink and nodded. "Yeah, it's different. There was a little variation today, though."

"Oh?" I prompted.

"Yeah," he said. "You know the El Cordoba at all?"

As a matter of fact, I did, from my visit there during an earlier case I'd worked on. I nodded.

"You know Brad, the day manager?"

'Oh, my, yes!' I thought. A hot looking hulk with muscles for days, and every one of them covered in tattoos, but with a really nice face. I nodded again.

"Well," Phil said "the client is toying with the idea of having me approach Brad for a three-way. I don't think Brad hustles, but if he'd be willing to go along with it, I sure wouldn't mind."

'Neither would I!' I thought, then had to force myself back to reality.

"You do lead an interesting life," I said. "Which brings me to one of the reasons I wanted to see you. I was wondering: are any of ModelMen's escorts bi?"

Phil looked mildly puzzled and thought a moment before answering. "Steve," he said. "He's married and has a son."

Steve! The Botticelli Man? I guess I was right about his androgyny, but it still caught me by surprise, somehow.

"Any of the others?" I asked.

"Good question," he said, then knit his brows a moment. "You know, Dick, I honestly don't know! Steve's wide open about it. I'd assume Matt was, since Billy told me he had a couple of kids, but I've never heard the other guys say anything at all about it. Why do you ask?"

Suddenly, his eyes widened slightly and he pulled his head back. "Jeezus!" he said. "The prostitute who was found in the Dumpster! Do you think...you think Steve...or Matt...?"

I raised my hand to try to slow him down. "I don't think or mean anything," I said, "but I have to consider every possibility, and this is one of them. Did you ever sense anything between Steve and Billy?"

Phil shook his head. "No. Like I said, Billy really dug butch guys and he always said Steve was just too pretty for him."

"Well," I said, "It occurred to me that the Glicks have gone out of their way to select escorts with the widest possible range of…experience…and it wouldn't be out of the question for some bi clients to want a bi escort for a bi three-way, say."

"Well, I think you could rule Steve out there," he said. "His wife is perfectly okay with him going to bed with guys— especially since it pays so well, but she puts her foot down about him having sex with other women. But I've honestly never heard it mentioned among the other guys. The Glicks keep a lot of things pretty much to themselves when it comes to who they select for what specific…specialties. When they first interviewed me they asked me all sorts of questions, but whether I was bi or not never came up. Of course, I guess I'd made it pretty clear to Mr. Glick that I was strictly gay when he first picked me up and mentioned his wife. One of the rules is that we're not supposed to discuss among ourselves what we do with our tricks—there's no reason to, usually. Probably you should ask the Glicks if any of the other guys is bi."

"I think I'll do that," I said. "Just thought I'd check with you first."

"Got any plans for tonight?" Phil asked.

"Not really, no," I said. "You want to do something?"

"Yeah," he said. "I'd really like to. Maybe grab dinner somewhere like we did the other night? And maybe go to a movie? God, I haven't done that since…in a long time."

"You got it," I said.

* * *

A nice night. We went for pizza, then to see the latest James Bond movie, then I drove Phil back to his car, near Hughie's. He was pretty quiet the last couple blocks, and I wondered if something was bothering him. Well, I figured, the best way to find out was to ask.

"Anything wrong, Phil?"

He shook his head. "Nah, not really. I just really miss not having somebody around to spend time with like…I used to."

"Well, all you have to do is call," I said.

He smiled and reached over to put his hand on my leg. "Thanks a lot, Dick," he said. "I had a really nice time." There was a long pause as we approached his car. "Would you…" he started to say, then stopped.

"Would I what?" I asked.

"Would you come spend the night with me?" he asked. "I don't mean to have sex, necessarily…" *Damn,* my crotch said. "I'd just really kind of like to be with somebody that I wanted to be with—it's really selfish, but you know, just for me."

And it suddenly struck me, probably for the first time, that I understood exactly what Phil's life must really be like—for him.

We pulled up beside Phil's car. "I'll follow you," I said, and he smiled again, then looked serious.

"You're sure you don't mind?" He asked.

"I'm sure," I said.

* * *

I can remember only one other time since Chris and I broke up that I ever actually *slept* with a guy without having sex. It was quite a revelation. I sensed that even my crotch understood that this wasn't the time or the place—that this was as Phil wanted and needed it to be: just for him. And I was pleasantly surprised to realize as we drifted off to sleep, Phil's head on my shoulder and arm across my chest, that it was kind of just for me, too.

* * *

After a quick run home to change clothes, I made a stop at the diner on the ground floor of my office building for a large black coffee to go, paused at the newsstand in the lobby for the morning paper, then up to the office, once again wondering, as the elevator creaked and groaned and shuddered upward, if it was going to make it.

No messages, either at home or at the office, from Tim or Lieutenant Richman about the discovery of another body, so I was fairly confident that I could look through the paper without finding any unpleasant surprises.

After taking my time drinking my coffee and doing the crossword puzzle, I decided to try the Glicks at home—I preferred not to call the ModelMen offices unless I absolutely had to. To my surprise, the phone was answered by a male voice not Mr. Glick's.

"Glick residence," the voice said, and I vaguely recognized it.

"Good morning," I said; "this is Dick Hardesty. Is either Mr. or Mrs. Glick in?"

"Oh, hi, Dick," the voice said. "This is Gary. I just came by to use the pool—you want to come join me?"

Remembering Gary stretched out on top of my desk, his pants around his ankles and his shirt pushed up almost to his neck made me very much want to join him. But business before, etc.

"Sounds great, Gary," I said, "but I'll have to take a rain check. Are either of the Glicks at home?"

"Yeah, Iris is…hold a second and I'll get her for you." I heard the sound of the receiver being set down, then a long silence, and finally a click and Iris Glick's voice:

"Mr. Hardesty! How nice of you to call. What can I do for you?"

"I was wondering if we might get together briefly—I have a question that can best be answered in person."

There was only a slight pause, and then: "Why of course. Mr. Glick is meeting with his stockbroker this morning, but he will be home for lunch. Could you join us? Say around 11:30?"

"Of course," I said. "Thank you for asking me. I look forward to seeing you."

"And we'll be eating by the pool, so if you'd like to come in through the side gate, it will save you a walk to the front of the house."

It wasn't until we'd hung up that it occurred to me that Gary might still be there for lunch. I didn't know how much he knew of the Glicks' business, but he *was* Iris Glick's brother. And if he was there, I could simply ask if any of the escorts were bisexual without pushing for a name at the moment, if they were reluctant for whatever reason to talk about it in front of Gary.

I was, of course, early getting to the Glicks, so decided to drive around the golf course. I'd never been anywhere near the Birchwood Country Club before, but I wasn't surprised to see that the clubhouse was a fairly good replica of Mt. Vernon— only bigger. And not being a golfer, I'd never really realized just how long it takes to drive around an 18 hole golf course. I pulled into the Glicks' drive at exactly 11:30.

I drove to the parking area and pulled in between a Lincoln Town Car and a silver Porsche so new it still had the dealer sticker in the window. My car sitting between them made me think of a dogfood sandwich. The side gate was open just far enough to let me know it wasn't locked, and I went in and walked toward the pool house. I noticed an umbrella table beside the pool was set for four, but no one was in evidence until I approached the front of the pool house. Inside, the little bar arrangement was still set up, and Gary, fully clothed, was sitting at one of the four stools, talking with Mrs. Glick.

"Mr Hardesty," she said brightly when she saw me. "Do come have a glass of wine. Mr. Glick is changing, and Johnnie-Mae is putting the finishing touches on lunch."

Gary got up for an exchange of greetings and a handshake, then moved behind the bar for a wine glass and a half-full bottle of something pink. (I'm afraid I flunked my Wine Snob course rather badly.) Whatever it was, I knew it had to be very expensive.

He handed it to me with a telegraphed-message smile.

"Did you see Gary's new toy?" Mrs. Glick asked, nodding toward the parking area.

'That explains the Porsche!' I thought. "Uh, yes, I did," I said. "Very nice, indeed."

"Well, it's a birthday present," she said in the "precious" tone of a matron talking to her poodle, and leaning forward to pinch Gary's cheek.

I immediately wanted to mention that my birthday is November 14th, but thought better of it.

"Happy Birthday, Gary," I said. "Just think...now you can vote."

"Thank you," he said, giving me a quick grin, while at the same time backing away somewhat awkwardly from Mrs. Glick's attentions. "Sis is very generous," he said, giving her a slow smile. "Oh, and Arnold, too, of course," he added, somewhat unnecessarily, I thought. "And I do like nice things." The latter comment was accompanied by a very interesting smile.

I would really have preferred that Gary weren't there—not that he didn't provide a welcome supply of eye candy and erotic fantasy, but again I wasn't sure how open I should be about the case in front of him.

At this point, Mr. Glick emerged from the house, followed by Johnnie-Mae pushing a covered caterer's cart which I assumed contained lunch. While she stopped at the umbrella table and began efficiently transferring things from the cart to the table, Mr. Glick came over to greet me. Even when he was dressed informally, as he was now, he still looked like an ad for a Distinguished Gentlemen's clothing store.

Gary went behind the bar to get Mr. Glick some wine, and when he returned, Mrs. Glick motioned us toward the table. Johnnie-Mae was just placing the last of the cart's contents on the table, and I was once again in awe of her efficiency. Whatever the Glicks were paying her could never have been nearly enough. We exchanged smiles, and she turned the cart around and headed back for the house.

Lunch turned out to be an incredible crab salad with a side dish of fresh fruit—slices of honeydew melon, cantaloupe, watermelon, and sprinkled with fresh raspberries.

We small-talked pleasantly through lunch, and Johnnie-Mae returned with coffee, then took the empty dishes back to the house on the same tray.

"So tell us, Mr. Hardesty," Mrs. Glick said as we drank our coffee, "what was it you wanted to ask?"

I glanced quickly at Mr. Glick and thought I noticed just a flicker of…what?… discomfort? …cross his face, but it was gone in an instant, replaced by his usual expression of complete composure. I felt suddenly very awkward, not really knowing what to say.

Gary caught on instantly. "Perhaps I should excuse myself," he said with a small smile, but making no effort to get up. Mrs. Glick reached out and touched his arm.

"Nonsense," she said. "I'm sure whatever Mr. Hardesty has to ask isn't privileged…" she glanced at me, "Is it, Mr. Hardesty?"

"Well, no…it's just a general question about the escorts' services."

"Please," Mr. Glick said, "ask."

I took what I hoped wasn't an obviously apparent deep breath. "I understand that each of the escorts is selected partly for their ability to cater to…specific…client requests, with each one providing a different area of expertise."

'Jeezus, Hardesty! You want to try that one again, in English?' my mind asked.

Mr. Glick gave a very small smile of amusement. "That's true, yes."

'Oh, to hell with pussyfooting,' I decided. "Are any of your escorts bisexual?" I asked.

There was a long silence, until Mrs. Glick said "Steve is, of course. And, we understand that some of the other escorts have had heterosexual experiences, yes."

'Which doesn't automatically make them bisexual,' I thought.

I recognized sidestepping when I saw it, and pushed ahead. "Yes, and I realize that a large number of your clients are themselves bisexual, but do any of your escorts specialize in requests for bisexual activity involving women?"

Another awkward silence, until…

"That would be me," Gary said with a smile, his eyes fixed on mine.

CHAPTER 10

I hope to hell my face didn't show the surprise the rest of me was feeling. But on reflection, how do you know if anybody's bi or not, unless they tell you? Nobody wears signs.

"Ah," I said, in yet another classic example of Hardesty non-statement. "And Steve?"

Mrs. Glick smiled warmly. "His wife would never allow it,"she said.

Well, if he did screw around with other women, he wouldn't be the first married man to do so, his wife 'allowing' it or not, I thought.

"There isn't really very much demand for that particular specialty," Gary said, still smiling, "but since ModelMen tries to cover every contingency…I'm here to serve, as they say."

"Actually," Mr. Glick said, "in light of the most recent terrible death and its obvious implications, Mrs. Glick and I thought that might be the gist of your question, and we agreed it might be good if Gary were here to directly answer any other questions you may have. Do you think the police will follow your same line of reasoning?"

I shook my head. "No way of knowing, really. I do know that Lieutenant Richman, though not officially a member of the homicide division, is pretty sharp—he's got a lot better feel for what goes on in the community than most of the force."

"So do you?" Gary asked, reaching for the coffee carafe to refill our cups.

"Do I what?" I asked, putting my hand over my cup to indicate I'd had enough.

"Have specific questions for me?"

"Well," I said, "we went over most of the basic ones before this bi issue came up. I just think it's a pretty good idea to understand that if I can see the potential link to ModelMen, the cops may well be able to do the same thing. The only wall we have right now is the fact that the police apparently aren't aware of ModelMen's escort branch. I think it's only a matter of time before Richman comes back to me on the escort service question, or somebody else decides to go retrace their steps to see what they've missed, and when they do...."

We all sat in relative silence for a moment, the only sounds being the water cascading down the little man-made hill surrounding the pool house, and the drone of a passing airplane.

"Gary," I finally said, "if I were you I'd go over your alibis for the nights of all three murders pretty carefully—you may well need them. I'd suggest the same to every one of the other escorts as well."

I turned to Mr. Glick. "You told me that the client Phil was with the evening Anderson was killed would be willing to come forward if necessary. I hope that's true, because Phil is a definite and obvious link between ModelMen and Anderson. If they track Phil down and he can immediately offer up the name of the man he was with that night, just the fact that he has a solid alibi may be enough to satisfy the police. You might consider alerting the client that he might be brought into all this."

Mr. Glick finished his coffee and set the cup down carefully on the saucer. He looked at me and smiled. "He already knows," he said, "and has told us to let Phil know that if he is approached by the police to give his name as the man he was with the night of Stuart's death. He agrees there is no reason why ModelMen need even be mentioned. He and Phil were together that evening. Period."

Why was I getting this strong sense that I knew who Phil's "client" was? No one had mentioned a name, just that the guy was a prominent fig...*shit, of course! That photo of Phil and Stuart Anderson taken with the senator and...Glen O'Banyon! Why Glen, you devil, you!* I don't think Glen O'Banyon customarily paid for sex, but in Phil's case, I'm sure he'd be willing to make an exception. Hell, almost any gay man in his right mind would consider it! And being with someone as prominent as O'Banyon would be about an iron-clad an alibi as Phil could possibly need. I made a mental note to ask Phil, just for my own curiosity.

I also made a mental note, in light of the connection between Matt Rushmore and Gary, to call Matt with a few more questions. I had a few specific things I wanted to check, and my crotch immediately jumped in with a question or two of its own.

* * *

As soon as I returned to the office, I looked up Matt's number and dialed it, not expecting to find him home, and therefore mildly surprised to hear him answer on the first ring.

"Matt, hi...this is Dick Hardesty," I said.

"Yeah, Dick, what can I do for you?"

I really wish hot guys wouldn't ask questions like that.

"I had a couple quick questions I hope you wouldn't mind answering," I said. "We can do it over the phone if you'd like."

"Sure," he said, "but I prefer to talk to people in person. Why don't you come over here? We can have a drink and talk about whatever it is."

While my crotch thought that was a great idea, my mind wasn't too sure. He was still very much a suspect-in-waiting.

So what's he going to do? Strangle you in his own apartment?

"Okay," I said, "if it won't be a problem."

"Nah, come on over," he said. "It's 4242 Harker, just north of Brookhaven. Know where it is?"

"Right off of Decorator's Row," I said. "I can find it. What time?"

"Five thirty?"

"Ok...I'll see you then."

We hung up and on a whim—hell, it wasn't a whim, that small part of me which wasn't totally ruled by my crotch was covering my ass!—I called Phil, ostensibly to make arrangements for going to Billy's memorial service Saturday. Luck was with me again, and he was home. We arranged for me to pick him up at around 10—the service was at noon, and it was about an hour's drive.

"Oh, and Phil," I said, as if it were an afterthought, "what can you tell me about Matt Rushmore's relationship with Gary?"

Phil thought a moment, then said: "Not too much, really. I know that he and Gary were a lot more than just old service buddies. Matt wasn't much of a talker, but I sensed something pretty strong between them—probably more from Matt than from Gary, now that I think of it."

"Anything happen to change that?" I asked.

"I don't know. It just seemed that things had pretty much cooled off between them just before Matt left. I do know that Matt's last client had been one of Gary's clients; no idea why he decided to go with Matt, but it's not unusual for a client to look for a little variety. And I can't imagine that making a difference in their relationship, whatever that might have been."

"Hmmm," I said, shifting the phone from one ear to the other.

"Any particular reason you're asking?" Phil said.

"Well," I said, "I've got a couple questions for Matt and I'm going over to his place shortly. I just wanted to see if you knew something I should follow up on."

"Oh, okay. But no, nothing I can think of."

"Well, thanks, Phil," I said. "I'll see you around 10 on Saturday, then, if not before, okay?"

"Okay. Take care of yourself," he said—which struck me as a rather strange thing to say.

Now don't get paranoid, my inner voice cautioned, *it's just a phrase.*

We exchanged goodbyes and hung up.

For some reason, I was increasingly curious about the relationship between Matt and Gary, and what might have happened to cool it. And that Gary had been with the client Matt had beaten up…did that suggest that maybe Gary was into a little "down and dirty" as Aaron called it? Maybe the client switched because Gary wasn't down and dirty enough. Hard to say.

Well, I'd find out.

* * *

The three blocks of Brookhaven just off Beech were known as Decorator's Row for all the exclusive furniture, art, and interior design shops concentrated in that area. Most of the stores were not open to the general public—as the discreet "To the Trade" signs on their doors announced, so foot traffic along that stretch was limited mostly to the occasional peasant looking enviously in the windows at the things they could never afford.

Harker marked the eastern boundary of Decorator's Row, and 4242 was a pleasant courtyard building with a fenced in small lawn edged with flower beds. Matt had not mentioned his apartment number, but I was able to find it easily enough on the list beside the door in the small alcove entry, and rang the buzzer. A moment later there was a responding buzz and the click of the door unlocking.

I found the right apartment and had just raised my fist to knock when the door opened to an impressive panorama of Matt Rushmore, wearing a white tank top and torn cut-offs that left little to the imagination.

"Hi," he said, standing back from the door. "Come on in." The apartment reminded me quite a bit of my own, in that neither Matt Rushmore nor I was likely to get hounding phone calls from House Beautiful wanting to come over. Not messy, but definitely "lived in." It was comfortable enough, but I didn't get the impression Matt had ever considered interior design as a profession. Functional, liveable. That about does it. But whereas I have a lot of—probably way too much—little personal stuff around my place, breadcrumbs leading to my past in reminders of certain people or places, I couldn't really spot anything that said "This is Matt." About the only thing unusual I noted were there were a lot of ashtrays around, most from hotels, from what I could tell, including one from the Montero. Well, we all have to have a hobby. And then I noticed a framed photograph on one wall of two little girls around six years old, obviously identical twins. I didn't have to ask who they were.

"Have a seat," Matt said, and I sat down on one side of a surprisingly comfortable if nondescript-looking couch. "Would you like a beer?" he asked, moving toward what I gathered was the kitchen.

"Sure," I said. "Thanks."

I heard the refrigerator door opening, then two soft "psshhhht" sounds. He returned a moment later with two uncapped beers, one of which he handed me before sitting down in a recliner across from me and pushing back with his arms to lower the back slightly and raise the leg rest.

"So what can I do for you?" he asked after taking a long swig of his beer and setting it on the small lamp table beside the chair.

I sat back on the couch and crossed my legs. "I'd like to hear a little more about ModelMen, from someone who isn't currently directly involved with it."

Matt gave a shrug. "Like what? If you're looking for me to drag any skeletons out of ModelMen's closet, don't bother. The Glicks always treated me fair, even when they canned me. I've got nothing bad to say against them. Like I told you, Mrs. Glick does tend to go a little overboard in favoring Gary, but that's probably natural. I think she still feels pretty guilty."

"Guilty?" I asked. "For what?"

"For dumping Gary when he was just a kid."

Dumping? I thought. And then I suddenly remembered that little raised-eyebrow smile Matt had given the first time we'd talked about Iris Glick showing Matt favoritism and the little light came on in my head! "Iris Glick is Gary's *mother*?" I said.

Matt just gave me a another raised-eyebrow look and took another swig of his beer.

"But why the charade?" I asked.

"Glick didn't want kids. His own or anybody else's."

"So he doesn't know?" I asked, incredulous.

"Why should he? Iris is 43; Gary is 29. Do the math." He looked at me for a moment and then said: "And if I were you, I wouldn't bring that particular subject up with *anybody*—and especially not Iris or Gary."

"How many other people know about this?" I asked.

He looked at me with a raised eyebrow. "No idea. I haven't told anybody anything," he said.

"Except me." I said.

He gave me an odd smile. "I didn't tell you squat," he said, and he was right. He hadn't come right out and told me anything. I got the impression that I wouldn't want to play poker with him.

"So," I said, deciding it was a good idea to move on to something else, "you met Gary while you were in the corps, I think you said."

Matt drained his beer and got up from his recliner, reaching out for my almost empty bottle. I quickly polished it off and handed it to him.

"That's what I said," he said as he went back into the kitchen. "Boot camp. A long time ago."

"Were you in four years?" I asked.

He came back into the room with two more beers and stood directly in front of me. He turned to one side to put both beers down on the table next to the couch, then grabbed my hand and pulled me abruptly to my feet.

"Let's cut the shit," Matt said. "You wanna get it on or not?"

No, Hardesty, you stupid shit, you don't, my mind yelled. *This guy could be a killer!*

Uh huh, my crotch answered as I watched Matt peel off his shirt.

* * *

On the drive home, my crotch was whistling a happy little tune while my mind was so pissed it wouldn't speak to me. And I had to admit, the mind was right. Why in hell do I do some of the things I do? What if Matt *was* the killer? Not only could I have ended up in a Dumpster somewhere, but that would mean I just had sex with the guy who had killed Billy—and Stuart Anderson, and that poor prostitute. But of course the odds were about...what's the population of the world? Five billion?...five billion to one against it.

And of course I hadn't learned nearly half of what I'd gone there to learn, though the revelation of Gary's being Iris's son and not her brother was worth the trip (not that the sex with Matt wasn't!). I realized in retrospect that Matt had played me like an accordion: hey, if you don't want to answer Hardesty's questions, just wave your dick in front of his face.

You're a stupid shit, Hardesty!

Well, mentally beating myself severely about the head and shoulders was an exercise in futility, so I forced myself back to the subject at hand: what I had found out. Other than the interest value of finding out Gary and Mrs. Glick's true relationship, I had no idea to what practical use that information could be put, or how it could possibly have any bearing on the case. But it raised a lot more questions as to the whole Glick family dynamics. That Mr. Glick apparently didn't know he had a stepson was interesting indeed. I wanted to know more about Iris Glick's background—and Gary's—but had no idea how to go about it, since I intended to follow Matt's advice and not mention it to anyone. But I made a mental note to arrange a little casual conversation with both Iris and Gary individually and then compare notes.

* * *

And then it was Saturday. I picked Phil up at 10 a.m. and we drove the 50 or so miles to Leeds, Billy's home town, in relative silence. We got there nearly an hour early, and stopped at a little diner just outside town for a cup of coffee neither of us really wanted or needed.

We got to the small yellow-brick church at about 20 minutes to noon. There were already several cars in the parking lot, including a new Lincoln Town Car and a silver Porsche I recognized as Gary's birthday present.

The church was small and simple and somehow comforting, as I assume all churches are supposed to be. Phil took me over to introduce me to Billy's mom and dad. Billy's mom hugged Phil warmly, and Billy's dad, though looking frail in his wheelchair, shook our hands firmly. I expressed my awkward but very sincere condolences, and Phil and I excused ourselves and went to a pew near the front.

The Glicks, in a typical act of extreme kindness, had sent Billy's folks a portfolio of all Billy's modeling work, which was displayed on a stand near the small urn containing Billy's ashes. It was open to two shots of a spectacularly beautiful Billy—one serious but calm, serene; the other with that big, sexy-sweet smile, eyes sparkling with fun, and life. I caught only a glimpse of them and had to turn away. Phil refused even to look. The Glicks themselves were in attendance as were all of the surviving escorts, who were presented to Billy's folks as—and were I suppose in fact—his friends from the agency.

I hate funerals, which is a truly stupid thing to say, I know. They're bad enough when the deceased had at least had a chance to live a complete life, but Billy.... And funerals always pry open doors within myself that I have worked very hard to keep closed and locked. I suppose it's a case of "ask not for whom the bell tolls..."

But the service was brief, and very dignified and I'm sure comforting to Billy's poor folks. The church's small choir—of which Billy had once been a member—sang "In the Garden" and "Amazing

Grace," and I sat next to Phil who, while outwardly composed, gripped my hand tightly throughout the entire service.

* * *

At the close of the service, the minister invited everyone to adjourn to the church basement where, in typical small-town tradition, coffee, cake and sandwiches were served by the church's Ladies' Auxiliary. It was a Norman Rockwell moment where the best of what makes us human was on display, and where there were no madmen and no Dumpsters.

* * *

As goodbyes were being exchanged in the parking lot, while Phil was talking with the Glicks, I managed to get a moment with Gary, telling him there were a few things I wanted to talk to him about, and asking him to give me a call when he had a chance.

On the drive back to town I invited Phil to spend the rest of the day with me—go to a movie, maybe, or just kick back, but he said he thought he'd rather just spend some time alone. I understood; I really didn't feel like doing anything myself. But I did suggest that we have brunch on Sunday, and he agreed.

"Tell you what," I said, "I think it's about time you started concentrating on you and the rest of your life. Why don't you call one of your friends and ask him to join us for brunch—give you a chance to start a little socializing outside ModelMen."

Phil gave me a very strange, somehow sad smile. "I don't have many friends," he said. "Billy was pretty much it—and you, of course. This business isn't the kind that lends itself to making friends, and I've been in it a long time. And there hasn't been much time lately for me to do anything other than work. Before that, when I was street hustling…well, you get friendly with some of the other hustlers, but the turnover is really high, and there's always too much competition going on. Probably sounds weird, but you're the first real friend I've had in years who wasn't in the business."

I just shook my head in disbelief. But I could see exactly what he was saying, and hard as it may be for me to comprehend, I was sure he was right.

"Well," I said, "You remember my friends Jared and Tim, from the parade? Maybe we could see if they'd like to join us for brunch. It'd be a start."

He looked at me and smiled. "Yeah, you're right...I've got to start meeting people outside the business. Both those guys seemed nice. Tim—he's the smaller one, right?" I nodded. "...he kind of reminds me of Billy, in a way."

I hadn't realized it before, but Phil was right. Tim and Billy didn't look anything alike, but they were about the same size and build, and both almost exuded an of devilish innocence.

"Well," I said quickly, "if that might be a problem..."

Phil gave a small wave of his hand. "Oh, no, no, not at all. I think it would be nice."

"Sure," I said, then had another quick thought: "They're really great guys. But...well, you know what Tim does for a living." I was thinking of the fact that Tim had performed the autopsy on Billy, and though I doubted Phil could know that, the thought undoubtedly occurred to him.

Phil smiled again. "Yeah, I know," he said. "But he struck me as someone I might like to get to know. We both have jobs that would turn a lot of people off."

"I'll give them a call," I said.

* * *

There were a couple calls on my machine at home: Bob Allen calling to say he and Mario were going out of town for a few days, Jared just checking in, and one from Tim, asking me to call. I didn't detect any particular note of urgency or any indication that he might have some more bad news, but I returned his call as soon as I'd deleted the messages.

"Hi, Tim, it's Dick," I said when he answered after the third ring.

"Like I didn't recognize the voice?" he asked, teasingly.

"I just got back from Billy's memorial service," I explained.

"Yeah," Tim said, "that's one of the reasons I called—just wanted to see how it went. How did your friend Phil take it?"

"It was a really nice service," I said, "and Phil did fine."

"I can't imagine how I'd have taken it," Tim said. "I only met them that once, but they seemed like a good team."

"Which," I said, "brings me to why I was going to call you even if you hadn't left a message. Phil and I are having brunch tomorrow and we were wondering if you might want to join us, if your busy social calendar will allow? Phil could really use some friends right about now."

"Sure," Tim said, then hesitated. "Uh, does Phil know what I do for a living?"

"Yeah, he knows," I said.

"And does he know I...ah...worked on Billy?"

"We didn't mention it," I said.

"Ok, great," Tim said. "I'll call in that rain check I took the last time you asked. Just let me know when and where."

"I'll do that," I said. Then, mildly irked at myself for being unable to resist dragging business into the conversation, I said: "Have you heard anything new about the murders?"

"Not much," Tim said. "The woman's body was claimed Friday by her ex husband; that's all I know."

And then I had another sudden wave of guilt for bringing up business. "Tim, I'm really sorry. It seems like I'm always pumping you for information."

"Not to worry," Tim said. "It's what you do. And I always enjoy a good pumping."

I laughed. "Yeah," I said. "I've read your reviews."

"So call me with the details for brunch."

"Okay. Talk to you in the morning. 'Bye."

The phone had barely fully touched down on the cradle when it rang, startling me. I picked it right back up. "Dick Hardesty."

"Dick, this is Gary. I just got back into town and wondered if you'd like to meet me for a drink. We can talk about whatever it is you wanted to know."

I glanced at my watch. It was still pretty early in the day for a drink, but I did want to talk with him. I thought momentarily about asking him over to my place—an idea my crotch seconded wholeheartedly—but realized that would not be a very good idea on several levels. I determined not to be distracted from my information gathering this time around.

"Sure," I said. "Now? And where did you have in mind?"

"I live fairly close to Venture," he said. "You want to meet there in about half an hour?"

"Okay," I said. "Just give me time to change clothes."

"That's just what I'm doing now," he said. "Take your time; I'll see you when you get there."

I made a quick call to Jared and left a message on his machine asking if he'd like to join Phil, Tim, and me for brunch and telling him to give me a call.

* * *

Gary was sitting at the bar when I walked in. Though it was still a long time until Happy Hour, there were more people there than I might have expected on an early Saturday afternoon. It had occurred to me, as I drove to the bar, that Mario, Bob Allen's new lover, was a bartender there, and if Gary was a regular at Venture, Mario might well know him. I'd have to check.

Gary turned around on his stool when I walked up beside him. "What are you drinking?" he asked, as he motioned to the bartender.

"Whiskey Old Fashioned, I guess," I said, and Gary passed that information on to the bartender, then handed him a bill when he brought the drink.

"Thanks," I said.

We talked for a few minutes about Billy's memorial and agreed that it had gone very well, and how hard it must have been on Billy's parents—he was their only child. I commented on how thoughtful it was of the Glicks to have given the portfolio of Billy's modeling work to his parents, and how much they must have appreciated it.

"Yeah," Gary said. "That's the Glicks for you—generous to a fault."

I wasn't quite sure how to take that. "Well," I said, "They've done pretty well by you. That was quite a birthday present."

Gary shrugged. "Yeah, I guess it was."

You guess? I thought. *I'll be happy to take it off your hands if it's a bother.* But all I said was:"It's nice to be so close to one of your family members. Have you and Mrs. Glick always been close?"

"Like peas in a pod," he said, and again I wasn't sure if there wasn't more than a little sarcasm in there. "I didn't see much of her there for a stretch," he continued, "but we hooked up again when she was working Vegas."

I noted the absence of the word "in" in that sentence.

"Where are you from originally?" I asked, hoping I didn't sound as though I were prying.

"Nebraska," Gary said. "Small farm town north of Lincoln. I was there until I joined the Marines, then went back for a year or two after, until I couldn't stand to hear one more cricket chirp. Bummed around for awhile, then found my way to Las Vegas"

"Ah," I said, half-teasing, "so you're a real farm boy."

He smiled and shook his head. "Not really. We lived in town. My grandpa had a gas station and bar there—we lived above the tavern."

"Must have been kind of tough making a living," I observed, taking the maraschino cherry off the little plastic pick and dangling it by its stem before eating it.

"You could say that," he replied, idly stirring the ice cubes around the rim of his glass with an index finger. "I helped my grandpa pumping gas, but if we filled up five or six cars a day, it was considered a big deal. The bar did okay, what with the locals not having too much else to do in what spare time they had, but with my grandparents taking turns running it, there wasn't too much I could do in there except sweep up and empty the garbage, stuff like that. I was too young to bartend, so one of my grandpa's cronies hired me to work part-time in his insurance office. Then when I graduated from high school, I joined the Marines."

"That's where you and Matt met, huh?"

He nodded, still looking into his glass, watching the ice cubes go around and around. "In boot camp. We got to be friends, then found out we had a…" he glanced up at me quickly, gave me a quick smile, then dropped his attention back to his glass "…a lot in common."

Like being bi? I wondered. But I got the impression I'd gone about as far as I could go for the moment without making it obvious I was prying. I'd already been able to figure out a few things by reading between his sentences. No mention of a mother or father—just grandparents. Referring to a "stretch" where he didn't see Iris. I wondered just how long a stretch it had been and how they had managed to reconnect after all that time, but couldn't really press him on it. And I wanted to know more about him and Matt—a lot more.

"It's nice to have good friends," I said, sincerely, "especially those who'll hang in there with you over the years. None of my business, but were you and Matt ever...well, more than friends?"

A slow smile crept over his face before he brought those fantastic sea-green eyes up to meet mine. "You could say that," he said.

Oh, what the hell: I couldn't resist. "I have to admit," I said, "I could have guessed Matt was bi, but you caught me kind of by surprise."

"So you think Matt's bi, huh?" Gary said.

I immediately felt more than a little stupid. "Well," I said, "him having kids and being that butch...." I decided I'd better stop before I made a complete idiot of myself.

"Let me tell you a little story about...a guy I know," Gary said. "This guy's old man was a psycho sonofabitch who was bound and determined *his* son was going to be a *real man* if it killed him. The kid always knew he was gay but he also knew without a question that his old man was enough of a psycho that he would, literally, kill him if he found out. So he did his best to be what his old man wanted. He made himself into a real jock—captain of the football team, that sort of shit. Then one night after a game during senior year, the team had a beer party at the kid's place—the kid's old man supplied the booze—and a bunch of his teammates set him up with the school's head cheerleader and resident slut. He couldn't get out of it, and he was just drunk enough to decide to try it. She got pregnant, but it was him who got screwed. He says it was the first time in his life that his old man was actually proud of him. The girl's parents demanded that he do 'the right thing' by their little girl, so they had a shotgun wedding. Blew his chances for a college football scholarship out of the water, of course, and he was so miserable he joined the Marines just to get away. But if that's what you think 'bi' is, I suppose you could call the guy 'bi'."

'Wow,' I thought. 'Maybe I should see if the local community college offers a course in Bisexuality 101.'

"And you?" I asked, knowing full well he hadn't been talking about himself.

He smiled again. "Me? Well, guys really turn me on, as you may have noticed. But so do women, and to the same degree. I guess you could say I'm an equal opportunity fucker." He gave me a big grin. "Hope that doesn't gross you out."

"Hell, no," I said. Actually, though I hated to admit it, he was within walking distance. I tried making a mental picture of an illustrated dictionary. Under "Butch" there was a picture of Matt; under "Gay" a picture of me, and under "Bi" a picture of Gary. Didn't really help.

Definitely time for a subject change.

"I understand you and Matt don't see much of each other anymore."

Gary shrugged. "Things change," he said.

I noticed both our glasses were nearly empty, and signaled the bartender for two more.

"So how about you?" Gary asked, apparently also wanting to do a little subject changing. "What's your life story?"

I gave him the Reader's Digest version, starting with my humble beginnings in a log cabin on the frontier up to my deciding to become a private investigator. I always find it kind of hard to talk about myself—I don't find me all that interesting.

When I thought I noticed his eyes beginning to glaze over, I wrapped it up.

"You caught many murderers?" he asked

That one sort of took me by surprise. "I don't know if 'caught' is exactly the right word," I said honestly, "but I've run into a couple, yeah."

"Interesting job," he said.

"So's yours," I observed.

"And you think the guy who killed Billy and those others is a bisexual?" he asked casually in a classic non-sequitur that somehow threw me a little off balance.

"It's crossed my mind," I said.

"And you think there's a link to ModelMen," he said, rather than asked. I didn't like where this was headed.

"I'm not sure on that one," I said, more truthfully than not. "That

Billy and Stuart Anderson had ties to ModelMen could just be a weird coincidence. The prostitute...well, that's a whole other story."

Gary had been watching me as I had earlier been watching him. "Well," he said, "if you think the killer is bisexual, and you think there's a link to ModelMen, that sort of narrows the field of suspects, doesn't it? Let's see...there's Steve and oh, yeah: me."

Now I was definitely uncomfortable. "I don't know enough to think anything yet," I said, hoping I sounded convincing.

Gary smiled and nodded. "When you do think," he said, more teasing than sarcastic, "you might keep something in mind."

"Which is?" I asked.

"Which is that the term 'bisexual' covers a whole lot wider a spectrum than most people realize. There are a lot more closet bi's than there are open ones. I wouldn't worry so much about the ones who aren't ashamed to admit it—it's the other ones I'd keep an eye out for."

He had a point, and despite the fact that that little observation opened the door back up to just about everybody except me, I allowed myself to relax a little. Which, of course allowed me once again to push aside the obvious fact that Gary might very well be a suspect, and let my crotch get its hopes up. The conversation had discombobulated me to the point where I had enough will power to keep from asking him if he wanted to go home with me, but I knew that if he'd suggested it, my nether regions would once again win out over my upper.

Fortunately, I didn't have to worry. Gary looked at his watch and said: "Ah, I'd better get going. Iris called right after I talked to you and asked me over for dinner. I was kind of hoping maybe you and I could...well, talk some more maybe at my place, but Iris's invitations are more like summonses and I'd told her I'd come. Can we get together again sometime? Maybe somewhere a little less crowded?" Considering there were maybe 8 people in the whole bar, I think I got the message.

Yeah! Yeah! my crotch said eagerly. "Sure," I said. "I'll look forward to it."

* * *

I stopped at the grocery store on my way home and splurged on a thick T-bone steak, a huge baking potato, and a carton of sour cream. If it was going to be a night at home, it might as well be a self-indulgent one.

Jared had returned my call to say that the Male Call was hosting a bike run Sunday, so he'd have to pass on brunch. Jared in full leather on a Harley—I quickly tucked that mental picture in my Future Erotic Fantasies file.

I made brunch reservations at Rasputin's—which was about equidistant for all three of us—for 12:45, then called both Tim and Phil to tell them.

I did my best to keep my mind off the case, but of course it didn't work. I was particularly bothered by this whole bisexual thing, for some reason—and I think it was because it made me realize that I wasn't as open minded and nonjudgmental as I'd always pictured myself as being. Finding out you're not exactly who you've always thought you were is unnerving.

And I found myself back with my jigsaw puzzle analogy. There were little bits and pieces of the case that I knew fit together somehow, though not only did I not know how, but I wasn't exactly sure which pieces they were. That the background of the entire puzzle was ModelMen, I was fairly certain. But I had the gut feeling that there was a lot more to the puzzle than the pieces already laid out indicated.

While I wasn't exactly an expert on murderers, the one thing I did know was that most of them were not stupid, and that very often what appears to be obvious at first glance turns out to be totally wrong on closer examination. And killers were also not above a little calculated misdirection. So since everything in this case pointed to the fact of the killer being bisexual, maybe that meant he wasn't.

'Oh, now that's a big help!' my mind said, scornfully. 'And maybe because you're sure ModelMen is involved, that means it isn't! You're custodial, Hardesty!'

* * *

Have I mentioned that I like brunch? I realized yet again, as Phil and Tim and I sat at the bar waiting for our table, that brunch was one of the few times when I always seemed to be able to step away from whatever case I was working on and just relax. Tim was being his usual effervescent self and I never ceased to be amazed at how someone with such a…well, gruesome…job could put it so completely aside when he wasn't working. I wished I could be a lot more like Tim in that regard. And Phil, too, seemed to be more relaxed than I'd seen him since Billy's death.

But even when I'm relaxed and having a good time, I manage to pick up on things, and I detected an uncharacteristic…well, shyness…between Tim and Phil. Shy is certainly not a word I could accurately use to describe either one of them under normal circumstances, but I sensed it nonetheless. I took it to mean they were mutually impressed with one another, and I couldn't have been happier. Maybe, if this P.i. thing didn't work out, I could open a practice as a matchmaker.

As soon as we were seated and had our orders taken, Tim excused himself to go to the bathroom. I took the opportunity of his absence to pull up one of the mental notes I'd made at the Glicks'. "So I understand you know Glen O'Banyon," I said, hoping it sounded like a casual remark.

Phil cocked his head and gave me a strange look. "Yeah," he said. "A really nice guy."

'Well, that got us absolutely nowhere, Hardesty,' my mind said. 'Just spit it out, for chrissakes.'

"You were with Glen the night Stuart Anderson…died, weren't you?" I tried, again, to make it more statement than a question.

Phil nodded. "You don't miss much, do you?" he asked with a smile. "Yeah, I've seen Glen a couple of times," he said. "But only that one night as a client. He took me out to dinner one night after that, but strictly as a one-on-one, not as an escort, and there wasn't any sex involved. Neither one of us would even think of breaking the Glicks' rules, and I cleared it with them first, of course."

Tim returned from the restroom and sat down, carefully removing his napkin from the table and arranging it in his lap. "Remind me next time we come here to bring my electric drill," he said.

Phil looked at him, head cocked in an unasked question. Tim grinned at him: "It's a great place for a glory hole, but they've got metal partitions between the stalls. I think I'll complain to the management."

"You've been spending too much time in the bus station," I observed, and both Phil and Tim laughed.

After brunch, we took my car and drove out to Jessup Reservoir, about 20 miles outside of town, and spent the remainder of the afternoon walking the forested trails along the shore, just talking and having a really great time. The subject of Tim's work...or Phil's...never came up.

But on the way back to town Tim, who was sitting in the back seat, leaned forward and said: "Would you guys like to come over to my place for dinner? I pride myself on my ability to call out for pizza or Chinese."

Phil sighed. "Hey, I'd love to, Tim," he said...and I got the feeling he really meant it... "but I've got...an appointment at 8:00. Can I have a rain check?"

I could almost hear Tim's mind saying: *Oh, yeah!* but he said, simply: "Sure. How about you, Dick?"

"Tim," I said, "your ability to call out for Chinese food is legendary! How could I refuse?"

I dropped Tim and Phil off near their cars and waved 'so long' to Phil; I waited while Tim pulled out of his parking space and followed him to his apartment.

* * *

"Phil's really a nice guy, isn't he?" Tim asked casually as we stood in front of his door while he rosaried his key chain looking for the right one.

"That he is," I said. "It appeared he thinks the same thing about you."

Tim shot me a quick look out of the corner of his eye as inserted the proper key into the lock, turned it, and opened the door. "Think so?" he asked.

"Yep." We both smiled.

* * *

Dos Equis beer, sweet & sour shrimp, snow peas and water chestnuts, and mounds of white rice soaked in soy sauce. They don't make gourmet meals any better. Tim and I sat cross-legged on the floor in front of his coffee table, eating and talking and laughing. No ModelMen, no murders. All in all, a damned nice day.

And when Tim, ever the gentleman, invited me to a little impromptu overnight pajama party (sans pajamas), it was a damned nice night, too.

CHAPTER 11

I was a little late getting to the office Monday morning, having needed to run home from Tim's to change clothes. There was a message waiting for me from Lieutenant Richman. Short and simple: "Captain Offermann and I would like to see you as soon as you can get here." Period.

Not good.

I didn't even take the time to drink my coffee; just put the lid back on and carried it out the door with me.

I was about halfway to the City Building Annex when I realized I didn't know where Captain Offermann's office was and whether Lieutenant Richman would be there or in his own office. I really didn't want to just walk in on Captain Offermann myself: I still didn't feel totally comfortable around him.

I checked on the office roster by the elevators to find Captain Offermann was on the 18th floor, so when I got on the elevator, I punched the button for Lieutenant Richman's floor first, hoping he might be in his office. If he wasn't, I'd go on up to Offermann's and take my chances.

I knocked on Richman's door, and there was no response. Opening the door, I looked in to find the office empty. Sighing, I closed the door and returned to the elevator.

I was duly impressed to find that Captain Offermann's office had a small anti-room complete with a secretary; a lady of a certain age with hair so jet black it had to have been dyed, and flaming red lipstick. I announced myself and she picked up a phone to let Offermann know I'd arrived.

"You can go right in," she said without a smile (apparently public servants are not required to smile if they don't feel like it), nodding to the only other door in the room. Taking a deep breath, I rapped once with my knuckle, then opened the door and entered.

Offermann, all Teutonic 6-foot-something of him, got up from his desk and extended his hand, which I walked across the room to take. I don't know why, but every time I looked at that man I kept hearing *Deutschland Uber Alles* in the back of my head. No sign of Richman, I was sorry to notice.

Offermann gestured me to a seat and said: "Lieutenant Richman will be here shortly." Luckily, he'd no sooner said it and sat down himself when there was another rap on the door and Richman entered, carrying a manila envelope which he handed to Captain Offermann before taking the seat opposite me. He hadn't even acknowledged my presence. Definitely not good. Offermann opened the envelope, removed a photograph, looked at it a moment, then slid it across the desk toward me. I leaned forward to take it, though I already knew what it was—a ModelMen head shot of Phil.

"Would you care to explain?" Offermann asked.

"I'm sorry?" I said. "Explain what?"

"The man in the photo."

"It's Ph…Mr. Stark," I said, hoping I looked puzzled. I wasn't.

"We showed this photo to several people at the Montero," Richman said. "They identified Mr. Stark as the man seen frequently in the company of Stuart Anderson. Stuart Anderson was your client. Mr. Stark is your friend. Stuart Anderson is dead."

"Have you talked with Mr. Stark about this?" I asked.

"We're interviewing him now," Richman said. "I noticed that Mr. Stark is a pretty big guy, and I'd wager his feet are considerably larger than Anderson's."

'Shit! The guy seen leaving the garage!' I was the one who mentioned to Richman that the guy had been wearing regular shoes, and speculated it was because his feet were probably larger than Anderson's. I didn't panic, because I knew Phil's alibi was ironclad. But I didn't want to let Richman and Offermann know I knew it.

"I'm sorry, gentlemen," I said, "but I really don't know where this is going."

Offermann sat back in his chair, his elbows on the arms, his hands about six inches in front of his face, fingertips touching. "Mr. Steiner and Mr. Stark were…roommates. You were an acquaintance if not a friend of Mr. Steiner. Mr. Steiner is dead. Mr. Anderson is dead."

"Did you know Mr. Stark had been seeing Stuart Anderson?" Richman asked.

"Yes," I admitted. "I told you Anderson had told me when he first came to my office that he had been referred by a business acquaintance but that he never said who it was. That's true. I only found out it was Phil...Mr. Stark...later."

"And just what sort of 'business' is Mr. Stark in?" Offermann asked.

Walking on eggshells time! I thought. "As you already know, he's a professional model," I said truthfully if evasively.

"And did you know he is also a male prostitute?" Offermann asked.

Care-ful, Hardesty. Care-ful. "I knew he had been a hustler, yes," I said. "That's how we met, actually."

"So you frequent male prostitutes, do you, Mr. Hardesty?" Offermann asked.

"No, I do not," I said, trying not to sound defensive. "I have never paid another man for sex. Phil and I met in a bar frequented by hustlers, near my office ..."

"Hughie's," Richman said in a quick aside to Offermann, yet again impressing me with just how sharp he was.

"...but I have never given him money," I continued honestly, "nor has he ever asked me for any. We became friends, although we hadn't seen one another for some time before Anderson showed up. In that time, Phil had managed to find a very legitimate and I imagine good paying job as a model. He's gone far beyond the stage of having to hustle tricks in order to pay his rent. I don't think it inconceivable that his relationship with Mr. Anderson was based on friendship, and I can't imagine that either of you gentlemen would hold his past against him. I know that when I had dinner with the two of them, they seemed genuinely comfortable and friendly with one another. If their relationship went beyond that, I would consider that was their business."

Oops! I thought. *Crossed the line a little bit on that one. Hope they don't catch it!*

As always when we were together, I was very much aware that Richman never took his eyes off me.

Offermann's smile was not exactly what I would consider warm. "An interesting story," he said. "But I fear the line of coincidence can only be stretched so far. What of Mr. Steiner's murder, and the fact that he and Mr. Stark were...roommates?"

He did it again: that damned pause before "roommates" as though he didn't believe it for a minute.

"Gentlemen," I said, "I would be willing to stake my life on the fact that Phil's having known Stuart Anderson has absolutely no relationship whatsoever to his being roommates with and best friend to Billy Steiner, or with Billy's death. And while I agree that coincidences do make weak alibis, let me ask *you* how you can possibly relate the most recent death of the woman to the first two deaths? I certainly can't." Richman had never officially told me about the knife, after all.

Neither Offermann nor Richman said anything for a full minute, until Offermann said: "Very well; you can go...for now. But be aware that we will be keeping a very close eye on you for your own protection. You do seem to have a penchant for becoming very directly involved with murderers."

'Whatever in hell that meant,' I thought. But I got up from my chair, followed by both Offermann and Richman, and shook hands with them both. I'd just about made it to the door when Richman said: "Just a minute, Dick—I'll ride down with you on the elevator."

I stepped into the hall, leaving the door open behind me, and heard a few muffled exchanges between the two officers, then Richman emerged and closed the door. We walked in silence to the elevators, and as the door opened, he said: "Let's stop by my office for a minute, okay?"

"Sure," I said. 'Part One of Interrogation completed; Part Two Beginning,' I thought.

Again silence until we entered Richman's office and he closed the door, motioning me to a seat. He walked around behind his desk and sat down.

"Okay," he said. "You want to tell me what's going on?" I opened my mouth to speak, but he cut me off. "I've gone way out on a limb for you more than once," he said, "but I've played a few games of dodge-ball in my day, and I know it when I see it. Do you think I don't know about your contact in the coroner's office? You know damned well that the knife stolen from Anderson's room was used to kill Laurie Travers. That was either one of the stupidest moves ever made or the killer damned well wanted us to know the killings are linked. Captain Offermann is no dummy, either, and you can be damned sure that if we'd have caught you in one outright lie up there, your ass would be in a cell right now. Now we can either talk, or you can get the hell out of my office."

Hey, he had a right to be pissed.

"You're right, Lieutenant," I started. "I know you've been a lot more supportive than just about anybody else in the department would have been, and maybe that's part of it. I trust you, but I'm not too sure where Captain Offermann stands. I know you've got a job to do, and a damned important one. But I've got a job to do, too. Now I'm going to go out on a limb with *you* and hope to God I'm doing the right thing."

I told him about ModelMen's escort branch, and the Glicks, their having hired me to protect ModelMen's interests, and their sincere concern for what was happening—and that the Glicks weren't a couple of sleezebag pimps taking advantage of either their clients or their escorts. I admitted to playing the semantics game occasionally, but that as an employee of ModelMen, Phil was not technically a hustler. And I told him again, and truthfully, that I wasn't sure yet what the murder of the prostitute meant in the overall scheme of the case, but that I sincerely hoped to find out.

"Now again," I pointed out, "no one can stop you from having the department step right in and take over the whole case, starting from scratch, or we can continue to work parallel. You know as well as I that if I'd mentioned ModelMen and its escort branch immediately, some of your colleagues would have turned it into a circus: finding the murderer would take poor second to rooting out which rich married men are paying other men for sex. The Glicks have promised me that they and the escorts will cooperate fully in exchange for not having to reveal the names of their clients. What possible good could come from ruining the reputations of a lot of decent men whose only crime is in perhaps not being 100 percent heterosexual?"

Richman just sat there staring at me, as though he were carved in stone. After a good 60 seconds of silence, he said: "I don't know if I can do that. I'm not in the homicide division, as you know."

"Yes, but Captain Offermann obviously listens to you and trusts your judgment. So can you try?" I asked. "All my clients and I want is for the police to not go charging into matters which do not directly relate to the case. By all means, interview the Glicks and the escorts. If your investigation of the prost…of Laurie Travers'… death leads you back to ModelMen, so be it. And if anything I find out from anyone associated with ModelMen should lead to her, I give you my word I'll tell you immediately. What do you have to lose?"

I stopped talking and I swear it seemed so quiet I could have heard a mouse sneeze. The silence was finally broken by the ringing of the phone on Richman's desk. He picked it up, still staring at me, and said "Lieutenant Richman." Silence, still staring, then: "Thank you," and he replaced the receiver into its cradle.

He sat back in his chair. "Glen O'Banyon, huh?" he said.

I wasn't exactly sure whether he was referring to Phil's alibi or the sudden linkage of the case to one of the most powerful lawyers in the city, but I nodded in either case.

"I'll talk to the Captain," he said. "But no guarantees."

"That's all I can ask for," I said. "And again, thank you." There was another long silence until I said: "Can I go now?"

Richman slowly nodded his head, and I got up from my chair and reached across his desk to shake hands. Neither of us said another word, and I turned and left.

* * *

From a corner phone booth, I called Glen O'Banyon's office. His secretary, Donna, said he was in court but was expected back within the hour. I asked her to please have him call me the minute he got in. Back in the office, I made a couple quick calls—first to Phil (no answer; I couldn't imagine the police would still be questioning him, but…), then to the Glicks' home, (Johnnie-Mae said they were both at the office), and finally to ModelMen's office, where I managed to speak to Mr. Glick and fill him in, briefly, on my meeting with Richman and Offermann. I suggested they prepare the escorts.

Then I just plopped down in my chair and waited for O'Banyon's call.

While I waited, I went mental fishing, trying to hook those elusive thoughts that kept darting back and forth beneath the surface of my consciousness. The police knew nothing, as far as I could tell, about Matt Rushmore, but there was only an outside chance that it wouldn't come up at some point. I had to find out more about him and his relationship with Gary, and Gary's relationship with Iris. I'd gotten some very strange signals from Gary on that latter score, and wondered whether the relationship were quite as rosy as it outwardly appeared. It struck me that someone whose mother had abandoned him as a child might well hold considerable resentment against her.

Sometimes thinking too much is self-defeating. There are just too many thoughts, too many questions…and too few answers. It boiled down to two extremely obvious—well, obvious to me at any rate—conclusions: either Anderson's and Billy's deaths were coincidental to their links to ModelMen and the death of Laurie Travers meant the killer was a faceless, unknown and unknowable psycho, or Laurie Travers' death was, somehow, tied in to ModelMen. If that were the case, it was pretty obvious—maybe too obvious—that the killer was bisexual. And since Gary was openly bi, that pointed directly to him. Once again, that damned trout in the milk.

Now, Gary didn't strike me as being particularly stupid: he could see the bisexual implications of the murders as clearly as anyone. So why would he go out of his way to tell me that Matt, the other "obvious" bisexual, and therefore the other obvious suspect, wasn't really bisexual? I mean, if I were Gary and I was the killer, I'd be pulling other bisexuals out of the woodwork to get the focus off myself. He did make that comment about 'It's the ones you don't know you should worry about.'

Aaron? Just because he's butch? Does that mean somewhere in the back of my mind I equate being butch with being bisexual? Lavender isn't exactly my favorite color either, but I know I'm sure as hell not bi. How about Steve? That thing about his wife not letting him screw around with other women was hardly enough to rule him out.

'Give it a rest, Hardesty,' I thought.

Luckily for me, the phone rang before I decided I was definitely in the wrong profession.

"Hardesty Investigations."

"Dick, it's Glen. Sorry I didn't call you the minute I got back to the office, but I had to give priority to a call from Captain Offermann."

"Everything okay, then, with Phil?" I asked. "I tried calling him when I got back from a meeting with Richman and Offermann, but he wasn't home yet."

"I know," O'Banyon said. "Apparently they were waiting for my verification of Phil's alibi before they released him. He should be home now."

I breathed a small sigh of relief. "Good," I said. I filled him in on my meeting with Offermann and then Richman, and told him I'd called the Glicks to prepare them.

"I appreciate that," he said. "They're next on my call list. I told Captain Offermann that I wanted to be present when the Glicks are questioned. I've been in trial all week, but fortunately it wrapped up this morning." There was a pause, and then: "And have you found out anything more about these killings?"

It was my turn for a pause. "Nothing at all solid, I'm afraid," I said truthfully. "Lots and lots of ideas and hunches and loose ends that are driving me crazy, though. Par for the course."

"Well, maybe we could get together for dinner some night, and you could bounce them off me."

"Thanks...I appreciate that," I said.

* * *

Eggshell walking is for the graceful; for the light of foot. I, alas, am neither. I had early in life given up any idea of seeking a career in the diplomatic corps, realizing I could probably quite easily manage to bring us into a war with Canada. So how to do what had to be done? How to ask Matt and Gary: "Hey, did either of you two guys happen to murder three people?" Or to ask Iris Glick: "So after you dumped your kid and took off, how are you two getting along?"

Well, I'd tiptoed around the subject with both Gary and Matt at one time or another. I'd never really had the chance to talk with

Mrs. Glick about her past and what, really, she knew about her little boy. I decided to start there.

I first called Phil to see how his interrogation had gone. Sure enough, the minute they found out Glen O'Banyon was his alibi for the night of Anderson's murder, they took on a different tone. When they asked, a little hesitantly, if O'Banyon had paid him for sex, Phil did a little tapdancing of his own—he told them "no", which was technically true since all financial transactions were handled through ModelMen. Glen O'Banyon's reputation as a top-flight lawyer overpowered even the fact of his being a fag. And, of course, they made it clear that even though Phil had an airtight alibi for the time of Anderson's murder, he still wasn't out of the running when it came to Billy's death, or for some totally inexplicable reason, Laurie Travers'.

With mild trepidation, I dialed the Glicks' and asked Johnnie-Mae if Mrs. Glick was by chance home yet.

"Why, yes, she is, Mr. Hardesty. She just came in. Just one moment, and I'll get her for you."

There was a moment of silence, and then Mrs. Glick's voice: "Mr. Hardesty…what can I do for you?"

"I was wondering if you'd been contacted by the police yet?" I asked, though that wasn't the real reason for the call, of course.

"My husband and I are meeting Mr. O'Banyon at police headquarters at 9:30 tomorrow."

"Ah." *Ah? That's all you can say: 'Ah?' Get on with it, stupid!* "I was wondering if it would be possible for you to talk with me privately for a few minutes between now and then."

"Privately?" her voice reflected just the slightest note of suspicion. "I…I suppose so, yes, of course. Mr. Glick has some business to attend to this afternoon, so if you'd like to come by now, we could have time for a brief chat."

"I'd really appreciate that, Mrs. Glick," I said. "I'll come right over, if that's convenient."

"Yes. Of course. I'll see you shortly, then."

We exchanged goodbyes and hung up. The fact that she hadn't asked the purpose of the meeting made me think perhaps she already knew it.

* * *

Johnnie-Mae greeted me at the door and showed me into the vast living room which I had only briefly glimpsed in my previous visits. Mrs. Glick was standing with her back to me, near one of the large French doors that opened on to a large terrace. Exactly what she was doing there, other than to recreate a scene from dozens of Hollywood movies, I had no idea. She turned as I entered the room and came over to greet me and usher me to one of two cream-colored settees flanking a fireplace large enough to roast an ox. The settees were so far apart that each had its own matching coffee table, and I was concerned that if she were to sit opposite me, we'd have to use semaphores to communicate. Instead, she joined me on the one facing the terrace doors.

She turned slightly toward me and smiled—did I detect just a touch of sadness in it?—and said: "And how can I help you, Mr. Hardesty?"

I took a mental deep breath and dove in. "I hope you'll excuse me if what I'm about to say intrudes upon your privacy, but there is certain information I really need, and you are the only one who can supply it."

She reached out and touched my hand, as if in sympathy. "I understand," she said. I suspected again she knew exactly where my part of this conversation was going. But before I had a chance to continue, Johnnie-Mae entered the room with a sterling silver tray upon which was a sterling silver coffee server, a matching creamer and sugar bowl, and two cups and saucers so fragile-looking they were almost transparent. She set the tray on the table in front of us, smiled, and turned and left without a word.

"Please, continue," Mrs. Glick said, leaning forward to pour our coffee.

I waited for a moment, watching her graceful pouring ritual and gathering my thoughts, then said: "I need to know more about Gary—specifically about his relationship with Matt and his relationship with you."

Without turning her head, her eyes darted to mine, then went back to the coffee server, which she carefully replaced on the tray.

"Gary's my son, you know," she said, handing me a cup and

saucer, her eyes on mine.

'Well, that certainly cut to the chase,' I thought. "Yes, I know," I said. I wondered how she knew I knew.

"I was sure you did," she said, "and therefore thought I'd spare you the possible embarrassment of having to ask."

She took a sip from her coffee, set the cup carefully on the saucer, and moved back slightly on the settee. "I was thirteen," she said, shaking her head slightly as if she couldn't quite believe it herself. "Thirteen. Gary's father was a roustabout in a carnival that played our local county fair. I never saw him again, of course, and never even knew his last name. There was never a question about abortion. What I'd done was scandalous enough; an abortion would have been unthinkable. And of course everyone in town knew. I'm rather surprised now, looking back, that I wasn't required to wear a scarlet 'A' on my clothes.

"To say that life was difficult for me is an understatement. A thirteen year old girl with a baby, in a small town in Nebraska, in those days! My parents never again looked me directly in the eye. I stood it as long as I could…until I was sixteen. I got a job as a waitress at a truck stop on the interstate about five miles south of town, and one day I just asked one of the truckers for a ride, and that was that. I couldn't take Gary. I knew my parents would look after him, and that he'd be much better off with them."

We both drank our coffee in silence for a moment. I sensed it wasn't necessary for me to say anything, and that she'd get on with her story in due time.

Finally, setting her cup and saucer on the tray, she again settled back on the settee and continued: "I was sixteen, pretty, and though I'd never finished high school, I was not stupid. I ended up in Las Vegas where I lied about my age and got a job in a casino. I worked hard, saved my money, took a correspondence course to get my high school diploma, then started taking courses at CCSN…" She gestured toward my still-half-full coffee cup. "More coffee?"

"No, thanks," I said, not wanting to distract her.

She gave a fleeting little smile, then continued her story.

"Then a little more than three years ago, there was a knock at my door." She paused, and her voice quivered ever so slightly as she said "and I opened it to see this absolutely beautiful young man standing there. I had no idea who he was, until he said, 'I'm Gary.'" She quickly looked away, then turned her head slightly and wiped at her eyes quickly with one hand.

"How had he found you?" I asked, not because I didn't think she was going to tell me, but just to give her a moment to compose herself.

She took a long, slow inhale, squared her shoulders almost imperceptibly, and took up her story: "One of the truckers I'd known when I worked at the truck stop had happened to see me in a show I was doing—actually, by that time I was pretty much out of the show scene, but had been filling in as a last-minute replacement for one of the girls who'd gotten ill. Anyway, how he ever managed to recognize me out of those dozens of other girls on stage I have no idea. But when he passed through Nebraska, he told everyone at the truck stop, and somehow the word got to Gary, and he came looking for me."

"You'd not been in contact in all those years?" I asked.

She shook her head. "No. Not once. There wasn't a day I didn't think about him, and wonder how he was and what he was doing, but I figured I had hurt him enough by leaving. I didn't want to remind him of it. And I'd managed to almost convince myself that maybe he didn't remember me, or didn't care. But here he was. He had no job, so I insisted he move in with me. I'd started an informal school for showgirls and others who wanted to improve themselves and their social skills. Gary began telling people we were brother and sister rather than try to explain our closeness in age. I got him a job selling insurance with a…friend…who was an executive at an insurance company—Gary had worked in insurance back home both before and after he got out of the service. He'd become one of their top salesmen."

Given Gary's looks and personality, that was hardly surprising.

"And when did you meet Mr. Glick?" I asked

She poured herself another cup of coffee, and I let her warm mine up before she continued.

"It was shortly after Gary arrived."

"And when did Matt enter the picture?" I asked.

"It was just about the time Gary took the job with the insurance company. He and Gary had kept in close contact since their Marine days, but it was within a month or two after I met Mr. Glick that Matt came to Las Vegas. He and Gary shared an apartment."

I wasn't quite sure how to ask the next question, but decided to just ask it. "Is that when you found out that Gary was bisexual?"

She took a long sip of her coffee and replaced it on the saucer before replying. "No—that was when I met Mr. Glick," she said.

Well of course! I thought. Pieces were falling into place with the velocity and impact of very large hailstones. *I'll bet anything that Gary hustled Glick! And then, when he found out Glick was both rich and bi, he introduced him to his 'sister'!! Jeezus!*

But where did Matt fit in to all this?

Patience, Hardesty, patience!

"Did Gary's being bisexual surprise you?"

She gave me an enigmatic Mona Lisa smile and shook her head. "Not at all. Oh, a bit at first, perhaps, but only because he was sleeping with just about every chorus girl on the strip. It just hadn't occurred to me that he might also be sleeping with the chorus boys, too."

Well, that little corner of the puzzle was fairly well filled in. Now to Matt.

"So then Matt showed up," I prompted.

"Yes. My apartment wasn't big enough for three, so Gary and Matt got a place together. It was quite obvious that they were…very devoted to one another."

"What sort of work did Matt do?" I asked.

"He got a job in security at one of the more…rowdy…off-the-strip clubs."

"He was a bouncer, then," I said. She nodded.

"You mentioned that they were…very devoted to one another. You mean you thought they were lovers?"

Mrs. Glick looked at me for a moment, as though she'd expected the question but still didn't know quite how to respond to it.

"I don't…I don't really know. Neither Gary nor Matt ever brought it up, so all I have are assumptions. I did sense a…bonding…that seemed very strong. Matt and Gary are very much alike in many ways; but I always had the impression that Matt…well…almost idolized Gary. I know that sounds very strange considering that they both are strong, confident, very…well, masculine...and don't express their inner feelings too openly. But I'm quite good at sensing things in people, and I also sensed that, while he never said anything, Matt felt a little stronger about the relationship than Gary did."

I took the last by-now-cool sip of coffee, shook my head again when she gestured toward the coffee pot, and set the cup and saucer on the coffee table.

"How so?" I asked, leaning back into the settee.

Mrs. Glick repeated my motion with her own cup and saucer, looking at them rather than me as she said: "I really don't know how to put it. Gary, for example, is Gary, through and through. But somehow I always had the feeling that's not the case with Matt. He's strong and secure on the outside, but I feel that deep inside he's quite another person. He uses his exterior as more a protective shell of some sort—protecting him from what I have no idea. And of course, it's easy to understand how Matt could become so attached to Gary: he's a natural born leader."

She turned toward me again, and looked me steadily in the eye. "I do assume, Mr. Hardesty, that our conversation will remain private between us, and that Mr. Glick need know nothing...of what we've discussed."

I nodded. "Of course," I said. "And I have only one more question. Again, I apologize for my bluntness, but I am rather curious as to why you never told your husband about your true relationship to Gary."

She sighed heavily, then shook her head slowly. "It's easier to tell a lie than untell it," she said. "Gary had...met...Mr. Glick, whose wife had recently died, and thought that it might help him get over his grief if he were to meet someone new. Mr. Glick, incidentally, was completely open with me about his sexual orientation, but assured me that he preferred the...stability...of a heterosexual marriage. Gary introduced me to him as his sister. Later I learned that Mr. Glick's first wife had been unable to have children, and he mentioned to me that he did not want any at this point in his life. So I never told him Gary was my son. We've never really discussed it since."

"And how soon after you left Las Vegas and moved here did Gary—and Matt—follow?"

She thought a moment before answering. "Almost immediately. Gary said that now that we'd found one another, he didn't want us to be that far apart again."

'Uh huh,' I thought. Something told me there might be a bit more to it than that.

"And did Gary continue selling insurance?" I asked.

Mrs. Glick shook her head. "Well, he is still getting commissions on his policy sales from Las Vegas; my husband was instrumental in introducing Gary to many of his wealthy friends, and it was shortly after we arrived here that the idea for ModelMen was formed, so he never felt the need to go back to it. With his modeling and the escort service, he does quite well."

I thought it was about time for me to leave, but as I started to get up, I had one of my little intimations-of-stupidity thoughts. *Jeez, you're stupid, Hardesty.*

"You know, Mrs. Glick," I said, "it suddenly occurred to me that I don't even know Gary's last name—or the last names of any of the other escorts for that matter, other than Phil's. I've never really had a need to know, but it might come in handy at some point—and so would their phone numbers, while I'm thinking of it."

She smiled. "Gary's last name is Bancroft—my maiden name; Aaron's is Aimsley; Steve's is Thomas, and Mark's is Neese. I have their phone numbers in the den."

"That's fine," I said. "I really should be leaving anyway."

We both got up and I followed her from the living room, across the foyer, and into the study. She moved quickly to the desk, opened a top drawer, and extracted a leather-bound address book. It was clear from her actions that she was super-efficient, probably a very shrewd business-woman.

When she'd finished, she smoothly closed and returned the address book to its drawer, neatly folded the page of names and addresses in half, creased it with the rapid swipe between thumb and index finger, and handed me the folded paper with a smile.

"Here you are," she said pleasantly, though I still felt like an idiot for having to have asked for them in the first place.

I smiled my thanks and once again followed her as she arced out from behind the desk and moved past me into the foyer.

She reached the massive double-door before I did and opened

the huge left-side door with just the slightest twist of her hand.

"Thank you for coming, Mr. Hardesty," she said. "I know I can trust your discretion."

"Of course you can," I said. "And I very much appreciate your cooperation."

I was of course aware we were once again doing our little etiquette pas de deux as, I'm certain, was she, but she seemed to take pleasure in it, and it gave me much-needed practice in the common civil graces.

* * *

I didn't have any trouble picturing Matt as a bouncer in "one of the more rowdy" Las Vegas clubs. Exterior or no, Matt was somebody you wouldn't want to mess with. But I don't think I would ever have pegged Gary as an insurance salesman.... Not sure why.

I was still going over the points of my conversation with Iris Glick when I walked into the office the next morning to find yet another call from Lieutenant Mark Richman.

Jeezus! my mind said, *he's spending more time with me than he spends with his wife.*

Yeah...You wish! another part replied.

I returned the call immediately, wondering as always what he wanted. I was getting to feel as though I were an unpaid member of the force. Well, as long as I didn't in any way compromise my clients' position, I could justify it.

"Lieutenant Richman," the familiar voice said.

"Lieutenant—Dick returning your call." I said.

"Glad you did," he said. "Thanks. Captain Offermann has asked me to sit in on his meeting with O'Banyon and the Glicks at 9:30, and we'll begin interviewing the...escorts...this afternoon. You know all of them, right? Spent some time with them?"

Not quite sure where he was headed, I replied: "Yes, I've met them all, and I've talked to each one of them about what they might know, but..."

"Any one of them we should be paying particular attention to?" he asked.

I thought about that one for awhile before answering. I was, after all, working for the Glicks and not for the police department. And while of the group, Gary stood out as the leading candidate for primary suspect, I still couldn't—and wouldn't—point the finger at him with any degree of certainty until I knew more. "Not really, Lieutenant," I said. And I wasn't about to mention Matt—I felt I was already walking enough of an ethical tightrope as it was. This was an investigation into ModelMen, its owners, and its escorts, and they had to be my only concern. If the police found out about Matt, that was fine, but they'd have to do it on their own.

"Hmm," Richman said, and I sensed he was aware of my position but had just given it a shot—and I couldn't fault him for that. "Okay. Just checking."

While I had him on the phone, I thought I might take a shot of my own. "Anything at all new on the pros…on Laurie Travers?" I asked.

"We have a few leads, yes. One of the girls saw her get into a car the night she was killed. We're tracking that down."

"You have a description of the car?" I asked.

"Fancy sports car—silver."

CHAPTER 12

Oh, shit! Well, there went the ball game! While Gary's Porsche was not the only silver sports car in the city, the "coincidence" of his having one, added to all the other ModelMen links, almost guaranteed it sure wouldn't take long before the cops zeroed in on him. Who was it who said coincidence only goes so far? I didn't like the thought, but it was starting to look like Gary might be the killer.

And you had sex with him, you stupid shit!

Look: I did it. I can't undo it. I even enjoyed it. Now shut up and let me think!

I tried. I hadn't said anything at all to Richman about Gary's new silver Porsche. There are lots of new silver sports cars out there, after all. Lots of them.

So let the cops take it from here, the rational part of my mind counseled. Good advice, I knew, while at the same time realizing that like a lot of good advice, I wouldn't take it. If Gary was guilty, I had to find out for sure on my own. Which, in itself, could be not only tricky but possibly downright dangerous. But there was still the very good chance that I was jumping to conclusions. There was still an awful lot I didn't know and wanted to— *had* to—know first.

But what if Gary *was* the killer? How could I confront him? Not alone, that's for sure…not even I would be that stupid, I hoped.

Ahead of the game, Hardesty, my mind said: *Way ahead! Slow down. We're way too far away from any confrontation to start worrying about it now.*

My mind was right, of course. Maybe get Gary and Matt together, privately…in my office, say. I'd never seen the two of them together, and maybe some of my other questions about their relationship might be resolved at the same time. I didn't want to let Richman feel I was going behind his back again. But no point in mentioning it until I'd made the arrangements.

"Well, thanks for the information, Lieutenant," I said, hoping he didn't notice that I'd sort of wandered off there for a second.

"So what have you got for me?" he asked.

If you only knew, Lieutenant! I thought.

"Nothing specific at the moment," I said, about half-truthfully, "but I've got an idea or two I'll have to mull over for a while before acting on. I'll keep you posted, I promise."

"I'll hold you to that," he said, then paused. "And keep in mind we're dealing with a sicko here—don't go trying anything stupid."

"I won't," I said.

There was another slight pause which said very clearly that he didn't believe me for a second, followed by: "I'll hold you to that, too. Well, it's time for me to meet Captain Offermann— the Glicks and O'Banyon will be here any time now."

We exchanged goodbyes and hung up.

* * *

It did pretty much seem like the case had been taken completely out of my hands, now. The police were slow, and they were a little dense at times, but they certainly were not stupid. They'd put the pieces together in short order.

As I'd said, I still found it almost impossible to think of Gary as being a murderer. Murderers are people you don't know; some badly lit sullen face with a two day beard stubble looking out at you from a "Wanted" poster or a mug shot. Not a beautiful photographer's model with sea-green eyes and a natural smile. Not right. Not right, and not fair.

Welcome to reality, Hardesty.

I looked at my watch: it was just after 10 a.m. The Glicks were still undoubtedly meeting with Offermann and Richman and God knows who else. I wanted very much to talk to Glen O'Banyon, but he was in the meeting, too. Since he was representing the Glicks, ModelMen, and by extension all the escorts, I felt I could talk openly to him under the laws of privilege.

I put in a call to O'Banyon's office and told Donna, his secretary, that it was imperative that I speak to him as soon as he could possibly do so. I was curious as to how Glicks' interview had gone, of course, but I also wanted to see if I might have set myself up for a possible obstruction of justice charge—unlikely as that may be—for not telling Richman immediately about Gary's Porsche.

God knows I couldn't say anything to the Glicks, or to anyone else. And there really was the possibility that I was way off base on this one. Just because Gary drove a silver Porsche—Richman didn't say a word about it's being a Porsche, or even a foreign car. Just a "silver car." But Gary knew Anderson and Gary knew Billy and Gary was openly bisexual....

I suddenly remembered that in one of my first talks with the Glicks, they'd said they did routine criminal background checks on all their escorts—but I wondered if that policy might have come along after they started up, and that it therefore may not have included Gary or Matt. On the other hand, Arnold Glick was a shrewd businessman and I didn't think he'd have let the fact of Gary's being related to his wife keep him from doing a check. I made a point to ask them as soon as I had a chance to talk with them.

* * *

Einstein was right: time is relative, and an hour can be an eternity when you're waiting for something. I was sure it must have been at least midnight when the phone finally rang, but the sun was still up and my watch said it was a few minutes short of noon.

"Dick," the readily-identifiable voice said, "it's Glen O'Banyon. I just got back from the Glicks' interview, and I've got to be in court at 2:00, but if you'd like to meet me at Etheridge's for a quick lunch at around 12:45...."

"Sure," I said.

"Good. I've got to run by my office for some court papers, so I should be just about on time. See you there." And he hung up.

Busy man.

* * *

Etheridge's is directly across from the City Building, and I'd met O'Banyon there several times while I'd worked with him on a previous case. He had what I could only think of as a permanently-reserved booth in the back of the restaurant—I'd never seen anyone else sitting there. The waiter, whose name I'd learned over previous lunches with O'Banyon was Alex, saw me come in and escorted me to the booth without my having to ask. I'd semi-hit on him one time while waiting for O'Banyon, and he'd made a point of subtly mentioning his other half, Jerry. Well, you can't win 'em all.

I was just pouring myself a second cup of coffee from the carafe when O'Banyon came in. He was about halfway to the booth when he stopped to talk with someone in one of the other booths. Finally he made his way to the back and sat down, as always first putting his briefcase on the side of the thickly padded bench closest to the wall. He reached across the table for our traditional handshake.

"Sorry for the delay," he said. "Judge Kurst had a question for me."

"No problem," I said.

He took his napkin from the table and put it on his lap, then reached for the coffee carafe. "You're looking good," he said. "Chasing murderers seems to keep you in shape."

"On the outside, maybe," I said.

He smiled and nodded. "So what's…"

Alex came up to ask if we were ready to order. Neither of us had looked at the menu, but even I fairly well knew it by now, so we just ordered our regulars: a caesar's salad for O'Banyon, the chicken and dumplings special for me. Alex smiled, gave me a quick wink, and left.

"…going on?" O'Banyon said, picking up in mid-question.

I hoped I wasn't going to sound too far out in left field, but figured there was no time to beat around the bush. "Well, first off I was of course wondering how the interview had gone. None of my business, probably, but that never slows me down."

He smiled again. "So I've noticed," he said. "It went quite well, I think. Captain Offermann suggested a possible conflict of interest in my representing the Glicks while 'being involved' as he put it, with one of their escorts and therefore their business. The fact of the matter is that I did not pay for Phil's…company…at any time. We met that evening he accompanied Stuart Anderson to Senator Marshfield's campaign fund-raiser. To say that I was impressed is something of an understatement. When he mentioned he was a model for ModelMen I called the Glicks the next day to find out more about him. The Glicks arranged, on their own, to have Phil spend the evening with me. I assume, of course, that they reimbursed Phil for his time, but that had nothing to do with me. We went out to dinner again a few weeks later, strictly socially, and strictly dinner." He sighed heavily. "I must say, though, that Phil is an incredible piece of work."

Indeed, I thought.

"But back to the Glicks's interview: it went as well as could be expected. If it had been merely Stuart Anderson's death, the police would have had a lot more reason to come down on ModelMen and its escorts. But with Billy Steiner's murder, that weakened that particular approach. And had it been merely Billy's death, the police would have had a lot stronger case for knowing ModelMen's client list on the grounds that it may well have been one of the clients. But with both a client and an escort dead....And then, along came Laurie Travers, and everything went back up into the air. So the result was mostly a fishing expedition. Lieutenant Richman raised the question of which of ModelMen's escorts were known to be bisexual. Not much grass grows under that one's feet, that's for sure."

"I think they're going to arrest Gary Bancroft," I said. "Probably fairly soon."

He had started to take a sip of coffee, but paused the cup halfway to his mouth and looked up at me without moving his head. "Yes, I'd think so too. What do you know that I don't?" he asked.

I told him everything I knew, suspected, conjectured. I told him of Gary's past—what I knew of it—of his being Iris's son, of having been abandoned when he was very young and of my assumption that Gary had some pretty serious anger issues. I realized full well that it was the fact that Gary was openly bisexual and the prostitute's death that had been the key—if she hadn't been killed, I don't know how long it would have taken me, if at all. I then proceeded to muddy the waters by telling him about Matt, about his tendency to play rough, about his still-not-totally-clear relationship with Gary. He was as good a candidate for Anderson's and Billy's murder as Gary was. But it was Laurie Travers' murder that tipped the scale toward Gary.

O'Banyon took his sip of coffee and returned his cup to the saucer. He looked at me without speaking for a moment, and then said: "And why did he kill Stuart Anderson and Billy Steiner?"

God, I wished he hadn't asked me that! I didn't have one single solid fact to back me up: just gut feelings and intuition—neither of which is considered to carry very much weight in a court of law. Well, I'd been right to go with my instincts often enough in the past.

Luckily, Alex arrived with our food and we concentrated on eating in silence for a few moments while I gathered my thoughts and tried to put them in some sort of order that would make sense to O'Banyon.

"I think," I said as I cut one of the dumplings in half and swirled it around in the cream sauce, trying to get a chunk of chicken to climb on board, "that if it was indeed Gary, he didn't necessarily set out to kill either one of them. With Anderson, I think it might have been something like spontaneous anger. Knowing as little as I do about him, Anderson apparently told just about everyone he came in contact with about his planning to send his eight-year-old son away. That could pretty easily really piss off somebody who'd been abandoned by his mother when he was even younger than that. I wouldn't be surprised if Billy was probably mostly an accident. Having an asthma attack while your face pushed into a pillow by somebody really strong on top of you, forcing you down…well…And that Billy refused to get fucked without a condom might have made the killer mad—he did it anyway, and Billy probably wasn't cooperating."

"And the prostitute?"

I sighed. "That's the rub. Why the hell would he steal a knife from Anderson and deliberately use it to kill a prostitute? I can't imagine either Gary or Matt—even if he's not totally gay as he says he is—being that stupid. I can't believe anyone being that stupid unless the killer is rubbing our noses in something."

"And I still keep coming back to the fact that of the three dead, one was gay, one bi, and one straight," O'Banyon said.

I shook my head slowly, as if trying to shake loose a thought or two I knew was in there somewhere. "I know," I said. "And it just doesn't make sense. But the fact of the matter is that the police will pretty much consider Gary the prime suspect, with Matt, as soon as they find out about him if they haven't already, a close second, and I don't know what to do about it."

Alex came to take our plates away, refresh our coffee and, at O'Banyon's request, leave the check.

"Do *you* think it's Gary?" O'Banyon asked when Alex had gone.

I shook my head again. "I really don't know," I said. "It's too obvious, in a way. There's an awful lot I still don't know and want to find out."

It suddenly occurred to me that, when it comes to investigating murders, the police have certain definite advantages in that they usually have a built-in objectivity: they don't know the suspect as a person, never spent time social time with him. 'And never went to bed with him,' my mind added.

O'Banyon looked at his watch. "Sorry, Dick, I've got to get to court. I'm sure you'll be able to get to the bottom of this mess. I really like the Glicks, and to think that one of their employees might be a murderer—and especially that it might be Iris Glick's...son—really boggles the mind. If there's anything you need from me.... Give me a call as soon as you find out anything, will you?"

"I will," I said.

O'Banyon looked at the check, reached into his jacket for his wallet, and extracted a bill, which he placed under the check. We rose to leave and, waving to Alex as he emerged from the kitchen with a tray of food, went out into the street. O'Banyon extended his hand for our customary handshake, but just as we were ready to release, he tightened his grip and his face grew serious.

"Be careful," he said, then released my hand.

I nodded and gave him a small wave as he headed for the crosswalk leading to the City Building. As I walked to my car, I noticed something...different...in the air, and realized it was the aroma of uncollected garbage. The sanitary workers' strike showed no signs of ending soon, and it was getting harder for average citizens to ignore.

* * *

Getting Gary and Matt together might take a little juggling—especially if, as both of them had indicated, there'd been some sort of rift between them. Just how deep the rift went I had no idea. I suspected it might go beyond Matt's feeling betrayed by Gary's not having intervened when Matt got fired from ModelMen. I tried calling Matt first and got his machine. I left a message for him to call me as soon as he could.

I then dialed Gary, and a sleepy voice answered on the third ring. "Hello?"

"Gary, it's Dick. Did I wake you?"

"Yeah, but that's okay. Had a late shoot last night. What's up?"

"I was thinking of getting together with you and Matt. I've got a couple questions and I can ask you both at the same time."

There was a brief pause, and then: "I don't think that's a very good idea."

"Oh?" I said, curious.

"I've pretty much cut all ties to Matt, and I prefer to leave it that way."

Now I was *really* curious. "Can I ask…?"

Another pause, then a sigh. "I don't want to talk about it," he said.

"Well," I replied, "I can appreciate that, but I'm afraid we really have to. Can I come by your place…now?"

There was a significant pause, then: "I've got to be at police headquarters at 4:30 for questioning. I suppose we could talk for a few minutes, if you really insist."

"I'm afraid I do," I said.

I suddenly realized I had no idea where he lived.

How the hell did anybody ever give you a license to practice, Hardesty? my little voice asked. "Where are you located?" I asked.

"Belamy Towers, apartment 2801." he said.

Belamy Towers? My, my! The boy lives well, I thought. Belamy Towers was one of the city's newest and most exclusive apartment complexes. Well, he said he liked nice things.

I realized, too, that my earlier concerns about not confronting him alone had more or less gone out the window, though I did think about calling Phil to let him know where I was going. But first of all, I wasn't anywhere near the point of confronting anyone about anything, and it was very unlikely that even if worse came to worse, and Gary turned out to be the killer, that he would try to off me in his own apartment. Besides, remember the odds: five billion to one that it wouldn't be Gary anyway.

* * *

Belamy Towers stood at the top of a hill overlooking the river and downtown. I'd imagine it had a spectacular view at night, and at 29 stories it was visible from almost anywhere in town. It was so new that they were still putting the finishing touches on the impressive lobby, all marble and mirrors, and only about half the tenants had moved in. Even though I'm sure Gary was in great demand as an escort and a model, I still questioned how he could afford to live here.

Then, as I waited by the elevators, I noticed a bronze plaque set in the wall: It listed the building's construction firm, the architect, and at the bottom were the words: "Glick Enterprises." Question answered.

The elevator had that overpoweringly *new* smell that hinted of sawdust and fresh laquer. The hallway of the 28th floor, when the doors opened with barely a sound, reflected the quiet elegance of the building. Thick burgundy carpet, simple but somehow dramatic lighting; floor-to-ceiling windows at each end of the hall, two doors on each side of the hallway to the left of the elevators, one door on each side to the right. Directly across from the elevator was another elevator, which I'd not noticed from the lobby. Two of the six apartment doors stood open, and out of curiosity I moved toward them just far enough to take a quick look inside. In one, carpet was being laid; from the other the smell of fresh paint and a section of dropcloth extending into the hall indicated the tenants had not yet moved in. I turned and walked back past the elevators just as the door to the one I'd not seen in the lobby opened showing it to be obviously a freight elevator. A really cute guy wearing white coveralls and a painter's cap emerged carrying several cans of paint. We exchanged smiles and a nod, and I reluctantly forced myself to head in the opposite direction to find Apartment 2801. I had no sooner rung the bell when the door opened to reveal a rather subdued looking Gary. He gave me a small smile as we exchanged a handshake and he showed me in. The small foyer, with parqueted floors, was painted the exact same shade as his eyes, and indeed, on two of the walls were a series of small seascape paintings. When we moved into the living room, I was more than a little impressed.

He had a corner apartment with floor-to-ceiling windows covering 2/3 of each of the two outer walls. The view was that of the river and downtown, of course, and again I could only imagine what it must look like at night. Either he had hired a top-notch interior designer, or Iris Glick had been right: Gary was a Renaissance man. In either case, he had fantastic and expensive taste. Perfectly balanced, from the small islands of carpeting in a sea of polished wood flooring to the mist-blue walls to the comfortable but obviously very expensive furniture.

"Like it?" Gary asked.

"Wow," I found myself saying, yet again demonstrating my worldly sophistication.

He managed a small grin. "Yeah, me too," he said. "It's a long way from Nebraska."

He motioned me to a seat, and I took one where I could look out the window. "Can I get you anything?" he asked, and I shook my head.

"I'm fine, thanks," I said.

He took a seat opposite me and leaned forward, elbows on his knees, hands folded. "So what did you want to see me and Matt about?" he asked.

I leaned back in my chair and took a deep breath. "Well, to be honest with you, I wanted to see the two of you together. The police are starting to zero in on ModelMen, and to blunt, you're going to be right up there on the top of their list, like it or not."

"Me, not Matt," he said.

I nodded. "Afraid it's heading in that direction."

"Because of the hooker," Gary said.

"Yeah, mostly."

"But how in hell can they tie her in with the other two deaths? Other than her and Billy both being found in a Dumpster...What did she have to do with that Anderson guy?"

Either he didn't know about the knife, or was pretending not to.

"The police apparently have some pretty good evidence of the link," I said.

He looked at me, eyebrow raised, and leaned even further forward. "Such as?" he said.

"I'm not sure," I lied. "The police don't exactly take me into their confidence." Which was largely true despite Lieutenant Richman's occasional sharing of information.

Gary unfolded his hands and sat slowly back in his chair. I decided to take a couple steps out onto the high wire. "Do you use prostitutes?" I asked, out of left field.

He looked at me a moment, then shrugged. "Yeah," he said. "I don't have to—I can get women just about anywhere any time I want them, but every now and then it's just simpler to go out and pick up a hooker. I do it mostly after I've been with a client who doesn't reciprocate. Sometimes I'm too horny to want to bother standing around in a bar for fifteen minutes hoping to score."

Fifteen minutes??

"And did you happen to pick up a prostitute the night Laurie Travers—that was her name—was killed?"

He looked decidedly uncomfortable and wiped his open hand over his face quickly. "Yeah, damn it!" he said. "I picked up a hooker, but the chances that it was the same one…I didn't ask her name, of course. Picked her up on McLeod and Spruce, drove her to an alley not far away. She blew me, I paid her, and I left."

"You left her in the alley?" I asked.

"No, of course not. I dropped her off at the corner a couple blocks away; near that all-night restaurant where the hookers hang out, on Cole."

"And did anybody see you drop her off?" I asked, realizing that it was a pretty stupid question.

Gary looked incredulous. "In that part of town? At that time of night? There are probably bums and winos and hookers lurking in the shadows all over the place down there, like some cheap vampire movie. How the hell do I know if anybody saw me, and how could I expect them to remember even if they did? There was a bag lady with a shopping cart crossing the street as I was coming up the block, but she was gone by the time the hooker got out of the car."

"Well, it's something," I said. *But not much,* I thought.

"Yeah," he said dismissively. "Like finding a needle in a haystack. Anyway, after I dropped her off, I came home. And as far as it being the hooker who got killed, that whole area is crawling with hookers; there's no way it could have been the same one."

"Well," I said, "I suspect the police may have a picture of her they'll be showing you, and if it *is* the same one...."

Gary shook his head. "This is bullshit!" he said. "How in the hell could they suspect me? Just because I'm bisexual?"

"I don't think it's just a matter of your being bisexual—but you did know Anderson and Billy and you and Steve are the only two escorts who openly admit to having sex with women as well as men."

Gary sat forward in his chair again. "That's ridiculous. I didn't kill that hooker! I swear!"

I decided that now would be a good time to switch the subject.

"And nobody has accused you of it," I said. "Let's not start jumping to any conclusions But like water running down hill, the police tend to take the most obvious route. They want a suspect, and like it or not, you're one of the most likely. But let's just wait to see what they ask you and where they think they're going with this. You can ask for Glen O'Banyon any time you want—but I'd probably wait until you thought it was necessary. You don't want to give the cops any reason to think you're covering anything up, and if you asked for O'Banyon the minute you walk in the door, they'd take that as a sure sign you felt you needed a lawyer."

Gary shrugged again. "Yeah, I guess you're right." He got up from his chair suddenly. "I could use a cup of coffee," he said. "I've got a pot in the kitchen. You want some?"

"Sure," I said, getting up to follow him, and appreciating the break in the conversation.

The kitchen, just off the dining room, was straight out of the set of a TV cooking show. Everything you could ever imagine a kitchen having, Gary's had. Designer pots and pans—the kind I very much doubted he'd picked up at K-Mart—hanging from hooks above the chopping-block counter next to the island stove; everything gleaming and spotless and obviously top of the line. Gary not only liked nice things, he had them.

He took two coffee mugs from a built-in rack under one of the cabinets and poured coffee from one of those fancy black, intricate-looking German coffee-makers. "Cream and sugar?" he asked, and I shook my head.

"No, thanks."

"A man after my own heart," he said.

Under other circumstances…quite possibly, I thought.

Handing me one of the mugs, he said "Shall we go back into the living room or sit in here?"

"Here's fine," I said, and we moved over to the small table near the window. Once we were seated, our coffee mugs in front of us, Gary moved forward in his chair, leaned forward, and put his elbows on the edge of the table, his arms crossed. We drank our coffee in silence for a minute or two, looking out the window at a bank of dark clouds tumbling slowly in from the west. I had the feeling Gary was deliberately staying silent, waiting for me to make the first move, so I did.

"Now, about you and Matt," I said.

Gary continued to stare out at the rolling clouds. "I told you, I really don't want to talk about it," he said. Then he turned those marvelous sea-green eyes to me. "And I don't want to be rude, but it just isn't any of your business."

"You're right," I said, wrapping my hand around the coffee mug and feeling its warmth. "It isn't any of my business. But I'm pretty sure the police will consider it   *their* business. You can talk to me now and maybe let me come up with some ideas of how to help you, because you can be sure you'll be talking to the police later. I'm sure they'll have found out about Matt by now, and I'd be willing to bet he'll be number two on their 'Likely Candidates' list. They're going to be very tempted to lay all three murders squarely at your feet—or Matt's."

"Well," he said, looking at me steadily, "If I had a choice…"

"You think Matt could have done it? Even the prostitute?"

He gave a dismissive shrug. "I wouldn't put anything past him."

"I thought you said Matt was strictly gay," I said, not a little disturbed—but I guess not really surprised—by his willingness to turn on his former…were they ever lovers or not?

He raised one eyebrow slightly. "You know that and I know that..." *Sort of...* my mind added, "but as far as the police are concerned, I'd imagine they might reason that Matt's got kids, therefore Matt fucks women, therefore he can't be all gay, therefore...."

He was right, of course. If I thought I'm pretty dense when it comes to the subject of bisexuality, imagine how it is for the cops—not one in a hundred has a clue.

Gary just shrugged again and took another sip of coffee.

"Look, Gary," I said, "I can't do very much to help you until I know everything we're dealing with. I don't handle surprises very well, and frankly I suspect that you and Matt have quite a few little surprises lying around."

Gary gave a deep sigh and settled back in his chair, index finger hooked around the handle of his coffee mug. Still looking at me, he slowly chewed his lower lip a moment before beginning. "Yeah, I guess you're right. But that's not my problem. Matt is."

???? I thought.

"Meaning?" I said.

Gary set his coffee down and looked at me, long and hard. "Okay, you want the whole story?"

I nodded.

Gary got up from the table and went to get the coffee pot, which he brought to the table and refilled his cup. He looked at my cup and raised an eyebrow, and I put my hand over it to indicate I'd had enough. I suspected that the last thing I was going to need would be something else eating at the lining of my stomach.

He returned the pot and came back to sit down. Cupping his hands around his mug, he leaned forward again, his forearms on the table.

"Matt and I were in the same class at boot camp. We met on the bus taking us to the base, as a matter of fact, and we had a little chance to talk before we got there. We sort of hit it off right away, but I could tell even then he had some serious attitude problems—he didn't strike me as the kind of guy who'd take shit from anybody, and I was right. Sure enough, the first night in the barracks, he got in an argument with another guy in our class over who had to take the top bunk, and Matt started to beat the shit out of the guy. I managed to pull him off just before the drill instructor came storming into the room, and the guy said he'd fallen out of his bunk. The D.I. didn't believe it for a minute, of course, but he couldn't prove anything, and a good, healthy fight proves you're a real man. The other guys in the barracks got the message pretty quick, and nobody messed with Matt after that.

"There were a couple more instances within the first week or two where Matt was about two inches away from being tossed into the brig or out of the corps. He was smart enough never to try anything with the drill instructors or other N.C.O.s, but with the other guys...I could tell it was only a matter of time until he got in real trouble, so I sort of took him under my wing, and tried to teach him how to get what he wanted with words rather than fists. He was a pretty fast learner."

He paused, whether to wait for me to respond or for him to figure out what to say next I couldn't tell. So I opted to jump in.

"And how did you...find out about each other?" I asked.

Gary gave me a small smile. "Well, it didn't exactly take a burning bush. I was certain about Matt within ten minutes of meeting him on the bus. He was just *too* damned butch not to be gay. Of course I have to admit that even I assumed he was bi; he'd showed me pictures of his kids while we were still on the bus. On our first weekend liberty, I asked Matt to go into town with me—I don't think any of the other guys wanted to risk being around him with that temper of his. We got a cheap hotel room, then set out to hit the bars and do our duty as Marines to get drunk out of our minds. At one of the hooker bars, a couple of the working girls were at the table with us, and things were going along fine. I suggested the four of us go back to our hotel room, but Matt backed out. The girl he was with said the usual 'What's the matter, honey, don't you like girls?' and Matt said 'Shit, yes I like girls. But I've got the clap, and I don't think you want to share it with me.' He didn't look at me, he didn't bat an eye."

Gary grinned. "I knew damned well he couldn't have clap—this was our first liberty and it would have been caught during his induction physical and he wouldn't have gotten into the corps."

We were both quiet for a minute, looking out the window. I finished the last bit of cold coffee in my mug. I got the impression

Gary was playing some sort of little control game. He knew I wanted him to continue, so he deliberately shut up, trolling for a response from me. I decided I'd bite my lip rather than play.

Gary glanced at me a couple of times, looking for something which I hope he didn't find.

Finally, he picked up where he'd left off. "The girl he was with just picked up her drink, got up, and left. I suggested to the one I was with that maybe she and I should go check out the hotel, and she agreed. I told Matt I'd meet up with him in a couple hours back at the room, and we left. Well, I was pretty hot to go, and it didn't take more than ten minutes for her and me to finish our business. Not two minutes after she left, Matt came in. I think now that he was probably standing in the hallway all the time she and I were in the room, just waiting for her to go. He came in, asked how it went and I was very careful to give him a detailed account, watching him as he got undressed for bed, and seeing his reaction. It sure wasn't hard to miss."

He looked at me again, smiled, and said: "So one thing led to another and we ended up spending the rest of the weekend in bed together."

"Interesting," I said.

Gary got up from the table, picked up our coffee mugs and took them to the sink. "Oh, that's not the best part," he said, and this time I took the bait.

"No?" I asked.

Gary rinsed out the mugs and, with his back to me, I heard him chuckle. "Nope. A week later both Matt and I came down with the clap! The hooker gave it to me and I gave it to him. He wasn't mad, though…it cemented our reputations as cocksmen with the rest of the guys in the barracks. I'm sure not one of them had a clue as to what was really going on."

Drying his hands on a dishtowel on a rack by the sink, he turned back toward me. "I've got to start getting ready for the interview before too long," he said. "You want to continue this conversation in the living room…or the bedroom?"

'Shit! He reads you like a book,' my mind said. 'Don't give in! Show some backbone!'

"Bedroom's fine," I said.

You idiot!

* * *

Sitting on opposite sides of the bed getting dressed, I said: "...and as you were saying...?"

"Matt again, huh?" he asked.

"Yep." If he thought a roll in the hay—one of the better ones in recent memory, I might add—was going to dissuade me from getting everything I needed regarding their relationship, he was wrong.

Gary stood up, hoisting his pants over his hips, still not looking at me.

"Okay, Reader's Digest version: we became an item. More of an item to Matt than to me, I soon found out, but I'd been up front with him right from the very start, and it didn't bother him. There are bi's who are what you might call 'serial bi's'—they'll go for long stretches being exclusively with one sex, then switch over to the other for a while. That's not me, and Matt knew it. I think he thought I'd see the 'error of my ways' and decide he was enough for me, and that we could...I don't know...Matt's not a white picket fence type guy, but I think that was basically the gist of it. For a guy who'd never really had much stability in his life or anybody who really gave a shit about him, I guess it's understandable.

"Don't get me wrong: I really dug Matt. We got along great. We had what I thought was a perfect relationship—Matt was there when I wanted a guy, and when I wanted a woman, I'd just go get one. Matt never said a word. After boot camp, we spent the rest of our tour of duty stationed at Camp Pendleton. About a week before we got out, Matt's old man died, and Matt got early release. We'd talked several times—well, actually Matt talked about it more than I did—about our maybe staying together after the service, but by the time we got out, I was beginning to feel a little ...well...hemmed in. I decided to go back to Nebraska to try to make it in the insurance business. We kept in touch—he'd call me a couple times a week wanting us to move somewhere together. I'll admit that I'd about had it with Nebraska, and I really sort of missed him."

We finished dressing and I followed him into the living room as he kept talking.

"Then I found Iris and called Matt to come out and join me in

Vegas. That was my big mistake."

"How so?" I asked.

He motioned me to a seat, but I shook my head—I knew it was about time for him to head down to Police Headquarters.

"Almost as soon as we hooked up in Vegas, Matt started getting a little too…well, clingy, for want of a better word. When I'd go out and pick up a woman, he wouldn't say anything, but it was pretty clear he didn't approve. He actually followed me a couple times—thought I didn't know it, but I did. I swear one night he was standing on the fire escape, watching us through the window."

If he was expecting a reaction to that one, he got it, though I tried not to let it show.

"Then we moved from Vegas to here and Iris and Arnold started ModelMen, and it just kept getting worse. Again, he never said anything when I'd go out with women; he's not the kind of guy to sulk or pout, but I could sense it. I felt like the life was being squeezed out of me. He always knew monogamy just isn't my thing with either sex, but he never really accepted it. I think it was his frustration with me that made him go too far with that client. And when he got fired and I didn't stand up for him, that about did it. We'd just been getting ready to move in here—again, Matt's idea, and we had already started moving some stuff in, as a matter of fact—and I told him it would be better for both of us if we just cut our ties and called it quits. He sure as hell wasn't happy about it: it was quite a show.

"So I moved out. But he just won't let it go! I swear he's been following me around, just like that time outside the window in Vegas."

He gave a slight shudder, then suddenly smiled. "I do miss the sex, though," he said. "Matt's great in bed…which I imagine you've found out for yourself."

Now that one came out of left field, but I suspected it fit in somehow with his need to control the situation by putting me off balance. I hoped to hell my face didn't show he'd succeeded.

"Your place or his?" he asked, again from left field.

"I'm not sure…" I started to say.

"Well, if it was yours, you should make a close check of your belongings."

I wasn't able to keep my eyebrows from moving toward one another in a combination of question and surprise. "Meaning what?" I asked.

Gary grinned. "Matt likes to collect things from guys he goes to bed with. You see his ashtray collection? Usually nothing big—though he did give me a Rolex he got from a trick once, before we started with ModelMen—it's just one of his little quirks. Left over from his days of stealing candy when he was a kid: his old man never let him have candy, so he'd take it."

Well, I filed that away in my mental trivia drawer, and looked at my own watch—which definitely wasn't a Rolex. "Well," I said, "I'd better get going. Thanks for a really interesting afternoon."

He walked me to the door and we shook hands before he opened it, his sea-green eyes never leaving my own. "My pleasure," he said. "Feel free to come by any time you have a...question."

I nodded, smiled, and went out into the hall.

The hunky painter was just emerging from the drop-clothed apartment heading for the freight elevator. He looked at me, smiled, and subtly ran his hand down to his crotch. I was tempted to ride down the freight elevator with him...maybe press the "Stop" button between floors and...? But instead I pressed the "down" button on the passenger elevator and deliberately avoided looking back at the painter.

Now that's progress! my mind voice said proudly.

No, my crotch answered: *that's stupidity.*

CHAPTER 13

'Well, so much for Gary's side of the story,' I thought as I headed back to the office. 'Now it's Matt's turn.' I neatly managed to ignore the fact that once again I may very well have just had sex with a murderer. I was getting pretty good at that.

* * *

I was hoping, when I walked in to the office, to find a message from Matt, and sure enough.... I called him back immediately without even sitting down at my desk. It was about ready for his answering machine to kick in when he picked up.

"Matt, hi," I said. "It's Dick Hardesty."

"Dick, yeah," he said. "I was kind of surprised to get your message. Is this business or personal?"

"Business, I'm afraid," I said.

Yeah, like that's ever stopped you! my little voice sneered.

"Ah, too bad. What have I done now?"

I tried to sound a bit more casual than I felt. "I really need to talk with you as soon as possible. Have you by any chance heard from the police?"

"The police? Why would I be hearing from the..." There was a brief pause, then "...Oh."

"I'm afraid so," I said. "Can I come over there, or do you want to come to my office?"

"Sure," Matt said. "Come on over. I probably should stay around and wait for a phone call from the fuzz. Or will they be coming to batter down my door and haul me away in handcuffs?"

I laughed—a bit forced, but laughed. "Nothing that dramatic, I'm sure. But I'm pretty sure they'll want very much to talk with you and it would be a good idea if you and I talked first."

"Whatever you say," he said. "I'll see you when you get here."

"Twenty minutes, tops," I replied. We exchanged quick goodbyes and I headed back out the door.

* * *

I'd no sooner touched the buzzer in the alcove of Matt's apartment building when the door buzzed open. Matt had his apartment the door open even before I reached it. He looked mildly worried.

"They called," he said as he motioned me into the living room, closing the door behind me. "They wanted me to come in at 9 tomorrow morning, but I told them I've got a Bleeker's catalog shoot from 6 a.m. to at least noon. So they made it 2:30 at the City Building Annex. I left ModelMen quite a while before all this started. I don't really know what I could tell them."

Somehow, I doubted that.

We sat on the comfortable sofa and Matt pulled a pack of cigarettes from his shirt pocket and offered me one. I shook my head. Either he'd forgotten I don't smoke anymore or it was a subtle teaser. He hoisted his hips to get at a lighter in his pocket, lit the cigarette with cupped hands, and took a deep drag, blowing it carefully out in a long stream well to one side of me. However, as cigarette smoke has an infuriating way of doing to nonsmokers, and particularly to evangelical former smokers, it stopped its straight trajectory and, caught in an air current, did a 150-degree curve directly into my face.

"Should I be worried?" Matt asked, leaning sideways to reach one of the two ashtrays on the table lamp beside the sofa.

"Well," I said, "that's one of the reasons I wanted to talk with you. And I have to be honest and tell you that from what I can see, I'm afraid you and Gary are running neck and neck on the cops' list of suspects."

He took another drag of his cigarette and held the smoke in as he said: "And why's that?"

I knew he knew damned well why that was, but decided to play along with him anyway.

"Mainly because you have a reputation as liking to play rough, because you went too far with that construction guy, because you broke ModelMen's rules and they fired you for it; because you knew Stuart Anderson and Billy…that's a start."

"And why would I kill that prostitute? I'm gay, remember? I don't have anything at all to do with women."

I nodded. "But you have kids which, in typical heterosexual male Breeder mentality means that no matter what you say, you can't possibly be really, deep-down gay. Probably just a phase. Fuck one, you can fuck 'em all."

Matt gave a short, derisive snort. "Yeah, I fucked one… *one*… and look where it got me," he said. "Believe me, one was more than enough to make me swear off women forever."

We were quiet for a moment, and then I said: "Tell me about you and Gary."

He stubbed his cigarette out in the ashtray and leaned sideways again to replace it on the lamp table. "I did," he said, not looking at me.

While realizing I was getting into a sensitive area with him, I decided I had to proceed anyway. "No, you didn't," I said. "You told me a little bit about Gary, but not very much about the two of you."

Matt twisted around slightly to be in a better position to look at me directly, resting his back between the sofa's back and arm.

"That's our business," he said.

I shrugged. "I'm afraid that's not exactly true anymore," I said, getting a slight feeling of "deja vu" from having had the same basic conversation with Gary earlier. "The cops, as I see it, have two prime suspects: you and Gary, and being cops, they're going to do their very best to pin these three murders on one or the other of you. I'd like to help you if I can, but I have to know exactly what's going on before I can even start."

Matt just sat there, face impassive, eyes locked on mine. I suspected he was, like Gary had done before, trying to see who'd blink first. It wasn't going to be me.

After a full thirty seconds of silence, he broke the stare and sighed. "He's going to set me up."

That one took me by surprise, though I'm not sure why. I suspected someone was setting up someone, but I had no idea who.

"For what?" I asked. "The murders?"

"Yes," he said.

"Why would he do that?" I asked.

He allowed himself a small, private smile. "You really don't have a clue about him, do you?" he asked. "Look, it doesn't matter who did those killings, Gary's going to be damned sure   *he* isn't the one who gets the blame. And if the only other convenient suspect is me, he won't hesitate for a second to make sure I take the fall."

"Then you'd better give me the whole story," I said.

He gave a resigned shrug. "Where do you want me to start?" he asked.

"Boot camp," I said.

* * *

I won't repeat the entire conversation word for word, but the gist of it made for some very interesting observations and speculations on my part. Matt's telling of the meeting on the bus the first day of boot camp was basically the same, but in Matt's version, Gary had spotted him even before they got on the bus and made it a deliberate point to sit beside him. Matt got pretty strong gay vibes from Gary even then, but being from a small town and without much gay experience, he wasn't totally sure. But Gary had shown him some attention, and while Matt didn't say so, I suspected that was all it took to hook him.

When I asked him why he had joined the Marines to begin with, he reluctantly admitted that he'd put his ex-wife's new boyfriend in the hospital after the guy told Matt he couldn't see his kids; the local judge gave him the option of going to jail or joining the military. He chose the latter, and went with the Marines because that's what his father expected him to do.

It was a little hard for me to ask some of the questions I wanted to ask, or to steer him where I wanted him to go, without letting him know I'd already gotten Gary's side of the story, and I didn't want to do that.

Again, I found it a little odd to be sitting on a sofa facing a guy so butch he'd make the Marlboro man look like a pansy but talking like a lovesick teenager. But from what Gary had told me about Matt's abused and loveless past, I'd imagine that's pretty much exactly what he was.

It was pretty obvious, just from the way he talked, that he fell for Gary in a big way, and that he was pretty sure Gary felt the same way about him. When I asked him when he found out for sure that Gary was gay ...*okay, okay, bi...* he also told the story of their first weekend liberty, but with significant differences. He admitted that Gary had talked an awful lot about women and led a lot of the barracks who's-had-the-most-pussy bragfests, but Matt really had no idea just what a bisexual was or was supposed to be. He just hoped that Gary might decide that Matt was all he needed. Sort of a reversal on the old "All you need is the love of a good woman" cliche.

Anyway, the first night of their liberty they went to the bar, and the scenario was pretty much the way Gary had described it. Matt wasn't embarrassed about making up the clap story; it was just his way of handling the situation, and he was pretty sure Gary knew it. And he wasn't even particularly surprised when Gary took the hooker back to their hotel room, again because he didn't have any experience to compare the situation with. He didn't say, as Gary speculated, that he stood in the hotel hallway waiting for the hooker to leave, but did say that when he came back into the room, Gary was sprawled out on the bed, naked, waiting for him. "Your turn," Gary told him.

After that, Matt was totally under Gary's control. From what I could tell, it didn't go nearly as far as a slave-master relationship—Matt more than held his own in the sexual end of the bargain—but it was Gary who made most of the decisions, and Matt was more than willing to do whatever Gary asked of him.

Matt verified that they'd talked a lot, as their military time was drawing to a close, about moving somewhere together. I suspected, as Gary had indicated, that Matt probably talked more about it than Gary did. And then Matt's dad died a week before their enlistment was up and Matt got an early release. It took Matt almost a year to sell the farm—the place was in serious disrepair and Matt spent all his time getting it into shape to sell. He and Gary kept in regular contact—again, I'd guess Matt called more often than Gary—until one day when Matt called and found Gary's phone had been disconnected. I could imagine how Matt must have felt.

A week later, Gary called Matt from Las Vegas, asking him to come out.

It was about here that Matt's story got a hell of a lot more murky and less easy to read what he was really saying. I got the feeling that there were definitely some large chunks that were being left out, but what they might be and why he was avoiding them I had no idea.

Having just closed on the sale of the farm and paid off all his father's debts, which left him with a total of $232.85, he packed up and drove his dad's ancient pickup truck to Las Vegas to join Gary.

Apparently Gary had been looking for Iris for a long time. His grandparents had not heard from her since the day she left her job at the truck stop. But Gary became obsessed with finding her. He'd talked to Matt about her a lot when they were in the Marines, and swore that one day he would find her, and that when he did, he would make her pay for having abandoned him. He didn't go into detail as to what sort of "payment" he meant to extract, but it appeared he'd done pretty well for himself since he and his mother had gotten together again.

It was Gary who'd introduced Matt to hustling. It was a quick way to make a few bucks, and while it was all new to Matt, it obviously wasn't to Gary. The first few times, they worked as a team, picking up high rollers at casino bars. But a lot of guys were understandably hesitant to go off with two very butch-looking tricks at once, so they soon started working separately. Matt wasn't wild about the idea, but since Gary wanted him to....

The key bit of information here, for me, other than the control Gary was exerting over Matt, was an incident Matt mentioned involving one of their first team-tricking incidents. They'd picked up a rich Texan who was already pretty drunk, and the guy was wearing a new Rolex. Gary had mentioned the Rolex, but not the fact that he and Matt had been together when it was taken. According to Matt, Gary pointed it out to him and, after they'd gone with the guy to his hotel room and done their thing, Matt just picked the watch up off the dresser, put it in his pocket, and later gave it to Gary. Gary was delighted, and that started a pattern: Matt would make it a habit of bringing home something for Gary after every trick—never money or anything as valuable as a Rolex, but just something: usually an ashtray from the john's hotel room but every now and then something a little special, like a crystal salt and pepper shaker from a fancy restaurant a john had taken him. Gary did, after all, like nice things.

As he talked, I began to feel as though I were being backed up into an open freezer. *Anderson's knife set!* But, if Matt killed Anderson and stole the knife set and gave it to Gary and Gary then used it to kill the prostitute...*Whoa, Charlie! Where's the logic?* No, it didn't make sense. Why would Gary use an exorbitantly expensive, easily identifiable knife to kill a prostitute? Unless Matt was right—Gary was setting him up.

What in the hell for? If Matt killed Anderson, he didn't need to be set up: if he did it, he did it—why kill someone else? And what about Billy? Why would Matt kill Billy? Shit, why would   *Gary* kill Billy? The only sure thing was that somebody had killed Billy. And Anderson. And the prostitute. But who? And why?

* * *

"So what," I asked finally, "broke you two up?"

Matt looked away and shrugged. "I got tired of being used," he said. "When he needed me, I was always there for him. When I needed him…. Anyway, I finally realized that as far as the two of us were concerned, it was strictly a one-way street: Gary's way. When I finally got up the guts to tell him 'no,' he dumped me."

"What did he want you to do?" I asked, knowing as I asked that it was none of my business and he probably wouldn't tell me. But I gave it a shot.

"It doesn't matter. It just finally dawned on me what a fucking idiot I'd been, letting him string me along all this time."

"And that was about the same time as your run-in with the construction guy," I said.

Matt nodded. "Yeah. It was a stupid thing to do. I knew it was wrong, and that my job would be in jeopardy. But I wanted to see if Gary would stand up for me. All he'd have had to have done was put in a good word with Iris. She could never say no to him, and if she'd cut me some slack, Arnold would have too. But he didn't. So that was it."

There was one other question I had to ask. "Do you have an alibi for the times of the murders?"

He looked at me like I was seriously retarded. "How in hell can I have an alibi when I don't even know for sure when they happened?"

Good point. Even I couldn't remember the exact dates. "Billy died, from what I know, the night of the Gay Pride parade: that would be Sunday, the…"

"…26th," Matt supplied. "I was home by myself. I don't like crowds, so I didn't go out at all that day. Great alibi there, huh? Who the hell ever thinks they're going to need one?"

I acknowledged his logic with a cursory shrug, and racked my brain for the date Anderson was killed. It was a Sunday, too…but one week or two weeks before the parade…? I mentally went backwards through the days between the murders and was surprised to figure out there was only one week between the two. I snapped back to reality to find Matt staring at me.

"The 19th," I said. "Anderson was killed on the night of the 19. It was a Sunday, too."

Matt moved his jaw to one side and furrowed his brow, thinking. "Sunday the 19th; that's a long way back: how the hell am I supposed to remember what I was doing? I was probably at home, alone. I…" He suddenly gave a slight start and a kaleidoscope of emotions washed over his face, from realization to anger. "The 19 Of course. That's my daughters' birthday! I called them to wish them a happy birthday and that cunt of a mother of theirs wouldn't let me talk to them! That fucking bitch!"

"What time was that?" I asked.

"I'd had an out-of-town shoot and didn't get back until about 9 o'clock. I called as soon as I got home, and that bitch told me they were already in bed and she wouldn't get them up. I was so fucking mad I couldn't see straight. Then Gary called—first time I'd talked to him in a week—to see how I was doing; like he gave a shit. He wanted to come over and look for something he'd left when he moved out. I didn't want to talk to him, so I told him I was beat from the shoot and was just getting ready for bed. But after he hung up, I just sat there getting madder and madder, and I decided to go out to the bars. Getting laid always helps calm me down. I was just ready to walk into the Male Call when this guy comes out and we take one look at one another and...I never made it inside."

"Did you get the guy's name?" I asked.

Matt pressed his lips together and shook his head. "No, damn it. I wasn't in any mood for conversation. I don't think we said more than ten words to one another all night."

"Did you go to his place, or did you bring him here?"

"We came here," Matt said. "He left about three in the morning."

"Had you ever seen him before?" I asked. "Did anybody see you together? What did he look like? What kind of car did he drive?"

Matt shook his head in exasperation. "Shit, man! When I set out to get laid, I don't pay all that much attention to detail. Big guy, about my size, maybe bigger; hot as hell. I'm sure I've probably seen him a couple times before in the Male Call but I can't be sure. I don't go to the bars that often. As for being seen, there were all sorts of guys coming and going, so I suppose somebody saw us together, but who the hell'd remember? He followed me home in his car, but I can't remember much about it—two-door, dark...blue, maybe, or black...American make, I think. Like I say, I had my mind on getting laid."

Great! I thought. The Male Call has a Sunday night beer blast from 9-11 and they always draw a big crowd. How in the hell could I—or anyone—track down one nameless, faceless number in a nondescript car out of the maybe 200 guys who were there that night?

The thought did occur to me that maybe Matt was just making up a story he hoped I'd buy. But if he was telling the truth, that would mean he couldn't have killed Anderson, which meant....

I had one of my out-of-nowhere thoughts. "Did Anderson have your phone number?" I asked.

He shrugged. "Not that I know of. I'm in the book, if he ever knew my last name. He never called me directly."

"Well, look," I said after a moment of trying to get my thoughts organized. "I'd suggest you go back to the Male Call tonight, to see if you can find the guy you were with the night Anderson was killed, or anybody who saw you together. The odds aren't good, but without that alibi, you're in deep shit."

I remembered that both Aaron and Jared frequented the Male

Call, and there was an outside chance…. Of course, if Matt had seen Aaron there, he'd have mentioned it. But I'd give them both a call, just in case.

I realized too that Matt would be more or less on his own when it came to the police. Since he was no longer employed by ModelMen, Glen O'Banyon wouldn't automatically be at his ready disposal. But I did recommend that if things got tight during the questioning, he ask to see O'Banyon anyway. It would be worth a shot, and I'd make a call to O'Banyon's office first thing in the morning to alert him.

I left a few minutes later, wishing Matt luck and asking him to call me as soon as he got back from the interview, and headed home. I was about halfway there when I realized that I'd been able to spend all that time talking with Matt without thinking about trying to get him into bed again.

Progress, indeed.

* * *

There was something missing, my gut told me: a very big piece of the puzzle, and I suspected it had something to do with the breakup—and specifically with what Gary wanted Matt to do that gave him the wake-up call. I still couldn't believe that either Matt or Gary could be a killer. Probably because I didn't want to believe it. On the one hand, everything pointed to Gary; on the other hand, an equally good case could be made that Matt did it—except Laurie Travers, which could have been a decoy killing. *Shit!*

I made a quick swing by the office to check for messages. There weren't any, which I took as a sign of "no news is good news." And by the time I got home, I realized I hadn't taken anything out of the freezer for dinner. I wasn't in much of a cooking mood anyway, so decided to give Tim a call to see if he'd like to join me for a quick bite (and, if things worked out, maybe a few other bites).

Tim answered on the second ring.

"Hi, Tim," I said. "Hope I caught you before you started dinner."

There was a slight pause, then: "Uh, yeah. Why?"

"Just wondered if you'd like to have dinner with me. Maybe try that new Chinese place on McLeod?"

Another pause. "Gee, I'd like to, Dick, but I've got a…I've got plans."

The *Aha!* response hit me. "Phil?" I asked.

"Yeah, as a matter of fact…" Yet another pause, then a hesitant "Would you like to join us?"

I'm dense, but not dumb. "No, thanks, Tim. Maybe we can all get together another time, with a little more advance notice."

I'm sure Tim was mildly relieved when he said: "Sure. I'll call you tomorrow, okay?"

"Okay," I said. "Give my best to Phil." I was sure he would; and his best, too.

I next tried Jared, both to see if he might like to join me, and to ask him about the Male Call. He wasn't home, so I left a message on his machine. Same with Aaron.

I opened a can of corned beef hash, covered it with catsup, and put it in the oven. Maybe I could have my own cooking show on TV one day.

At 9:30, the phone rang. I assumed it was Jared or Aaron returning my call. I was wrong.

"Dick, this is Gary," a very unhappy-sounding voice announced. "The police just left—they showed up with a search warrant and practically ransacked the place."

"What were they looking for?" I asked.

"The warrant was for my bedroom, for chrissakes!" he said. "I guess they just wanted to snoop around. They were mostly interested in my pillows! Even after they took the damned pillows off the bed they wanted to know if I had any others around. Yeah, like I collect pillows! I told them no, but they weren't satisfied until they'd torn the place apart. I don't know what the hell they thought they were doing, but it doesn't look good. I just wanted to let you know. You think I should call O'Banyon?"

"Definitely," I said. "Try to stay calm, and wait to see what O'Banyon has to say. They probably just wanted to rattle your cage. Obviously they didn't find anything incriminating enough to arrest you on the spot."

"Yeah," he said. "Some consolation."

"Well, like I say, try to relax," I said. "I'll talk with you tomorrow."

"Okay," he said, and hung up.
Pillows? As in eider down?

* * *

I got to the office early Tuesday morning and tried to hold off thinking any more than I already had about the police search of Gary's apartment. I forced myself to take plenty of time to drink my coffee, read the paper—the sanitary workers strike was apparently about to be settled to the workers' satisfaction, the mountains of garbage piled up all over the city undoubtedly a factor—and do the crossword puzzle before calling Glen O'Banyon's office and leaving a message for him to call me at his earliest convenience.

Though it was still early, I took a chance and called Gary to see how he was doing. He hadn't had much sleep, but seemed in much better spirits than he'd been in the night before. He did say he missed his pillows, though he didn't seem concerned as to why they had been taken.

I then called the Glicks to check in and see if they'd encountered any surprises during their interview. I found it very interesting that Mrs. Glick did not mention the searching of Gary's apartment, and I could only assume Gary hadn't told her, for one reason or another, so of course neither did I. As to the interview, Mrs. Glick assured me, it had gone very well and she was favorably impressed by Lieutenant Richman. She suspected that even Captain Offermann might have been just a little intimidated by Glen O'Banyon's presence, but that the questioning had been courteous and did not get into areas they were not comfortable discussing. Offermann did bring up the subject of ModelMen's client list, but dropped it when O'Banyon reminded him of the only condition the Glicks had placed on their cooperation.

The phone calls took up all of about 45 minutes, leaving me with little to do but sit back and wait to hear from Matt to get some idea as to where the police might be going with the case. I toyed briefly with the idea of calling Lieutenant Richman, but decided against it—I didn't want to get too chummy with the police, nor did I want to give Richman the idea I was pressing him.

Have I ever mentioned that patience is not one of my greater virtues? Just sitting around waiting for something drives me to distraction, but I didn't have much choice. I didn't want to try to call Aaron this early in case he'd been up late the night before; Jared was at work, as was Tim—unless he was still in bed with Phil.

I tried sitting back and thinking about the case: what I knew for sure, what I didn't know, what I suspected, what I still had to find out. I went trolling for those elusive hunches that kept darting around the periphery of my mental vision, as usual without success. About the only thing I accomplished was to become more frustrated.

O'Banyon called around 11:00 and I told him of my conversation with Matt, without going too deeply into detail, and asked if Matt might be considered under the umbrella of O'Banyon's availability to ModelMen escorts. He said he'd of course respond if Matt called on him and we could work out the fine points with the Glicks later if necessary.

* * *

Around noon I went downstairs to the coffee shop on the ground floor and was surprised not to see either Eudora and Evolla working the counter; it was the first time I could ever remember their not being there. I asked the harried waitress what had happened to them and was told that Eudora had had a mild stroke, and that Evolla was at home taking care of her. I felt oddly sad; although I had never exchanged a single non-order-related word with them in all the years I'd been coming into the diner, they had somehow become a block in the foundation of my daily life.

Somehow the day passed. Matt's interview had been scheduled for 2:30 and I had heard nothing from him by 4:30. I resisted trying to call him and was just getting ready to leave for home when the phone finally rang. I practically snatched it off the cradle.

"Hardesty Investigations."

"Mr. Hardesty. This is Arnold Glick. I thought you should know Gary has been arrested for the murders of Stuart Anderson, Billy, and that…woman."

CHAPTER 14

Though the fact that Gary had been arrested was hardly unanticipated, it still came as something of a shock.

"Mr. O'Banyon suggested I call and let you know," Glick continued. "My wife and I are on the way to police headquarters to meet him now. We hope to have him released on bail."

I wasn't sure what I could or should do at this juncture, so managed to say: "Thank you for calling, Mr. Glick, and please let me know what if there is anything I can do to help. You have my home phone number, and I'll be there in about an hour. Please convey my concern to Mrs. Glick. I'm sure Mr. O'Banyon will do whatever he can."

* * *

I'd no sooner hung up when the phone rang again.

"Hardesty Investigations."

"Dick, this is Mark Richman. I'm really going out on a limb here, but I think we should talk. Privately."

"Of course, Lieutenant," I said, hearing my voice floating like a cork on a mental sea of confusion.

"I understand you've arrested Gary Bancroft," I said.

"Word travels fast," he replied. "And of course that's what I want to talk with you about. But not over the phone."

"Well," I said, "I promised the Glicks I'd be at home shortly. Would it be possible for you to come to my place? I gather you weren't thinking of meeting at headquarters in any event." I readily admit that from time to time since I'd met Lieutenant Richman I'd entertained several erotic fantasies of luring him over to my apartment and vigorously demonstrating that heterosexuality was not the only game in town. The current scenario wasn't exactly what I had in mind however.

"Right," he said. "Your place is fine. I can meet you there in half an hour."

"Fine," I said, and heard him hang up before I could give him my address.

'Like you think for one minute he doesn't know it?' my mind asked. And I realized that of course he did—Richman was, yet again, no dummy. I wondered what else he knew about me that I didn't know he knew.

* * *

Traffic was a bitch, and I'd barely gotten into my apartment when the buzzer rang—the good Lieutenant, I guessed…rightly. I'd been very curious, ever since he'd called, as to exactly *why* he'd called. Obviously, he wanted something from me…but what? And whether he was here on his own or as some sort of envoy for Captain Offermann, I wasn't sure, though I had my suspicions. Well, I'd soon find out. A quick glance at the answering machine showed I had messages, but I didn't have a chance to check them before there was a knock on my door.

Seeing Richman standing there in all his civied glory set off a little flash-powder *"Poof!"* of erotic fantasy, but even I knew this wasn't quite the time for it. We did our customary handshake and, closing the door behind him, I gestured him to a seat. "Are you officially on duty," I asked, "or can I offer you a drink?"

He shook his head as he settled into my favorite chair. He sure looked like he belonged there, and I had to shut the door tight on the my little fantasies toy box. "I'm just on my way home," he said, "so while I'm not officially on duty, I'd better not. Maybe next time."

Next time! I could almost hear the fantasies beating on the lid of the box, wanting to get out.

I sat on the sofa, facing him, leaning forward with my elbows on my knees, my hands folded. "So what can I do for you?" I asked.

Richman was silent for a moment, staring at me as he always did. I assumed he probably did that with everyone, but…

"We did arrest Gary Bancroft," he said, "but I'll wager we won't be able to hold him long with Glen O'Banyon in the case."

"Then why did you arrest him?" I asked. "Obviously, you have more than…" I almost said "than the fact that he drives a silver

Porsche" but caught myself in time—I didn't want to remind Richman that I'd never told him that Gary drove a silver sports car—"…circumstantial evidence."

Richman suppressed a very slight smile, and his eyes never left my face. "Okay, Dick," he said, "I'm not sure when we're going to stop playing these little games with one another—I know you knew about Bancroft's car, and I'm not particularly happy that you didn't tell me, but the fact is we need your input on this whole mess. You know Bancroft, you know O'Banyon, you're a friend of Stark's, you're working for the Glicks, and you knew Anderson and Steiner. You know just about everybody involved in this case, you know them a hell of a lot better than we do *and* this whole thing is interwoven around the gay community—not to mention the bisexual community, if there is such a thing. We're like Alice at the tea party here, and you're the White Rabbit."

"Nice analogy," I said, and we exchanged a quick smile.

"Well, you know what I mean," he said. "And our problem is what it has always been; the police department is simply not as qualified as it needs to be for dealing with the gay community. You aren't a member of the force, but you're our closest link with the community. So—and this goes no further than the two of us, understood?" I nodded "—I've been authorized to let you in on certain facts of the case in exchange for your honest input."

I sat back on the sofa and crossed my legs, my right ankle on my left knee. "Go ahead," I said.

Richman took a deep breath. "I suspect you already know a lot of this, but we'll go through it from the top so as not to miss anything: Gary Bancroft knew Stuart Anderson and had…spent time with him. A set of very expensive knives was given to Stuart Anderson by a supplier the night he died, but was missing from Anderson's room when his body was found. Judging from his car and where he lives, Bancroft obviously has pretty expensive tastes. He was seen picking up Laurie Travers the night she was killed—one of the hookers who had seen Laurie get into the car thought she remembered two numbers from the license plate. Two random numbers out of seven didn't do us much good, but when we finally found out yesterday afternoon—no thanks to you, I might add—that Bancroft had a silver Porsche, those two numbers just happened to match two of the numbers on his plates. Laurie was stabbed by a very expensive knife from the same manufacturer of the set taken from Anderson's room, which was conveniently left near her body. There were no prints on the knife, of course, which made us wonder why the killer would bother to wipe the murder weapon clean and then leave it where it could be found." He paused. "Following me so far?"

"Every step of the way," I said, uncrossing my legs.

"Good," he said. "Based on the identification of Bancroft's car, we got a search warrant for his apartment yesterday afternoon, as you undoubtedly know. However, what you probably don't know is that, thanks to the sanitation workers' strike, we were able to search the Dumpsters behind Bancroft's building. They hadn't been emptied since the morning after Laurie Travers was found."

He looked at me with another slight smile. "Would you care to guess what we found in one of them?"

I hope I looked appropriately puzzled—largely because I fairly well was.

"A red leather case designed for a set of six Antonio Vivace knives. There were only five knives in the case."

* * *

'I've got to hand it to you, Richman,' I thought. 'You sure do know how to work a crowd.'

"So you arrested Gary." I could hear the cell doors slamming shut behind him.

"It seemed like the logical thing to do," he said, dryly. "As I say, O'Banyon will probably have him out in a matter of hours. But if, as we suspect, the pillows turn out to be Eider down…"

I sensed his hesitation, and picked up on it: "However…" I said.

He sighed again, and shifted his position in the chair. "However," he continued, "from what we can tell, the knife case had no fingerprints on it, which strikes me as more than just a little odd. We're doing further testing now, of course, but if indeed there are no prints… O'Banyon will be able to get Bancroft released just on that. And especially now with this new element."

"And that element is?" I said, feeling rather like one of Socrates' students, prompting the master along. (*"Tell us, Socrates...."*)

"Matt Rushmore," he said. "There's an outside chance arresting Bancroft might have been a little premature. I've got a very strong feeling about this Rushmore guy, and from what Bancroft said and what little we picked up from the Glicks and the others we've interviewed.... You know him too, of course, and I was curious why you'd never mentioned him?"

I felt a mixture of embarrassment and defensiveness, but we were doing one of our eye locks and I didn't want to be the one to break it. "Mainly because..." I hesitated, looking for a diplomatic way to put it "...I am not, as you've pointed out, a member of the police force and I didn't feel it was my place to go around pointing fingers at anyone until I'm pretty damned sure I'm right. My main concern was and is my clients: the Glicks, ModelMen, and their current escorts. But believe me, Lieutenant, if I had solid evidence against Matt—or Gary, for that matter—I'd have come to you."

I had no idea whether or not he was convinced—his expression never changed, but he did break off the stare as his eyes moved to the flashing red light on the answering machine. He looked at it just long enough for me to know he was looking at it, then brought his eyes back to mine.

"So now that we're aware of Rushmore," he continued, "I suspect we've—I'm talking about the police here—run head-on into that damned gay/straight brick wall. As far as the old school in the department is concerned, you're gay or you're straight. Guys who go both ways throw them for a loop. Bancroft was hard enough for them to figure out, but as far as they're concerned, I think, he's straight. He looks straight, he acts straight, he has sex with women: he *is* straight." He heaved a quick sigh. "But when Rushmore, who looks and acts like a football player and has two kids, says he's strictly gay, that's pretty much beyond their comprehension and they wonder what he's trying to pull."

We were both quiet a moment, and Richman's expression reflected his concern.

"So I need your help," he said, finally. "I don't have a problem grasping the concept of being bi..." *Fantasy time!* "...but there's a hell of a lot I don't understand. Bancroft is doing his level best to pin the murders on Rushmore; Rushmore's claiming Bancroft is setting him up. And it's pretty obvious, to me at least, that something's going on between the two of them that neither one will talk about.

"Bancroft claims he was having dinner with Mrs. Glick on the night Anderson was killed, and she verifies that he didn't leave until nearly midnight; Anderson and his killer entered the Montero's garage at 11:15. Rushmore says he picked up a trick that night outside the Male Call, but he can't prove it, which puts the ball in his court. Neither one can come up with a solid alibi for Steiner, but we have plenty of evidence to nail Bancroft to Laurie Travers."

He shook his head slowly. "There are too many holes here," he said. "Too many little things that we can't even guess at. I really need your help here."

Well, the case had reached the stage where I didn't have much to lose by telling him everything I knew. I could readily see that so much of what was going on was, in truth, a "gay thing" the police had no idea of how to deal with, let alone understand. And I felt that I could trust him not to take unfair advantage of anything I said.

"Everything off the record?" I asked. "Strictly between you and me?"

He nodded. "Agreed," he said.

I settled back on the couch and said: "Okay, Lieutenant, here's what I know…."

* * *

I don't wear a suit of shining armor, I don't ride a white horse, and I'm sure as hell not one of those detective novel p.i.'s who can look at a cigarette butt and tell you what size shirt the smoker wore and what college he'd gone to. I may be short on brilliant deductive reasoning, but I've been pretty lucky at following my hunches and gut reactions. Finding killers I can handle; apprehending them was a job for the police. But if I was in a position to provide information to enable them to do so, I was obligated to provide it.

Whether or not Richman followed everything I told him, or understood it, or agreed with it, I couldn't say. But he did listen to every word without comment or objection.

"…which brings us to right here, right now," I said. "There are still a few things I want to find out, and I hope that you might be able to find a way to give me a little time to do it."

I knew full well by now that Richman was Captain Offermann's *de facto* leg man on this case and that, much as I might want to think that he was sitting there because of my irresistible charm and sexual appeal, he was there with Offermann's full knowledge and approval.

"I can't promise anything," he said, "but I'll see what I can do."

"That's all I can ask," I said.

Richman glanced quickly at his watch. "Oh, oh," he said, slapping his palms on his knees and leaning forward to get up from his chair. "I'm late for dinner. My wife's going to be really pissed—not that she's not used to it by now."

As I was getting up from the couch, the phone rang.

"Go ahead and get it," he said, offering me his hand for our parting handshake. "I can let myself out. But keep me posted."

"I will. For sure," I said as I picked up the phone. "Dick Hardesty," I said as Richman closed the door behind him.

* * *

"Did you get my message?" the voice asked. Luckily I recognized it immediately as Matt.

"Sorry, Matt. I had a…visitor…the minute I walked in the door and I haven't had a chance to check the machine. How did it go with the interview?"

"I fucking knew it!" he said, without explanation.

"Knew what?" I asked, though I didn't have to ask.

"He's setting me up! I told you that's what he was doing, and I was right. That fucking bastard!"

"Hold on a second," I said. "Tell me everything that went on. Who interviewed you? What did they want to know?"

"Know?" he asked, the bitterness clearly evident. "They seem to *know* everything; they mostly *told*. Two detectives…Carpenter and Couch, I think their names were…took me into one of those interrogation rooms with that fucking two-way mirror. I don't know who the hell all was behind there watching me. They told me how

I'd gotten fired from ModelMen and why, my 'specialty' with clients, my temper—they even had my police file from back home, when I beat up that sonofabitch boyfriend of my ex-wife's. And a lot of it was stuff only Gary could have told them; stuff from our Marine days, the Rolex. That I'd had the hots for Billy—even that I hate to wear condoms, fer chrissakes! What the hell does that have to do with anything?"

I felt the hair on the back of my neck stand up. Why? Phil might have mentioned it, but I was betting on Gary: and if that was the case, why would he have said anything about that unless he knew the autopsy would show that Billy'd been fucked without a condom?

I forced myself to put that thought on hold and got back to the subject. "Did you go to the Male Call last night, to look for the guy you were with the night Billy died?" I asked

"Yeah," he said, his voice still echoing his anger and frustration. "Stood there for two fucking hours, hoping he'd come in. He wasn't there. The cops think I just made him up so I'd have an alibi. I'm heading back there tonight, just as soon as I calm down a little. I've got to find him. He can prove I couldn't have killed Anderson."

"Well, obviously the cops didn't think they had enough to arrest you, or they would have," I said, trying to sound reassuring. I wondered if he knew they'd arrested Gary, but decided not to mention it unless he did.

"They're just waiting," he said. "Gary'll come up with something. You watch."

I could certainly empathize with him, but…"Matt," I said, "I still can't figure out why Gary would turn on you like that. So you broke up. Too bad, but Gary definitely doesn't seem like the type—and I hope you'll excuse me here if I hit some sort of nerve—to be vindictive over the end of a relationship."

Matt's short laugh didn't have a hint of humor in it. "A 'relationship'? I was the only one who ever thought there was a relationship. Gary never gave a shit about me. He conned me from day one; I was nothing to him but a fucking go-for, and the minute I stood up to him he does this."

The thought occurred to me that it all sounded just a bit melodramatic, but that might be partly because I had still never adjusted to the huge gulf between the ultra-butch facade Matt presented to the world, and the all-too vulnerable guy inside.

"You never did say what he wanted you to do that you wouldn't," I said.

"Nothing," he said abruptly. "Never mind. It's not important."

I was pretty certain that it sure as hell was important. "I think it must have been. I can't imag…"

"Drop it," he said. "Okay? Just drop it." The tone of his voice made it clear he meant it.

"Okay," I said. Which of course I had no intention of doing. I'd find out one way or the other, somehow.

There was a rather awkward pause, and then Matt said: "Well, I gotta go down to the Male Call and look for that guy. You just watch yourself around Gary, you hear me? And don't believe a word he says. Especially about me."

We hung up and I once again found myself staring at the receiver in my hand wondering for the umpteenth time exactly what was going on.

* * *

A couple of the things in my conversation with Lieutenant Richman were idly circling around in the back of my mind. What were they?

Ah, yes: Gary's alibi for the night Anderson was killed. He'd been having dinner with Iris, and didn't leave until around midnight. Is there a flaw in this picture? Would Iris Glick have lied to cover for her son? Unlikely, but even if she did, Mrs. Dabbs would be able to verify what time Gary left.

Then I remembered: Sunday is Johnny-Mae's day off. And Mr. Glick was out of town. That meant only Gary and Iris were in the house.

What else about Gary and that night? He was there when Stuart Anderson called asking for Phil. I'd naturally assumed Iris had taken the call: but what if she hadn't? And Gary had called Matt around 9:30—just about the same time Anderson called.

Gary was setting Matt up! My mind raced off on its own scenario: Gary answers Anderson's call and talks him into letting Gary come over instead of Phil. *Where was Iris?* Who knows…

putting the dishes away? Getting more coffee from the kitchen? Gary then calls Matt to make sure he was home alone and wouldn't have an alibi! Matt had told him he was going to bed early. Gary makes some excuse and leaves, meets Anderson somewhere and rides to the hotel in Anderson's car, and then....

Nice story. Only one small question: why? Did Gary mean to kill Anderson? If he didn't, why would he have bothered to call Matt? And if he did intend to kill him…again, why? Just to set Matt up for a murder? 'Come on, Hardesty!' What in hell reason would he have to do that? Because Matt wouldn't do something he wanted him to do? A little unlikely, I'd think.

Obviously, the first thing to do would be to have another little talk with Iris Glick. I'd have to wait until morning—Gary may or may not still be in jail, and in either case the Glicks would be preoccupied. It could wait until morning.

Now, as for Matt and his alibi. I really didn't know whether he actually had one, or if he had indeed made it up. But if he was telling the truth and could locate the guy and the alibi stood up, that would pretty much get him off the hook and nail Gary as the killer. I decided to call Jared on the outside chance he might have gone to the Male Call that night. I dialed his number, and got his machine. I left a message for him to call me as soon as he could.

Still working on outside chances, I gave Tim a call. It was remotely possible that Jared was over there.

The phone rang three times and I was about to hang up when I heard the receiver being lifted and a rather breathless "Hello?"

"Tim—hi, it's Dick. Jared isn't by any chance over there, is he?"

"No…I haven't talked to him in a couple of days, actually. I heard the phone ringing just as I was coming in the door. I had an early…date."

"Phil?" I asked, taking a not-so-wild guess.

"Yeah," Tim said, just a little hesitantly. "He has to meet a client at 10, so we went out for an early dinner. We, uh…"

He didn't have to say anything else. "I get the picture," I said.

"Well," Tim added hastily, "we're not exactly registering china patterns at Marston's, but we do seem to be…uh, getting along okay."

"Just take it as it comes," I said, truly delighted to think of the two of them getting together. "But I've got my fingers crossed for you…for both of you."

"Thanks, Dick. Really. This is all new to me, as you well know—it's new to Phil, too, I guess—but so far, so good."

Tim didn't ask about the case—probably too preoccupied thinking about Phil—and I didn't necessarily want to bring it up at the moment, so I didn't. We talked randomly for a minute or two more, then hung up with the usual promises to get together soon.

I watched the late news, waiting to hear from Jared, and when I didn't, I went to bed.

* * *

It had been a restless night, but I got to the office on time to find a message consisting of three words: "Warman Park, 12:30."

Here we go, I thought.

Well, if I had to meet Richman at Warman Park at 12:30, I'd damned well better try to talk with Iris Glick before that, so I called immediately. Mrs. Dabbs answered the phone and then put me through to a very tired-sounding Iris.

"You'll have to excuse me, Mr. Hardesty, but it was a very long and difficult night. I'm afraid I didn't get much sleep, if any."

"That's understandable, Mrs. Glick," I said. "Was Gary released?"

"Yes, thank heavens," she replied. "Mr. O'Banyon was able to use his influence to expedite the process, and he was released around 11:00. A terrible night!"

"I'm sure," I said, "and I'm sorry you had to go through it. Is Gary there with you now?" I sincerely hoped he wasn't.

"No, he insisted on returning to his apartment."

Good!

"And Mr. Glick?"

"He had a business meeting at 9. I told him to cancel it—he is the Chairman of the Board after all, but he insisted."

Better!

"Well, I know this is not a good time, but something has come up and it's really imperative that I speak with you again for a few moments. I won't take much of your time, I promise."

There was a long pause, and then: "I…well, all right. I don't mean to appear rude, Mr. Hardesty, but I'm quite upset and very tired. I hope you understand."

"Completely," I said. "I'll see you in about 20 minutes, then."

"Very well. Goodbye."

I picked up my coffee—I hadn't even taken the lid off yet—and left the office, locking the door behind me.

* * *

Mrs. Dabbs showed me once again into the vast living room where Iris Glick sat on one of the sofas in a very expensive housecoat, drinking coffee. She looked tired, though she had obviously taken the time to put on her makeup and pull her hair sharply back into a pony tail.

"Would you like some coffee, Mr. Hardesty?" Mrs. Dabbs asked as she stood aside to let me enter the room.

"No thank you, Mrs. Dabbs," I said. "I won't be staying very long."

She smiled, nodded, turned, and moved off toward the back of the house.

Mrs. Glick did not even try to get up to greet me, and instead I walked over as she set her coffee cup on the saucer on the coffee table, and leaned forward to take her extended hand. She then patted the sofa cushion beside her, and I moved around the coffee table to sit down.

"What do you want to know, Mr. Hardesty," she asked, her voice weary.

"Tell me about the night Stuart Anderson was killed." I said. "You were having dinner with Gary. Was there any particular reason?"

She picked up her cup and settled back onto the sofa. "Not really," she said. "Mr. Glick was out of town on business, and Gary had been…well, not at all himself…since he and Matt…since he had moved into his new apartment. I thought a quiet evening with just the two of us would be nice."

"Sunday is Mrs. Dabbs' day off, isn't it?" I asked.

She looked at me quickly, then away. "Yes, but I'm a very good cook, as is Gary. We made a little adventure out of it."

"And when Stuart Anderson called, who answered the phone?"

"Why, I did, of course" she said. "We have a private line for clients, and no one other than Mr. Glick or myself is allowed to answer it. Stuart said he'd finished his business earlier than he'd anticipated—from the music in the background I gathered he was calling from the restaurant—and wanted to know if Phil might be available. I told him Phil was occupied, and asked if he might like to spend time with one of our other escorts. He said no, he could wait until Phil was available, and I scheduled him for the following evening at 8:00, their usual time. We chatted for a few moments during which he asked about Mr. Glick and I mentioned that Gary and I had just finished dinner. As you know, Gary had spent some time with Stuart when he first became a client, and Stuart always asked about him. When I said Gary was here, Stuart asked to say hello, so I put Gary on the phone."

"And did you hear anything of their conversation?" I asked.

She shook her head, leaning slightly forward to return her cup to its saucer on the coffee table. "No. Gary reminded me, as he took the phone, that the creme boule needed attention, so I went into the kitchen. When I returned just a few moments later, Gary was on the phone with Matt. I didn't hear their conversation either, but when he hung up, I could tell Gary was very upset."

"What do you mean by 'upset'?" I asked.

She leaned forward to adjust the coffee cup on its saucer, and wiped at an imaginary crumb on the table with the edge of her hand. She did not look at me.

"Gary is always very much in control of his emotions," she said. "When he is upset, he becomes withdrawn and sullen. I could tell he was definitely upset by something."

"And he left here at what time?" I asked.

"As I told the police, it was nearly midnight."

I was quiet for a moment, looking at her, and was well aware that she would not meet my eyes. I hope her lie was not quite so obvious to the police.

I gave her a small smile. "I know what you told the police, Mrs Glick," I said. "But what time did he really leave? I'm on your side, remember."

She carefully smoothed out the lap of her housecoat before

answering. "I really don't remember," she said. "Really. We had our dessert but he hardly said a word. Finally, he excused himself and said he really had to spend some time alone. As I've said, Gary does not show his emotions readily, but I know he was very distressed by his...parting...with Matt. So I understood his wanting to leave, and I did not look at the clock."

"And so when you heard of Stuart Anderson's death...?" I prompted.

"Both Gary and I were heartsick!" she said. "We realized immediately that it would be very likely that the police would find out about ModelMen. Gary had been the last person to speak with Stuart—the police's assumption that he might be responsible was axiomatic. That Gary's disagreement with Matt—which happened after he spoke with Stuart—was the only reason he left earlier than he had intended would mean nothing to the police. And since I had not looked at the clock when Gary left, I can't say for sure that it *wasn't* nearly the time I told them."

She fell silent, and I joined her in it for a few moments, realizing she wasn't going to like my next question. "Is it at all possible that Mr. Anderson might have asked Gary to take Phil's place for the night?"

She sat upright as though she'd been slapped. "Impossible!" she said. "I asked Stuart if he wanted another escort, and he said no. If he'd wanted Gary's company, he certainly would have asked for it. And Gary would never make arrangements with a client without clearing it through me. Never."

Unless he knew you'd never find out about it from Anderson, I thought.

Seeing how upset I'd made her, I decided it was time for a diplomatic withdrawal.

"Well, thank you for your time and honesty, Mrs. Glick. I really didn't mean to upset you; but I'm sure you understand that in order for us to help Gary, we can't afford to be taken by surprise by something the police may come up with."

She nodded, then rose with me and walked me to the door of the living room.

"Gary did *not* do this, Mr. Hardesty," she said emphatically. "I know my son."

Ya think? my mind asked, rather sadly.

CHAPTER 15

I parked in the underground garage at Warman park at 12:15, and emerged to find that a thick cloud cover had rolled in and it looked like it might pour at any second. We hadn't made any contingency plans for meeting anywhere else, and I didn't have a raincoat or umbrella with me, so all I could do was hope for the best. The usual picnickers and book readers and fountain sitters had more or less disappeared in anticipation of the rain.

Sure enough, it started to sprinkle, and I moved to the cover of a large elm just opposite where we customarily met. I could hear the rain hitting the leaves above me, so I stood with my back against the trunk debating on whether I should stay or make a run for the parking garage entrance about 200 feet away. I was just opting for the latter when I saw a familiar form come sprinting down the walkway toward the fountain, followed by a curtain of heavier rain. He saw me, motioned toward the garage entrance, and kept running. I joined him, and we hit the doorway just as the rain became a downpour.

"Good timing," I said as we stood behind the heavy glass doors and watched the machine-gunned raindrops ricocheting off the sidewalk. It showed no signs of being merely a passing shower, so I said: "You want to come down to my car? We can talk there, and I can give you a ride back to headquarters when we're done."

"Sure," he said as we turned and went down the stairs.

He was slightly in front of me, and I had a chance to see him from, literally, a different angle than usual. He was in civies, and I sure liked the way he moved.

Oh, fer chrissakes, Hardesty! my mind snapped. *He's straight! Get used to it!*

We found my car and, being the gentleman that I am, I opened his side first, then moved around to the driver's side as he leaned across the seat to unlatch the lock from inside.

"So," I said when we'd settled in, "what's new?"

"We're going to arrest Matt Rushmore." he said.

"For…?" I asked, thinking *Didn't we just play this game with Gary?*

"For the murders of Stuart Anderson, Billy Steiner, and Laurie Travers."

"Based on what?" I asked.

Richman moved around so that he could better face me, one shoulder resting against the door, the other against the back of his seat. "Based on his interview, his having no credible alibis for any of the murders, and the fact that the knife box, even though it was found behind Gary Bancroft's apartment building, had no fingerprints on it. We think Rushmore planted it there."

"And Gary's silver Porsche?"

"Good point," he said, "but Bancroft swears Rushmore's been following him—some 'jealous lover' business, I gather. He figures Rushmore saw him drop Laurie off, picked her up himself, and did her in. We've been spending a lot of time interviewing the regulars who hang around Cole and Prentice, where Bancroft claims he let Laurie Travers—he did identify her from her picture, by the way—out of the car and we found a bag lady who thinks she saw a woman get out of a 'light colored' car at about the same time."

"And did she see anybody else pick Laurie up?"

He hesitated for a moment. "Well, no…but…"

Gee, a hooker getting out of a 'light colored car' on a corner near a coffee shop frequented by hookers. Bet that doesn't happen often, I thought.

I shook my head. "That hardly seems like a steel-clad case," I said, and Richman, watching me as always, gave a little smile.

"True," he said. "From what we can tell, the weapon used to kill Stuart Anderson is still being carried around between the legs of his killer. But we have the murder weapon for Laurie Travers and all we needed was the pillow that suffocated Billy Steiner. The pillows we took from Bancroft's apartment were filled with goose feathers. That, no fingerprints on the knife case or the murder weapon, and what Bancroft had to say about his…ex-friend… pointed us toward a set-up by Rushmore. We were able to get a search warrant for his apartment early this morning to get his pillows, and guess what? It looks like they're filled with Eider down."

"How in the hell can you tell the difference?" I asked. "Feathers are feathers."

He smiled again. "Not quite. Eider down is distinctive in several regards, including a predominance of black and white feathers. The lab is making the final analysis now."

"But you haven't arrested him yet?" I asked.

He looked at me without expression for a full minute, then said: "No. If the lab says it's definitely Eider down, we'll formally arrest him then. I thought you might want the chance to talk to him first, to see if you can pick up on anything that might let us cement the case."

I rolled down my window about halfway—it was getting uncomfortable in that car, in more ways than one. Having rolled it down, I turned back to the good Lieutenant. "I'm afraid I don't like this, Lieutenant. I'm not a police informant, or some snitch." I was really surprised at how strongly I felt about being used by the police department. Richman could have unzipped his fly right then and offered me unlimited sex in exchange, and I'd still have said 'no'—which gives you an idea of just *how* strongly I felt. Lieutenant Richman just looked at me and the corners of his mouth curved up just the slightest bit.

"No," he said. "You're not a police informant, and you're not a snitch. What you *are* is a private investigator who doesn't want to see a guilty man go free, or an innocent one go to prison. The fact is that right now, we don't know for sure what the hell to believe. Is Bancroft setting Rushmore up? Is Rushmore setting Bancroft up? You know these guys one hell of a lot better than we do; you can see things we can't. That's all I...we...want: the truth."

I managed to calm down as he talked. He was right, of course.

"And let me ask you," he said calmly. "What were you were intending to do if...or let's make that 'when'...you do figure out who did it? Wrestle them to the ground? The police have to come into it at some point. Now, let me turn the tables on you a little, and use one of your favorite arguments: if you want us to take over the whole case from this point on, fine. We can and we will. You can just walk away. But I think I know you well enough by now to know you could never do that. And we both know you have a better chance of bringing this to a head quicker than we do, and you can see things we can't when it comes to the gay community."

I heard myself giving a deep sigh, and I nodded. "So what do you want from me?"

Richman returned the nod. "First, I...we...don't want you to do anything stupid. No heroics. Just remember the guy we're after kills people. All we want is that when you are really sure which one of these guys did it—or even if you are sure neither one of them did it—you just give me a call and let us take it from there. Agreed?"

It was with a surprising degree of effort that I managed to say: "Yeah."

"Good." he said, and smiled. Then he did something that really surprised me: he reached out with his left hand and slapped my right leg, lightly. Under almost any other condition, my crotch would be yelling "Whoopee!", but not now. It was a pat on the leg. Period.

But my little inner voice still managed to say: *Damn!*

We'd said just about all there was to say, so after a minute or two of relative silence, I asked if he wanted me to drive him the two blocks back to headquarters, and he said "yes."

* * *

I decided to call Matt from the office—I wanted to check for messages anyway, and when I did, I found one from Jared.

"Hi, Dick: Jared. Sorry I've been missing you, but I've been really...busy. I'm on my lunch break, but I'll give you a call at home as soon as I get off work, okay? See ya."

Nothing from the Glicks. Nothing from Gary. Nothing from Phil or Tim, but I put two and two together on that one. I had no idea whether Matt might be home or not, but I gave it a try, and was surprised when he answered on the first ring.

"Matt: Dick. Just thought I'd check in and see how things were going."

"They searched the place," he said. I didn't tell him I knew.

"And?" I said.

"They took my pillows. My fucking pillows! And I just figured out why! What a fucking idiot!"

"You want to talk about it in person?" I asked.

"No," he said,. "I think I'm going to go over and have a talk with Gary."

I didn't like the tone of his voice, and I definitely didn't like the implication.

"Hold on a second," I said. "That's a really bad idea and you know it. Why don't you let me come over and we can talk about it? I can be over in less than fifteen minutes. Can you hold off that long?"

There was a moment of silence, then: "Yeah," he said, "I guess so. But I'm not making any promises after that."

"Good," I said. "That's all I can ask. Just try to calm down, and I'll be right over. Stay there."

"You better make it fast," he said.

I was halfway around my desk heading for the door as I hung up.

* * *

Matt had the door open by the time I reached his apartment after ringing the buzzer. He motioned me in with a jerk of his head. He looked really pissed.

"He's done it this time," he said, his voice a study in barely-controlled anger.

"Okay, so tell me about it," I said.

He led the way to the couch, and I sat down. He started to sit, but apparently changed his mind and walked to the window, looked out for no reason I could tell, and walked back again. He just stood there, his hands on the back of the chair in front of me.

"When Gary moved out of here and into his new place," he said, first taking the time to light a cigarette and offer me one (I was tempted but declined), "he left most of the furniture. None of it was good enough for his new place. He conned Iris into buying most of what he needed, including a fancy new bedroom set." He looked at me and almost smiled, but not quite. "That woman is on one enormous guilt trip, and Gary milks it for every penny he can get.

"So then the day after the Gay Pride parade, he calls me up and says he wants to come over to pick up some stuff he left. Asks if he can trade me for the pillows off our bed; bitches because the ones he bought are too damned soft. He knows I always thought the ones we had were like rocks, so I said 'okay.' I knew fucking-A well that he was going to try to—" he paused, took a long drag off his cigarette, and leaned over to stub it out quickly in one of the several ashtrays on the lamp table beside him. He never finished his sentence, and I found that fact more than a little intriguing. Try to what? But I decided to let him continue, and ask questions later.

Even though he'd only halfway smoked the last cigarette before putting it out, he lit another.

"Anyway, he comes over with a suitcase and these two huge pillows and starts looking around in the closets for a couple shirts and stuff he'd left. He asked me for some coffee, so I went into the kitchen to make it. I don't know what all he took, if anything. I noticed he'd put pillowcases on the pillows, which I thought was kind of odd—Gary's not the domestic type. I found out why that night when I went to bed. I bunched one up and a little puff of feathers shot out of one corner. The thread had come loose and there was maybe a half inch hole, which I fixed with a safety pin. I was pissed to think Gary knew damned well it was torn, but he figured he could just pass it off to good old Matt, who'd be too stupid to realize he was being pissed on again—it's classic Gary."

He looked at me, long and hard. "Billy was killed with a pillow, wasn't he?" he said.

Again, I felt that cold chill. I nodded. "From what I know," I said.

"I guess Gary's right," he said, "I *am* stupid. I never put two and two together; the cops never told me how Billy died and I never knew until they came in to get those fucking pillows."

He was quiet for a moment, then sighed.

"So I've had it," he said, calmly. "I've got no alibi at all for the night Billy was killed, I can't find the guy I tricked with the night Anderson died, and as far as the cops are concerned my being completely gay doesn't mean shit since I've got kids—they probably think I spend most of my free time on Pussy Patrol: hell, that's what *they*'d do if they had the chance. So unless I can find that guy, I'm really, really screwed—and they'll probably arrest me before I can find him."

His assessment of the situation was, I knew, pretty accurate.

Time to take the plunge.

"Okay, Matt," I said, readjusting my position on the couch so I could face him more directly. "We're pretty much down to the wire, here. I want to believe you, and if there's anything I can do to help you, I will—I promise. But I know damned well that there's more going on here than you're willing to tell me, and unless I know everything, you're going to take the fall."

He took a long drag off his cigarette and stubbed it out quickly in one of the several ashtrays on the lamp table.

"Won't do much good," he said. "I can't prove anything and nobody will believe it, anyway."

"Try me," I said. "And start by telling me just why Gary is trying so hard to set you up."

He shrugged, then sighed. "You're sure you want to hear it all?"

"I'm sure," I said.

He took a deep breath and began:

"I told you that even when we were in the Corps, Gary was obsessed with the fact that his mother had dumped him when he was a kid. I told you he swore to get even when he found her. It wasn't a matter of *if* he found her; I knew he would."

He reached into his pocket for another cigarette and, finding the pack empty, he went into the kitchen for another. When he returned, he sat down again, opened the new pack, and lit another cigarette before continuing.

"Gary played me from day one," he said. "I think he had his plan all laid out even before he met me. If it hadn't been me, it'd have been some other sucker. He led me on, and I let him. I knew he liked women too, and that didn't bother me: apples and oranges. But whenever he talked about the future, it was always 'we'—him and me.

"And then he found Iris, and called me. Shit, I was like a little kid, and I couldn't wait to get out to Vegas to be with him."

He looked at me and gave me a sad little semi-smile. "Sounds pathetic, doesn't it? Well, when you've lived all your life being something you're not, and when you've never had anybody who really gave a shit about you, you're pretty open to somebody who makes you think they might actually…well, you know."

I knew.

"So I got to Vegas, and I met Iris—who turned out to be a pretty decent lady in spite of what she'd done to Gary. Even though I'd always known Gary was a real con man, I was surprised at how he worked Iris. Even I thought he'd changed his mind about 'getting even.' They were like best buddies, and Gary never said a word to make me think otherwise. Of course, I never brought the subject up—I was just glad he'd found her and assumed that when he got to know her, he let all that other shit go."

He sighed and remained quiet for a moment. I wasn't about to butt in.

"We used to hustle the casinos to make extra money," he continued, "and that's how Gary met Arnold Glick. Most of the guys we hustled were pretty well off, but Arnold was really loaded! And when Gary introduced Arnold to Iris…. Well, I should have started getting wise right then, but I didn't."

He paused and glanced at me just long enough to check my reaction to all this, I guess, and then continued. "So I'd found a job working as a bouncer at one of the strip clubs and Iris got Gary a job with some executive she knew at an insurance company, and Iris and Arnold got married, and everything was fine. Gary was doing pretty damned well selling insurance—con men make good salesmen—and he convinced Iris that she and Arnold should take out huge policies on one another. Arnold is getting up there in years, after all. I thought he did it just because it would really boost his commissions. He already had her wrapped around his little finger."

He looked at me as if to see if I was still with him. I was.

"So then one of Arnold's real estate ventures…the plans for Belamy Towers…really took off and he decided to move here. Iris insisted that Gary and I move, too. I'm not really sure what Arnold thought of that idea; he's sure no dummy, but he doesn't say much, and just lets Iris have whatever she wants.

"About the time of the move, Gary brought up the subject of a male escort service. It was a natural—he and I both hustled, Iris had had that little 'school' as she called it, Arnold had quite a few rich bi friends. So that's how ModelMen got started."

I'd begun to have an inkling of where all this was headed, but set it aside to concentrate on what Matt was saying.

"And then Arnold sold off a couple of his business interests back in New York, and made a killing." He paused for a second. "No pun intended. And that's when Gary sprang the trap on me. He waited until one night just after we'd had sex. Again, I should have seen something was coming. We'd taken a week off and gone to Hawaii, and all the time there, he never once took off with a woman: it was just him and me, and he kept talking about everything 'we' were going to do in the future.

"So, as we're lying there, Gary tells—not asks, tells—me what we're going to do: we're going to kill Iris and Arnold. Calm and casual. Nothing to it. We'll kill Arnold first, so all the money will go to Iris—that was just in case Arnold has some relatives we don't know about who might put a claim on the money if they both died together. Then we'll wait awhile and kill Iris so all the money will go to us. 'Us,' he said! I realized at that instant how fucking stupid he thought I was, that I'd fall for that!"

He looked at me again for my reaction, but I was too zeroed in on what he was saying to register one. I was in my mind-as-sponge mode, just soaking it all in.

He sighed, put out his cigarette, and started to reach for another but apparently decided against it.

"Part of me wanted to think he was joking, of course," he said, "but he wasn't. I just lay there beside him and listened to him talk. He wasn't just thinking out loud. He'd had it all figured out since God knows when and was just waiting until the right moment to tell me. After sex is always good.

"Now, Gary's spent a lot of time studying Iris. He knows exactly how she reacts to things, so he could be almost positive the scenario he worked out would work exactly as he planned it."

He paused again, looking at me. I didn't say anything, but let my eyebrow ask the question.

"Arnold doesn't like opera," he said. "Iris loves it. So Gary would buy tickets for himself, Iris, and me for a Sunday night, when Johnnie-Mae was off. Arnold would stay home alone. We'd make a point of going over during the day Saturday so I could drop some hints that I wasn't feeling very well— probably coming down with the flu, I'd say. Iris would be concerned, of course; she does enjoy the role of mother hen. Sunday evening, we'd pick her up at the house and I'd do my 'I'm really feeling rotten but I'll be brave' routine. Iris would insist we not go; I'd insist that she'd been looking forward to it. Gary would suggest I go home to bed while he and Iris went ahead to the opera. Iris would object, but I'd say it was a good idea, and she'd go along."

As happens so often when I'm fascinated with something, I sat there, completely tuned out to the world, only seeing Matt's face, only hearing his voice.

"So they drop me off here, on their way to the opera. I come into the apartment and wait. As soon as they get to the theater, Gary suggests they should call to see how I'm doing. Either Iris will want to call, or Gary will be sure she gets on the phone. I say I'm feeling worse and am going to go right to bed. If Iris doesn't suggest I leave the phone off the hook so I can sleep, Gary will.

"They go in to the opera, I leave the apartment by the back way, drive my car—which I'd have parked a block or two away earlier—to Arnold's via back streets, pull up through the service alley. Gary's left the pool gate open. I go in, kill Arnold, make it look like a break-in and robbery, and go home. Gary arranges for Iris to insist stopping by the apartment on the way home from the opera, and there I am, fast asleep in bed, the phone off the hook."

I found myself shaking my head—I'm not sure if it was in disbelief or because of the intricacy of the scheme, and the fact that I could see it actually might work exactly the way Matt described it.

He counterbalanced my head shake with a slow nod, and continued. "The furor dies down, I've got a pretty good alibi supported by the grieving widow, and Iris inherits the Glick fortune. We wait several months—once Arnold is dead, Gary can afford to bide his time for awhile, especially to avoid suspicion—and then Iris has an 'accident'. A fatal one, of course. The exact details of that part of the plan he hadn't worked out yet, but I was sure he would."

Now it was his turn to shake his head. "And he actually expected me to go along with it! I do the dirty work: I kill Arnold—and I'm sure Iris too when the time came—and then we get the money. Oh, sure…like I'm actually dumb enough to believe that? I told him 'no,' I wouldn't have any part of it. I think that really blew him away. Here he's been grooming me to be his lap dog ever since that first day on the bus in boot camp, and I tell him 'no.' He dropped it for the moment, but kept coming back to it; how 'we' could have anything we wanted, do anything we wanted, go anywhere we wanted. And when I'd say 'no,' he'd just clam up and go out for the night and pick up a woman. Sometimes he'd bring her back here and fuck her in the guest room, hoping I'd get jealous, I guess. I knew he was sending me a message. He started getting more and more insistent until one night we had a really big fight about it. That was just a couple days before I went with that guy who got me fired. My own fucking fault for letting Gary get to me."

Apparently figuring he'd talked long enough without getting some feedback from me, he fell silent until I asked: "And you think Gary killed three people just to get even with you? I'm sorry, but..."

Matt shrugged. "See? I told you. Let's just forget it."

No way, Charlie! I thought. "Hey, no...I'm sorry," I hastened to say. "I want to hear it all. Go ahead, please."

He looked at me as if he wasn't sure but then shrugged again and continued. I guess he figured that if he had a chance of anybody buying his story, it would be me. It sure as hell wouldn't be the cops.

"I'm not saying he set out to kill anybody just to get even with me," he said, "but it sure turned out that way. Anderson may well have been some sort of accident for all I know, but once he was dead, Gary wasn't about to risk taking the blame. Not when I was available. He stole that knife set because he knew I...uh...like to take a souvenir every now and then. Those were pretty expensive knives. Maybe he thought at first he could just keep them and tell anybody who might ask that I'd given them to him. Either way, he saw it as a perfect way to get me to do what he wanted."

How would he know about the knife set? I wondered, but decided to wait to see if he was going to have an explanation.

"He called me a cohoping to get me to change my mind. Kept saying how he missed me, how we could still be a great team. I didn't buy it, and that pissed him off. Gary's not used to not getting whatever it is he wants...especially not from me. I'd try to shift the conversation anywhere but where he wanted it to go—ask him about the guys at ModelMen; made the mistake of telling him I was thinking about giving Billy a call. The next thing I know, Billy's in a Dumpster. I should have known right then that Gary had done it, but…"

"Do you have any proof?" I asked. "Other than the pillow exchange?"

Matt reached again for his cigarettes, apparently thought better of it, then changed his mind and fished the pack out of his pocket, removing a cigarette, replacing the pack, and lighting up. "I've got to stop this damned habit," he said. "It's going to kill me."

He blew out a long stream of smoke and waited a few seconds before answering my question. "I didn't," he said, "until after the hooker got killed."

"How's that?" I asked.

"I was looking for something and checked my footlocker in the closet. Haven't opened it in months. But when I did, there on top was a red leather case I'd never seen before. I opened it up, and there were six velvet-lined compartments with five really expensive-looking knives; when I saw that, and that one was missing, I knew. I remembered that Anderson had a bunch of stores that sold kitchen stuff, and I knew that Gary liked expensive things. He'd taken it, used one of the knives to kill the hooker, and then planted the box where he didn't think I'd ever look, but knew the cops would if they searched my place."

We were both quiet for a minute, my mind like a backed up sink slowly letting all this information drain into my memory. Something…*something*…wasn't right.

Matt was watching me, waiting for my reaction, but I was too busy at the moment trying to absorb it all and figure out what that *something* was.

"When I found the knife set," he said, "I knew what he was up to. If I refused to go along with killing Arnold and Iris, he could use the knife set—I still didn't know about the pillows, of course, stupid jerk that I am—to frame me for murders I didn't commit. So I wiped the case off after I picked it up, to get rid of my fingerprints—I knew they couldn't be on the knives—then waited until that night and put the case in the Dumpster behind Gary's building. Then I stopped at the hardware store and bought a new set of locks for the door. That sonofabitch thinks he's getting in here again to plant some more shit on me, he's got another thought coming!"

* * *

Feeling a little bit like a punch-drunk fighter who's just gone 15 rounds, I left Matt's apartment shortly thereafter, after managing somehow to tell him not to do anything foolish, and to just wait to see what the examination of the pillows showed—though we both knew damned well what that would be. I was pretty sure he'd calmed down enough by the time I left that I didn't have to worry about him going after Gary right then. I assured him that I would do whatever I could to try to find his alibi trick, though again I realized that would be next to impossible even if I was convinced there *was* an alibi trick, which I wasn't, totally.

I felt like my head was carrying around a ton of rocks.

Did I believe him? It made sense. I could, with relatively little effort, see Gary as the master manipulator Matt painted him as being. The plan to kill the Glicks was a shocker, but again....

But just as likely, I knew, was that it was Matt who was doing the manipulating here; that he was the one out to get even with Gary for having dumped him. Hell hath no fury like a lover scorned.

What about the pillows? It was just as likely that Gary had taken the old set of pillows when he moved from Matt's apartment, and that Matt had bought the Eider down as replacements, especially if Gary, who'd been the leader throughout their relationship, had indeed liked hard pillows. Matt probably would have gone along with hard pillows.

But Gary hadn't appeared to be the least concerned when the police took the pillows off his bed. Maybe because he knew they weren't the right ones? Chalk one up in Matt's column.

Matt admitted he had been thinking about calling Billy. What if he had?

Shit!

* * *

It was just after 3:30 and though it was a little early for Happy Hour at Ramón's, I decided that my need for a Happy Hour made it worth jumping the gun a little. Jared had said he'd call me when he got off work, and though I wasn't sure of his schedule, I knew that often Ramón's was his last stop of the day, so thought I'd risk it. Sure enough, as I pulled up in front of the bar, I saw Jared's truck just turning into the alley leading to the back door. I hurried inside, waved to Jimmy, who was waiting on a customer near the front door, and moved quickly to the back to where Jared was rolling in a dolly stacked with beer cases. He seemed surprised to see me.

"Dick, hi," he said. "I was going to call you as soon as I got home. Glad to see you couldn't wait to see me, though."

We exchanged grins. "Right as always," I said. "But I did have a question that sort of can't wait."

"Oh?" he asked, stepping around from behind the dolly. "What's that?"

I quickly outlined the situation of Matt's having picked up a trick at the Male Call the night Anderson was killed but not having gotten the guy's name, and asked if Jared might have any idea of how I could track him down.

Jared shook his head. "Didn't get the guy's name, huh?" he asked. "Gee, I'll bet that's the first time *that's* ever happened at a gay bar. I do it all the time. I did it myself a couple weeks ago—I was just coming out of the place and ran into this…"

"Whoa, there!" I'm afraid I practically yelled. "What night? What time? What did the guy look like?"

Jared looked at me as though I were more than a little demented. "Don't remember exactly when it was," he said. "A Sunday, I think. Maybe around ten…eleven…thereabouts. Real hot number; butch as they come—and did he ever! Can't describe what he looked like from the neck up in all that much detail. We went to his place over off of Brookhaven. I remember he had a big 'U.S.M.C.' tattoo on his left bicep. I did my best to lick it off, but…That help?"

'Oh, Hardesty,' my mind sighed, 'somebody up there really likes you!'

"Jared, if you only knew!" I said. "I owe you, big time! You want anything, you got it!"

"How about a couple hours in the sling for starters?" he asked with a wicked grin.

I didn't know if he meant him or me, but at that point it didn't matter.

"Like I say, you got it!" Part of me hoped he'd say "tonight," because I really, really needed a break. But I knew full well that while my crotch may be into it, I wouldn't be. Those damned rocks in my head.

"I've got a date tonight," he said, to my relief, "but how about Saturday?"

"Great!" I said. With luck, this case would be over by then. "Your place or mine?"

He looked at me with a raised eyebrow. "You got a sling?" he asked.

"Uh, no…" I said, knowing he knew full well I didn't.

"Then mine," he said, reaching out to punch me quickly on the arm. "Seven thirty? I'll order in a pizza."

* * *

I had a quick drink after Jared left, talked with Jimmy for a few minutes, asking how Bob Allen and Mario were doing, and tried to make small talk, but I just wasn't in the mood.

Matt had his alibi, and Gary Bancroft, Gary of the sea-green eyes, Gary of the great sex, had killed three people and had designs on at least two more: his mother and unacknowledged stepfather. I had sex with him on the very same bed where Billy had died, though my head had not been resting on the same pillow. I didn't like that thought one bit.

All your fault, my head scolded my crotch, which pretended it didn't hear.

I would call Lieutenant Richman first thing in the morning. He'd been right that it wasn't my place or authority to actually arrest Gary, and I certainly wasn't about to go over and confront him. I'd done that once before in an earlier case and was damned lucky I didn't end up dead. Nope. No confrontations. I felt very sorry for the Glicks, but no more sorry for them than I felt for Stuart Anderson or Billy or even Laurie Travers, though I'd never met her.

But again, *something* wasn't right. There: that little flash of movement in the shadows in the back of my mind. What was it?

* * *

I wasn't really hungry, but I knew I had to eat something, so I went through the drive-through lane of a fried chicken place and got two breasts, extra crispy, a cup of mashed potatoes with extra gravy, and a side of cole slaw. When the smell of it, all the rest of the way home, still didn't make me hungry, I knew I was in trouble.

What the hell *was* it?

I ate dinner, looked at the television for a couple hours (I can't say I actually watched anything), and went to bed.

Why would Gary do it? I could see him killing Stuart Anderson—he choked the guy to death during sex. He obviously didn't like the guy very much to begin with, but hired men don't have much of a say in who they go to bed with. The client pays, the escort obliges. And Gary didn't strike me as the kind of guy to turn down money if it was offered. Either Anderson had asked him over, or Gary had suggested it; it didn't matter.

Anderson almost definitely had told Gary, as he told anybody else who would listen, that he was sending his kid away, in effect abandoning him. He'd have had no idea that wasn't the thing to tell a guy whose mother had dumped him when he was even younger than Anderson's kid. From what everyone said, Anderson was strictly vanilla when it came to sex. He didn't suck cock. Well, I can see where if Gary mentioned it and Anderson said 'no', Gary might have gotten pissed, which led to the bruise marks on his inner arms. Maybe Gary was trying to teach him a lesson, and got carried away.

And Matt was probably right; with Anderson dead, Gary decided to frame him for having had the balls to refuse to go along with Gary's plan to get the Glicks' fortune. The wedding ring being shoved up Anderson's ass? Gary knew Matt had pretty strong feelings about bisexuals who he didn't feel had the courage to at least admit what they were. And he stole the knife set because he knew that fit Matt's pattern, and while he may well have intended to keep it and say Matt had given it to him, after Billy's death he decided to plant it and the pillows in Matt's apartment. It made sense.

There it is again! That damned glimmer-thought. Come on out, you bastard! It darted back into the shadows.

Billy. Poor, sweet Billy. Why in hell kill Billy? Gary knew Matt had the hots for Billy—all the other escorts knew it, too, except maybe Phil. Matt had told Gary he was going to try to get together with him. Undoubtedly it was Gary who Billy had the date with, but didn't want to tell Phil because he thought Phil didn't approve of escorts dating one another. Gary's a big guy, probably pretty damned strong, too. Caught up in the heat of sex, pushing down on Billy's shoulders at the base of his neck, if Billy had a sudden asthma attack, he might not have been able to let Gary know. Billy was pretty vocal during sex, I remembered. Maybe Gary just didn't know what was really happening. Exchanging pillows with Matt and planting the knife set guaranteed tying Matt directly to all three deaths.

Yeah, but Billy wouldn't get fucked without a condom. Gary knew Matt refused to wear a condom; maybe it came off or it broke or he took it off halfway through the sex, and Billy wasn't aware of it?

No! No! Think!

Laurie Travers. Why would Gary kill Laurie Travers at all, let alone use a knife he'd stolen from Anderson? It didn't make any sense. None.

I sat bolt upright in bed.

That's it!

I looked at the clock: it was nearly 7 a.m. I hadn't even been aware I'd fallen asleep.

* * *

It was early, but I couldn't wait. There was one other thing I had to know. I dialed Gary's number and prayed he'd be home. Just before the answering machine kicked in, I heard Gary's sleepy voice. "Hello?"

"Gary, it's Dick. I'm sorry to get you out of bed, but I...uh...I wondered how things were going, and if you've heard any more from the police."

"Not a word," he said. "I just want this damned thing over and done with. This waiting around for a knock on the door's a pretty shitty way to live."

Though it had never happened to me, thank God, I could certainly empathize with him. "Well, you can be sure if they thought they had enough to re-arrest you, they would. So it's again a matter of no news being good news."

"Let's hope," he said.

I decided now was the time to ask my question: "There's something I wanted to ask you," I said. "You still have the keys to Matt's apartment, right?"

There was a very slight pause, then: "No, I did have, but he changed the locks on me."

"Exactly when was that, do you remember?"

Another pause, then: "Not too long after Billy died."

Bingo!

"Ah, okay," I said. "Thanks. I was just curious. I'll let you go, then. Take care and we'll talk later."

"Sure," he replied. "See ya."

We hung up.

I knew.

* * *

The question was: now that I knew, what was I going to do about it? What solid proof did I have? None. What solid proof did the police have? They had evidence, but proof? But that was more their job than mine. I was sure Gary would continue to blame all three deaths on Matt, and Matt would blame all three on Gary. But with Jared to provide Matt an alibi for the night of Anderson's death, if anyone were to take the fall for all three, I was pretty sure it would be Gary.

The one thing I sure as hell wasn't, was satisfied. Maybe I'd read one too many old fashioned detective novels, but part of me really wanted to have a dramatic confrontation... I could imagine everybody together in the Glicks' vast living room, Iris in a black, floor-length gown, the men all in tuxedos, sipping brandy and smoking cigars around the fireplace as I stood before them in a woolen sweater with a cowl collar, smoking a Sherlock Holmes meerschaum pipe (cherry tobacco) which I would use as a baton to emphasize important points, and awed them all with my brilliance. I could see eyes darting nervously from one person to the next as I laid out the evidence, narrowing down the suspects. Everyone trying to look calm and sophisticated, but breathless with anticipation. Richman and the cops, guns drawn, standing just outside the door waiting to burst into the room when they heard me say: "And, ladies and gentlemen, the killer IS..."

Unfortunately, life just ain't like that.

But my little scenario did give me an idea, and I called the City Building Annex and asked for Lieutenant Richman's extension. It was barely 8 a.m., but I knew from our past early morning breakfast meetings that chances were good that he would be there. Luck was with me.

"Lieutenant Richman," the voice said.

"Lieutenant, I need a favor," I said, and I told him everything.

It took some convincing, but he put me on hold while he checked with Captain Offermann, then came back on the line.

"You're sure you want to do this?" he asked. "It would be a lot simpler if we just brought both of them in for questioning here."

"I don't think that would do it. Without something more solid than what I gather you have now, this case can drag out for a long time and you still might risk letting a killer go free."

Richman sighed. "Okay," he said; "go for it."

I hung up and immediately dialed Matt's number, hoping that he would be home. Again, luck was with me.

"Matt," I said, "it's Dick. I just talked to my contact at the police department, and...well, you and I had better talk right now. I'm afraid they're getting ready to issue a warrant for your arrest for all three murders, but I convinced him to hold off until I could talk to him in person—I have an appointment to meet him at noon, but I think I've figured out a way to prove you didn't kill those three people if I can just verify one thing. Can you come over to my place at, say, 10:00? There are a few things I have to check on first."

"Aren't you afraid I'll just take off?" he asked.

"Not unless you want to prove beyond a doubt that you

are guilty," I said. "And I'm sure you're not."

There was only a slight pause and then: "Okay, I'll see you at 10."

We hung up and I dialed Gary's number, fairly sure he'd still be home. The phone rang four times, and I heard his answering machine kick in: "You've reached…" *Shit!*

I was just about to hang up when I heard the receiver being lifted: "Gary here."

"Gary, Dick," I said, vastly relieved.

"Sorry, Dick," he said, "I was in the shower. Something else you need to know?"

"Yeah, I just got a call from my contact at police headquarters," I said, with no little sense of 'this is a recording.' "I'm afraid they're getting ready to issue a new warrant for your arrest for all three murders, but I asked him to hold off until I could talk to you. I think I can change his mind if you could just verify one thing. He wants to see me in his office at noon, and he's giving me until then. Can you come over here at 9:30, say? I've got to make a few phone calls and tie some things together between now and then."

There was a long pause, and I was afraid he sensed something and wouldn't come. But then he said: "Okay: I'll be there."

"Great; I'll see you then."

My stomach was holding a butterfly convention, but it was too late to back out now.

As I hung up, the door buzzer rang, and I went to ring them in and open the door. Richman had worked quickly. When a heavy-set guy in work clothes appeared, carrying what looked like a large tool box, I motioned him in. "Set it up wherever you want," I said, as he looked around the living room, then went to work. When he left, I walked over to the window and looked down at the street, watching as he got into a blue van parked at the curb. It did not drive off.

* * *

At 9:35 the buzzer rang again.

Show time!

I opened the door and stepped aside as Gary strode into the

room. "You want some coffee?" I asked.

He shook his head. "No, I want to know what's going on. What's all this bullshit about an arrest? What do they have they didn't have the last time they tried to arrest me?"

I realized I had to do some fancy footwork to stall for time. "I don't think it's what they have," I said. "They didn't tell me, but I think it's a who."

I thought Gary was about to explode.

"That fucking son of a bitch!" he spat.

I gave him a quick, traffic cop "Halt" gesture. "Hold on just a second," I said. "You don't know that it's Matt and I don't either. That's why I wanted to have you over here. I wanted to..."

"He's coming over, too?" Gary asked. "I told you I don't want anything to do with that sick bastard!"

I went over and sat in the chair facing him. "I understand," I said. "But things have reached a point where the only way we're going to be able to resolve all this is for me to talk to you both at the same time. So just be cool, okay?"

Fortunately, at that moment, the buzzer sounded again, and I got up to answer.

When I opened the door and Matt saw Gary, I thought for a moment he was going to turn around and walk away, but then he tentatively stepped inside and I closed the door.

"What the fuck is *he* doing here?" Matt demanded. "Is this another part of the set-up? You two little fuck buddies getting together to screw me? Well, it ain't..."

I raised my hand. "Calm down, Matt," I said. "Nobody's out to screw anybody. If we're ever going to be able to figure out what's going on, you two have to talk to me! So let's all just sit down and talk this out, okay?"

Matt reluctantly sat down. His eyes had been locked on Gary's since he came in, and even without the matching scowls, I could feel the tension between them.

Gary was on the couch, Matt in the chair I'd just gotten out of. I moved the other chair so I could face both of them, and sat down.

"Okay, guys," I began. "Now here's the way I see it. It's all pretty sketchy and it gets a little complicated, so please, hear me out all the way before you say anything. Let's start with the knife set...

"Gary took it after Anderson died...."

Gary leaned quickly forward on the couch and opened his mouth to say something, but I raised my hand to cut him off.

"Bear with me a second here, okay? I don't know for sure what happened, except that Anderson ended up dead." I addressed myself to Gary, though I could still see Matt out of the corner of my eye. "You must have been pretty pissed at him—if I were to guess, it would probably be because he was planning to abandon his kid the way Iris had abandoned you. And I'd guess his trying to hide the fact that he was bisexual by taking off his wedding ring when he was around gay guys ticked you off, too. That's probably why you shoved his ring up his ass after he was dead."

I could see Matt's eyebrows raise in a look of surprise. He hadn't known about the wedding ring incident, of course. Gary sat back on the couch, staring at me with those beautiful sea-green eyes.

"The fact that you've got pretty expensive tastes probably influenced your taking the knife set in the first place, and I'm not going to speculate on why you decided to plant it in Matt's apartment. But it was probably after...after Billy's death."

I was amazed that I could be sitting there talking about these things as calmly as I was.

"Again," I forced myself to say after a moment's pause, "I don't know the circumstances of Billy's death, and I don't need to, but I'd imagine it was after Billy died that you decided to plant both the knife set and the pillows. The fact that you hadn't been concerned with the police having taken the pillows from your bed—old pillows on a new bedroom set—meant Matt was right about the reason you wanted to switch."

I didn't think there was much point in bringing up the whole scheme to kill Arnold and Iris, or Gary's intent to blackmail Matt into signing on to it. That was between Matt and Gary. My purpose now was just to lay out the facts of the deaths.

I shifted my attention slightly to include both Gary and Matt, who until now had just sat there without saying a word.

"But I really couldn't figure out why Gary would kill Laurie Travers," I said, looking from one to the other, but really speaking more now to Matt. "He didn't have to. He'd planted the evidence. So why had he killed Laurie Travers?"

Both of them sat motionless, expressionless, but almost radiating hostility. There was no answer to my question, so I answered it myself:

"Simple; he hadn't." I said.

I now turned my full attention to Matt. "You had said you'd found the knife set after Laurie Travers had been killed, and that one of the knives had been missing. But it couldn't have been. Gary planted the knives the day he came over with the pillows—he was setting you up in case the police came after him. Gary couldn't have removed one of the knives before he planted the set: that would have meant he intended to use it to kill someone else, and there was no reason for him to do that if he'd already framed you for the first two."

Both of them were staring at me now, silently. Kind of disconcerting, but I forged ahead, again looking from one to the other as I talked.

"Matt, you always said Gary's being with women didn't bother you, but Gary said it did, and I strongly suspected he was right. You wanted Gary all for yourself. And believe me, guys, as a dyed-in-the-wool Scorpio, I can attest to the power of jealousy. Gary had said he was sure you had been following him around. I believe that, too."

Matt's face remained expressionless, but I could swear he was blushing. I turned back to Gary.

"Matt found the knife set, undoubtedly just as he said he had; just not *when* he said he had. He realized that it would frame him for Anderson's death, so he decided to turn the tables. He knew you liked hookers, so probably followed you, taking one of the knives with him, until he saw you pick up Laurie Travers and drop her off. Then *he* picked her up, took her somewhere, and killed her, leaving the wiped-clean knife near her body to assure the killing would be directly linked to Anderson."

The flush in Gary's face was not from blushing, but from anger. His eyes narrowed and all but bored holes through Matt, who returned the stare calmly.

"Murder's what you read about in books or in the newspapers. It's what *other* people do; not people you know. I know you two; at least a little bit. I found it really difficult to think that three people are dead because of something you guys did…" I shook my head. "Well, anger and jealousy and a really fucked-up past can combine in pretty strange ways. Matt, I imagine you probably felt sure the fact that you are gay would rule you out as a suspect in Laurie Travers' death, and because the knife was a direct link to Anderson's death, throw it all on Gary. The rationale about being gay and therefore being ruled out as a suspect in Laurie Travers' death worked pretty well with me, too, for a while. But then I realized that Laurie Travers' murder may not be related to having sex with her, and if so, the sex preference of the killer wasn't important."

To be honest, I was amazed that I'd gotten as far as I had without some sort of outburst from one or the other, but they just sat there, listening. And that fact made me increasingly nervous. Well, I wasn't about to let them know *that* little fact, so I kept right on talking, addressing myself to Gary again.

"Matt probably thought the cops would pick up on the connection to you a lot faster than they did," I said, "but luck was strongly on his side when he dropped the knife set into the Dumpster behind your building. If it hadn't been for the garbage strike, the Dumpster would have been emptied long before the police got the search warrant for your apartment."

I'd just about run out of steam, and I was even more aware that they were now both looking at me like a cobra watches the guy with the flute. Not a pleasant feeling.

As if on cue—which in fact it was—the phone rang.

I got up from my chair. "Excuse me, guys," I said. "I'll take it in the bedroom." I then walked into the bedroom and closed the door behind me, feeling a little lightheaded. It was Richman, of course.

"Want to listen?" he asked.

"Yeah, please," I said.

There was a pause, a bit of static, and then an oddly hollow sound. And then, in a voice obviously held low but more than making up in intensity what it lacked in volume, I heard Gary:

"You stupid, stupid son of a bitch!" he hissed. "You were stupid the day I met you and you're still stupid. We could have had everything…everything…and then you had to blow it all by killing that fucking prostitute!"

"So I was just supposed to sit back and let you frame me for that Anderson guy and Billy?" Matt asked, his voice equally low but more calm.

"I'd never have done that!" Gary answered. "Anderson was an accident! I was pissed at him for being such a ball-less bastard who would throw his own kid away but was too high and mighty to suck cock. Well, he sucked it. I didn't mean to kill the bastard. And how the hell did I know Billy had asthma? We had an argument when I wanted to fuck him without a condom and he started to wheeze a little, so I put on the damned condom and turned him over on his stomach and took the condom off when he wasn't looking. He must have sensed it, because he started to turn over, but I just pushed him down and did my thing. After a few minutes, he relaxed and I thought he was enjoying it. But he was dead, for chrissakes!"

"So you planted that evidence on me just in case, huh?" Matt said. "If you think I'd buy that for one second I'm a hell of a lot more stupid than you claim I am. You think I wanted to kill that girl? When I found out what you'd done to me, I didn't have any other choice."

There was another moment of silence, and then Matt said: "So what do we do now?"

Another brief pause, then Gary's voice: "Nothing right this minute. We can't kill Dick right here and now…"

Jeesus H. Kryst! I felt a wave of panic so strong I almost didn't hear Matt say:

"What the *fuck* are you talking about?" His voice echoed his incredulity. "I'm not going to kill Dick! Maybe you're developing a taste for murder, but I sure as hell ain't. One was way, way too many for me!"

"Dick is the only one who knows enough to tie all the ends together. With him out of the way, we'll just stick to our stories and they won't be able to prove anything."

"For chrissakes, Gary, you're insane!" Matt said.

"No, I'm not." he said. "We can't just do it here, but it's got to be done before he goes to the police at noon. Let me think…."

"Lieutenant?" I said into the phone, hoping he could hear me. "Are you there?"

"Yeah, I'm here, Dick," he said. "Hold on just another minute till we find out what Gary comes up with, then go back in there. And be cool."

Oh, sure, I thought.

Gary was saying something: "…how you hot-wired Jamison's car at Pendleton? We'll leave here, you go to that office building parking lot a couple blocks away and get us a car. I saw Dick's car parked on the street. When he comes out to get in to it, we'll do a hit and run. I'll follow you, you ditch the car, and we're home free."

"You don't seriously think that will work, do you?"

"What choice do we have?"

Richman's voice said: "Go."

I hung up the phone and returned to the living room, trying very hard to pretend I hadn't just heard these guys plotting to kill me.

"Sorry," I said. "A client."

"So what happens now?" Matt asked again.

"Well," I said, "to be honest with you, I'm hoping you'll turn yourselves in. Kind of stupid of me, I know, but it will go a lot easier on you if you do. Even if you stick to your stories, one or the other of you will go down eventually."

"Well," Gary said, "I think we'll just let them earn their money." He got up from his chair. "Nice try, though."

Matt got up, too. "Gary's right, I guess," he said. "Maybe they'll never be able to get enough hard evidence on either one of us. I don't have to tell you I wish none of this had ever happened."

"I know," I said, and odd as it may sound, all things considered, I firmly believed him.

As Gary reached for the doorknob he turned and gave me a big smile. "Take care of yourself, Dick," he said.

There was a knock at the door.

The End

YOUR PRIMARY SOURCE
for print books and e-books
Gay, Lesbian, Bisexual
on the Internet at

http://www.glbpubs.com

This book is Number 4 in the Dick Hardesty Mystery Series
Finalist in the Lambda Literary Awards 2002

- - - - - - -

Number 1: The Butcher's Son***$14.95
Finalist in Lambda Literary Awards 2001***
Number 2: The 9th Man $14.95
Number 3: The Bar Watcher $14.95
Number 5: The Good Cop $15.95
Number 6: The Bottle Ghosts $15.95
Number 7: The Dirt Peddlar $15.95
Number 8: The Role Players $15.95
Finalist on the Lambda Literary Awards, 2004
Number 9: The Popsicle Tree $15.95
Number 10: The Paper Mirror $15.95
Finalist in the Lambda Literary Awards, 2006

Available as print book(s) directly from the publisher:

GLB Publishers
P.O. Box 78212
San Francisco, CA 94107

with author-signed bookmark (add $3.00)

(for shipping in US—add $2.00, for Canada—add $5.00)
(For Overseas—add $10.00)

or as an e-book (download file) from the Web Site
in your choice of formats:
http://www.glbpubs.com

Credit Cards and checks honored